Mind Guerrilla

MARTIN TRACEY

Copyright Martin Tracey 2015

Martin Tracey has asserted his right under the Copyright, Designs and Patents Act, 1988 to be the author of this work.

All rights reserved.
No part of this publication may be reproduced, stored in or introduced into a retrieval system, or transmitted, in any form, or by any means (electronic, mechanical, photocopying, recording or otherwise) without the prior written permission of the author in line with publishing guidelines.
If you wish to read this work you are kindly advised to please purchase a copy. Thank you for respecting the hard work of the author.

All characters and names in this publication, other than those clearly in the public domain, are the product of the author's imagination and any resemblance to actual persons, living, dead or undead, is entirely coincidental.

Cover artwork by Ares Jun 2015

Printed by CreateSpace, An Amazon.com Company

ISBN: 1518818978
ISBN-13: 978-1518818974

*For sufferers of Multiple Sclerosis
everywhere*

Also by Martin Tracey

BENEATH THE FLOODLIGHTS

ACKNOWLEDGEMENTS

Thanks to Ares Jun for a top quality cover.
Thanks to fellow author Dawn Torrens for helping me to gain the courage and insight to fly solo.
Thanks to everyone who continues to live the dream with me - one way or another. Your perpetual support remains invaluable.
Thanks to Paddy Considine, Shane Meadows and Quentin Tarantino for leading the way on what revenge can look like.
Thanks to John Lennon. You will sadly never know the inspiration that you have been to me – including some of my ideas for this work.
Thanks as always to my family – none of this is possible, or means anything, without you.

And of course…
Dear reader, I thank you for engaging with my work.

Please support the charities either mentioned or relevant to
the themes within this work:
Birmingham Dogs Home
Multiple Sclerosis Society
The White Feather Foundation

CONTENTS

Part I Walls and Bridges

Part II Bigger Than Jesus

Part III Crippled Inside

Part IV Trojan Football

Part V Milk and Honey

PART I
WALLS AND BRIDGES

CHAPTER 1

The year 2011

"Ahh, Detective Inspector Stone, I'm so glad you could join us," said Detective Superintendent Ben Francis in his legendary deep-pitched voice, somewhat absent of humour and slightly annoyed at his DI's less than speedy arrival.

"Sarcasm is the lowest form of wit you know, sir" replied Judd, instantly wishing that he hadn't. Banter such as this was common place in the world of Birmingham and District CID, though Judd Stone usually knew better than to aim it at a superior officer. The banter served as a necessary channel of deflection, a coping mechanism, to assist with the brutal reality of dealing with the most horrific crimes imaginable in order to simply earn a living. However, Judd Stone was about to discover that simple banter was going to prove fruitless in counteracting the particularly chilling and incredible events that had preceded his arrival.

Faced with much more pressing issues than chastising his Detective Inspector, the Detective Superintendent didn't bite back too sharply at Judd's counter. "On the contrary Stone, I find sarcasm a very satisfying pastime indeed, and fortunately you supply me with constant windows of opportunity to indulge myself."

"Yeah, where have you been, Stone? You were called for well over an hour ago."

The unwelcome intruder to the conversation was Detective Inspector Lionel Scarrow, a sleazy and untrustworthy man with an unusually wide and unattractive face that somehow managed to rest on a strikingly contrasting slender neck and frame. On the rare occasions Scarrow managed a smile, his mouth appeared to host more teeth than seemed humanly possible. Scarrow struggled with banter as the words he projected were seldom intended to be well-meant. Any attempt at good-humoured mockery was usually let down by his distinct satisfaction at being malicious and down-right nasty. Scarrow just couldn't help himself. Judd loathed the man.

Nevertheless, Judd realised that on this particular occasion, Scarrow did have a point. The fact remained that he had taken an unusually long time to reach the scene and no doubt Ben Francis's sarcasm had been fuelled by Judd's lack of punctuality. Judd was never going to explain himself to the little weasel known as Lionel Scarrow of course, but Judd genuinely respected Francis and realised that perhaps he did owe him an explanation. Fortunately the DSI didn't press Judd for the reasons behind his late entrance; the matters at hand were clearly far more important. Just as well really, Judd didn't imagine that his superior would be too impressed to learn that one of his detective inspectors had switched his mobile phone to silent in order to prevent being disturbed whilst he successfully wrapped up a game of poker to the tune of £2000 winnings in the attic room of The Black Swan, a Victorian back-street boozer situated less than a 10 minute walk away from where they were standing now. Judd also hoped that the minty-fresh gum that he was chewing was enough to camouflage any stench of alcohol that may be present on his breath.

Suddenly a fresh voice entered the vicinity.

"Detective Inspector Stone was detained coming to the scene as he kindly stopped by to assist me in getting here. Do you want to criticise me for being late too, Scarrow?"

Lionel Scarrow's wide face reddened dramatically when he witnessed Detective Chief Inspector William Chamberlain struggle to enter the scene with the assistance of his two walking sticks, his left leg characteristically dragging out of sync with his once common gait. Judd acknowledged his DCI's generous white lie with a wink and a smile. Unbeknown to both Scarrow and Ben Francis, William Chamberlain had actually arrived independently to the crime scene courtesy of a traffic patrol car. Judd and William held an enormous amount of mutual respect for one another and enjoyed a strong personal friendship. Like Judd, William detested Lionel Scarrow.

"Thanks for coming, William; I didn't expect you to actually attend the scene as I had planned for Judd to inform you of proceedings."

"There's life in this old dog yet, Detective Superintendent."

"Very well, William. I appreciate you being here." Ben Francis acknowledged the determination of William Chamberlain with a smile born from a genuine respect for his DCI. The outstanding mental ability that Chamberlain possessed was never in doubt, but Ben Francis was becoming increasingly concerned at William's physical abilities which were becoming more and more compromised by his progressive illness. Nevertheless, now that he was here, Francis knew that William's input would be valuable.

"So what have we got this time?" enquired Judd, lighting a cigarette and keen to establish as to why he had been summoned to this luxury apartment that overlooked the canal network of Birmingham's city centre.

"What we have, DI Stone, is a murder executed way beyond anything we have ever experienced before on this force, certainly to my memory at least. The methods used in killing this poor girl are both extreme and bizarre," replied Detective Superintendent Francis, choosing to ignore the cigarette smoke that was unintentionally swirling its way towards him from the direction of his detective inspector. Making exceptions for Judd Stone was a common occurrence for Ben Francis. Although Francis himself was a strict disciplinarian, he also had the good sense to know that Judd Stone was a very efficient detective inspector, in spite of his rough edges and often unorthodox methods in executing his duties.

DSI Ben Francis was an extremely intelligent black man who had been adopted at an early age and raised by very loving white parents, which gave him the ability to be very non-judgmental in life and to approach situations with a much-evened state of reasoning. Even now, decades later, Francis still felt the pain of his parents for the ridiculous unpleasantness they had been subjected to for their choice of child. But he knew that the relationship he had with them was so strong and productive it had made no sense for those ignorant members of society to have ever challenged his family's existence.

These days, Francis was a leading activist in the police force for promoting equality, diversity and inclusion. His strong levels of tolerance of other people and his uncanny ability to unsuspectingly motivate the best actions from the members of his team were his forte. Before embarking on a successful police career, where his credentials and high achievements in traditional academic subjects had quite rightly enabled him to storm up the promotional ladder in the force, Ben Francis had studied degrees involving Psychology, Sociology, Philosophy and Theology, all to an extremely high educational standard which helped shape his very balanced outlook on life. All of this admirable intellectualness and open-mindedness enabled Ben Francis to make allowances for his Detective Inspector, especially as he empathised with the tragedies that Judd Stone should never have had to deal with in his personal life.

"Extreme and bizarre, you say, sir?" said Judd. "Poor girl! Well, in my experience, if unusual methods are being performed during the killing, more murders will surely follow. You know what I mean, collecting shoes from the victims for instance has happened before now. These crazy types of killer never stop at a single victim. We only need one more murder and we will have a definite serial killer on the loose, so we need to stop this psycho before he gets the label he no doubt desires."

"Wow, there are no flies on you are there, Stone? Detective school at least taught you how to count and state the bleeding obvious."

"How would you like to count the seconds it takes 'til you pass out with the pressure of a size ten boot pressing against your scrawny little throat, Scarrow?" retorted Judd, clearly losing patience with his counterpart and unable to share the levels of tolerance that his detective superintendent was capable of.

"Come on, ladies, leave your personal baggage at the door; this is a serious murder investigation and I need your tiny little brain cells to focus on the task at hand. I don't need them overloaded by playground squabbles. Is that clear?" Feeling the need to ease the situation between both his DIs, even Ben Francis's patience could be stretched to the maximum by DI Lionel Scarrow. Ben Francis suspected with regret that his earlier mocking of Judd may have given Lionel Scarrow a perceived licence to be an even bigger arsehole than usual, which mostly lent itself to pushing the buttons of Judd Stone.

"Yes sir", replied Judd and Lionel, untypically in unison for once.

"Besides," continued Ben Francis, "If Judd, is correct, it looks as though we are dealing with a potential serial killer, and on my watch stating the bleeding obvious is allowed as any holding back on thoughts or opinion could prove to be detrimental to the investigation – no matter how insignificant they may initially seem to be. I expect all my officers to share their views in an environment without fear of ridicule, engaging in constructive dialogue so that this investigation can move forward. If we apply ourselves correctly then perhaps we can prevent this maniac from killing again and therefore he won't have the opportunity to become the serial killer he is most likely hoping to become.

"My very presence here tonight highlights the seriousness of what we are up against. As we are all here, I believe it's a good idea for the four of us to examine the scene together to see what we make of the horrific methods inflicted by the killer. However, after tonight Detective Chief Inspector Chamberlain I want you to be the Senior Investigating Officer on this case with Detective Inspector Stone assisting. You may call upon Detective Inspector Scarrow, if you feel that his assistance would support you. However, with the current spiralling drug situation and gangland gun crimes on the streets of Birmingham at this present time, accompanied with the ever increasing financial cuts imposed on us by the powers that be, we are having to spread ourselves a little too thinly lately for my liking. Nevertheless Gentlemen, I want you to do whatever it takes to catch this basket case sooner rather than later and that's an order."

"Yes sir, thank you sir. I'm sure Judd and I have sufficient resource between us for now. We will of course recruit some help from the detective constables and Detective Sergeant Mistry can always be relied upon. We'll leave Scarrow to rid the streets of drugs; I think he has a particular aptitude for understanding how the low-life of Birmingham operates."

Lionel Scarrow inwardly scowled as he felt sick at his exclusion on the murder enquiry.

"Very well, William. Now we need to be careful about releasing the details of the killing to the media. That way we won't get any crank calls from daft buggers claiming to be the killer simply because they want to make a name for themselves. The unusual methods that have been used in this murder will have every twisted wannabe around calling us. We still need the assistance of the media and the public, but for now at least, the less people understand of the gory details, the more likely we are of targeting potential suspects, and I'm hoping that the unusual and specific evidence that is presenting itself will simply serve to become the killer's downfall. If we need to change our approach at a later date and actually utilise the knowledge of the bizarre acts of cruelty by making them explicit then so be it. But there can't be many individuals who would choose to kill in this manner and I don't want to muddy the waters at this stage. I'm afraid that we are dealing with one sick bastard, Gentlemen."

"So where is she?" enquired Judd.

"She's in the kitchen. But be warned, the poor girl has suffered some truly horrific inflictions."

Detective Superintendent Ben Francis led the men along a tastefully decorated hallway, themed in various shades of lilac and lavender, including some very expensive looking abstract artwork, which in the circumstances curiously projected a very soothing effect. Judd helped William walk a little quicker by allowing his friend to link his arm as they walked. Typically, Lionel Scarrow offered no assistance at all. On the short journey along the stylish hallway, the *convoy* of CID detectives passed by two uniformed police constables who stood either side of a glossy walnut table which hosted a vase of fresh flowers that complemented the colour scheme.

A prolonged existence in the B.A.D CID had a habit of hardening its partisans, but what the detectives were about to witness was enough to shock even them, despite being amongst the most hardened detectives that had ever served in the British police force.

As they entered the glossy kitchen area, the blood-soaked girl was instantly facing them. Judd noticed that her eyes were open and eerily seemed to stare straight at him, but the knife protruding from the poor girl's unclothed chest confirmed that her young life had been cruelly taken away from her.

The scene of crimes officers, or SOCOs as they were more commonly known, were beavering away, meticulously gathering what evidence they could with their usual professional detachment to try and establish some forensic evidence and other clues to the poor girl's demise.

Although clearly lifeless and partially mutilated, her beauty could still be poignantly captured by a beam of streetlight that chinked through the small gap of the wooden, horizontal window blinds.

The girl's arms were spread-eagled, each of her hands pinned to the wooden door of a kitchen cabinet by a respective knife having been forced through her palms. It seemed clear that the killer wanted to create a depiction of a crucifixion.

The corners of her mouth had been slit with a blade or similar sharp object, giving the appearance of an exaggerated inane grin similar to that of the Joker character from the Batman comic stories. Judd recognised the marking as that of a *Chelsea Smile* from his distant days when he flirted heavily with football hooliganism, before finding his correct path in life as a police detective. However, he found it difficult to understand as to why the markings of an act of football hooliganism should be married to a mock crucifixion.

And in spite of the undoubted violence that had resulted in this tragic situation, Judd found himself reflecting on the still form before him, and his thoughts likened the girl to that of a smiling butterfly, captured in a moment of beauty just like a butterfly would be in a lepidopterist's collection.

"What on Earth could be the reason for portraying the girl in this manner?" asked William Chamberlain, speaking aloud the thoughts of all four men.

At this point none of them, not even Detective Superintendent Ben Francis, could offer any kind of explanation.

Cassie Parker had seemingly become the first known victim at the hands of a potential macabre serial killer, unless they could somehow stop him before he killed again. It wasn't going to be easy.

"Who found her?" asked Judd.

"One of the cleaners, a young Polish girl," answered DSI Francis. "Cleaning is included as part of the service charges in this fine establishment. She was doing an unusually late shift."

"Unusual enough to be a suspect?" Enquired DCI William Chamberlain.

"No, we are not treating her as a suspect. She informed us that she prefers to clean the corridors, the stairwell and lift area in the later hours of the day as she feels a little nervous when most of the residents' rooms are empty in the daytime when they are usually out at work or whatever, but tonight she noticed that Cassie's door had been left open. I'm keeping an open-mind, but as you can tell by the gruesome scene we have before us Gentlemen, I doubt very much that one lady could do this to another female, and our slender Polish cleaner could simply not supply the brutal force required to succeed in a killing of this nature. She's been comforted by welfare - the experience has shaken her up quite badly I'm afraid," answered Ben Francis.

"I'm not surprised, poor cow," said Judd. "With the door left ajar and with the body not being dumped in the nearby canal or even further afield into an inconspicuous rural area, I'd say that our killer wanted this body found."

"Oh, most definitely. Our man has taken great pride in the displaying of this body. The burning question is *why*?"

Judd searched his brain to try and make sense of it all. Was this girl a specific target with the *Chelsea Smile* and *crucifixion* somehow being connected to her with a specific meaning? That would suggest that she in fact knew her killer. Or was she just a random victim, a convenient window of opportunity for the twisted fiend who was worryingly still at large? Judd's hunch was the latter.

But why display her in such a manner?

Judd tried to mentally piece together what he already knew. He understood the slitting of the mouth to be known on the football terraces as a *Chelsea Smile*, a technique of inflicting pain on rival supporters made famous by the hooligan element of Chelsea fans known as the Chelsea Headhunters, but the victim certainly didn't strike Judd as being involved in the world of football hooliganism. Cassie lived in very affluent surroundings within a luxury apartment near Birmingham's Brindley Place. Judd understood that the Royal Borough of Kensington and Chelsea was also an extremely affluent area so was the *Chelsea Smile* a jibe at the affluence of the victim and nothing to do with brawling football supporters? It seemed a far more likely explanation.

Judd also realised that the *Chelsea Smile* was a technique used in the world of gangland London in the traditional sense, when gangsters who were predatory in the notorious times of the Krays for instance would mark their victims with the disfigurement of their mouths as a useful reminder to the world that the victim had dishonoured the wrong gangster. These techniques of long established East End gangsters were distinctly different to the current trend of gangland killings that were plaguing the streets of inner-city Birmingham where a gun or knife was used to maximum effect resulting in death inspired by the *preachings* of so called *Gangsta Rappers* (the change of spelling deliberate by those involved as a means of clear identity) through their Rap music which was often perceived by outsiders as inflammatory, though the rappers themselves often countered with protests that they were simply reflecting the reality of the struggles of inner-city life through their lyrics, with never an intention to promote such territorial crime. Indeed, some rappers from the Birmingham area were now actually creating lyrics that vehemently spoke out against gun and knife crime in an attempt to diffuse the current spiralling situation. Nevertheless, the reality remained that the youth belonging to the inner-cities of the UK, and Birmingham in particular, as B.A.D CID knew only too well, had chosen to adopt this way of life from their glorified and misguided interpretation of how the gangs of Los Angeles and New York behaved by marrying aggressive hip hop music to violent gang crime as the seemingly only means of survival.

Confident that the present-day Birmingham *gangsta* was not seemingly responsible for the serial killings at hand, Judd realised that the marking of the *Chelsea Smile* in the traditional world of East End gangsters was usually reserved for the male population, keeping to the values of old school gangsters where women would not suffer such a fate. Furthermore, the intended dishonour of bearing the mark across the victim's mouth and face could only have been realised if the recipient was purposefully kept from death in order to walk the streets in permanent humiliation. Judd was therefore puzzled as to why this marking had been placed on Cassie, breaking with old school tradition and of course placed on a victim who had intentionally being killed.

But this wasn't Chelsea, the East End or anywhere else in London for that matter; this was Birmingham in the Heart of England so to Judd, it suggested that the killer was most likely to be a local man, unless he had recently moved into the area from London. London had always had its fair share of serial killers: the notorious Jack the Ripper, who outfoxed the Victorian methods of policing; Dennis Nilsen, the unassuming individual who dismembered his victims in the north London suburb of Muswell Hill and John Christie, who buried his victims around the residence of 10 Rillington Place in what is now the wealthy suburb of north Kensington, interestingly not too far away geographically from Chelsea. But Birmingham fortunately had never been as acutely exposed to serial killers – usually. One thing was for sure, B.A.D CID had been dealt their biggest test for a number of years.

As Judd found himself once more looking into the beautiful blue eyes of the dead girl, signifying such a tragic waste of life, he felt overwhelmingly compelled to catch this twisted bastard and put a stop to the killings, for he was convinced that more were planned.

But where should he begin?

What real leads were there?

There seemed no apparent motive or reason evident for the bizarre killing, and there was certainly no suspect at the moment, but there was undeniably some unhinged individual still out there who was seeking great pleasure in taking the lives of young attractive and wealthy women, by stabbing them in the heart, slitting their mouths (more than likely while they were still alive) and pinning them upright in the style of a crucifixion. Was the style of killing even meant to reflect the crucifixion of Jesus Christ for some bizarre reason? Or perhaps something entirely different? But again why the *Chelsea Smile?*

Judd had enough experience to know that it was not going to be as simple as looking for a misogynist from a contrasting background to the dead girl. Judd had prided himself on his instincts for cracking cases and his unorthodox style of getting results. His success rate was second to none, but his methods of policing were not always well received by the hierarchy and DCI Chamberlain had often needed to save him from disciplinary action by appeasing the chief superiors of the force on his behalf, including the Chief Constable.

But no matter what methods could be used to succeed in solving this mystery, at present Judd could only draw a blank.

And more worryingly, as he looked at the desperation on the faces of his colleagues, including of course his two very capable superiors DSI Francis and DCI Chamberlain, Judd realised that all that anyone had to offer at this present moment in time was to do what DSI Ben Francis had not altogether discouraged - *to state the bleeding obvious.*

CHAPTER 2

The year 1986

She lay awake trembling.

She hoped that tonight she was not going to be the *chosen* one. She really couldn't face it. The other girls in the camp felt privileged to be chosen, they hoped for it even, ached for it with their whole being. But not Tilda. She didn't believe like they did.

Like they did.

She believed in God of course, but she knew that the virtual prison in which she existed wasn't God's way – it couldn't be. Though she was meant to believe it was. Tilda wasn't stupid; she allowed *them* to believe that she believed. She certainly felt stupid to have ended up in this mess though. How could she have allowed herself to be at the mercy of these misguided fiends?

What they actually *were*, even now she didn't quite know. Although she knew the label that everyday society would choose to give them. She knew now it was too late. They claimed to follow God, but they were not Christians of any description, or any other form of acceptable religion from what she could see. They sometimes referred to themselves as a *Church,* but they were in no way aligned to Tilda's romantic notion of a building nestled in the English Countryside. She dared not speak her conclusions aloud, but she had come to realise that they were nothing more than a religious cult. And what would her big brother think if he knew where she was and what she had been subjected to? It would break his heart for sure. She had not been allowed contact with either him or the outside world for well over 2 years now.

Sometimes they took turns. She particularly hated those nights; she felt so violated and was often left with a significant degree of pain – both physically and mentally.

Sometimes, most times, it was just Eli the so called leader of this farce. All the others hung on his every word, placed him on a pedestal, genuinely believing him to be the divine messenger of God. This is why the other girls were so happy to willingly give themselves to his desires.

Eli had two right hand men in the form of Boris and Jaden.

It had been Jaden, the youngest of the three men who had recruited Tilda a few years earlier. In truth, and she felt ashamed now, she fancied him at first. What teenage girl wouldn't with his charming southern-states drawl, deep chestnut eyes and well-toned physique?

He had seen her, preyed on her as she waited for her bus on Birmingham's New Street. Her bus stop was directly outside the cinema. She had been shopping and Jaden had witnessed the bulky album sleeve tucked under her arm, her small hand struggling with the responsibility of holding it safe.

"*Upstairs at Eric's,* an interesting choice for the name of an album don't you think?"

Tilda had never heard a voice like it in her short life and as she turned to see who had spoken, the glossy-white smile that greeted her simply melted her heart. She gave an embarrassed giggle, much as young and unconfident girls do when in the presence of someone who has made the effort to give them some attention.

"I don't know why the album is called that. I prefer the album title of *Fantastic* by Wham!, I got that album last week. It really is fantastic actually as is George's singing, but I like the voice of the lady who sings in Yazoo too; she has a really lovely voice."

"A lady named Alf I believe, as equally a strange name for a lady as *Upstairs at Eric's* is for an album. I agree she does have a very pleasant voice. Do you sing at all?"

"A little," answered Tilda shyly. In truth she loved to sing and she was good at it too. If the singing talent shows of today's TV had been around in the eighties, and if Tilda had ever had the confidence to audition she could surely have done very well.

"I knew you did. I bet you have the voice of an angel. You certainly have the face of an angel."

Tilda simply blushed. This boy had shown her more attention in the past couple of minutes than any of the boys at college ever had.

"George and Alf - they sound more like two old men who sit in your English country pubs instead of two cutting-edge pop stars."

"Yes, I suppose they do," giggled Tilda.

"Forgive me; I must be forgetting my manners in the presence of such beauty. My name is Jaden. How do you do?"

Tilda shook Jaden's outstretched hand and felt a thrill go up her spine at this simplest of touches from the opposite sex. Her experience of boys was very limited in spite of her pretty looks, which she had never truly realised that she possessed.

"Jaden, that's nice. It is certainly not an old man's name. My name is Tilda."

"Tilda, that's a lovely name."

"Are you American?"

"Easy to tell, huh?"

"Your accent is very strong, but I like it very much."

"That's good to know."

"Why are you in Birmingham?"

"I am part of the show that it travelling the UK. Well I say show - it is more of a travelling convention. We are trying to spread the good word of the Lord."

"Oh, I have seen a big tent placed up in the park near Witton Lakes. Is that you guys?"

"Yep, that's us; we are there until Sunday night. Come along and drop in; we would all love to see you. We have a choir and I would love for you to come and sing a few songs with us."

"I would love that."

"That's great - how's about Saturday at 3? But, as I say, any time is fine."

"Saturday at 3 is fine. I'm pretty bored on a Saturday afternoon. My older brother goes to watch football matches so I'm usually left twiddling my thumbs and just listening to my music."

"Don't you have many friends, Tilda?"

Tilda looked to the floor and curled a strand of her hair behind her ear. "No, I got bullied at school a lot. It's better now I'm at college, I don't get the nasty comments anymore but not a lot of kids speak or hang out with me."

In truth Jaden had already noticed Tilda's obvious vulnerability by the way she hung her head, shying away from the world. There was no sparkle of self-confidence in her eye; he had evaluated her as being typical prey, the sort of girl that Eli had instructed him to look out for.

"That's too bad, Tilda. I think you will enjoy meeting up with us on Saturday though. We will have a swell time."

Jaden lent forward and gently kissed Tilda on the cheek; she got a pleasant yet curious smell of pine or cedar wood. She wasn't sure if it was his cologne or his natural scent. She certainly wouldn't be surprised if this wonderful boy could generate a lovely smell all by himself.

The following Saturday she went to the convention. It was the worst mistake of her life.

Now three years or so later, Tilda's heart sank as she heard the door creak open allowing a stream of light to enter the room. She felt sick as the smell of pine and cedar wood drifted towards her.

Tonight was going to be Jaden's turn.

Meanwhile in a flat in the East End of London, the baby boy slept peacefully as the proud mother stood over the cot giving her baby's wisps of downy blond hair a gentle and loving stroke. The mother's own hair by contrast was a little ruffled following the activity she had not long engaged in with the famous footballer in the next room, and her own blonde colour was courtesy of a bottle, although it could not be denied that the golden shade suited her pretty and pronounced features.

As her fingers tenderly made the slightest contact with the baby, he gave out a little sigh that babies do when in a contented sleep, possibly even being able to sense that the security of his mother was nearby. She turned away from her pride and joy and turned to the well-known footballer who had by this time got dressed and exited the bedroom. She smiled at the man with the household name, his hair sporting a long curly perm at the back of the head, a style that many footballers sported in 1986. His hair was also blonde and like the baby's it was his natural hair colour.

The footballer was top goal scorer for a successful London club, and he was guaranteed to be selected for the England squad that was destined for Mexico to take part in the forthcoming World Cup Finals.

He could have the pick of almost any woman, he knew that and his huge ego encouraged and allowed him to indeed indulge in many liaisons with the opposite sex. He didn't need to pay for a woman's services. Due to his position of fame sex was readily available to him - not least from his wife, but this lady before him offered a sense of danger that excited him. After all, when a man has everything a sense of danger and excitement is often all that remains to keep him stimulated in life. And she was good at what she did of course, worth every penny.

She always hoped that their encounters would lead to something more; she hoped he would fall in love with her and take her and the baby away from their less than perfect life. She hoped that he wouldn't always want to pay for her services but instead the time that they shared in the bedroom would occur from a proper relationship. A relationship that she hoped could one day evolve into something more meaningful.

She knew she pleased him, even did things for him that she wouldn't do for the others, things that she knew his wife wouldn't do for him either, but she didn't understand that in his mind this cheapened her and without the aspect of danger their relationship would be dead in the water.

But she had always been a little mixed up. She had always been a fantasist and this romantic notion that she had of setting up a happy home with this footballer was sadly never going to happen.

The footballer walked over to her, his blonde locks bobbing with each charismatic step and then he kissed her on the cheek. "I've left the money in the room, thanks for a great time. I'll see you soon."

She smiled. "Aren't you going to say goodbye to the baby?"

"Oh err; I don't want to wake him."

"You can just look at him can't you? Acknowledge he exists."

"Yeah sure." The footballer took a quick glance at the sleeping infant. "Cute little mite. Anyway I must be off. I've got a training session to go to, I hope I still have some energy left."

She watched the door close and she rested on the bars of the cot while she lit a cigarette. She smoked it, swiftly blowing the smoke away from the direction of her baby.

Not long after, the doorbell rang. She quickly straightened her hair with those expert fingers of hers and finished the cigarette. The footballer had broken her heart again, leaving her mood slightly low, and she hoped it wasn't going to be one of the clients that unnerved her, the ones that she simply viewed as a business transaction, gritting her teeth as she went through the motions all in the quest to get money to feed her and her baby.

In addition to the footballer, her diverse list of clients spanned across all spectrums. One thing she had learned about prostitution was that it didn't discriminate; it affected and enticed all walks of life.

Instead she hoped that perhaps it was one of the other clients that she could pin her hopes upon, one of the other clients that she fantasised could take her away from all this. She had a pecking order in her romanticised imagination, starting with the footballer, but there was at least one other client who she felt could easily fit the bill. And he came from an even more unlikely source than that of a married footballer. Following this latest rejection by the footballer she hoped it was going to be him at the door.

As it turned out it was.

CHAPTER 3

DCI William Chamberlain watched with interest as Judd Stone unceremoniously dumped his fourth and final spoon of sugar into his mug of tea.

"I really don't know how you do it, Judd?"

"Do what? Look so irresistible to women?"

"No, take four sugars in your tea."

"Well, I can't understand why you don't take any sugar in yours."

"Well that's easy; I'm sweet enough."

"You? Sweet? Well I suppose you are if your definition of sweet is an overweight and balding hulk!"

"Okay, if not sweet then cuddly."

"Cuddly? If you say so."

"Well Sab thinks I'm both."

"She just feels sorry for you, mate."

"Jealousy, it's such a terrible thing."

Judd just smiled, as usual allowing his friend to have the final word on the matter. It was never easy winning a dispute with William, either a light-hearted one or otherwise. He finished pouring the milk into the two mugs of tea that he was preparing, before stirring them and bringing them over to the table where William was sat.

It was the first tea break that they had taken away from their desks since starting work around 5.00 am that morning. The archaic yet accurate clock that hung high on the police canteen wall displayed the current time at 11.49am. It had been a long and frustrating morning.

"Thanks, Junior," said William as Judd placed the mugs on the table. William's mug was a specially weighted one that assisted with his occasional hand tremors. In reality, William would benefit from drinking through a straw as he could often lose grip of his mug, but it had taken Judd all of his efforts to persuade his proud friend to finally succumb to using a weighted mug. One of William's favourite sayings over the past several years as his illness slowly continued to take over his body had been: "I may have MS but MS does not have me!" It was an attitude that had to be admired.

In truth, William should have scaled down on his duties long before now due to the effects caused by the Multiple Sclerosis, but to William he simply viewed his job as being his life so any suggestion of diminishing his workload would only prove to make him unhappy. Whatever quality of life he did or didn't have was irrelevant in his mind. He could either struggle into the workplace and enjoy the interaction with his colleagues, especially Judd, or deteriorate at home in his apartment which he shared with nobody. There had never been a Mrs. Chamberlain as William had always been married to the job, although he did have a passionate affair with a certain married lady once named Evelyn Craig.

To William, the choice to come into work was a no-brainer even though his colleagues were genuinely worried about his well-being. But then again they were glad to have him around the workplace, not only because of his infectious personality but also because in spite of his physical difficulties he still had a lot to offer the job, and they learned from him daily. The crime fighting ability of his brain was incredible. Second to none in fact, certainly within and even beyond the Birmingham and District Police force.

But so far this morning not even William's experience and intellect had been able to conjure up anything of any worth to offer the murder investigation.

"What are we going to do William; we have been busting a gut all morning and so far come up with Jack shit?"

"Patience my dear boy; Rome wasn't built in a day you know, a lead will present itself just when we least expect it."

"I hope so, but this particular investigation is just so damn freaky. I mean where does this psycho get off depicting women in the style of a crucifixion and slitting their mouths?"

"I know what you mean, Judd; it is a curious one all right and one that is going to test and stretch us to our limits. It crossed my mind that it could be a resurrection of the Peaky Blinders, due to the type of infliction across the face, but it doesn't really add up. I'm just trying to grab onto something, anything in fact to make some sense of this."

"Peaky Blinders?"

"Have you never heard of them?"

"No."

"In late 19th century Birmingham there was a notorious pool of gangsters known as the Peaky Blinders, so called because they used to sew razor blades into the peaks of their trademark flat caps, and then remove their headwear in order to slice the eyes of their enemies in the territorial brawling of the day. They were a particularly violent bunch, but although not totally averse to giving their women the odd slap to keep them in check, killing a piece of skirt wasn't their style."

"And the infliction on Cassie is across her mouth, not her eyes. A similar approach to mark the face but perhaps a case of so near, yet in reality, so far."

"Exactly, Judd - I got kind of excited when I first put two and two together, especially as this is Birmingham, but the Peaky's territory was Small Heath and Bordesley Green, they may have strayed into Digbeth and the Bull Ring but if we are dealing with a Peaky copy cat the choosing of a luxury apartment in Brindley Place doesn't make much sense. The pinning of the spread-eagled arms also puts doubt in my mind, mixing religion and murder in such a visual way was never on the Peaky's agenda from what I know. I'll keep an open mind but the Peaky Blinder theory will stay at the back of that open mind for now as I'm not convinced."

Judd placed his mug with the slogan *God must be a woman because a man wouldn't put balls on the outside* to his lips, and took a sip of sugar-loaded tea before speaking again.

"It sounds as though it is worth considering William, and even if the killing is not related to the Peaky Blinders there still may be a gangster connection yet with the slitting of the mouth."

"Sab is working hard on the case bless her. She's been doing door to door enquiries in the apartment block of Cassie Parker and even the bars and restaurants in and around Brindley Place, but she phoned me a couple of hours ago to say there wasn't much to go on. It seems everyone was walking around with their eyes shut last night."

"Any other leads?"

"None of any considerable worth. I've allowed that joker, Scarrow to do a bit of snooping across the various church communities to discreetly enquire if they have any obvious weirdos in their congregation in light of the crucifixion depiction, if that's what it is, simply because I can't stand to have him round me in the office. His drug bust has seemingly hit a brick wall."

"If Scarrow does find a lead we will never hear the end of it."

"He has got more chance of enjoying a candlelit dinner

with Sab, and you know she hates him as much as we do, but to be honest if he could put a stop to these poor girls being killed, especially in such a sadistic way I'd be the first to shake his hand."

William noticed the familiar air of sadness and guilt in his friend's eyes. "You are always the same when the victims are female aren't you my friend? You can't afford to get emotionally involved Judd. I care about what happened to this poor girl too but you can't let your judgment become clouded."

"Yeah, I know, but this job has a knack of constantly reminding you of how life is so unfair at times."

"Life also has a funny habit of balancing itself out too. Cassie Parker appeared to be minted remember."

"That doesn't mean she deserved to die!" snapped Judd, amazed at the callous words of his friend.

"No, of course she didn't deserve to die, I didn't mean it like that, but she may have some awful hidden secret that we haven't discovered yet and that is why she was targeted. We are still waiting for the relevant authorities to get back to us to try and determine how she made her money as her career choice seems to be shrouded in mystery at the moment, but you know how that type of information can take an eternity to get to us. My money is on her being an antique or art dealer who shafted the wrong person with a fake piece of art of some description. I'm convinced that her wealth led to her death somehow."

"It more than likely did but that doesn't explain the nature of the killing. I know we have seen plenty of crimes committed in an attempt to achieve financial gain, but remember with this case we don't believe that anything was taken from the scene of the crime. Also Cassie had not found it necessary to take out any life insurance policy as she was still in her mid-twenties, and as far as we can tell she was single so there was no hubby or boyfriend likely to profit from her death. We know that with most murders the victims end up to have known their killer but if this is a random slayer it makes our job a thousand times more difficult. It's weird, William - no matter how much I analyse the gory details of the murder, this macabre killing still doesn't make a lot of sense."

"Which fuels my theory of it being a grudge killing, although I agree the nature of the killing is most peculiar? If the murder is down to a miffed art collector Cassie may not have been displayed as a crucifixion at all, it may be she was displayed as Da Vinci's Vitruvian man."

"Da Vinci's Vitruvian Man! What, and the slitting of the mouth is meant to represent the smile of the Mona Lisa no doubt! You've been reading too much Dan Brown mate. If we are meant to explore other theories in addition to the poor girl seemingly being *crucified*, then perhaps we should consider that the outstretching of her arms is meant to make the victim appear as if she is flying, or it did cross my mind that the poor girl had been displayed like a beautiful butterfly would be in a collection?"

"Now you are using your loaf, Judd. What have I always taught you? Think outside the box, expect the unexpected. Of course the killer could have simply pinned her hands to the cupboards for convenience, to prevent her from fighting him so he could carry out his hideous crime. Or perhaps to prevent her from scratching him and obtaining his skin and therefore his DNA under her fingernails. But I think the likely scenario is that he killed her before displaying her in the manner that he did, it would have been easier for him to do so if she were already dead. We will have to wait for the forensic specialists to confirm. There just has to be some kind of a secret we haven't unearthed yet which will connect all of this together."

"A secret. But what?"

"That's what we need to discover. Hidden secrets are not uncommon amongst the human race. You have one and I still see that it eats you up my friend."

"Bollocks does it."

"Bollocks, it doesn't. You do not have to try and make amends every time we come across a female victim. It wasn't your fault what happened to that girl all those years ago. When are you going to realise that?"

"But it was my fault, William."

"How was it your fault? You were being a gentleman."

"Yeah, the one fucking time I was being a gentleman and a girl goes and gets raped."

"It wasn't your fault."

Just then an excited Detective Sergeant Sabita Mistry rushed into the canteen which unwittingly brought a close to the now awkward conversation.

"I think I've found some vital information boys. At last we have a lead on this awful case."

CHAPTER 4

"So what have you got Sab? Enquired Judd.

"We're all ears, Detective Sergeant."

Sabita Mistry could hardly contain her excitement as she sat between her two colleagues at the circular table. Although they were her superiors she preferred to think of them as friends.

"Well, PC Worth and myself were getting nowhere fast making door to door enquiries around the victim's apartment block, you know the kind of stuff, *'oh everyone keeps themselves to themselves around here, we hardly knew the woman, I didn't notice anything unusual last night'*, they are a right stuck-up bunch living in that apartment block I can tell you, looking down their nose at you as if to say *'how dare you interrupt my plans for today'*. The fact that a girl had been murdered seemed immaterial!

"Anyway, so we went on to ask around a few of the bars and restaurants but we were still hitting a brick wall, so I decided that we should stop for a coffee and a panini at one of the Italian cafes in order to recharge our batteries. Whilst I was supping on my cappuccino, with a much needed additional shot of espresso, I kept thinking about the one apartment where there had been no answer

- the one opposite Cassie's which was number 23. I kept thinking that if someone had been in that apartment last night they may just have seen or heard something. So anyway, PCs Samstrong and Purcell are guarding Cassie's flat at the moment, and I left them instructions to call me as soon as anyone returned to number 23. To his credit Samstrong did just that.

"So anyway, Worth and I get back to the apartment block pronto to find this beautiful young lady in floods of tears being consoled by Purcell with all the effort he can muster."

"Purcell? He usually has the compassion of a crocodile," said Judd.

"Exactly, so you can begin to realise the physical attractiveness of this lady. I noticed that she had the most golden suntan you had ever seen and an expensive looking suitcase with her, so I guess that she had just returned from a holiday or an overseas trip of some description."

"We'll make a detective of you yet, Sab."

Sab ignored William Chamberlain's attempt at humour and continued with the same excitable vigour. William and Judd had often affectionately commented on how the detective sergeant could *talk for England*.

"This lady is screaming hysterically, *'no not Cassie, poor Cassie it's all my fault, it's all my fault, I should never have left her.'* So I take her inside to her apartment, relieving Purcell of his duties, and make her a cup of tea. The finest Ceylon tea you have ever tasted incidentally, and she eventually calms down to a level where she can speak to me. Due to the circumstances she got really candid; especially when I explained to her that she wasn't in any kind of trouble with us and we just wanted to catch Cassie's killer. It seems the death of her friend enabled her to be really helpful; she just totally crumbled with the seriousness of the situation. She told me how she has just come back from a trip with a millionaire businessman, she didn't want to tell me his name mind, but I assured her that his identity could be protected if we do need to speak with him, and she explained how he had paid for her to accompany him on his private yacht in the Aegean Sea for the past three weeks. She and Cassie had always looked out for one another considering their line of work and the ironic thing is Fleur, that's the lady's name by the way, was the one they were both worried about as she was the one out on the ocean with nobody else but this millionaire guy."

"What do you mean considering their line of work? Why do art dealers need to look out for one another? Unless their methods of doing business have criminal elements of course. And why did you have to reassure her that she wasn't in any kind of trouble?" said William.

"Art dealers? They are not art dealers, sir."

"So what are they then?" enquired Judd with genuine interest.

"Do I really need to spell it out for you? They were, or Fleur still is at least, prostitutes."

"Prossies, no way. Cassie wasn't a junkie hanging around on street corners. She was minted."

"Judd, don't be so naive. These are your top-end of the market type of hooker, the real high-class prostitutes, although they prefer to call themselves escorts. They earn a fortune doing this sort of work, entertaining rich businessmen or airline pilots for instance; the list of clients is endless and from all walks of top-brass life, just as long as they can afford the price for their services."

"Cassie, a hooker! Blimey I never expected that," said Judd. "Mind you I didn't think that she was an art dealer either."

"It was just one line of enquiry," said William. "I should have considered that the victim could have been a high-class escort sooner than this though. Damn, due to the unusual nature of the killing I was trying too hard to think on an abstract level. The type of hooker we usually have dealings with is indeed at the lower end of the market, it seems society is evolving all the time including in the West Midlands. Because escort agencies are in effect legal establishments we very seldom have the need to get involved. This now explains the unforced entry into the property because it is likely that the killer was expected to make an appearance."

"So that is why they looked out for one another - Cassie and Fleur - in case they got a dodgy client?" enquired Judd.

"Yeah, Fleur told me that they always let one another know of their whereabouts and who they were with, especially when entertaining away from their luxury apartments. You see, although they were at the higher end of the market, these girls don't actually work for an agency which would have safeguarding mechanisms in place to protect their girls. Therefore, as Fleur has been away on this trip for the past 3 weeks, Cassie has been working at risk as only she would know whom her clients have been. Okay, they are high-class prostitutes but working within this 'self-employed' type of approach still leaves them vulnerable."

"This is good work, Sab. Is there anything else we should know?" enquired William.

"I was just coming to that. I've been re-checking all the incoming numbers to Cassie's mobile phone and one number in particular has turned up on a few occasions on the records. So there is a high chance that this number could lead us to a client of Cassie's."

"And quite possibly the killer," said Judd. "However, surely she had regular clients anyway."

"Granted, but this number definitely contacted Cassie the night before she was killed."

"Who is it registered to?" asked William.

"I don't know yet, and I can't be bothered to wait for the phone provider to get back to me so I have thought of something else."

"Yeah, they could take a while to unearth any helpful information," said William. "So what do you have in mind,

Sab?"

Sabita presented a mobile phone from her pocket and introduced the item by musically voicing the traditional blast of *ta-da*. "This is the mobile phone of Cassie Parker."

"With the suspect's number inside?" Smiled Judd.

"Whatever you are proposing Detective Sergeant, I'm sure that it isn't going to be standard procedure," said DCI William Chamberlain with a wry smile.

"Of course not, just how we like to do business if I'm not mistaken? You two have always led by example in providing innovative solutions to problems, especially if it cuts out all the red tape bullshit. Of course I'll ensure that the phone is bagged in the usual way in due course, but there's no rush is there?"

The three detectives smiled at each other as Sab punched in the number.

After three rings it was answered.

"Hello, Benedict Hudson-Pigott speaking. How are you, Cassie?"

CHAPTER 5

Detective Sergeant Sabita Mistry hadn't fully appreciated the implications of her impulsive actions in using the phone that once belonged to Cassie Parker to contact the suspect. In her rashness she had forgotten that Cassie's number may flash on the screen of the suspect's own phone if he had chosen to save her details in his contact list. She was now concerned that her actions could be warning the killer that they were on to him. Her two superiors, Judd Stone and William Chamberlain, instantly read the panic in her pretty face. She needed to act fast.

"Oh, err, Benedict. Hello. This isn't Cassie, but thank you. You have now informed me who this phone belongs to. I found it down by the canal in Birmingham's Gas Street Basin and I was randomly just phoning numbers to see if I could trace the owner, you're the only success I've had. I am so grateful that you answered my call. I've tried five previous stored numbers but no-one answered. It seems that you are the only knight in shining armour, thank goodness. So the phone belongs to a girl named Cassie you say?"

"Err, yes I guess so."

Sab detected an element of unease in the man's voice.

"You sound like a nice man. Perhaps if you know Cassie I could meet up with you so that you could return the phone to her? I'm not interested in a reward or anything."

"Why don't you ask me for Cassie's address then you could just pass it on to her yourself?"

"Well, I guess that could happen, but what if Cassie didn't want you to give me her address? I mean, I know I've found her phone but she may not take too kindly to you revealing her address to me, after all I am still a stranger to her really. As you are her friend, and to make things easier, I suggest that we meet so that I can give you the phone to pass on to her."

"I never said that I was Cassie's friend."

"Oh, I just presumed that you were, as her number was stored in your phone."

"No, I'm not her friend exactly, in fact it's not really any of your business is it?" The man's tone was becoming increasingly unpleasant, enough to be able to send a chill up Sab's spine which was not an easy thing for someone to achieve.

"It is not my intention to pry; Mr. Higson-Pudgett was it?"

"Hudson-Pigott."

"Yes, sorry. I just want Cassie to be reunited with her phone again. So where is the best place to meet you?"

"You are not asking me for Cassie's address because you know where she lives already don't you? I'm not stupid; you are the police aren't you? You are trying to trick me."

Sab felt her stomach squirm. These weren't butterflies flying around inside her they were pterodactyls. Admirably she kept her composure.

"Why would the police be phoning you Benedict, have you done something wrong?"

"I'm not admitting to anything. You can't prove anything."

"Mr. Hudson-Pigott, I'm not the police."

"Well if you are not the police thank you for finding Cassie's phone. I hope that you get it to her somehow, but I don't really want to give you her address. Like you say, she may not want me to give it out to strangers."

This bastard's hiding something. Sab thought to herself. *Even if he now believes that I am not from the police he doesn't want to lead me to the dead body in case I can connect him to the murder and be able to assist them with their investigations. Even though he deliberately left Cassie on display I doubt that he would actually want to get caught. Alternatively, as he initially suspected that I was the police using Cassie's phone he must have assumed that we have discovered the body.*

"It would make life a lot simpler I feel if we were to meet, and then I could just pass the phone on to you to give to Cassie. I'm really not interested if the police are looking for you or not."

"I'm extremely busy over the next few days; you really do need to find some other way to get the phone to Cassie if that is your true intention."

Just then Sab heard another voice at the end of the phone in addition to Benedict Hudson-Pigott's. She strained to hear the words but the voice sounded detached and slightly disembodied. Then Sab heard a pattern of three musical tones followed by the same exact voice repeating the same exact message that it had just aired again. Sab was able to hear enough of the words to identify the source.

Then Benedict Hudson-Pigott spoke again. "I really do have to go now. Goodbye."

The phone went dead.

"We need to get to Birmingham Airport and fast."

CHAPTER 6

Judd Stone hadn't bothered to place the detachable flashing blue light onto the roof of the unmarked police car as it sped down the A45 towards Birmingham Airport. Several roadside speed cameras had flashed as the speeding car moved well above the recognised speed limit of 40 mph for the dual carriageway, causing Judd to mischievously snigger to himself as he pictured his colleagues in Traffic Division being annoyed with him when they needed to complete the inevitable reams of paperwork to excuse his actions whilst on official duty.

Only Sab had jumped into the car with him. There simply wasn't time to assist William into the car, which was required due to his lack of physical dexterity.

"So what did you hear over the tannoy, Sab?"

"Well, it was a little muffled but I definitely heard the words *final call* and *Bangkok Airport*, so it could well be that our killer is getting on the plane for Thailand in order to flee his horrific crime. He promptly terminated the phone connection following that tannoy announcement."

"If he is boarding for that last call to Thailand, I estimate that gives us a maximum of about 20 minutes to reach the airport before the plane leaves the runway. I'll be there in ten!" As Judd spoke, he swerved dramatically to avoid hitting a hackney carriage; the driver aggressively sounded his horn with a high level of venom. Judd responded by releasing one hand from the steering wheel, quite a skill considering the high speed in which he was travelling, in order to give the taxi driver the V sign. During the remaining journey to the airport, the scene was re-enacted with several drivers who took exception to Judd's reckless driving style. Judd also failed to stop at several traffic lights that were displaying red.

Being an avid Beatles fan, Judd admired the decision to rename Liverpool's airport to *John Lennon Liverpool Airport*, and in spite of the urgency and focus he required to get to Benedict Hudson-Pigott, Judd still found time to search his brain for a suitable candidate to be associated with his own home city airport.

He pondered with both the titles of *Lenny Henry Birmingham Airport* and *Julie Walters Birmingham Airport*, but then quickly ruled them out of the race on account of them technically not being Brummies in the purest sense, with Lenny coming from Dudley and Julie originating from Smethwick.

Besides, he liked to keep with the idea of a musician earning the accolade and quickly recognised Robert Plant to be a very worthy candidate, but as the Rock God originated from nearby Stourbridge, Judd's strict criteria of being Birmingham born and bred also ultimately ruled out the Led Zeppelin front man. Judd decided therefore that there could be only one possible candidate, arguably Aston's most famous son – John Michael Osbourne, better known to the world as Ozzy Osbourne.

"Hey Sab, if they were gonna rename Birmingham Airport in honour of Ozzy Osbourne, you know like they did with John Lennon for Liverpool Airport, should it be called *Ozzy Osbourne Birmingham Airport* or *John Osbourne Birmingham Airport* because John is Ozzy's real name in case you didn't know?"

"Neither. It should be called *Matthew Boulton Birmingham Airport*. That man did a lot of important work to help put Birmingham on the international map, and people heavily associate Birmingham with the success of the Industrial Revolution in which Boulton played a prominent part. He was also a key member of the Lunar Society, so called because the members met each month in line with the displaying of the full moon, and so as a member of the society he was one of a group of local geniuses who were incredible experts in the arts, sciences, and theology of the day. Members of the Lunar Society also included James Watt whom Matthew Boulton worked with to develop steam engines. Boulton also founded the Soho Mint, set up of course in Birmingham, and he improved Britain's coinage no end by using copper to make pennies and other coins. In comparison to Boulton's sustained achievements, you have to ask yourself why Mr. Osbourne would be considered to be a more worthy candidate."

Judd hadn't banked on the history lesson from his Detective Sergeant, and he was a little surprised at her impressive knowledge, which as a Brummie himself he was a touch ashamed to realise he was ignorant to a lot of what she was talking about.

"Err, well articulated Sab, but hasn't Matthew Boulton already got some colleges or something named after him in Birmingham? Besides, let's just keep with the idea of a musician if we can, although I am not for a second dismissing the achievements of any of the Industrial Revolutionists. I simply feel that a successful Rock or Pop musician is a much more universal subject of fame to be able to connect with an international audience."

"Okay, I take your point on the college thing. I guess Matthew Boulton can't have his name placed on all Birmingham based projects, and the achievements of other Brummies do need to be recognised. But you are on dodgy ground if you want to use Birmingham musicians; I mean, clearly Liverpool could only really name their Airport after

John Lennon, or possibly one of the other Beatles maybe, but Lennon is a totally unrivalled Liverpudlian as an achiever in both life, and sadly death, as a musician, a political activist and even an icon. But why would Ozzy rank above Jeff Lynne or Bev Bevan of ELO fame? Or Roy Wood for instance? Or Tyseley's founder Wings member Denny Laine? Both Lynne and Laine have had connections with former Beatles remember. And then there's Great Barr's Steve Winwood, not to mention the group UB40. It's too subjective; there is no clear front runner for Brummie musicians."

Judd was beginning to wish he had never started this conversation.

"Okay Sab, let's just pretend for argument's sake that Ozzy has surpassed his achievements as a musician and has found a cure for tropical diseases or something equally as impressive. Would you rename the airport as *Ozzy Osbourne Birmingham Airport* or *John Osbourne Birmingham Airport?*"

'Oh, that's easy. *Ozzy Osbourne Birmingham Airport*, that's what he is known as so that's what it should be called."

"Thank you."

Shortly after deciding the renaming of Birmingham Airport, Judd reached the road traffic junction at South Yardley, which could take you back into Birmingham city centre or west towards Stechford, east towards Solihull or of course the direction that they were facing towards the airport and Coventry. The notoriously congested traffic junction didn't disappoint and Judd was reluctantly forced to bring the Peugeot to a halt.

"Shit. How long have we got?"

"7 minutes to take off I reckon," answered Sab.

"Shit, shit, shit," repeated Judd as he banged his fist on the steering wheel with evident frustration.

"We are not going to make it, Judd."

"Oh, yes we will."

Judd noticed that the traffic on the opposite side of the dual carriageway was moving quite freely, unusual for the time of day as that traffic flow was heading towards the city centre. He allowed the traffic in front of him to move another few feet, so that he had just enough room to manoeuvre the car across the grass verge and into the flow of traffic coming in the opposite direction.

"Hold on tight, Sab."

Sab gave an embarrassed smile to an old lady in a Ford Fiesta who stared into the car with a sheer look of disbelief on her face.

Then the driver of an oncoming Audi slammed the brakes on when he saw the Peugeot speeding the wrong way down the dual carriageway, and although the Audi driver slowed down dramatically, he couldn't help but catch the tail end of Judd's Peugeot, sending it into a crazy spin, and causing some damage to the rear of the car.

Judd fought to control the car as it span around furiously with bits of metal flying off, but he successfully managed to bring the car under control and fortunately made progress of about 100 yards unchallenged against the incorrect flow of traffic. But the drama was not over, and soon Judd and Sab were unsurprisingly faced with another life threatening situation as an articulated lorry began to head straight towards them. The lorry was hurtling down on them like an express train out of control and Sab found no assurance from seeing the look of horror on the face of the lorry driver who was now so close that she could even see the whites of his eyes, his orange-coloured baseball cap and the fact that he was holding a half-eaten sandwich in his right hand.

In the near distance, Judd noticed an opening to a petrol station, realising it was their only chance of escape. In record time he just about managed to manoeuvre the car into the station forecourt exit before the lorry squashed them flat. Judd scraped the Peugeot along the red and white *no entry* sign, resulting in a dreadful screeching sound and causing sparks to ignite from the side of the car as the connecting metals wrestled with one another. Fortunately, the Peugeot went unchallenged by any exiting vehicles from the petrol station.

Judd continued to drive the battered Peugeot through the horse shoe shaped forecourt, and successfully out of the actual entrance to the petrol station, miraculously still avoiding incoming traffic.

Soon after, it was proven that Judd's rash actions had achieved the objective that he had set out to accomplish and he felt a great feeling of satisfaction that he had escaped the traffic jam and returned to the correct side of the road - much to Sab's relief.

Not long after, Judd approached the entrance to Birmingham Airport complete with its sign that identified the airport and welcomed its visitors. Quickly picturing a replacement sign of "*Welcome to Ozzy Osbourne Birmingham Airport*", Judd shot the red light at the entrance and sped the car at high speed around the curious statue that decorated the traffic roundabout, with Judd again quickly taking a mental picture of a statue of Ozzy being erected in all his glory replacing the current statue that stood there.

The tyres of the Peugeot screeched loudly as Judd continued rapidly past the long stay car parks and was soon able to park the battered car unceremoniously on a zebra crossing outside the departures building, nearly knocking a platform of suitcases off a passenger trolley being pushed by a startled man half its size.

An armed policeman in bullet proof uniform approached the Peugeot convinced that he was witnessing a terrorist attack in the style of parking a car loaded with explosives at the passenger entrance to the airport foyer. The vigilant policeman was about to point his machine gun at the two *terrorists* as they got out of the car when Judd was quicker on the draw and flashed his badge shouting: "CID, don't even fucking think about it. In fact laddie, we may well need your help." Judd was more than convincing in his hurried explanation and in a split second the armed policeman had decided to believe Judd's claim to being CID and was quickly updated by Sab as they all ran towards the departures lounge. In truth, the young policeman became quite thrilled in being able to assist the CID.

The airport was currently in its usual busy state with swarms of holiday makers and pockets of sharp-dressed businessmen present, which compromised Judd's, Sab's and now PC Steven Cornfield's mission to locate Benedict Hudson-Pigott. Sab had discovered the policeman's name as she briefly explained the urgency of the situation to him, and in spite of the hysteria of the situation, Sab was able to digest how attractive the young officer was with his athletic build and deep chocolate brown eyes, which were perfectly set into his pleasant, if somewhat rotund, slightly unshaven face.

As the trio ran through the crowds of people, the unsuspecting public were letting out noises of gasps and conversational uncertainty, alarmed to see an armed policeman being led to an obvious imminent confrontation of some description.

When they reached the entrance to the departures lounge, they were frustratingly greeted by a congested snaking queue of many people going through the laborious but necessary process of being security checked.

Clearly needing to get beyond this queue to reach the lounge and hopefully Benedict Hudson-Pigott, Judd decided to flex his authoritative muscles by holding his ID badge aloft and crudely announcing at the top of his voice, "Police. Get the fuck out of the way!"

Gaps were indeed made for the trio to pass as people breathed in, stepped back and even assisted by lifting the canvas belt designed to keep people in an orderly queue. But the queuing public's co-operation was mainly owed to the presence of PC Cornfield's machine gun rather than to Judd's crass announcement

Judd did have the courtesy to apologise as he unintentionally stepped hard onto the unprotected foot of an overweight man in clear holidaying mood, complete with Hawaiian shirt and lime-coloured shorts that clashed hideously. The man had been required to remove his shoes in order for them to be scanned for potential explosives, and he yelped when Judd had come down on his foot in full force as the detective inspector dodged between the queues of people. Once over the obstacle of the colourful and overweight holiday maker, Judd continued to create havoc setting off the security alarm as he raced through the screening area with metal about his person a plenty. Sab and Cornfield, who were in close proximity, also triggered the security alarm.

Finally they reached the open plan of the departures lounge complete with sitting areas, shops and eating places, which was again full of life with swarming human beings. The quantity of people made their task even harder as they realised that they still didn't know exactly where Benedict Hudson-Pigott was located amongst the crowds – or what he actually looked like. They were forced to draw to a halt while they helplessly scanned the faces of the people before them.

They had only stopped for a fraction of a second when Sab's mobile phone rang.

"William. Hi."

"Sab, I've managed to check the departures for Bangkok Airport online and the next flight is scheduled at 13.05pm. It is an Emirates Flight and has the code EK698."

Sab checked her watch; it read 13.03 with the second hand all too obviously ticking away.

"Thanks sir, we had better get our skates on."

"Good luck, Sab."

The phone went dead. William Chamberlain realised time was running out for his two detectives.

Sab ran for the nearest information screen with Judd

and Cornfield hot on her heels.

The flight was within the first 3 detailed on the screen.

"Damn it," she said. "We need Flight EK698. Boarding has closed and it takes off in less than two minutes. We need gate 19."

"I know where that is. Follow me," announced PC Cornfield, pleased that he could offer something to the cause.

Once more holidaymakers looked on astonishingly at the sight of three police officers, one armed, running across the departures lounge. Unfortunately, gate 19 was one of the furthest to get to and when they eventually did reach their destination all three hearts sank as they looked through the large glass pane that gave a shielded view on to the runway below. The dejected three law enforcers looked on helplessly as an airbus began to leave the ground bearing the large lettered branding of Emirates.

CHAPTER 7

"Was that definitely flight EK698 to Bangkok?" Sab asked the bewildered airport employee who moments earlier had carried out her duties of checking the passengers' boarding passes and passports for the now airborne flight.

"Well, yes it was. Is there a problem, madam?"

Sitting neatly underneath her petite uniformed hat, her brunette coloured hair was tied in the most perfect ponytail that Judd had ever seen, strikingly complemented by emerald green eyes that could twinkle in any given shade of light. Rarely looking for meaningful love, but always an admirer of the opposite sex when warranted, Judd couldn't help but notice how pretty the girl was and felt a compulsion to somehow put her at ease.

"Allow me to introduce ourselves Miss. I'm Detective Inspector Judd Stone of B.A.D CID and this is my colleague Detective Sergeant Sabita Mistry." PC Steven Cornfield required no introduction as he stood there in undeniable Airport Police uniform brandishing a machine gun. "Please don't be alarmed, we do not suspect that there are any explosives on board or anything as sinister as that, however, we may need to ask for the plane to turn around and come back to Birmingham as there may be, err, someone on board that we need to talk to." At this stage, Judd saw little point in revealing that *the someone* on board was a suspect in a murder investigation. "Can you tell us if a Mr. Benedict Hudson-Pigott was on board? We strongly suspect that he may have been."

The brunette hesitated somewhat, a victim of *brainwashing* techniques in data protection training. However, she felt that she needed to co-operate when Judd felt it necessary to flash his ID at her with a warm smile, the mixture of the two actions having the desired effect.

"Of course, just give me a second. I can check on the computer."

Everyone was in anticipated silence for what seemed like a long 7 seconds.

"Benedict Hudson-Pigott you say?"

"Yes," barked an impatient Sabita Mistry.

"No, there appears to have been no one of that name on Flight EK698."

"Are you sure?" asked Judd.

"Yes, quite sure. I have all the details of the passengers' right here."

"Yes of course. Forgive me, Chloe," apologised Judd quite unnecessarily. Chloe's response hadn't been hostile at all. By this time Judd had noticed the brunette's name badge.

Sabita felt like throwing up at Judd's approach.

"I wonder if he has booked in under another identity."

"I wouldn't expect so, Madam. Our passport and checking-in procedures are very robust."

Sab forced herself to smile at the acknowledgement of the comment; again it hadn't been delivered with any hostility from Chloe.

"Are you able to check if there is an Benedict Hudson-Pigott scheduled on another flight from this airport?" enquired Judd. "If there isn't then we will have to assume that he has used a false identity and we will still have to request the return of the Bangkok flight."

"Just give me a couple of minutes, it is not that easy to scroll through all of the airlines but I'm sure I can check through a general search. The system can be a bit slow as it trawls the data."

"We appreciate your co-operation," said Judd sincerely.

Chloe smiled as she tapped and clicked away.

"Ahh, here he is. Mr. Benedict Hudson-Pigott. He is booked on a flight to Newark Airport. Business Class. It doesn't take off for another 40 minutes but the passengers should be boarding soon. I'm sure with such an unusual name this must be your man."

"It must be him. It's certainly not as common as John Smith, and I bet you get loads of them passing through the airport every day?"

The pretty girl giggled and instantly felt more relaxed as she realised she wasn't going to have to get involved with calling back the Emirates plane.

"What gate is it please?" asked Sab, now a little more accepting of Chloe considering the helpful information she had provided.

"Gate 12, it's a Continental Flight scheduled to leave at 13.53pm.

"Okay gang, here we go again," instructed Judd. "Thank you Chloe, you have been very helpful."

"My pleasure, sir."

No matter how reluctant Judd had been to leave such a pretty face he raced as fast as he could towards Gate 12 with Sab and PC Steven Cornfield in close proximity.

When they arrived, the queue was already taking shape to board Flight COA45, which would shortly be departing for Newark Airport in New Jersey. The flight was mainly used for people to visit New York City.

To prevent causing alarm, Judd asked PC Steven Cornfield to discreetly remain in close proximity of the queue to make it appear as though he was simply on a routine presence for a flight to the USA, not an altogether surprising sight since the tragedy of 9/11. Judd didn't want their suspect spooked causing him to abandon the line, yet there remained a possibility that the armed police officer may have to be called into action. Meanwhile, he and Sab would wait patiently at the passenger disembarkment point as the passengers handed over their details for checking one by one; eventually hoping that Benedict Hudson-Pigott would unsuspectingly present himself right into their hands.

Judd showed his badge at the airport for the third time today, though this time much more discreetly, and explained the mission to the female Continental employee responsible for checking the passports and boarding passes of departing passengers, who was equally as co-operative as Chloe had been at the Emirates check-point. Unfortunately for Judd, however, Ethel was nowhere near as attractive as Chloe had been, due to her over peroxided hair, baggy eyes and jowly facial resemblance to a bulldog.

Judd and Sabita tried to be as inconspicuous as possible as they positioned themselves slightly behind the checking point for departing passengers. First up was a loud and brash native of New York clearly depicted by her accent. Accompanying the elderly lady were what Judd and Sab took to be her two grandchildren, one a girl and one a boy, both still of a pre-adolescence age and who had the mark of being *spoilt bastards* plastered all over them.

Next up was a fairly non-descript, painfully thin gentleman who quickly became a lack of interest to Judd and Sab when Ethel wished *Mr. Jones* a pleasant flight. Judd wondered if Ethel's deliberate attempt to distinctly make each passenger's name heard for the benefit of him and Sab was being played a little too obviously.

Mr. Jones was followed by what Judd took to be a same-sex couple, rather than simply friends, as their body language indicated something to him that suggested such a relationship. When one of the girls, a *Miss. Judy Thomson*, whom Judd estimated to be no older than her mid-twenties, flashed him a flirtatious smile, he was forced to reconsider his opinion.

Miss. Judy Thomson and her companion Miss. Cindy Hanley were followed by a balding overweight gentleman in a blue, pinstripe suit, who had a grey mackintosh coat draped over his right arm, with the same hand holding a black leather brief case, whilst the left hand was securing a half-eaten BLT sandwich which was intermittently shovelling the food into a heavily chomping mouth.

"May I see your passport and boarding card please, sir?" asked Ethel politely.

"Of course, my apologies," replied the man, his face a little red, not from embarrassment but more likely due to an unhealthy lifestyle twinned with high blood pressure. The words were still audible in spite of the volume of BLT that was churning in his mouth, and Sab's attention instantly heightened at the recognition of the sound of his voice from the phone call earlier, guiding her to glance a knowing look and discreet nod towards Judd.

The man balanced the remains of the sandwich in his teeth as he fumbled for his passport and boarding card in the huge pocket in the seat of his trousers. Soon after he produced the required documentation.

The hesitance displayed by Ethel was enough to signal to Judd and Sab that this was indeed their man, but moments later confirmation was forthcoming as she returned the passport and boarding card with the well-rehearsed phrase, "Thank you Mr. Hudson-Pigott, enjoy your flight."

The fat man did not have time to take a step forward and a look of horror filled his red face as his blood pressure climbed up the scale when Judd approached him and said the words: "Benedict Hudson-Pigott, I am arresting you for the murder of Cassie Parker. You do not have to say anything but anything you do say will be…"

Suddenly Sab's phone rang and she swiftly answered it. Judd momentarily moved his attention away from the suspect and saw the colour drain from his sergeant's face.

"What is it, Sab?"

"It's William; they have found another dead woman."

"Displayed in the same manner?"

Sab nodded.

"Exactly the same manner?"

Sab nodded again.

"Do we have a name?"

"Olive Jenas."

Judd turned back to his suspect and began to engage once more. "Slight correction, fatso. Benedict Hudson-Pigott, I am arresting you for the murders of Cassie Parker and Olive Jenas. You do not have to say anything but anything you do say will be taken down and used to bury your sad fat arse! Comprendez?"

But Benedict Hudson-Pigott was unable to say anything as his gob-smacked mouth was still full of a half-eaten BLT Sandwich.

CHAPTER 8

Interview Room 3, Handsworth Police Station, Birmingham

Benedict Hudson-Pigott looked like the proverbial rabbit stuck in the headlights as he sat opposite Detective Inspector Judd Stone and Detective Sergeant Sabita Mistry. It was DI Stone who particularly frightened him with his menacing stare. The deep-rooted anger which was evident behind Stone's eyes screamed a message of *don't even think about fucking with me*.

The fat man got the distinct impression that the detective inspector could react violently and suddenly at any given moment, coupled with an unpredictable temper. It was clear to the suspect that Stone was one angry copper, stimulated no-doubt by something dark lurking within his past. He was similarly convinced that the intimidating DI Stone would be more than willing to step outside of the law if required in order to achieve his desired result.

He didn't realise just how accurate his assumptions of DI Stone actually were.

Attempting as much as possible not to make eye contact with the harrowing detective inspector, Hudson-

Pigott couldn't help but wonder what it was hidden deep within Judd Stone that troubled him so greatly to fuel such an intimidating and menacing exterior.

"So why did you do it?" asked Judd nonchalantly as he leaned back on his chair causing it to balance on its two rear legs, a habit that had stayed with him since his school days.

"Do what?" answered Hudson-Pigott, his face as red as severe sunburn.

"Kill those two girls."

"I didn't. I swear. In fact I'm most upset that they are dead. I was very fond of them, especially Cassie. But for all I know, perhaps you are trying to trick me and they are not really dead. You just want to catch me out." In spite of his attempted assertiveness, Benedict Hudson-Pigott wondered if throwing accusations at Detective Inspector Stone was such a wise thing to do.

"So you do admit to knowing both girls?" asked Sabita Mistry.

"Yes of course I know them and you know full well that I do otherwise I wouldn't be here. I'm a highly successful businessman so I am not stupid, Detective Sergeant. You can stop this charade of telling me that the girls are dead as some sort of tactic to shock me into confessing to paying them for their err… services. I admit it, I have paid them. I'm sure this could have all been sorted without the need for me to miss my flight."

Judd Stone slammed his chair back to the floor on all four legs causing the startled suspect to jump. Judd proceeded to pick up an A4 sized wallet from the desk that separated the detectives from the anxious Hudson-Pigott. Never diminishing his menacing stare away from the trembling fat man, Judd freed the contents from the wallet and placed two graphic photographs of the victims that had been taken at the scene of each murder onto the table, facing them towards Hudson-Pigott.

Hudson-Pigott began to shake even harder and more

visibly at the sight of the photographs. Once he had processed the reality of what he was seeing before him he gave out a loud gasp, appearing to genuinely fight back tears as he forced himself to look at the two girls who he had personally known to be so beautiful in life, now having their appearance so cruelly compromised in death, by a succession of demonic slashings.

"So it is true. They are dead. The poor, poor babies. Who on Earth could do this to them? And why are their mouths disfigured in such a manner?"

"We were hoping that you could tell us that," said Judd.

"You can't possibly believe that I am capable of doing this? Not to these poor innocent girls. I am a respectable businessman not a monster."

"We have evidence to suggest that your mobile phone number has been logged as contacting these girls the night before each of their murders. How do you explain that?" asked Sab.

"The night before they were murdered? Do you mean to tell me that just the very next day after having the pleasure of the company of these lovely girls somebody killed them?"

"That's exactly what we are saying, and what's more we think it was you that killed them, but we managed to catch you in time before you fled the country hoping to make a new life for yourself in the good old US of fucking A. Do you really think we would pull you off a flight just because you've shagged a couple of hookers? Now stop pissing us about fatso or I'm going to start getting really angry. Why did you do it?"

Hudson-Pigott flinched at the detective inspector's venom. "Look, I realise now that this is very serious. I didn't ask for legal representation before because I genuinely thought that you were arresting me for simply using the services of these poor girls. I admit to giving them money for sex, but I swear to you, I would never harm a single hair on their heads. These girls were very special to me. I wish I had known that I was seeing them for the last time; I wish I could have done something to help them. Now if you truly are questioning me about murdering these poor women then I'm going to have to ask for my lawyer to be present."

Judd Stone leaned back in his chair again, frustrated at this recent turn of events. "Okay, we will arrange for your lawyer to be present if you want to play it that way, but it's only delaying the inevitable."

"And what is that?"

With aggressive momentum Judd returned the four legs of the chair to the floor once again. "That we bust your fat arse for killing these girls you sick piece of shit." Stone banged the table with his fist. "I need to get some air, Sab."

"Interview suspended." Sabita Mistry followed her detective inspector out of the door leaving a bewildered Benedict Hudson-Pigott alone in the interview room.

Once outside, the two detectives began to discuss the situation.

"Is he bluffing or did he do it? He doesn't look like a killer."

"It was his mobile number that was in touch with these girls before they got killed, Sab. It's got to be him surely?"

"Come on Judd, you know as well as I do that that in itself is not enough to make this thing stick to him. It's just circumstantial evidence, although I admit it's a major coincidence."

"The thing is we have very little else to go on. There was no semen found inside the girls because their profession obviously dictates the use of a condom for protection. Or perhaps the killer, whoever he is, did not even have sex with them. It is not clear that sex was in any way a motive for the killings.

"The killer used gloves to inflict the injuries so there are no fingerprints on the knives at the scene, and we basically have zilch in the way of DNA, just a few fibres possibly passed from clothes. But if fatty in there admits to being with the girls then his fibres would be on them anyway so that could prove useless. And forensics has drawn a blank on finding skin under both of the victims' fingernails; the poor cows were unable to put up a fight which at least for their sake suggests that they were killed quickly."

"Unless he somehow managed to pin them to the wall before killing them."

"If that were the case it doesn't bear thinking about. I'd hate to think that they suffered those inflictions whilst still being alive. Anyway, Hudson-Pigott has admitted to knowing them and admitted to being with them. What we need to do is prove he killed them."

"But perhaps he didn't kill them. Okay he pays for sex; he funds an illegal profession, but a killer? He seemed genuinely shocked Judd that he was up for murder and he seemed genuinely upset when he looked at those photographs of the victims."

"Okay, okay, he doesn't strike me as being in the same ball park as he Yorkshire Ripper either. Let's stall for a bit. Arrange for Leighton to make Hudson-Pigott a cup of coffee and allow him to phone his brief. Ask William to fill in for me while I pop out for a while. It will take William an eternity to get to this station anyway, and once he is here his diplomatic approach may work wonders in getting fatty to cough if it is him who did do the killings?"

Leighton was the resident data statistician for the Handsworth based police station where Birmingham and District CID often interviewed their most serious suspects. A pleasant scouse with a great head of thick ginger hair, Leighton was something of a connoisseur with the coffees of the world and Sab and Judd liked to sample whatever he had to offer when they were working from Handsworth.

"Okay, I'll sort everything here. Where are you going then?"

"I'm going to go and have a friendly chat with your

friend, Fleur. Hudson-Pigott may have frequented her company in the past to utilise her services too. We are running out of options here, hopefully she may be able to enlighten us a bit more with this particular line of enquiry."

The rear window of Fleur Kennealy's stylish apartment looked out onto one of Birmingham's least used canals. Judd Stone was intrigued at the stillness of the murky water which he knew was in sharp contrast to the hustle and bustle of city life just a stone's throw away. He turned to face the host once she re-entered the room.

"The kettle's boiling Detective Inspector, it won't be too long."

"Please, call me Judd. I can't wait to sample your Ceylon tea, my colleague Detective Sergeant Mistry informs me that it is a taste to die for." Judd inwardly kicked himself for his inappropriate and clumsy choice of phrase, but thankfully Fleur didn't seem to mind as she gave an understanding smile from her heavily decorated lips. Judd had realised that putting the kettle on had been a good excuse for Miss. Kennealy to put a bit of slap on too. When he first arrived, Judd could determine that she must have clearly been crying for hours before, and in line with her chosen profession she must have an inner self-preserved necessity of always trying to look her best in the presence of a man, even if he wasn't a customer. Judd had noticed her beauty on immediate impact and found her to be attractive with either her make up in place or in her initial eau-naturalle state of appearance.

"Fleur, I know this is a stupid question but how are you feeling?"

Fleur gave another little understanding smile before answering. "Oh, you know. Okay I guess in the circumstances. It's just such a shock. Cassie was more like a sister to me than a friend. Please just promise me one thing, Detective Inspec — err, Judd. Please make sure you find the bastard who did this to her."

"I promise. In fact, if you don't mind, I would like to ask you some questions about a man we currently have in our possession."

"You have him already?" For the first time Judd was able to notice a glimpse of the sparkle that would usually be associated with Fleur's deep-blue eyes.

"We believe the man we have could be the killer, although to be honest we are now not as sure as we initially hoped when we first arrested him. Does the name Benedict Hudson-Pigott mean anything to you?"

Fleur searched her mind for a couple of seconds and Judd felt guilty as he took the opportunity to view her well-rounded breasts that were bursting from her designer blouse. "Benedict Hudson-Pigott, oh yes, he wasn't one of my, err, clients but he was a regular of Cassie's. Is he the man you are holding?"

"Yes, he is Fleur; did Cassie ever speak much about him?"

"Well when we chat, err, I mean chatted," the pain was sadly obvious in Fleur's face as she was resigned to speaking of her friend in the past tense. "When we chatted we didn't usually go into much detail regarding our clients, you know we serve a purpose for them, and they serve a purpose for us, and we leave it at that. Cassie and I did always inform one another who we were entertaining, simply for security reasons, but Benedict was one of the few clients that she actually quite liked so she would actually speak quite a bit about him."

"Go on."

"Well, she always found him to be kind of sweet really. She wasn't in the slightest bit physically attracted to him; I mean you've seen him haven't you? I've met him once or twice and he was always very charming, a bit shy really. Anyway, Fleur used to tell me how he had told her about his wife, who one day just point blank refused to have sex with him anymore. His wife told him that she no longer respected him, as a man you know, and he wondered what the hell was suddenly wrong with him. They had separate bedrooms and everything, but his wife insisted that they kept up the pretence of their marriage with neighbours and family because they were very prominent figures in their village, somewhere very nice in the Cotswolds by all accounts.

"The poor bugger eventually discovered that she was having an affair with the landlady of the village boozer, yeah a woman! He stumbled upon them with their tongues down each others throats after last orders one night. He had coincidentally entered the pub after a tricky business trip and wanted a night cap to soothe his nerves. The pub was empty, and he thinks they didn't realise that the front door was open, but instead of confronting her he sneaked back out of the pub, went home to his single bed and to this day his wife doesn't know that he knows her secret. Apparently, even in this liberal day and age the scandal would cause her a lot of grief in that particular village community, they're a bit narrow-minded it would seem, so he just goes along with his charade of a marriage. He would rather protect her than upset any apple cart, no matter how justified he would be.

"He is loaded too. Cassie used to tell me how he always paid her more than the going rate and for the minimal amount of services - if you catch my drift. His cheat of a wife is living off his money and his good will. He has every right of course to expose her and kick her out of the house, which he owns outright with no mortgage to pay, but he told Cassie how he couldn't do it as he wanted to protect their only child. They have a daughter who lives nearby with her own family you see, Cassie says his daughter means the world to him.

"Apparently, he gets great pleasure from being a philanthropist. He gives lots of money to charity and even gets actively involved with fundraising events. Once he turned up at Cassie's place with a hideous long beard which he had grown for some kind of fundraising forfeit."

"This man certainly doesn't sound like a killer, assuming what he told Cassie was all true of course. However, history does tell us that the most unsuspecting people can still turn out to be murderers."

"I honestly can't believe it's him, Judd. Cassie had been seeing him for near on a decade and he was one of her cast-iron clients, so why would he suddenly kill her now after all this time?"

"I don't know. A sudden rush of consciousness, perhaps?"

"What did he owe his wife? Bugger all I'd say?"

"True enough, I suppose. However, we know he was also in touch with the second victim, so if he was so fond of Cassie, like you say, why would he look to other err, ladies for their services?"

Fleur was amused at Judd's clumsy attempts at articulating the subject of prostitutes, and she took his attempts to skirt around the subject as an indication that he didn't wish to offend her, and therefore he probably fancied her.

"Well, Cassie had other clients. Some good and some bad. But I guess she couldn't always be available for Benedict if she was already pre-booked. I know that Benedict lived in the Cotswolds and he used to give Cassie a call if he was due to fly out from Birmingham on a business trip, but due to the nature of his work this could be very sporadic. Perhaps Cassie was otherwise engaged and so he chose to use a different girl?"

"Yeah, maybe." Judd reluctantly realised that if Hudson-Pigott was a regular user of Birmingham Airport for business trips, it was highly possible that he wasn't using the flight to Newark Airport as a reason to flee the country. "So you think we have the wrong man?"

Fleur shrugged her shoulders, which made her breasts shake, and Judd found himself surmising if she was wearing a bra or not. "You're the detective," she said.

He felt useless. The more he listened to Fleur's details

of Benedict Hudson-Pigott the more he began to convince himself that he wasn't the killer. Judd even found himself beginning to feel a little sorry for him.

A click could be heard from the open-plan kitchen. "Oh, that sounds like the kettle's boiled, do you take sugar in your tea?"

"I take four, thanks."

"Four! Doesn't that give you a sugar rush?"

"Looking at you, I don't need sugar to give me a rush."

There. He'd done it. Then immediately wished that he hadn't. He was interviewing a witness in a murder case for Pete's sake; this wasn't an occasion for flirting.

"Well, perhaps we should take our tea to bed then?"

A feeling of relief swept over Judd, pleased that Fleur hadn't been offended at his flattering yet risky remark. "Bed, you say?"

"Yeah, to be honest I don't feel like being on my own too much."

"I don't think I could afford your prices, Fleur."

"Who said I would charge?"

"Well, the thing is I don't think I should be having any type of a relationship with a potential witness in a murder trial. There are protocols to follow you know?"

"And who said I'd tell?"

"Well, in that case, why don't we just skip the tea altogether."

"That's just what I was thinking," and with that, Fleur's tall slender frame rose up from the chair that she had been nestled in and she strutted over to Judd with a sexy swagger, every movement of her perfect swinging hips mesmerising him. Before she reached him she tossed her auburn hair back to make way for her well-structured face to come closer to Judd's, and she took a long, seductive time, looking into his eyes before she eventually kissed him.

In spite of his incredible satisfaction following the very

capable services applied by Fleur, Judd now felt slightly uncomfortable as he sat up in her huge bed between luxurious red-coloured sheets, wondering just how many other men had entered this arena of pleasure. He began to fondle the sheets to better appreciate their smooth texture, something he had been oblivious to in the previous hour or so.

"Don't worry; they *were* clean if that's what you are thinking. I always change them after every satisfied customer and besides, I haven't slept or entertained in this bed for the past three weeks remember."

"So is that how you see me, just another customer?" teased Judd.

"Now stop searching for compliments, I've already told you that I'm not charging and I don't always so freely engage in such a variety of pleasure for the men who share my bed. No that's not quite right, I have chosen to *share* my bed with you, but when I'm entertaining my clients I'm not inviting them to *share* it, I'm simply carrying out a business transaction. When it's business I perform on a strictly supply and demand basis, and that's only if I'm comfortable with the request to supply. Any escort will tell you that emotions never, ever enter the equation. I hope that you noticed that with you all my barriers came down, an escort has to have her own life too you know, and she is capable of wanting sex for her *own* pleasure occasionally."

Escort, Judd chuckled inwardly at Fleur's description of her profession.

"Now who is fishing for compliments? Don't worry, I have no complaints with what just occurred, in fact it was amazing!" said Judd genuinely. "Are they silk by the way?"

"No, but they look and feel good don't they?"

Judd couldn't disagree.

Suddenly Fleur sat bolt upright, retrieving her head from the soothing resting place that had been Judd's chest as she had played with his chest hair. In spite of her sudden and obvious anguish, Judd couldn't help but admire the physical beauty before him as the red sheet fell to Fleur's waist allowing her perfectly formed breasts to swing in exposed enchantment. Hooker or not, he felt a sense of macho pride that he had managed to engage with such a beautiful specimen of the female form. His mind momentarily raced as to why she had chosen to become a hooker as opposed to a successful glamour model, and then he quickly concluded that it could well have been the world of the latter that had actually introduced her to the world she now found herself to be living in.

"What's wrong, Fleur?"

"Something has just occurred to me. Whilst I was telling you how I don't do anything for my clients that I don't feel comfortable with."

"Go on," said Judd gently as he placed a hand of reassurance on the warm and smooth skin of her back.

"Well, it may be nothing but I think I should mention it, you know after what happened to Cassie."

"Please do, it may help, you never know. Sometimes the most unlikely information we receive helps to crack the most serious and horrific crimes, and besides I'd better make sure that I carry out some of my official duties here today don't you think?"

Fleur smiled, but then her expression quickly returned to an air of seriousness. "Well, there is this one customer I have quite regularly, his name is, oh no will he get into trouble? Will I get into trouble? If he knows I've said anything to you he could get a bit heavy?"

"Fleur, everything you tell me will be confidential, and besides if it could help Cassie..."

"Okay, well as I said I have this one fairly regular customer, his name is Eddie Goode, not that there is much *good* about him from what I can tell, although he always pays me well."

"What does he do for a living if he can pay you so well?"

"He is a lawyer?"

"A lawyer? Eddie Goode. The name doesn't ring a bell?"

"No, I don't think you would have come across him Judd, he specialises in medical malpractice. He is very successful in winning cases where he can prove that a hospital or doctor has been negligent, often resulting in the death of patients. He often wins the grieving family thousands of pounds. He is very good at what he does, but he always unnerves me when he rubs his hands together with a huge smile on his face when he discovers that another unsuspecting patient has died at the hands of medical negligence. It's almost as if he is glad that they have died because it gives him a chance to line his pocket."

"Some of which he passes on to you; sorry I was just thinking out loud, I didn't mean to cast any aspersions. With some of the stories that you hear on the news, I can see how he is making his money."

"Apology accepted. Well Eddie is a very tense man; he often lets his work get to him. Even though he welcomes the suffering of patients to keep his employment status alive, he gets very angry at the bureaucracy of the system and how most tragedies could so easily have been avoided. He often says that he would like to see justice achieved by simply putting those responsible in a room with the family so that they could apply some suitable justice of their own."

A man after my own heart, thought Judd. "So he is an angry kind of a guy?"

"Very much so, that's why he has two very distinct outlets. One is to frequent escorts like me, and although he isn't disturbingly rough if you know what I mean, he is very much a Wham! Bam! Thank you Maam! Kind of guy. He certainly doesn't get his money's worth in my opinion. It's like he just needs some sort of release."

"Okay, so he likes to put it about a bit with high-class hookers, err escorts, what's the other outlet he has? You said he has two."

Fleur looked a little uneasy. "Are you sure that he won't know I've said anything?"

"You have my word."

"Well, he likes to get involved in physical fights; in fact he often comes to see me on a Saturday night if I'm available following a good punch up."

"Yeah, I guess Saturday night is generally the night for fights to occur once the morons who participate in such activity have a sniff of the barmaid's apron. The lads in uniform are always very busy on a Saturday night."

"Well, the significance to it being Saturday is not because of Birmingham's night life, it's more to do with football matches being played on a Saturday."

"Football matches? You've lost me."

"Eddie Goode is a football hooligan, although he prefers to call himself an *orchestrator of violence associated with football*. The man's in complete denial, he is nothing more than a glorified football thug."

In denial, a little like calling yourself an escort instead of a prostitute perhaps! Judd decided it was best not to share his thoughts aloud.

"An orchestrator of violence associated with football. Sounds very grand."

"Exactly. Okay, so Eddie is not your regular football hooligan I guess, he doesn't walk down the street with his football scarf on shouting *'come and have a go if you think you're hard enough'*. Remember he is a very educated man and he is also a very well presented man, I very rarely see him not wearing a suit. He arranges pitched battles between rival football supporters, basically whoever is playing his team, I forget which team it is now, but then again Eddie is never really interested in the football, just the fighting. He gets off on it. It's another release for him. I can't get my head around it; there is this sophisticated network in place where key representatives, like Eddie, from all the clubs around the country communicate with one another on mobile phones, social networks and e-mails to arrange pitched battles, usually on deserted sites far away from the football grounds themselves. And the amazing thing is its top businessmen like Eddie making it happen, *orchestrating* the event. It's sheer madness. Eddie wades in and has a good ruck but his main objective seems to be to lead streams of unsuspecting gangs of youths who look up to him as some sort of Mr. Big for some reason, into some terrible episodes of violence, sometimes leading to serious injury. But Eddie tries to reassure me that most of the time it's just a harmless good old-fashioned punch up and everyone lives to tell the tale in the pub afterwards."

Judd felt his insides squirm as he recalled his own distant experiences, when he was himself an aggressive youth who would get involved in pitched battles in the name of football. Judd felt ashamed to think that he could once have been referred to as being a bonafide football hooligan.

"So, this Eddie clearly likes a bit of violence on a Saturday afternoon, but that doesn't necessarily make him a killer, Fleur. Has he ever harmed you?"

"No, never. I wouldn't exactly say that he has got a high level of respect for women; but Eddie is pretty much old school in his way of thinking. He would never dream of raising his hand to a woman. No, I don't think Eddie's the killer but something happened about 6 months ago that unnerved me quite a lot."

"Go on, babe, you are doing really well." Judd reassuringly stroked the small of Fleur's back; he could see that it wasn't easy for Fleur to talk about the experience.

"Well, Eddie had booked me for my services this one particular Saturday night, and he turned up full of beans, or full of something for sure, I know he uses cocaine quite a bit, anyway he was really excited and I guessed that he must have had a particularly enjoyable episode of violence some time earlier.

"The thing was, he turned up with this other guy and straight away I didn't like the look of him. He had really sly, shifty eyes. Eddie assumed that I would be up for a wild time with two guys at the same time but I told him straight away that I wasn't playing with two. Looking at this creepy guy I wouldn't have even wanted him alone either, no matter what he was willing to pay. Eddie seemed more disappointed than angry and I felt a bit guilty when I saw the smile leave his face, but as I told you, I don't get involved in what I don't feel comfortable with. Eddie even apologised for assuming that his pal could tag along. I told him that an apology wasn't required and that I'd be happy to see him alone again in the next few weeks. He gave me two hundred pounds simply for my inconvenience and I told him that he didn't have to pay me anything, but he insisted.

"Then as Eddie and I began gently talking with one another the other guy starts kicking off, getting really nasty you know. He was shouting things like *'what are you paying that scrubber anything for she didn't even drop her knickers for us'* and crude stuff like that, he was really disrespectful. He said to Eddie *'why don't we smack the bitch about a bit, she'll put a show on for us after a couple of slaps'* and I felt really threatened. Eddie turned on him and told him to shut his mouth and then the psycho got really weird quoting stuff from the Bible and saying that *'I was an instrument of the devil'* and *'would burn in hell for my sins'*."

The mention of the Bible aligned with violence found Judd once more picturing the disturbing scene of when he first witnessed Cassie depicted as a crucifixion.

Fleur, who was by now visibly shaken, continued to reveal her distressing experience to Judd. "Eddie got into a real heated argument with this guy and they were still going at each other down the corridor after Eddie had pushed him out of the apartment. Eddie managed to apologise to me once more before I could thankfully close the door behind them. I haven't heard from Eddie or this other guy since."

"You don't know this other guy's name?"

"No, sorry. Eddie never introduced him. Do you think he may be the killer?"

"Who knows? He may just be another nasty little football hooligan with a big mouth, but I'll check it out. You did the right thing in telling me."

Just then Judd's mobile phone rang.

"Stone."

"Judd, its Sab. Where the hell are you, you've been gone ages?"

"Let's just say I've been very thorough with my enquiries," answered Judd, cockily shooting a wink and smile towards Fleur.

Sab guessed what had taken up his time being familiar with the lifestyle that her superior indulged himself in; she decided not to press the matter further.

"Well, we all may have to consider getting more thorough with our enquiries. Hudson-Pigott's got an alibi that checks out for each of the murders, and when we picked him up at the airport he was genuinely scheduled to go on a business trip to New York. He wasn't it seems fleeing the country as we originally suspected."

"I don't think Benji is our man either."

"Oh, so you're enquiries have been quite productive then," said Sab with an air of sarcasm.

Judd chose to ignore the banter. "How do his alibis check out then?"

"Well, on the actual night of the killings of both Cassie and Olive he was with different escorts who are both very much alive. We've checked out his movements with them and once we promised them that their liaisons were free from scrutiny they were willing to confirm that he was definitely in their company. He phoned Cassie and Olive on the night he saw them, to check the appointment was still valid without any last minute complications; but he did not have a booking with them on the actual night they died. Benedict's quite a creature of routine in many ways it seems. He actually originates from Solihull and he likes to come and spend time in Birmingham by himself whenever he can. He has a bit of a crap life at home by all accounts..."

"Yes, I've heard."

"...so before he flies off on a business trip, usually from Ozzy Osbourne Airport..."

"Very funny"

"..he comes and stays in a hotel here, wanders around his old haunts, checks out the city centre and the canals and sees a high-class prostitute, or two, the night before his business trip, or if his diary allows several nights before his business trip, to help relax him before the stress of his work overseas. He is a very successful Chartered Accountant in high demand by companies all over the world. He prefers to fly from Birmingham Airport when he can as he finds Heathrow and Gatwick too big and overwhelming; in spite of his high profile job he likes things very simple whenever possible."

"Birmingham Airport is just as commutable as London if not better for a guy who lives in the Cotswolds. The fact he knows the two girls doesn't necessarily mean he killed them, there are probably lots of guys who have paid for their services and have had the pleasure of been entertained by both women." *And Fleur no doubt.*

"I think Cassie was his favourite, he liked to see her if she was available but his business trips were often arranged at short notice and Cassie's diary wasn't always free. We know he called Cassie on the night before her killing, and he admits to seeing her on that very night even though his DNA is nowhere inside her as he admits to always using a condom. He is a bit sweet really, I think he respected the girls and is genuinely upset in particular by Cassie's death and he is glad to have had the chance to see her so close to her passing. He does in fact admit to seeing both girls on the night *before* their killings but he has just been unlucky to have been with them so close to their deaths."

"I don't know about describing him as sweet myself, but Hudson-Pigott does seem a very nervous kind of guy, I just put that down to the fact that we had arrested him for two murders."

"Yeah, but like William pointed out to me earlier, Hudson-Pigott's behaviour didn't sit right with him. History dictates that the personality of a classic serial killer sees them as calm, collected, methodical and very assured in what they do, even at the time of their arrests and when sentenced. Just look at Sutcliffe, Nilsen, Manson, Lecter – the list is endless."

"So I guess that just because his phone number has appeared twice in connection with each of the prostititu... erm ladies' phones, it doesn't automatically make him the killer. It ties him to them but all we have at the moment is circumstantial evidence. We were right to follow the lead up though even for elimination purposes."

"Yeah I guess so. William also pointed out why such a meticulous serial killer would be as stupid to leave a mobile phone trail anyway. This brings me to my next point."

"Go on."

"On the *actual* night of the killings the two victims were contacted each time by a traceable telephone line."

"So our man has been stupid, whoever he is."

"Not exactly, they are from two different lines."

"Yeah, but they are still traceable. The phones must belong to someone."

"No Judd, they are both traceable but they are both different because the clever little sod used telephone boxes."

"Telephone boxes! Blimey, I didn't think there were any left nowadays in this age of mobile phone technology."

"There aren't many but this sly dog sought them out. Hudson-Pigott phoned the girls the night *before* the killings but the night before isn't the link here Judd, the psycho we are looking for used the phone box on the *actual* night of the killings no doubt to ensure that his victim would be at home, possibly on speck rather than a pre-arranged appointment. I need to tell you something else too."

"I'm all ears, spit it out Sab."

"Well boss, I suspect that you are with Fleur at the moment. That girl had a lucky escape because her landline was called from the same phone box just five minutes before the call to Cassie was made. If she hadn't have been swanking around the Aegean Sea, you wouldn't be nestled beside her right now."

Judd looked towards Fleur who fortunately hadn't overheard Sab's comments. His heart sank when he thought how this beautiful and warm specimen before him could have suffered the same fate as her poor friend.

"I'm determined to catch this bastard, Sab and when I do he will be lucky to make the fucking court room because I'll have his balls for cufflinks." Judd composed himself, not wanting to alarm Fleur too much who had noticed his anger. "I'm not too concerned about the lack of potential identification from the phone boxes. In spite of your sarcasm earlier Sab, my enquiries have been very productive today as it happens. I think I have a very strong lead on another suspect. I'll fill you and William in later."

"Okay, what shall I do with Benedict?"

"Mmmm, see what William thinks is best, but I say just let him go. But tell him he can't leave the country and we may still need him to help us with our enquiries at a later date. For now let the poor bastard still think he may be considered as a suspect but we don't have enough evidence to charge him with. You never know, he may still be connected in some way even though it now seems unlikely. Oh, and you may wish to remind him that paying a lady for sex is still a crime in this country no matter how dressed up it is."

Fleur hit Judd with a pillow for that last remark.

"Will do, boss. See you later."

The phone went dead.

"So are you going to arrest me, Detective Inspector?"

"I haven't seen any money exchange hands today?"

"But I've admitted to being an escort."

"Yes you have, but being an *escort* isn't a criminal activity as far as I understand. No I'm not going to arrest you Fleur, although I would like to put you in handcuffs."

"Anytime."

Judd leaned over and kissed Fleur gently on her forehead before jumping out of bed to retrieve his clothing.

"Sorry Fleur, I really need to get going now."

"Will I see you again?"

"Yeah, I may need to ask a few more questions."

"That's not what I meant."

"Yeah, maybe why not?" After learning from Sab that the killer had tried to reach Fleur he was determined to protect her somehow.

Fleur sensed that Judd wasn't exactly proposing marriage to her here. "Don't sweat it Judd, it's an occupational hazard I'm afraid trying to get a regular boyfriend when you are in my line of work."

"Believe me Fleur, it can be an occupational hazard trying to hold down a relationship in my line of work too."

"I'd like to give it a try."

"Believe me Fleur, not with me you wouldn't. I can be bad news. But I promise you that you haven't seen the last of me." *Not while there is a psycho out there hell bent on crucifying high-class prostitutes.*

CHAPTER 9

As Judd approached The Seraph Public House he closed his mobile phone shut in sheer disbelief, barely able to digest the information that he had just received from William. His fears of a serial killer being at large were well and truly realised as he agonisingly heard how a third victim had now been discovered, and one that had no known ties whatsoever to Benedict Hudson-Pigott.

Kez Raven had been found in identical circumstances to Cassie Parker and Olive Jenas. A *Chelsea Smile* had been slashed across a once pretty face and her outstretched arms pinned to the wall in the style of a crucifixion.

A crucifixion still seemed to be the most logical depiction, but with the tally of victims rising, it fuelled the theory nagging at the back of Judd's mind that the serial killer was perhaps forming a collection of beautiful butterflies.

To make matters worse, Kez Raven had been found in Sutton Coldfield, not only another affluent area of the West Midlands, but the area where both Judd and William lived. With a murder now being committed in their own back yard, Judd found the situation to be particularly frustrating.

Judd was currently around twelve miles away from the scene of the latest murder. Nestled not far behind a cluster of Victorian terraced houses, The Seraph Public House sits about two and a half miles south-east from Birmingham's city centre. Nearby is a typical south Birmingham bustling main road of shops, dotted amongst numerous restaurants of Eastern origin, making the location of The Seraph quite deceiving if you were to approach the pub via an alternative direction instead of the main city centre traffic routes. The Seraph Pub itself stands alone. Desolate and detached from its nearest neighbour of a mechanics yard.

When Judd had first witnessed the horrific scene of Cassie Parker, with her arms spread apart as if nailed to a crucifix, it was initially difficult to comprehend why the dead girl had been displayed in such a manner. But once he had quickly noticed the poor girl's involuntary grin crafted into her face by her killer, in what was known in the world of football violence as a *Chelsea Smile*, his gut feeling had been that the murder had some sort of connection to football hooliganism. Of course, Judd also recognised the facial marking as something akin with East End of London gangland, but the fact that these murders were happening in Birmingham confused this theory. He didn't initially go with his gut feeling, something totally untypical of Judd Stone, mainly for fear it was too much of an absurd speculation. After all, why would the tactics of a football hooligan which were specifically used on opposing male football supporters suddenly be untypically depicted on what was now realised to be a high-class prostitute? Similarly, Judd struggled to logically place either the crucifixion element of the murder, or perhaps the depiction of a captured butterfly, in line with the world of football hooliganism.

There remained these two clear peculiarities to the murders. The pinning of the arms and the slashing of the mouth. If Judd were to concentrate on the latter trademark of the killer for now, coupled with the information provided by Fleur around football hooliganism, he was beginning to conclude that his gut feeling had some relevance after all. At the very least, Judd had decided it was now a theory that was definitely worth investigating, and the reason for pinning apart the victims' arms would perhaps become clearer in time.

As Judd approached The Seraph Pub there was no traditional swinging English Pub sign to welcome him, just huge murky letters on a mustard background identifying the name of the structure. Judd guessed that the letters would have originally been brilliant white in colour when originally placed sometime in the 1960s, but lack of maintenance over the years had enabled the industrial city grime to discolour them somewhat. Regarding the absence of a traditional pub sign, Judd thought it was just as well. The name of the pub was ironic enough; any picture depicting an angelic figure would be a step too far for this rough back-street boozer. Judd was more than familiar with the pub's notoriety due to his line of work, and in a more distant past as a pub where rival football hooligans gathered.

Before making the final decision to cross the threshold of the pub, Judd looked behind him to compose his thoughts before entering *enemy territory* in more ways than one. The sky was perfectly clear and he could see the steeple of St Martin's Church in the Bull Ring pointing up towards heaven. Perhaps that was how the pub originally got its name, he thought, because it was positioned in line with the church and he began to wonder if this pub was once a friendly and innocent establishment that simply served the heart of its community. Whatever its history, these days the characters that frequented the pub were far from angelic.

Continuing to momentarily scan the city skyline, Judd could also see the glistening silvery, circular shapes that covered the locally dubbed "Mother Ship" building, a structure that had caused much debate and had strongly secured a means of identity for Birmingham. The contemporary appearance of the "Mother Ship" building was in sharp contrast to the pub's architecture and it was clear that such a structure could not have been in existence at the time of the pub's erection in the late 1800s. Birmingham was now a lot like this, a contrasting sight of modern and older buildings, including some listed. Judd loved every brick of his home city, excluding perhaps The Seraph pub.

Judd finally plucked up the courage to enter the establishment and pushed open the ancient frosted-glassed door as if he was a cowboy entering a Wild West saloon. Judd could see that the place couldn't have benefitted from any type of refurbishment for more than twenty years or so, chillingly transporting him back to his days of football thuggery. Days which he would rather forget, ashamed of his own inclusion in such a mindless activity.

As he entered the pub further, Judd could recognise that all eyes were upon him, though reassuringly not too many as there was only about eight people in total dotted around the place. At some point the decision had been made to knock the Snug, Bar and Lounge area into one large open plan room, which done nothing to project a welcoming atmosphere. Judd made a point not to stare too much at the inhabitants, but just enough to have his wits about him, and as he perched himself on a bar stool he caught a glimpse of an elderly man in a herringbone tweed cap. He had a red swollen nose as a testament to his years of propping up this bar no doubt, and a grey to ginger stubble on his harsh-looking face. Judd realised that although this old boy was obviously past his prime in terms of brawling he would still be up for the challenge with anyone who cared to have a go.

"Afternoon," offered Judd. The elderly man didn't answer him but at least he decided to turn his evil stare away from Judd.

He caught a glimpse of a couple of other *gentlemen*,

equally as rough looking with craggy features and battle scars decorating their scowling faces. As far as Judd could tell there was a distinct absence of any female representation in the pub. This was no more evident than behind the bar where any hope of a welcoming cheery barmaid was replaced by a skinny, unkempt man wearing a jumper that looked as old as the pub's decor. Impossible not to notice the greasy state of the barman's long hair, Judd wondered if the last time he had washed it was the same day that he had purchased his jumper. If it hadn't been for his matching dark moustache, Judd would have taken the black colour of his hair to have been caused purely by the amount of grease in it.

As Judd approached the bar he could see by the crude writing on the chalkboard that was propped on the mahogany surface that the only food outside of crisps, nuts and pork scratchings that was on offer, was ham, or cheese and onion cobs, priced at a fairly reasonable £1.50. However, Judd quickly considered if the price could be perceived as a bargain, on account that it could well have been the greasy barman who had been responsible for providing the cuisine.

"What can I get you?" asked the barman.

"A bottle of lager please, don't worry about a glass." Judd felt it safer to drink out of a bottle than from a glass allegedly washed in this pub.

The barman didn't engage in any type of conversation as he reached for a bottle from the fridge and forced open the top with a rusty opener, releasing a hiss as the bubbles fizzed up the neck of the bottle. A cold smoke swirled out of the top.

"Cheers," said Judd, as the skinny barman finally handed it to him.

"That will be £2.75," said the barman. Judd still couldn't help but wonder when his jet-black greasy hair had last had a wash.

"Three quid mate, keep the change."

"Thanks. I don't think I've seen you in here before."

"No, I usually drink in *The Watering Can*," lied Judd, knowing that *The Watering Can* was also a pub accepted as being a fellow hooligan establishment on this side of the city. "But a mate of mine tells me this is the place to be if you want your finger on the pulse of any match day activity, and I'm not talking about on the football field if you know what I mean."

"I won't argue with that."

It's hard to imagine at the moment, thought Judd, as the pub seemed so deserted.

"The same mate tells me I need to speak with a guy called Eddie, so that we can be involved in the serious rucks; we are a bit fed up with just picking off the odd random fan as he walks down the wrong street in his woolly scarf."

The scruffy man looked at him wearily. "How do I know you are not the old bill?"

Judd laughed out loud and when he spoke he seemed to address the whole pub, complete with open-hand gestures. "Do I look like the filth? Come on, do me a favour."

"Okay, I guess not. So you want to speak with a guy called Eddie? Eddie who?"

Judd knew the man was still testing him. "Eddie Goode of course, he is the main man right?"

"He isn't here today."

According to Fleur's description, Judd began to wonder why such a sharp-dressed individual such as Eddie Goode would ever choose to drink in a shithole like this one.

"No of course not, he'll be at work I guess. He does a very worthwhile occupation by all accounts."

"I wouldn't know about that."

Just then a voice came from behind Judd; it was one of the two chaps he had spotted moments earlier. "The Welsh boys are coming on Saturday. They always want a piece of English meat, even more so when they are playing us. Something's going down at 11 o'clock down by Millennium Point. The stupid police thought by making the game a 12.00 o'clock kick off it would stop the trouble occurring. Fucking idiots."

"Wow that sounds great. I'm much obliged mate. I'll be there."

"Most of us will be meeting here; we will still have a few beers before we kick their heads in. Gordan always opens up for us no matter how early the kick-off is."

Judd wasn't sure if this latest reference to *kick-off* was referring to the football match or the arranged battle at Millennium Point.

"Meeting here you say? I might just do that." Judd proceeded to down the entire bottle of lager in one long swill. It had the desired effect of impressing his audience.

"Ah, lovely. Much obliged, Gordan. Right then. Saturday it is."

CHAPTER 10

DCI William Chamberlain was sitting at his desk watching his silver pen roll back and forth across the glossy surface. His hands were positioned snugly on his lap, his fingers comfortably entwined. Every now and then he allowed his gaze to move away from the scribing instrument and instead turned his attention to the metal balls of his Newton's Cradle as they rhythmically struck against one another causing a hypnotic clicking sound. Using only the power of his mind, William often found himself performing activity such as this to unwind in-between his demanding detective duties.

The first time that he had become aware of his *powers* was at the tender age of five when he went to the school toilet unattended. After securing the bolt and subsequently taking a much needed pee, the young William discovered that he was unable to unlock the door after the rusty metal of the bolt and catch had fused together too harshly for a boy of his physical strength and age to move. William the child had begun to panic convinced that he was destined to a life inside an inept and filthy toilet cubicle. Like all children at that age he never possessed the foresight to realise that eventually someone would come along and set him free.

His tiny fingers had attempted to wiggle the bolt free, even causing them to bleed, but it was no use. The bolt simply would not budge. The skin on his fingers had begun to painfully erode and became sorer with each attempt to free himself, but once he realised that his physical strength was no match for the metal he discovered some kind of unexplained inner strength instead to serve his quest.

The young William didn't know where this inner strength had arrived from, or why he had even begun to contemplate this new approach at freeing the bolt, but he had felt a sudden necessity to calm himself down and to focus his eyes and mind on the rusty metal. With tears of frustration in his eyes, William stared at the bolt willing it to move. Then eventually, millimetre by millimetre, the bolt had begun to slowly shift, until eventually using only the power of his mind and concentration William remarkably unlocked the bolt and freed himself from the toilet cubicle.

Strangely enough, William chose not to discuss the experience with anybody else, and in terms of displaying feats of mind control, William's childhood passed by fairly unremarkably. It was when he stumbled upon his years of adolescence that William's acts of telekinesis began to become more eventful.

Before the days of remote-controlled handsets, William was already turning the television on and off and switching channels from the comfort of his armchair. But he would never perform such a task whilst his mother, or anyone else for that matter, was in the room. In fact to this day William Chamberlain has chosen never to share his amazing talent with anyone else!

Certain people have however, inadvertently been affected by William's telekinesis. Like the time the school bully, Sam Gibson was leaning back on his chair during a Geography lesson. He and everyone else in the classroom had thought that the spotty lummox had simply overbalanced causing him to hit his head quite heavily on the wooden floor beneath, but William sniggered to himself knowing that he had provided Gibson with more than a helping hand with his painful misfortune.

Furthermore, as the teenage William became increasingly aware of the desirable attributes of the opposite sex, he found great pleasure in mischievously lifting the skirts of schoolgirls aloft for a look at their panties and thighs. The embarrassed girls were always left wondering where a sudden gust of wind had come from on such a pleasant day!

At the age of fifteen, William decided that he needed to try and understand this talent of his that he had either been blessed or cursed with, and as his adolescent years came long before the introduction of the internet and its infinite research opportunities, he eventually found answers through the discovery of a book in Birmingham's Central library entitled *Opening The Doors of Parapsychology* by Professor Clement Wagner. Wagner explained in his book, unsurprisingly to William as it happened, that telekinesis was an ability to use the power of the mind in order to move a matter over distance. For William, the confirmation at least reassured him that he wasn't some sort of weirdo, especially as the book supplied a handful of examples from other telekinetic artisans reaching from the deep southern states of America all the way across Europe to Russia. In fact the book revealed that the term telekinesis was coined as far back as 1890 by a Russian psychical researcher by the name of Alexander N. Aksakov. Through further research, William discovered that before telekinesis had been identified, historically the movements of objects were believed to be solely carried out by mischievous ghosts or demons, much like a poltergeist might move objects. Although still by no means universally recognised by all in society, through researching a plethora of literature, William discovered that the concept of the minds of certain living individuals performing telekinetic movements was much more widely accepted than he first thought.

In more recent times, William had indeed been able to take advantage of the internet to discover further case studies and analysis relating to telekinesis, but these days he tended to research the other *condition* that now influenced his life - his suffering of Multiple Sclerosis. In spite of now having this opportunity at his fingertips to search the entire World Wide Web, the websites that defined Multiple Sclerosis did little to enhance his understanding of what had already been explained to him by his doctors and specialists.

William understood that around 100,000 people in the United Kingdom shared his neurological condition with him. The suffering resulting from damage to myelin, a protective sheath that surrounds nerve fibres of the central nervous system. This damage to the myelin interferes with messages that the brain sends to the other parts of the body, effecting William and thousands like him with simple everyday movements and difficulties in walking. At times, William even found the ability to bear his own weight on standing a major challenge, or lifting a conventional mug of tea to his mouth.

William also understood that he was suffering from the progressive strand of the condition where the unfortunate prognosis was that he would gradually get worse over time. For many other MS sufferers they could go through long periods of remission showing no signs whatsoever of compromised brain messages, but could then fall into a temporary state of relapse when the MS effected their movement for a short while. For William, there was only a continual deterioration of dexterity with no welcomed periods of remission.

William had been diagnosed for close to 20 years now and he realised that Multiple Sclerosis generally effected young adults, the fact that he was now in his early fifties and still going, though not going strong, did make him wonder whether he had been able to at least slow his progressive illness down somehow, therefore displaying some form of *mind over matter*. If so it would have to have been attributed to his positive attitude working subconsciously with his telekinesis. But William was an intelligent man, he realised that whatever powers of the mind he possessed he could not ultimately keep the MS at bay forever, realising with each passing day that his condition was deteriorating and his lifespan would always be below the national average.

Sadly, the one thing that the Word Wide Web had frustratingly not been able to offer was a tangible cure for his condition. With all of today's technology readily at our fingertips, and in spite of all of the amazing medical advances that had occurred over recent years, there was still no known cure for Multiple Sclerosis. William could locate an abundance of support groups that were available; all offering a valuable variety of assistance, but William did not take advantage of any of them. It simply wasn't his style.

It also wasn't his style to get in touch with the Institute of Noetic Science and its various off-shoots concerning his ability to move objects with his mind. He had discovered the institute whilst browsing the internet and was content that it was a credible organisation which had been formed by astronauts to encourage and conduct research of the human potential to control things by the power of the mind. William knew that he could provide invaluable evidence to these people but he wasn't prepared to make himself some kind of guinea pig for their benefit, besides he still hung on to the hope that one day his *secret weapon* of mind power could be used to great effect in catching criminals. If he became a well known "circus freak" how could he ever hope to utilise his *secret weapon*? The promise of strict confidentiality by the institute did little to reassure the natural cynic in William.

It was what frustrated William Chamberlain the most, the fact that his telekinetic powers had never seemingly enhanced his ability to perform as a detective. He unnecessarily beat himself up time and time again on this point, for even putting his powers of the mind to one side, his existence as a *regular* human being had enabled his career to be exemplary in impressive achievements and recognition as a crime fighter.

Although the messages sent from William's brain to his nerves and limbs didn't always function effectively due to his Multiple Sclerosis, William was beginning to realise that in spite of his deteriorating physical state his telekinetic powers seemed even sharper and greater than ever. William didn't know whether to be further frustrated, or even amused at the irony. He was slowly discovering that as his bodily condition deteriorated he was being able to perform more and more tasks with the power of his mind - an unlikely connection of human potential that no doubt the Institute of Noetic Science would be very intrigued to learn about.

He watched his pen roll back and forth once more before sending it into the air for a complete somersault, then allowing it to land completely upright balancing delicately on its nib.

Perhaps I should give them a call after all? He contemplated.

CHAPTER 11

The stretch of land that links the Birmingham districts of Nechells and Digbeth is primarily taken up by Curzon Street, a large highway that once consisted of a number of small businesses and traditional public houses. These days Curzon Street can proudly boast to being home to the impressive contemporary development of Millennium Point. Millennium Point has many features in store behind its remarkable glass frontage. There is the Think Tank where children can interactively learn about urban science and environmental issues such as recycling. Or if kids prefer to indulge in a less educational activity, they can either pop up the stairs or use the exciting glass elevator to reach the state of the art cinema where they can watch the latest film releases in glorious 3 dimensional High Definition. The cinema definitely becomes a favourite location for children and their families every passing December where it shows re-runs of *The Polar Express* allowing the 3D animation to truly come to life.

Millennium Point is also the venue for many of Birmingham's finest budding actors and actresses to develop their craft and nervously perform their carefully rehearsed pieces, hoping to secure a Distinction or Merit in their Dramatic Arts examinations.

Immediately outside the structure of Millennium Point there is ample pedestrianised space, and Birmingham City Council have often utilised the forecourt to host many different events. During the 2008 football World Cup Finals a huge screen was temporarily erected to televise the matches that England engaged in, allowing the strength of Birmingham based well-wishers to unite and get behind their national team, alas only to typically end up disappointed and dejected when England once again failed to rise to expectations as they embarrassingly crashed out of the competition at the hands of Germany in the form of 4-1 losers.

On New Year's Eve 1999, the space was also utilised in order to welcome the next 1000 years; forming a firm tradition to stage New Year celebrations every 31st December at the Millennium Point forecourt where hundreds of excitable Brummies brave the sub-zero temperatures to watch the latest pop stars of the day entertain them into the New Year. One concert unfortunately ended unexpectedly when scores of excitable teenage girls raced forward to try and get close to their latest musical heroes in the form of singing boy band JLS. The swarming crowd caused a barrier to give way and this unfortunately resulted in many shocked fans requiring extensive hospital treatment.

Ironically, in striking contrast to the impressive construction of Millennium Point, less than 200 yards away moving towards the Nechells end of Curzon Street, sat at the time an extensive wasteland where out of favour pubs had become derelict since the smoking ban of 2007, and once vibrant warehouses had been bulldozed to make way for new exciting developments in the wake of the success of Millennium Point. However, these visions of structural magnificence had yet to materialise in the early 2010s, possibly due to the severe economic climate of the time, causing developers to rethink their optimism for building and construction. On the other hand, one man's loss often becomes another man's gain, and this large area of desolate land complete with scatterings of broken bricks, metal and other debris served as a perfect battleground for warring football hooligans.

In light of the information received by Judd during his initial outing to The Seraph Pub prior to today, Judd had met with Eddie Goode and his self-acclaimed 'Barmy Army' at the backstreet dive, but had purposely arrived at 10.30am, just as the hooligans were leaving to march onward to the battlefield in Curzon Street. This enabled Judd to refrain from having to engage in any pre-battle conversation with Eddie Goode or his cronies to avoid any potential suspicion. Judd felt it unwise to place himself in a vulnerable position where he would have to answer awkward questions regarding his sudden appearance as a comrade.

Things had gone well so far. The craggy-faced man who was in The Seraph Pub during Judd's first visit, turned out to be a builder's labourer named Hank. Hank had recognised Judd, foiling Judd's attempt to blend in inconspicuously, and he quickly introduced Judd to Eddie as a fellow supporter to the cause. The leader of the pack was so animated and clearly focused on leading his troops to the clash with the Welsh contingent, a quick acceptance of *"welcome aboard squire"* and a strong handshake was all that took place between the two men.

As the gang of about forty or so thugs made their way along the two mile journey, Judd decisively blended in with the swarm of bodies, intentionally keeping away from Eddie's line of sight who was out front strutting like a proud peacock.

Judd scanned as many stony-faces in the crowd as possible, and wondered which one of these animals could be the potential killer of Cassie Parker, Olive Jenas and Kez Raven. Some faces were covered by scarves in an attempt for the thugs to either disguise themselves from the ever-present CCTV, or to make their appearance more threatening. Judd was under no illusion in understanding the levels of violence that these individuals could indulge in, but he still found it extremely difficult to conceive if any of them could really be capable of stabbing a girl, slicing her mouth into the shape of an inane grin and subsequently pinning her innocent hands to the wall. That simply wasn't what made football hooligans tick, no matter how mindless their usual purpose was. Nevertheless, his experience had taught him that the best way to catch a criminal was to keep an open mind, expect the unexpected and to embark upon spinning a web of layered evidence, just like a spider spins a web of silk thread. Then he had to simply wait patiently until the unsuspecting villain inadvertently presented so many clues that he, or she, found themselves stuck in the web until Judd considered the time was right to come along and eat them up - metaphorically speaking. That was why he wasn't initially rushing to interview each and every thug in the gathering of the 'Barmy Army'; as surprise was often the vital tool that allowed Judd Stone to get his man. For now, the Detective Inspector was content to remain undercover and inconspicuous, soaking in observations like a sponge, until the telling moment presented itself for Judd to pounce.

For a moment, Judd could be forgiven for believing that he had been catapulted back in time as he once again mingled amongst the once familiar mob of football hooligans. They passed a small and terrified gathering of mixed-gendered teenagers dressed in retro clothing, and Judd quickly realised that their mode of dress was due to them being recent visitors to The Custard Factory, a hive of activity where vintage clothing could be purchased from shops and stalls selling items from yesteryear, whilst the soundtrack of live retro bands blasted out. The mob of football hooligans were themselves in fine voice as they chanted their songs of the terraces, and even managed to drown out the excessive barking that could be constantly heard from Birmingham's Dogs Home which soon followed the Custard Factory on their journey to the battlefield.

Judd noticed Eddie momentarily refrain from the chanting in order to speak on his mobile phone, no doubt to communicate with the leader of the Welsh crew to inform them that the clash was now imminent. Judd found it curious how the grisly battle of rival football hooligans could be arranged in the style of a business meeting; it was certainly different from the distant days when he had indulged in football hooliganism. The luxury of mobile phones were not an option back then and gangs used to simply target well-known pubs of rival fans, or randomly wander in the vicinity of local parks and town centres, in the hope of finding a section of contenders who were up for trading sporadic acts of intense and mindless violence. The world of football hooliganism had definitely evolved; it all seemed so organised these days to Judd.

Once past the noisy dog's home, the mob were soon pounding the pavement of Curzon Street, and Judd momentarily spun his head around to catch a glimpse of The Mother Ship building from a different and more clearer angle than was on offer from the view from The Seraph Pub. The urban sun was shimmering off the metal plates that covered the structure making it appear even more like an alien spaceship than usual, seemingly radiating the customary aura of light often associated with countless UFO sightings.

They were soon marching past the Millennium Point too, which was unusually and fortunately void of significant family activity on this particular Saturday morning. After that, the crew banked left towards the wasteland which was soon to become the battleground for two sides of football hooligans.

Eddie led the Brummie party from the west of the derelict site and as the thugs gathered amongst the rubble and abandoned bricks, the Welsh hooligans appeared with perfect timing from the east. The Welsh were led by a stocky man with thick black hair and a goatee beard. He momentarily had his hand inside a leather jacket that matched his hair colour perfectly. Judd quickly surmised that the Welsh man was either reaching for a weapon of some description, or was most likely securing his mobile phone into an inside pocket after liaising with Eddie Goode, who by now had also secured his own phone.

Just beyond the Welsh mob, Judd could see the old Nechells dairy, the rows of two-storey council flats and the musical instrument store complete with its painted murals of famous rock stars which greeted vehicles on a second by second basis as they manoeuvred around the adjacent busy traffic island. In closer proximity was the canal, but Judd figured that the crude wire fence should just about be strong enough to prevent the warring hooligans spilling into the filthy water.

For what seemed like an age but in reality was closer to thirty seconds, the two rival mobs simply stood about 50 yards apart across the derelict arena, sizing one another up until Eddie Goode broke the deadlock by shouting across to his Welsh counterpart.

"Are you sure that you're boys are up for this, Hywel? You took a bit of beating last time around as I recall."

Blimey, thought Judd. *Things have changed. These hooligans are even on first name terms!*

A broad Welsh accent shouted back at Eddie with the same equal confidence as that of the Birmingham man.

"You got lucky last time Eddie, that's all. Of course we are up for it. Do you think that we have come all this way to kiss and make up with you?"

Eddie simply smiled and then stepped to one side whilst Hywel mirrored his actions. This gave the unspoken signal for the two sets of rival hooligans to commence combat and they quickly charged at one another.

Judd hoped that the battle would at least reveal some clues to who the killer could be, as so far he had been unable to determine anything in relation to the murders. He was hoping that he would witness the actions of a madman keen to use an unusual pattern of football violence, most notably in the use of a *Chelsea Smile*. Obviously this would mean some poor Welsh man being badly hurt and scarred for life, but Judd squared this in his mind by convincing himself that if a football hooligan was willing to partake in such a vicious and senseless activity then he couldn't really complain if he were to discover a blade being sliced across his kisser, especially if the horrific actions led Judd to the killer of at least three innocent women. It was a trade off that didn't play too much on Judd's conscience.

Judd quickly realised that to somehow stay out of this bloody battle when he was so intricately caught up in the middle of it was not going to be an easy accomplishment. He glanced across at Eddie Goode and Hywel who both stood on the sidelines like two conceited roman emperors as their gladiators knocked seven shades out of one another.

At one point Eddie was approached by two young hoodies chancing their arm, but Eddie expertly knocked them to the ground with a respective crack to each of their skulls from a small baton type instrument, that was so swiftly placed back into his inside jacket pocket, that Judd did not even have time to realise what he had actually used to silence the two chancers.

"Cheeky bastards," grunted Eddie, as the two novices lay motionless with blood seeping through their hoods.

So far Judd had managed to stay on the fringes of the battle, occasionally throwing a punch here and there as a means of self defence, but still he did not see a single knife drawn in the battle - let alone anyone inflicting a *Chelsea Smile*.

He had witnessed Hank convincingly wade through the army of Welsh hooligans capably breaking noses or hitting his opposition so hard that they either retreated altogether or went off to choose a more easier opponent. Then suddenly Judd did see a knife appear. However, the blade was drawn from one of the Welsh boys who had taken exception to Hank easily putting him down. As the Welshman regained his standing position he drew the knife from the inside of his boot and Hank simply froze to the spot not quite sure how to deal with the situation without getting stabbed.

Eddie Goode was standing about twenty yards or so away from the incident and when he too saw the blade he was slightly worried that this could be the end of the road for one of his most loyal and capable fighters. It crossed his mind to race over and steam into the cheeky bastard himself, the rules had quite specifically been agreed with Hywel beforehand that blades would not be used.

But Eddie Goode did not need to trouble himself with getting his hands dirty as he watched the new recruit leap into action and come to the rescue of Hank.

For some reason not yet clear to him, Judd Stone the undercover detective felt a sudden impulse to disarm the knife wielding hooligan. Content that the murder suspect was not expected to appear from the Welsh side of the battling hooligans, in a split second Judd quickly analysed that the man with the knife was simply a football hooligan crossing a boundary.

Whether it was the instinct of a policeman to disarm a knife wielding hooligan Judd wasn't too sure, but for some reason he felt some type of allegiance to Hank, with his endearing country and western name and his quick acceptance of Judd into the crew. Judd impulsively entered the conflict in order to save the life of the craggy-faced Hank, taking the knifeman completely by surprise as he punched him in the side of the jaw, causing his legs to instantly buckle and he dropped to the floor like a spilled pack of cards. The thug's lack of consciousness on impact enabled Judd to easily retrieve the knife.

"Thanks mate," spoke a genuinely grateful Hank.

Judd simply nodded and raised half a smile.

That particular incident was over in such a short amount of time, so why did Judd continue to fight following his knock-out punch?

He had successfully disarmed the Welsh hooligan and put him out of action for the near future, so there appeared no further need to continue fighting, but with the adrenalin rushing Judd became more and more involved in the battle, punching and kicking his opponents to dramatic effect like there was no tomorrow.

But surely Judd had been left little choice?

Once he had punched the knifeman to the floor, the injured hooligan's comrades had approached him keen to avenge their friend, so Judd had had no choice but to defend himself.

Had he?

And of course if Judd hadn't partaken in the battle surely this would have compromised his cover? It certainly wasn't the first time that Judd had been required to indulge in unusual activity in order to protect a false identity to ultimately secure an arrest.

But Judd seemed very comfortable in this particular activity, and perhaps for him it wasn't so unusual.

Of course Judd also knew the law well, and he knew the part about using reasonable force, but on more than one occasion Judd had been guilty of using excessive force as he waded into his opponents. He simply didn't care. It looked as though he was even enjoying it, but again that was surely to make his undercover activity appear so convincing.

Wasn't it?

One thing was for sure, Eddie Goode had been watching his latest recruit from the wings of the battle and he was impressed with what he had witnessed. Very impressed indeed.

Then suddenly the noise of battle cries was interrupted by the sound of police sirens.

CHAPTER 12

The Birmingham mob had returned to The Seraph Pub victorious. It was true that the fight with the Welsh contingent had been more closely fought than their previous bloody encounter, but it remained a fact that Eddie Goode's 'Barmy Army' was yet to be taken in their own back yard.

Judd had hoped against hope that the police wouldn't have been alerted to the fight, though he realised that there had always been a strong possibility. He had purposely chosen not to inform his colleagues, wishing to remain undercover on an unofficial basis until he felt the timing was right. The last thing he wanted was for his cover to be blown by a policeman who recognised him, especially in the precarious situation he would be found in – fighting in a pitched battle between football hooligans.

The wasteland near Millennium Point was by no stretch of the imagination an arena positioned behind closed doors and there had always been the risk of a well-meaning member of the public alerting the authorities.

Immersed in the heat of the battle, Judd almost failed to get away in time from the police vans or 'meat wagons' as they were affectionately known back in the days of

Judd's initial football hooliganism antics.

The sirens that had entered the fracas had also belonged to ambulances as well as police vehicles, but fortunately there weren't too many wounded individuals to attend to, and those hooligans who suffered minor injuries managed to run away. The amount of numbers involved in the incident had been a challenge enough for the arriving policemen and out of a potential eighty or so arrests only fourteen were made, ten of these being Welsh. Eddie took pleasure in recognising that he hadn't suffered a large amount of casualties in his crew, although it didn't sit comfortable that Hank could well have been one of them. Eddie had been grateful for Judd's quick thinking and intervention.

"Well done lad, you did really well out there. Let me get you drink, what'll it be?"

"Bottle of lager please," answered Judd.

"Not a problem. You certainly made an impression mate and thanks for getting Hank out of trouble."

"I was never in trouble, I had the situation firmly under control," claimed Hank.

"Yeah right. That Welsh geezer was about to drive a blade into you until our new recruit here saved yer bacon."

"Yeah, I guess so," conceded Hank quickly. "Thanks mate. I guess I owe you one."

"No problem," said Judd. "Why ain't you gone the match now the brawl's over."

"Simple," answered Eddie. "We ain't got any tickets." Then turning to the greasy barman he said, "Hey Gordan, a bottle of lager for our new recruit. What's your name anyway, squire?"

"Err, Judd."

"Judd, that's a good name."

"American like mine," said Hank. "My dad was a big Country and Western Fan, and he also liked the guitar band The Shadows, so Hank was a natural choice of name for him."

"Mine was a big Beatles fan. It's actually Jude on my birth certificate, you know after *Hey Jude*, the song, but after a while he thought he would change it to Judd as he thought Jude sounded too much like Judy." Judd had lied. In truth he didn't know how or why he had been christened Judd and he never knew who his father was having grown up in children's homes. Spinning a yarn about his name being connected to his favourite band The Beatles was an easy enough tactic for Judd, as he felt it wise to keep up the camaraderie for a little while longer at least.

"Judy wouldn't be an appropriate name for someone who hits as hard as you," remarked Eddie. "Your dad did the right thing; the name Judd passes the building site test all right."

"Building site test?" enquired Judd, a bit mystified as Eddie passed him a bottle of lager. Judd noticed that no money changed hands between Eddie and Gordan and assumed that Eddie either had a tab, or more likely had acquired the privilege of not needing to pay for his alcohol on these premises.

"Yeah, you know the building site test," offered Hank. "If you have a son you have to ensure that if he was employed on a building site nobody would take the piss out of his name if there was the need to shout it across the site."

"Oh, okay. Makes sense I guess," though Judd wasn't convinced that the name *Hank* would actually pass the building site test.

"So what's your game then Judd. Are you a brickie on a building site?"

Judd took a swig of lager before throwing the question back at Eddie.

"What do you do?"

"Me? I'm a lawyer. I specialise in medical claims."

Judd smiled inwardly at the irony, just as he had done when Fleur had informed him of Eddie's occupation. "A very worthwhile profession. It obviously pays well," Judd caught site of a very expensive diamond encrusted watch on Eddie's wrist as he too took a swig of lager.

"Yeah, it has its advantages. So what do you do?"

Judd took a longer swig from his bottle of lager realising that he could no longer avoid the question. It would be easy to lie but Judd decided that there was now little point in staying undercover. The killer hadn't presented himself during the fight as Judd had hoped for and there had been no *Chelsea Smile* inflicted during the battle, therefore he realised that his only hope of unveiling his suspect was perhaps to question Eddie Goode, who would undoubtedly be his best if not only source of information.

Judd, Eddie and Hank had fortunately moved away from the hub of bar activity and the unspoken respect that surrounded Eddie had ensured that they wouldn't be crowded by fellow hooligans who knew better than to invade the personal space of their leader.

Confident that only Eddie and Hank was in ear-shot, Judd let the bombshell drop.

"Perhaps I should introduce myself more formally to you chaps; after all we have built up such a bond."

The two hooligans frowned.

"Detective Inspector Judd Stone at your service."

The two hooligans were now gobsmacked.

"You're a fucking copper?" snarled Eddie.

"I'm afraid so."

"You've got some fucking front coming here alone."

"I thought we were best mates now, Eddie," said Judd exercising one of his favourite pastimes - sarcasm.

"That was before I knew you were old bill. What's to stop me setting my boys upon you right here and now?"

Judd stepped closer to Eddie before he replied in a far more menacing tone. "You could set your boys on me Eddie, but now you have seen what I'm capable of you know I'd take you out before they reached me and you wouldn't want that would you? Think of your reputation. You may think your something special but in my eyes you are just another glorified football hooligan."

"I may be a glorified football hooligan but I can tell you've been around this scene before. You were loving it out there."

"Very good Eddie. Perhaps you too could make a detective."

"Never in a million years."

"Never say never, Eddie."

"I should fucking kill you."

This only prompted Judd to move his face even closer to Eddie's, almost daring the lawyer to make a move. Even relishing the prospect.

Just then Hank joined the conversation. "Come on guys, we don't want this. Judd saved my skin remember Eddie, and just think about things for a second. He scarpered along with the rest of us when the meat wagons arrived."

"The fact that this pig saved your life Hank is the only reason why I haven't had him torn from limb to limb."

"You need to relax Eddie," said Judd. "It's obvious I'm not here for you or your pathetic little outfit. If you want to bash out the brains of fellow imbeciles every Saturday then be my guest. I'm here on much more serious business and I would like your co-operation."

"And why would I want to help the filth?"

"Because I could equally change my mind and have my colleagues come down here and bust your sad little butts, and you Mr. God Almighty would lose your fucking job as a high-flying lawyer. Besides, once I tell you why I am really here I think that you will want to help me."

"Let him speak Eddie," said Hank.

"Okay, but this had better be good, copper."

"Now, I know that you like to engage in bouts of extreme violence but that seems mostly amongst well-organised sections of football hooliganism, which if I know you correctly Eddie, wouldn't stretch to slicing up women."

"Don't insult me. I don't hit women."

"Just as I thought, but do you know of any one in your contingent who would get off on slicing girls?"

"I don't grass."

"You also respect women."

"I still don't grass."

"Perhaps a charge of GBH and conspiracy to create a riot will help you to be a little more co-operative."

Eddie paused for a moment as he digested Judd's words of persuasion. "So what's this all about then?"

"I'm investigating a series of murders."

"And they are all women?"

"Yes, and believe me what they had to suffer would even make your blood run cold, Eddie."

"Slicing up women, that's not right. But why come to me? You know that's not what I would condone from any of my boys."

"Can I trust you Eddie, Hank?"

Hank nodded immediately, eager to learn any detail that he could of the intriguing murders. The request of trust from Judd, actually seemed to strike some kind of allegiant chord with Eddie, and he was content that Judd wasn't here in order to get him. "I never thought I would say this to a copper but on this occasion, yeah, you can trust me."

Judd was keen to offer just enough detail to steer Eddie into identifying the fiend who accompanied him that night to Fleur's apartment, but wanted to ensure that Eddie didn't know that Fleur had been the source of information. Judd was keen to protect her.

"What I am about to reveal to you is not yet in the public domain, so if it gets around I know where it came from, and I may not be so reasonable about your little hooligan outfit next time I come visiting."

"Don't worry, you have my word. Hank, I can see no reason for you to still be here with us at the moment. Go and chat with some of the other guys."

Hank appeared disappointed that his curiosity was not going to be satisfied; nevertheless he snuck off like an obedient puppy.

"There, I trust Hank with my life but now you are just telling me. Does that give you some reassurance?"

"As much as I can expect I guess. The victims in question all had their mouths split by a blade."

"A Chelsea Smile?"

"A Chelsea Smile."

Eddie scratched his head, genuinely appearing as if he was willing to help in any way he could. Judd had seemingly been successful in protecting Fleur by throwing out the generics of the football hooligan marking. "And the sick bastard has done this to a woman?"

"To three women at least, as far as we know."

"Okay, there was one guy but he isn't here today. In fact we weren't overly keen on his outlook on life so I kindly asked him to fuck off and leave us alone."

"Tell me more, Eddie. Please."

"Well, he was a bit of a charmer at first, coming into The Seraph splashing a bit of cash and buying us drinks. His accent was distinctly from down south and he told us how he was a main boy down in London and how he used to get involved in the fights on behalf of one of the London football clubs, I forget which one now. He said that he had come up to Birmingham to work but still wanted the buzz of fighting on a Saturday afternoon. He said that he had always had a soft spot for our team as his grandmother was from Birmingham, I'm not sure if that's true or not, but we decided to let him into the crew anyway. Looks like I need to get a bit smarter with allowing new recruits to join us, aye Judd?"

Judd offered a smile at the remark. "Go on Eddie."

"Well, he also liked to tell us how his dad was a proper East End gangster. I thought it was a load of crap really but some of the more vulnerable guys in the outfit got caught up in the romance of East End gangland and looked forward to his stories about his old man. But he was always the outsider of the group - you know - he always seemed a bit detached. A bit vacant. He was definitely a bit fucking weird in my book. During the rucks he would be quoting passages from the Bible as he laid into the opposition, saying he needed to cleanse them of their sins and all sorts. A right fucking weirdo.

"Then he would begin to preach at us, lecturing us that what we done every Saturday was also a mortal sin and we would all rot in hell. Why he felt exempt from it all I couldn't tell you because he would fight like the rest of us. But he said he saw himself as a warrior of God, cleansing the streets of football hooligans."

The insight into this weirdo's character and odd-religious behaviour established a clear link in Judd's mind to the way the dead girls had been tragically portrayed as a crucifixion. It seemed if this guy was the killer, then he was on some sort of warped mission to rid the Earth of his perception of sinners - with football hooligans and prostitutes clearly fitting the bill.

Eddie continued. "He said that football was a sinful game, made up of narrow minded capitalists and sinners, spouting on about overpaid footballers cheating on their wives with prostitutes or whatever."

This was further affirmative information for Judd, and he hadn't even prompted Eddie to go down the religious route. Judd had not needed to reveal the crucifixion element of the murders which was a welcome bonus.

"He was a contradictory little prick really. A real hypocrite, and a blatant misogynist too. He was always slagging women off, saying that they were sinners for so willingly opening their legs to footballers; he had no respect for women at all. He especially hated WAGS.

"Then he began to bring knives to the scraps, something we don't encourage on the battlefield. We prefer a good old fashioned punch up and I had organised with Hywel today that no knives should be brought, so that little wanker who pulled one on Hank was bang out of order. So any way, he was bringing knives along and he started to become more random in his behaviour, having a go at us quoting all this biblical religious crap. He even pulled a knife on Jonah, one of my young lads, in the toilets in this very pub, threatening to slice his dick off because he had heard how he had cheated on his girlfriend with a lap dancer. Then he said he was going to find the lap dancer and teach her a lesson for being such a sinner exposing her flesh so easily. Fortunately, Hank and I walked into the bogs in the nick of time and managed to disarm the psycho. So that was the last straw for me, I told him in no uncertain terms to piss off and never to return, and if he did it would be him who would be on the receiving end of a good hiding."

Eddie hadn't told Judd about the incident with Fleur; probably for fear of revealing to a policeman that he frequented prostitutes, but it didn't matter. Judd was convinced that Eddie had confirmed that this was his man.

"What was his name?"

"Graham was it, or Garry? No Gareth, I think. Yeah, Gareth. We never knew his last name."

"Where did he live?"

"You know what? I honestly don't know. He never told us."

"You've been really helpful Eddie, thank you. I mean it."

"Well, I've helped you so it's only fair that you help me. I reckon I could use a copper to my advantage if he were to permanently join the crew."

"Thanks for the offer but I don't think so."

"Come on, you loved it getting stuck in up at Millennium Point. I can tell that you've been involved in football hooliganism before and you were getting the taste again."

"Yeah, I was involved in it once but then I grew up."

"Bollocks."

"Aren't you a bit old for all of this, Eddie? Don't you worry about losing your job?"

"It gives me a release from my job. By doing this I get some sanity back from all the stresses of dealing with twatty barristers and lawyers who are so far up their own arses when they brush their teeth they can give their shithole a scrub at the same time. It wears you down I can tell you."

"Why not simply go to anger management classes?"

"Very funny."

"Besides, I used to fight for the other side of the city".

"The weaker side."

"That's a matter of opinion. How do you define weakness?"

"Not fighting for us."

"Well I'll have to remain weak then because I'm not fighting for you again."

"More's the pity."

CHAPTER 13

"Okay I'll do it," said Sab with genuine conviction.

"I'm not so sure; I don't like putting you in danger."

"She will be wired Judd, and we can set up a camera in the room. We will only be seconds away from her should this Gareth fellow get nasty. He may not even be our killer yet."

"I still don't like it William. A second is all it takes to drive a knife into someone."

"Can I change my mind?" half-joked Sab.

"It was your idea initially, Judd," said William.

"I know, I know. But I didn't think it through properly. I can't have anything happening to Sab on my conscience."

"Ahh, I never knew you cared Guv," teased Sab. "Listen, I can see no better way of catching this murdering prick so I say let's do it."

"And use you as bait, Sab? I don't like it."

"What alternative is there? The only lead we have is an ex-football hooligan called Gareth who is seemingly from London and both could turn out to be false offerings. Even if our footy hooligan is the killer we don't even know if that is his real name or if he really is a Londoner," said Sab.

"And so far his self-narrated theory of being the son of an East End gangster is drawing a blank. The London Met have provided us with details of all the Champions league equivalent of East End gangsters from the last thirty years, and no sons of these notorious criminals are named as Gareth or even seemingly living outside of London," said William.

"Exactly Judd, so we have to do it. *I* have to do it."

Gathering his thoughts, Judd turned away from the team to face the incident wall. The other DCs in the room chose not to offer an opinion to the proposal of Sab going undercover, most likely thinking it a necessary risk whilst at the same time not wishing to commit to playing any part in placing Sab's life in danger either.

All of the incident rooms in B.A.D HQ purposely didn't include windows to ensure maximum focus could be dedicated to the respective investigations. Judd stared at the three photographs of the victims digesting the reality of their wasted lives.

He also mentally assimilated the supporting information that ran along each photograph, hand-written in colour co-ordinated marker pens on the wipeboard, coldly reflecting the graphic details of this tragic investigation.

The title of the investigation had been underlined twice in black ink - *Operation Dakota*, the computer generated name for this particular investigation which had been randomly churned out by the computer in Scotland Yard. These randomly selected titles never bore any resemblance to the respective investigation.

He then studied the map of the West Midlands and its strategically placed pins to depict the scenes of the three murders, a text book approach to assist in establishing a pattern or any geographical linkages to the killings.

Judd returned his attention to the photographs once again and focused on the faces of the girls He was desperate to avenge their deaths, and he wanted to bring their killer to justice more than anything else. The Family Liaison Officers had done a wonderful job in supporting the families of the victims and the families had indeed recognised their efforts, but Judd knew only too well that until the killer was caught and put behind bars the family members could never really have any type of closure. Judd realised only too acutely that their lives could never be the same again, but seeing the killer brought to justice was now the best outcome they could ever wish for, and he was determined to see that through.

The pathologist had confirmed that with all three murders not a single scrap of DNA had been found under the victim's fingernails. The victims for some reason hadn't put up a fight, or had been prevented from doing so, and the team were downhearted once they had learned the news that traces of the killer's skin could not be retrieved from the victims' fingernails.

It was possible that the killer had used rohypnol, often referred to as the "date rape drug" but this would be impossible to trace in the bloodstream of the victims if the autopsies had taken place after 24 hours. The killer would have needed an opportunity to slip the drug into something for the girls to unwittingly ingest it, a possibility if free-flowing alcohol was part of the escort service. If he had used rohypnol to allow his victims to lose consciousness, the killer would have needed to lift their weight to pin the victims to the wall, this wasn't an impossible task and it would have allowed him the freedom to stick knives into them and to inflict the *Chelsea Smile* unchallenged. Judd hoped against hope that the girls were not conscious to endure the sick torture inflicted upon them, but he feared that such a sadistic killer would have revelled in seeing the painful reactions of his torture as he carved knives into his victims.

Unfortunately, obtaining any crucial DNA from the scenes was proving a substantial challenge, in spite of the best efforts of the forensic scientists who were working round the clock to try and discover something of use. This lunatic, although clearly disturbed, had still been smart enough to cover his tracks extremely well.

Without any telling DNA evidence present, reluctantly Judd could see no other way but to utilise his Detective Sergeant in order to try and catch this maniac. It seemed that the best option to catch the killer any time soon was to bring him to them. Judd turned to face the team before fixing his eyes squarely on Sab and he smiled at his Detective Sergeant wishing there was indeed another way. "You're a good copper, Sab."

Sabita Mistry was an attractive girl, not in an obvious way that made heads automatically turn when she entered a room, but her skin was soft and naturally a beautiful shade in colour due to her ancestry. Her breasts and rump were a near perfect shape, complemented by a small waistline and shapely legs, but her assets often went unnoticed due to the clothing she wore as part of the job. Although she wasn't required to wear a uniform, she chose to wear clothing that she could perform comfortably in, such as loose trousers and baggy tops. Things were about to change for Miss. Mistry to ensure that her attributes were much more easily recognised.

The Birmingham and District CID realised that the killer was contacting the escorts from a series of phone boxes dotted across the city. Although the numbers of phone boxes were limited these days, they were still scattered across a wide geographical area and there was simply not enough human resource available to have each and every one of them placed under permanent surveillance.

The plan was to replace many existing 'business' cards and flyers that were routinely placed in phone boxes offering a gentleman a good time, with cards inviting potential clients with a promise of "eastern paradise" in the company of the sultry Enigma (aka Sabita Mistry). B.A.D CID didn't necessarily believe that the killer used the vehicle of cards and flyers to reach his victims; therefore a discreet newspaper advertisement was also listed in the personal columns of local newspapers as a simultaneous ploy to entice the killer to make contact with Enigma. Either way it was hoped that the killer would be suitably enticed to give Enigma a call and to set up a liaison. Then dangerously for Sab she could hopefully catch the culprit just as he was about to commit another act of murder – on her!

Of course even if the phone boxes could be substantially resourced, there was nothing to suggest that the killer was anyone who collected a card in order to engage with prostitutes anyway, and even this little plan of setting a trap with Sab as the bait could yet prove fruitless.

The decision had nevertheless been made to take this approach as a reasonable attempt of drawing the killer to them, knowing he would most likely use a phone box to contact his next target even if he ignored the marketing cards.

In each of the phone boxes across Birmingham, a secret and discreet camera had been hidden so that the B.A.D CID at least had a chance of seeing the face of the possible killer once he entered to take a card, or indeed used the phone box to make that call to Enigma, or even another targeted victim.

Using Sab as bait and the escort marketing card strategy was a gamble, but one that could pay off. However, Judd was seriously worried for Sab's safety even though there would be significant measures put in place to protect her.

It was typical of Judd Stone to agonisingly worry about the safety of a woman who was close to him.

He didn't think he could face losing another one.

CHAPTER 14

"So let's see what we've got, Leighton," said William Chamberlain.

Leighton, the police station's resident data analyst, and somewhat of a computer game geek, had had his duties temporarily escalated to allow him to help assess the CCTV surveillance of Birmingham's phone boxes.

"Hold on a moment, Leighton. I'd rather check out one of these cards that we have placed in the phone boxes." Judd picked up the first in a stack of surplus identical business cards that 'promised a night of eastern paradise' courtesy of the exotically named Enigma. "Hey, are those really your tits, Sab?"

Sab presented DI Stone with a playful slap across his arm. "As you can see from the photo Guv, the face of the individual is pixelled out, unlike the breasts of course which you have predictably noticed, proving the success of our intent to attract the attention of a Neanderthal male who only thinks with what's in his trousers."

"Ouch!"

"Sorry to disappoint you, but the picture is not me. We used a local model from Tipton. Hey, Leighton, I bet a quick search of the film will soon produce footage of DI

Stone entering one of the phone boxes himself, searching for a card so that he can get in touch with a suitable lady of the night?"

"I'm afraid Detective Sergeant, I have no such footage of Detective Inspector Stone but there are some characters that certainly do take notice of the cards. Allow me show you," said Leighton in his Liverpudlian accent.

Leighton had wired the digital images of who entered the respective phone boxes to project onto a 50 inch television screen that was positioned on the wall of the meeting room.

"Firstly, this is the evidence presented from our camera in Livery Street near the Jewellery Quarter. As you can see our surveillance has been somewhat sabotaged by the mindless morons you see before you."

The screen portrayed two youths wearing baseball caps picking up the entire pile of cards and walking out with the lot stuffed into their pockets, before one of them casually urinated in the phone box before leaving.

"I doubt very much that this pair are our killers, but by taking the entire stash of cards we cannot really determine any clues as to whether our killer used this particular phone box in the following 48 hours or not. I can tell you that an elderly lady used the phone box the next morning, followed a few hours later by a young mother with a child in a pushchair, and that is the extent of the activity so far in this particular phone box."

"Okay, so it is extremely unlikely that our killer has used the jewellery quarter phone box. What do the other cameras have to offer?" enquired Judd.

Leighton manipulated the images on the screen with the use of the controls on his laptop and switched the camera from Livery Street to the recordings of a phone box in Moseley Road, coincidentally situated not too far from The Seraph Pub. He fast forwarded through some non-eventful footage and then slowed the images to show an Asian man with an ill-fitting handlebar moustache sat uncomfortably against his particularly bony face. The team watched him enter the phone box and proceed to dial a number.

"Have we bugged the phones so that we can hear the conversations, Leighton?"

"Yes we have Judd, just don't inform the Human Rights brigade."

The Asian man proceeded to have a conversation in what was clearly his native language.

"Any ideas to what he is saying, Sab?" enquired William.

"Yeah, it's a slightly different dialect than I am used to but I can make out that he is telling somebody that his mobile phone is out of charge, hence the use of the phone box."

"Anything else?"

"Nothing too Earth shattering to our enquiry it seems. He is saying that he wants his car booked in for the brakes to be checked and is negotiating a decent price on any potential work."

"I doubt he is our man based on that evidence," said Judd.

"It's like finding a needle in a haystack. This guy hasn't even taken a card. What about the phone boxes we suspect were used to contact our three victims, Leighton?"

"Well, DCI Chamberlain, there is some footage at those particular phone boxes but again pretty non-eventful stuff I'm afraid."

"What about cutting live to one of the phone boxes that our killer has previously used?"

"Sure I can do that Judd, but I think we should bear in mind that the killer may never use the same phone box twice for his phone calls to the victims. He has certainly used a different one each time so far. Also with the use of mobile phones so evident these days, watching the phone boxes live can be very uneventful, hardly anyone uses them."

"Which means that if our man is to still use a phone box to target his next victim the search should be narrowed down quite dramatically? Stay with me Leighton, I've just got this hunch to cut to a live phone box. Access the one in the city centre, by the ramp between Waterstone's Bookstore and McDonalds. Even if our man doesn't show it could still be entertaining watching the hustle and bustle of what's on offer there."

Leighton manipulated the images once more and within seconds he had cut to the live camera of the phone box that Judd had selected.

For a few minutes no-one even entered the phone box and the four police workers had to be entertained by the diverse population that passed close to the phone box.

"We may as well stop watching the live camera and just catch up with the recorded images again. We are wasting time here," said DCI Chamberlain.

"Hold on a second, Guv. Someone is entering the phone box."

"You are right Sab, lets see what occurs," said Judd.

The camera showed somebody of slightly less than average height and build enter the phone box but he or she was wearing a hoodie with the hood firmly covering their head and much of their face. The string had been pulled so tight that the smallest hole had been left to aid with breathing and seeing only. This concealing attire immediately stirred suspicion in the police team.

A gloved hand then took a card from the pile. The unknown person pondered it for a moment, their shielded face clearly off camera as they read the contents of what the exotic Enigma had to offer. After a few seconds they reached out for the handset of the phone, waited a further few seconds and punched in the numbers of the card.

"Bingo!" said Judd Stone punching the air. "I knew I had to go with my hunch."

A mobile phone in Sab's possession rang once, but the team's excitement was rapidly distinguished as the screen before them showed the person replacing the handset before Sab had even had time to answer.

A frustrated Judd Stone threw a pencil at the screen as he watched the person slip away from the phone box.

"Talk you bastard, why didn't you talk?"

"It's okay; he took the card with him. Our man will phone again," offered a decisive DCI William Chamberlain. "All we have to do is wait."

CHAPTER 15

William Chamberlain had been correct.

Whoever had entered the phone box wearing the very concealing hoodie, had indeed dialled the numbers on the card once more.

However, in order to contact Enigma the hooded suspect had ironically chosen not to use a phone box.

A report had come in regarding the theft of a mobile phone from a 15 year-old schoolgirl who had been waiting alone at a bus stop. The schoolgirl had given a description of a man of slightly less than average build, who concealed most of his features by wearing a hood pulled tight around his face.

It was true that much of the random and opportunist acts of crime that came by Birmingham and District Police were often carried out by chancers fitting this description, but the victim's account still seemed far too coincidental for the team to ignore, especially when she detailed a pair of evil-looking eyes that peered through the small canvas window made by the hood. The stare had been so menacing it had been enough on its own to scare the poor schoolgirl into handing over her phone without a struggle.

If this hoodie-clad individual had been the killer, the

schoolgirl didn't yet realise just what a narrow escape she had had by simply having her phone taken. She could so easily have had her life taken as well.

When Sab had answered the call, the distinct menace in the voice had been enough to make the hairs on the back of her neck stand up, and she was convinced this caller had to be their man. It was soon established that the call had come from the schoolgirl's stolen mobile phone, but the trail rapidly ran cold. The mobile phone had most likely been destroyed immediately after the brief conversation with Sab, leaving no trace of its whereabouts from there on in.

Of course, the team were wily enough to realise that calls could be received from a variety of individuals who had taken the information regarding Enigma from any number of respective phone boxes, and it was even feasible that the hooded individual whom they had spotted on the camera was not the killer or even the same one who had stolen the phone.

Nevertheless, it seemed the dots were beginning to join.

They initially assumed that their break would come from those calls instigated by the newspaper advertisements, this being a more likely avenue for the killer, knowing that the higher end of the sex market would be more inclined to advertise this way. Sab had indeed received six other calls since the advertisements had gone live, but these had easily been detected, derived from landlines which prompted the routine deployment of police constables to make enquiries at the homes of the unsuspecting callers, which produced nothing too remarkable in the way of results. Some of the callers became suitably embarrassed when they had to explain their actions to the constables in front of their wives! It was extremely unlikely that a killer who had so far been able to convincingly cover his tracks so well would have been so naïve as to use a traceable home-based landline.

It was agreed that the call from the stolen mobile phone, most likely by the individual wearing a concealing hoodie, was the call that stood above any other in terms of suspicion to the B.A.D CID. Taking the call and the preceding events very seriously, a rendezvous had been set up for Sab to 'entertain' the caller and thus enable capture of the psychopath before he struck again. It felt right that this could well be their killer.

The B.A.D CID had taken the decision for Flat 43 Church View House, to be the site of the enticement. The location fitted the bill of being positioned in an affluent area of the West Midlands which would maintain the killer's expectations of Enigma being an escort of the up-market kind, yet a surveillance team could easily stay well-hidden in the old church yard that sat opposite the apartment block.

Crucially, there were few options available for the suspect to make his getaway should he get spooked, and this was a valid reason to hold the rendezvous on the fourth floor to limit an escape route even further.

A team had been set up in flats 42 and 44, either side of flat 43, complete with concealed live CCTV monitoring, so if the need to intervene became apparent it would take only a moment for the police to obtain access to the apartment. DCI Chamberlain had made it crystal clear to his colleagues that his command would be imminent the moment DS Mistry's life was placed in danger and decisive action would have to be swiftly forthcoming.

William was to assist in the team occupying Flat 44, as was Judd.

"I hope that this can never be conceived as entrapment," stated Judd, sweat forming on his brow.

"Never, this is good old fashioned undercover surveillance. Thanks to your trumped-up football hooligan Eddie and the young lass Fleur, we have enough evidence to at least suspect this fellow called Gareth and we are all in agreement that is precisely who will show tonight in spite of the lack of facial ID thus far. Besides, without any DNA evidence how else are we going to catch this bastard before he kills again? If we can catch him in the act, about to commit a murder, there is not a jury in the land who won't convict this piece of shit, while all the jigsaw pieces regarding the other murders will simply fit together."

"Anyway, I'm sure we can leave out certain 'methods' of how we have come about setting this 'trap' in the paperwork, aye boss?"

"The case file will have all that it needs to have," said William Chamberlain with a mischievous smile and a wink. "Our priority is to get this scumbag off the streets and away from killing innocent girls."

"Too true William; I just don't want this psycho to get off with a technicality, you know?"

"You worry too much, Judd. By the way, are you still up for going to the match on Saturday?"

"Bloody hell, William. I wish I could be as relaxed as you are. How can you think about football at a time like this? I still don't like putting Sab in this position."

"It's the only way. We all agreed, including Sab remember. Well, are you coming to the match?"

"Does Lionel have a silly face?"

"You bet he does."

"Well I'm coming to the match then, obviously. The fact that I get in for free plays a huge advantage."

"I can always find another carer to accompany me into the disabled stand, and then you would have to pay to watch the game."

"No other sucker would put up with your company, William. Seriously I think it should be a cracking game."

Judd Stone's history of attending his local club's football matches had taken a diverse journey. As a small child he had ached to attend the matches, even standing outside the ground on a Saturday afternoon as he tried to guess what was happening on the pitch on the other side of the wall. He would listen to the reaction of the crowd to gauge what was happening in the thick of the action. The stadium was only a stone's throw away from the children's home where he once resided and the young Judd used to beg the staff to take him to the games, but they used to laugh at him, making a point that there were simply no funds to accommodate taking anyone to football matches.

When Judd was thirteen-years-old he was taken in by foster parents, but his foster dad was as unsympathetic to his cause as the staff at the care home had been, claiming that football was a game for 'poofters' and that young Judd should aim to follow a more manly game such as rugby. The fact that Saturday afternoons clashed with drunken lock-ins at the local pub also prevented 'Dad' from ever having an appetite to take his fostered son to a football match.

It had been Mr. and Mrs. Craig who had fostered Judd up until the age of 18, after which he just became a member of the family. Evelyn Craig would have loved to have formerly adopted Judd before his 18th birthday, but her useless husband Jimmy would never allow it as that would have compromised the payments provided for fostering. Jimmy welcomed this injection of money, not to support the boy whom he was fostering, but to help fund his excessive time spent in the pub.

At least in the long run Evelyn had got what she wanted - Judd to be her son and neither she nor Judd needed a legal declaration on a piece of paper to recognise that fact. Judd chose not to adopt the name Craig as he hated his foster father too much, and besides, just like a legal declaration, a name was unimportant compared with what was in his heart for the woman he considered to be his mother.

Judd didn't only like to watch football he was quite good at playing it too, scoring many goals for the school football team. When Judd reached 15 he secured himself a regular line of cash via a local newspaper round, and with the odd fiver sneaked to him by the ever-caring Evelyn,

Judd was at last able to cheer his local team on from the terraces with his schoolmates.

At the age of 16, Judd had been spotted by a scout for one of the top London football clubs and had earned himself an apprenticeship. In spite of this achievement, Judd had been disappointed that his local club had failed to notice his talent, but he took comfort that a player that originated from his local team, Marlon Howell, had moved on to prove his worth at the London club and was now scoring goals for fun - not only for his club but also in the national side for England. Unfortunately for Judd, his own football career was very short-lived and didn't work out as it should have done, which sent Judd into a downward spiral of depression and bad behaviour recognising that he had ruined his chance of becoming a professional footballer.

By his 17th birthday, the disillusioned Judd Stone had embraced the darkest element of football. Hooliganism. Always handy with his fists, Judd was instrumental in giving the opposing supporters a good kicking on a Saturday afternoon. Much of this fighting was fuelled by Judd's anger of never feeling belonged during his short life, in spite of the efforts that Evelyn Craig could muster in light of her controlling husband. The frustrations of living with a detached and nasty foster father also played its part, but the straw that broke the camel's back was losing out on his dream to play professional football. Judd dealt with such things in the only way he knew how - by hitting out.

The hooliganism in Judd's life went well into his 18th year, his attendance at matches now being funded by unemployment benefit, although his time watching and cheering the footballers on the pitch was becoming less and less important for him. The primary aim for attending matches was to indulge in brawling with the opposition.

Fortunately for Judd, his date of birth had enabled him to miss the most prolific years of the football hooliganism disease of the 1970s, but it was still very much apparent in the 1980s, as demonstrated by the Heysel Stadium disaster on 29 May 1985 when a wall collapsed segregating Liverpool and Juventus fans who had gathered for the European Cup Final. Some 39 Italian and Belgian fans were crushed or trampled to death which brought a 5 year ban on all English clubs being allowed to play in European competitions. Astonishingly, a decision was made for the cup final to still go ahead and Juventus won 1-0 from a second half penalty.

Unfortunately, other 1980s' footballing atrocities occurred. This included another wall collapsing, this time at St Andrews, the football ground of Birmingham City. Blues were hosting Leeds United on that catastrophic day, with the collapsed wall resulting in the tragic death of a young boy. In 1987 Wolves fans rioted across the seaside town of Scarborough, with one fan even falling through the stadium roof. Unfortunately, like most youths not directly involved with such appalling events, Judd was able to mentally distance himself from these terrible acts of violence and their horrific consequences, it was only as he got older that he realised how terrible the whole football hooligan movement had been.

On one occasion, Judd was caught beating a rival supporter with a piece of wood. Luckily Evelyn knew the arresting officer very well, a then Detective Sergeant William Chamberlain who was intricately involved in tackling the increasing trend of football hooliganism across the country. When Evelyn was informed by DS Chamberlain that her son (she always referred to Judd as her son even though it was never a legally-bound connection) was lucky to escape a prison sentence, thanks largely to his influence, the red-haired lady wept at the prospect of Judd being involved in such a violent way of life. Judd hated seeing his mom so upset and he quickly realised that he had lost sight of the reasons why he had originally wanted to attend football matches. He promised to make something of his life and to restore Evelyn's faith in him. With DS Chamberlain's guidance and influence Judd promptly signed up for the police force.

Judd instantly liked the older man by some 13 years and was aware that William's connection with his mother was more than just a simple 'friendship'. Judd was pleased that his mother could find the happiness she shared with William that she could never have with Jimmy.

William was a few years younger than Evelyn, but she had always been a very attractive woman. She had a much defined bone structure to her face which always gave the impression she was younger than she actually was. Judd could see a zest for life in her that had been suppressed until the inspiration had came from her relationship with William. There was also the appearance of a sparkle in her eye that had never been present before he came. Judd's respect for William would never diminish as the years passed.

Jimmy eventually died of a sudden heart attack whilst supping at his local pub, but Evelyn sadly didn't outlive him for long. She was killed by a drunken driver who also killed himself in the process by wrapping his car around a lamp post. This incident robbed Evelyn of the years of happiness she deserved. Ironically the accident occurred outside the football ground where both Judd and William now cheer on their team.

The tragic loss of Evelyn to both Judd and William only proved to bond the two men's friendship even further as years went by, and in many ways the wiser and less impulsive William became the father that Judd never had, even though the years of age difference would usually be associated with a big brother-type relationship. Judd never knew who his real father was and his estranged birth mother had died of a drug overdose when Judd was three years old and living in children's homes.

Judd turned his back on football hooliganism in an instant. He soon enjoyed attending the terraces for the right reasons again with his mentor and friend William

Chamberlain at his side. At the time William was yet to realise that he had Multiple Sclerosis. Workload permitting, they had even managed the odd trip to Wembley and away games when their team had been destined to appear at such stadia. When it comes to supporting the local football team in more recent times, Judd accompanies his friend in the disabled enclosure of the football ground, a telling symbol of how Multiple Sclerosis has now affected William Chamberlain.

Back in Flat 44 Church View House, the two men continued to discuss the forthcoming events of Saturday's football match when they were interrupted by a stunning sight that appeared from the bathroom.

"Blimey, do we have a new copper on the force? I don't recognise this babe," said an open-jawed Judd.

Sabita Mistry had emerged from the bathroom with her dark hair tied up on top to resemble what could be described as a beautiful, dark pineapple with fountains of strands falling delicately over her heavily made-up face. Wearing a short figure-hugging and low-cut midnight blue coloured satin dress, with black frilly bra straps purposely on display at the shoulders, the detective sergeant had been transformed from a pretty but slightly frumpy police woman to a sultry and deliciously stunning young sex-kitten! For once Sab's usually hidden assets of shapely breasts and buttocks could be appreciated as they protruded from her snugly wrapped midnight blue form. Her lips were full and bright red and her eye shadow was an exact shade of her dress which complemented her dark sparkling eyes perfectly. The balance of beauty and sexiness had been achieved to perfection, only the highest price paid could warrant a night with this lady.

"Sabita, you look absolutely beautiful."

"Thanks William, but don't you mean Enigma you look beautiful?"

"Sab don't put yourself down. That is you standing there not some high-class hooker called Enigma. William is right. You do look beautiful. And your legs, I never knew that you had such gorgeous, shapely legs and—."

"Okay Judd cool down, you'll embarrass the poor girl. Seriously Sab, how are you feeling?"

"A little nervous, I guess… Damn, who am I kidding? I'm bricking it. But I'm determined."

"That's my girl," said William.

"Wow, suddenly I wish you were my girl Sab."

"Keep on dreaming, Stone."

"From this moment on they can only be sweet dreams about you."

"Pass me a bucket will you, William? I think I'm going to be sick."

CHAPTER 16

Sabita Mistry had taken sufficient time to acquaint herself with the layout of Flat 43 Church View House knowing that she needed to give the impression that this accommodation was her own. Sab particularly recognised that both the bedroom and kitchen were significant rooms that she needed to appear to be familiar with in order not to spook their suspect. As she soaked in the layout of the rooms, its colour scheme and other elements, her professionalism and experience couldn't fully suppress a chill from running up her spine as she contemplated what had happened to the three murdered women within their respective locations.

Sab's thoughts were broken when a buzz came over the intercom causing her to startle. An acute feeling of anxiety rushed through her body like an internal tidal wave. Sab knew that this was it. There was no turning back now.

"Come on Sab, you can do this," she said, offering herself encouragement.

She moved forward and picked up the receiver.

"Hello."

A monotone voice replied to her.

The same spine-chilling voice that Detective Sergeant

Sabita Mistry had heard at the end of the stolen mobile phone.

"I have an appointment with Enigma."

Sabita felt her stomach squirm to unimaginable proportions but with every ounce of her professionalism she refused to let her nervousness show and released the door to let her visitor enter. "Yes, I have been expecting you. Please come in." Sab surprised herself at how sultry she even managed to sound.

The two minutes or so that it took for the visitor to enter the lift and eventually reach the door of Flat 43 seemed like an eternity to Sabita Mistry. She waited in the hallway, staring at the closed door, hoping that somehow, something would intervene to prevent the appearance of the suspect. Sab's stomach continued to squirm and the palms of her hands began to erupt with clamminess.

In spite of all the hidden cameras and microphones, and the knowledge that a substantial amount of police colleagues were only moments away, Sabita felt very much alone as she waited for the inevitable knock at the door.

Even though she expected it, Sab couldn't help but gasp as that knock at the door finally materialised.

Sabita found herself glued to the spot, fear paralysing her and preventing her from moving forward. The visitor was required to knock again.

Even the sound of his knock sounded sinister. A deliberate trio of well-executed heavy staccato strikes that chilled the stillness of the moment.

Despite her apprehension, Sab knew that she couldn't allow her visitor to knock for a third time and she plucked up the courage to hasten and open the door. She greeted her visitor with a smile that strikingly belied her inner fears, her acting proving worthy of an Oscar or BAFTA.

"Welcome, sir. How nice of you to come. Please come in and make yourself comfortable."

The visitor didn't speak but simply gave the most minimal of nods. His eyes never left Sabita's the whole time he entered the flat and closed the door behind him. He was wearing a canvas; parka coat with the hood pulled up and tied tightly around his face, so tight Sab couldn't even see the colour of his hair through the faux-fur lined window. But there was no mistake in seeing his eyes. He stood with his back to the door for a few moments maintaining his chilling stare as if to signal to Sabita that this door now belonged to him and it was a barrier to the outside world unless it was he who chose to open it.

In Flat 44 William looked at Judd. "We're on."

"Can I get you a drink, sir?" offered Sab, praying her voice was still free of nervousness. "Please come and sit down."

The visitor remained at the door, his evil eyes staring at Sabita. This time he slowly shook his head.

"Oh, okay. No drink. That's fine."

Still leaning against the door, the visitor slowly began to move his eyes up and down Sabita, clearly intending to make her feel uncomfortable. His eyes seemed to penetrate her clothing and his stare was almost tangible as it slowly crept over her breasts, hips and legs making Sabita feel invaded and violated without the need for the visitor to physically reach out to her.

Then suddenly he moved forward causing Sabita to gasp.

"Are you afraid of me?"

"Should I be?"

He didn't answer. Instead he just smiled. Like his stare even his smile was sinister.

"I think we could get better acquainted if I knew your name? After all you know that mine is Enigma."

After a few seconds he spoke. "Gareth."

Bingo!

"Would you like to sit down?" offered Sabita again, pleased the dots were joining up but a little surprised that Gareth had decided to seemingly provide his real name. Then chillingly she realised it didn't matter what name he gave if he was deciding to kill her.

"Why are you not showing me to the bedroom? Isn't that where your work takes place?"

"Well your fee includes me providing you with a full service of companionship. I offer you drinks, good company and conversation at this price; it's not just about you having sex with me. I aim to provide you with a fully holistic and pleasant experience."

"A pleasant experience you say? Oh, I'm sure that you will provide me with that."

"I'm pleased to hear it."

An awkward silence fell once more until Gareth began to move further towards Sabita. She managed to resist flinching as he began to stroke her hair.

Sabita tried to offer a smile that she hoped appeared genuine, but she wished this creep would refrain from touching her at all. She knew that she was not expected to literally have sex with this monster, but she needed to somehow allow Gareth to believe that she was forming a relationship with him in order to entice him into providing an opportune moment to arrest him.

"You are beautiful."

"Thank you"

"Very exotic looking. I doubt very much that you are a Christian looking at your appearance."

"Well I don't see how my religion is relevant, but actually I was raised as a Hindu."

"Don't get defensive, Sab," said William Chamberlain who was monitoring every word and movement. "Don't blow it. Keep your cool."

"A Hindu. I see. On the contrary I think that religion is very relevant. I mean, I don't know much about your God but tell me, does Hinduism promote the existence of prostitution?"

Sab forced a smile. "No, but I have to make a living. I keep my religious beliefs and my work very separate. Besides I do not look upon myself as a prostitute, but more of an escort."

"An escort. Oh forgive me, you are nothing like a prostitute at all then," said Gareth sarcastically.

"Are you a Christian, Gareth?"

"I am."

"I didn't think that paying ladies for sex is something that is accepted in your religion?"

"Who says I pay ladies for sex?"

"So why are you here then?"

Gareth purposely contrived another awkward silence and fixed his sinister stare onto Sab once more, deliberately delivered to unease her. Eventually he spoke.

"To the bedroom then is it?"

"If you wish. We can talk after perhaps." Sabita was finding it more and more difficult to play the perfect hostess to this scary creep.

"We'll see."

"After you Gareth. It's the first door to your left." There was no way that Sab was going to turn her back on this psycho.

Gareth smiled and walked past Sab brushing against her disrespectfully. He didn't look back as she watched his slender figure disappear into the bedroom.

Sab didn't want to, but she knew she had to follow him. Knowing that there were cameras set up in the room allowing her colleagues to monitor her safety did little to reassure her.

Taking a deep breath, Sab plucked up the courage and also entered the bedroom. Still in his parka, Gareth was standing at the far side of the room.

"Please come in," he said, appearing to forget that the bedroom was meant to be Sab's.

"Are you not going to take your coat off?"

"Are you not going to take your dress off?"

"Of course." Sabita moved slowly due to her reluctance to comply, which ironically gave the impression she was expertly teasing her client. She removed the dress south over her shapely breasts and dropped it to the floor as she stepped out of it in her high heels. She looked stunning as she stood there in a black laced underwear set, which Sab had cleverly ensured would cover her most sacred places. Nevertheless, she felt very exposed and uncomfortable, but kept reminding herself that what she was doing was necessary to put this monster behind bars.

Time to get sultry again Mistry. She told herself.

"So do you like what you see, Gareth?"

"I see Mary Magdalene, the filthy whore," came a mono-toned sinister reply that actually disappointed Sab considering her efforts.

"Excuse me?"

"Forgive me Enigma, I just like to speak dirty that's all. I'm sure that you are used to all sorts of weird and wacky requests in your profession. Whips or costumes for instance. I just like to speak dirty, that's my bag. Is that okay with you Enigma?"

"I guess so."

"Lie on the bed then bitch."

"I would prefer you to take your coat off, after all how can you erm, interact with it on?"

"I can simply undo it. If I want to that is. I like to leave it on when I *perform*. Like I said I'm sure that you are used to weird and wacky requests?"

Sab wasn't sure she wanted to go through with this. How was she going to get enough information from him without having to have sex with the man? The previous killings didn't necessarily indicate that sex had actually been part of the event, but this seemed to be Gareth's intent tonight. Unless it was simply part of a plan to control and humiliate her? Sab had already gone further than she wanted to by removing her dress, there was no way she was going to remove her underwear for this horrible individual. Besides, when her colleagues did recognise the need to intervene she wasn't altogether thrilled at the prospect of them seeing her naked either.

"I want you to get on the bed, Enigma."

Reluctantly, but in the character of Enigma, Sab got on the bed appearing as provocative as she could.

"Good, now remove your bra."

"Please remove your coat first; it's freaking me out a bit."

Gareth suddenly became angry and exploded in stark contrast to his previous quiet and deliberate menacing demeanour. "I told you that I like to leave my coat on," he screamed. He flung his arms out and knocked the plant pot on the floor smashing it instantly. The problem was it was the plant pot that was hiding the camera for William and Judd's benefit in room 44.

"Shit, we have lost the picture," said Judd.

"It's okay we can still hear what's going on and the other guys can see what is happening from Flat 42," said William.

"*I* prefer to see what is going on. I'm going in."

"No, it's too soon." William began to communicate by radio to his colleagues in Flat 42; DI Lionel Scarrow was leading the team in that particular room. "We have lost our picture in here Scarrow, so things have changed. You are no longer waiting for my signal so it is now your call Scarrow. I'm sure that you will relish your temporary promotion to DCI. Now listen carefully, you let me know when Sab is in danger, okay? And then we go in and nail this joker. We need to get enough evidence on this prick to make it count – but Sab's safety is paramount. I repeat Sab's safety is paramount."

"Roger that," said a smug DI Scarrow, more pleased with his sudden escalation of authority than the fact that Judd and William had lost a camera to Sab's room. William knew that it wasn't an ideal situation but he saw little option as Scarrow was now the most senior officer with the ability to physically see what was happening.

"My apologies Enigma, I didn't mean to lose my temper." Fortunately Gareth had not spotted the wires within the smashed plant pot.

"It's okay."

"However, you need my help to take you away from this life that you lead. You need me to deliver you from this existence. You need me to deliver you from evil."

"What do you mean?"

"You are living a life of sin."

"So what do you propose? How will you save me?"

"All will be revealed in good time." Gareth placed his hand in his coat pocket and searched around for a few moments. He quickly realised that the small bottle of rohypnol was missing. How could he have been so stupid? He must have dropped it somewhere, he was sure he had it. Never mind, he would continue without it. Perhaps it would be fun to slice this one while she could watch, but he knew that he needed to be careful not to give away any DNA. His thick coat would perhaps prevent her from scratching his skin and he was going to burn the coat after his work was done any way. Fortunately he had quite a grand collection of hooded garments.

Meanwhile in Room 44, Judd Stone was becoming increasingly agitated with the situation. "I don't like this Guv. I'm going in."

"It's too soon, Judd. Scarrow will let us know when the time is right. Meanwhile just listen to what's happening."

Gareth Banks continued. "Tell me Enigma, do you like cooking?"

"Yes, I guess so."

"Why didn't you take up a profession as a cook then? Much more dignified than being an escort don't you think?"

"I guess it doesn't pay as well."

"Ahh, and there it is - money. Everything always come down to money doesn't it in this day and age? Money is the root to all evil don't you know? Tell me, what sorts of knives do you have in your kitchen, Enigma?"

"Knives. Why do you ask?"

"Just curious, I have worked as a chef myself you see. Different knives do different things, slice fruit, chop herbs, slice bread you know what I mean? Only a certain type of knife is able to cut through flesh though."

"That's it I've heard enough."

"No Judd, it's too soon. He hasn't done anything yet… Scarrow is Sab in danger in there?"

"No Guv, they are just talking at the moment."

"The second that you think Sab is in danger you let us know, do you understand, Scarrow?"

"Yes Guv, it's all under control."

"I'm trusting you, Scarrow."

Back in the bedroom of flat 43, Sabita's stomach increasingly churned. This guy was weird and she didn't know where this situation would eventually go, even though she knew she had an army of colleagues surrounding her.

"Perhaps I could go and take a look at what knives you have in the kitchen. Would you object to that, Enigma?" Gareth had returned to his slow and deliberate menacing delivery of speech.

"Well, it's a bit unusual for you to go and leave me to look at knives; I mean I am lying here in my underwear. It's not something that usually happens to me."

"But you said that I could have an entire holistic and pleasant experience did you not? Well at the moment I would like to study your knife collection. Perhaps you could remove your remaining underwear for when I return in a moment."

Scarrow was watching everything and he felt the need to communicate with his DCI: "He is leaving the bedroom; I'll let you know when he returns."

William: "If he returns with a knife we wait until he threatens her or at worst makes a move towards her, but if it's the latter we had better act damn quick. I'm afraid simply holding a knife and talking about a knife isn't enough to charge this psycho. Sab's been briefed on the situation and she is no mug. She knows how to disarm someone. She knows that she needs to get him to say something more incriminating - then we have got him. However, Scarrow, as you know if she shouts out the code word 'Geronimo', we go in regardless."

Scarrow: "Roger that, Guv."

Judd: "I don't trust Scarrow to get this right."

William: "He will. Even he won't want to put Sab in danger."

Judd: "If he does put Sab in danger, it is me who you will be placing on a murder charge for killing my scumbag colleague."

Scarrow: "We have cut to the screen in the kitchen Guv; he is indeed looking through the collection of knives. He has placed gloves on now and is admiring the knives one by one, scrutinising them, caressing them as if they are items of diamond-encrusted jewellery or something."

Judd: "If he has put gloves on he is obviously looking to kill Sab and leave no trace."

William: "Very likely, but at the moment the jury would simply be led to believe that they were dealing with an eccentric ex-chef who likes to discuss kitchen knives whilst wearing gloves."

Judd: "I don't like it."

Scarrow: "He is leaving the kitchen and going back to the bedroom. He has one almighty big knife with him in his right hand and has placed several others in the pockets of his parka."

Judd: "That's it. I'm going in."

William: "No wait, Judd it's too early. Just a few seconds more so we have some real shit on this guy."

But William's words were in vain. Judd had been in a situation before where he could have saved a young girl from harm and he wasn't keen to let it happen again.

Sabita gulped hard as Gareth stood at the doorway grinning as he caressed the knife in his gloved hands.

"This is a lovely specimen," he said.

Genuinely concerned for her life, Sabita wondered if now was a good time to call out the code word to signal a rescue from her colleagues, but she realised that a few seconds longer was probably all it needed to have enough evidence to convict this monster.

"So Gareth, do you usually use knives when you visit prostitutes? I mean, do you actually use them on anyone? Do you like to cause them harm?"

Good girl, thought William as he listened in.

But before Gareth had time to answer and incriminate himself, he was startled to hear the door of Flat 43 being kicked off its hinges, and as he turned to look up the hallway he saw a 6ft 2 inch manic individual come hurtling towards him at a tremendous pace. Gareth didn't even have time to raise the knife to protect himself as Judd flew at him feet first, connecting with Gareth's torso, sending both his victim and the knife spilling onto the floor in separate directions.

Already severely winded, moments later Gareth was losing consciousness as his attacker stood over him grabbing the scruff of the parka with one hand to perfectly align his head to the point of attack, while Judd proceeded to punch him in the face with his other hand over and over again. During the assault Judd had also managed to rip open the cord of the hood and release a bigger target to aim at.

Seeing the rage in his fellow DI's face, Lionel Scarrow thought better to intervene when he entered the room and ordered three of his officers to attempt to persuade Judd Stone to stop beating the suspect to a pulp. Judd eventually released his victim as his colleagues somehow managed to pull him away, leaving the bruised and battered suspect in a state of semi-consciousness.

Judd turned to Sabita who had protected her modesty by wrapping a sheet around her underwear-clad torso.

"Are you okay, Sab?" he asked.

Sab smiled, "Yes thanks, Guv." Of course Sab realised

that Judd had entered the vicinity a moment too soon as it seemed she may have been able to have teased some incriminating evidence out of Gareth, but she was grateful all the same to her DI and was glad that the horrible situation was over. "Geronimo."

Judd also smiled as Sab released the code word signalling that his female colleague was glad for his intervention. A groan could be heard from the direction of Gareth Banks' battered heap.

William was unable to get to the scene in any great haste due to his medical condition, but once he arrived and realised what had occurred he simply radioed across to DI Tam Jennings who was leading the team in the graveyard opposite the apartments. "It's okay Tam, your men can stand down. DI Judd Stone has the situation firmly under control."

CHAPTER 17

The world-renowned London based football club had decided to have a little fun by blending the young apprentices with the senior squad members for a training session. Eagerly ceasing the opportunity 16 year-old Judd Stone, who appeared stronger and more mature for his tender years, was beginning to make a marked impression.

It filled Judd with enormous pleasure to be able to share the field with the likes of Marlon Howell, a prolific and popular striker who had previously made his name at the Birmingham based team that Judd had always supported since a small boy. Howell's very presence had inspired Judd to make an impact on the training session.

Like many youths of the 1980s, Judd had even copied Marlon's hairstyle that had been dubbed the footballers' perm. The hairstyle consisted of the hair being left natural but flicked on the top with a mane of curls falling down the back of the neck beyond the shoulders. At today's training session, Judd had managed to emulate his hero even further by scoring four goals - the exact same amount as Howell had achieved.

The usual banter associated with footballers soon surfaced as Howell's team mates ribbed him with remarks such as "Watch it Howell, that kid's gonna take your jersey."

Watching with interest from the sidelines was the team manager, the coaching staff and a girl who worked in the ticket office called Bonnie.

Bonnie was 19 and Judd fancied her like mad.

Content with the input from his squad, the manager blew the final whistle to signal the end of the training session and called the players, both apprentices and professional, to gather round.

"You young lads done really well today, especially our young goal scorer Stone here, therefore as you have matched the senior players of the team I feel that they are obliged to take you all out tonight to the West End and show you a night on the town. They can treat you to a show or something because you have earned it.

"I like my players to bond so tonight you have my permission to go out and enjoy yourself, but not too much, remember you are always representatives of the club. I want anyone under the age of 18 to drink soft drinks only. I don't want anything appearing in tomorrow's papers that shouldn't. Is that clear?"

"Yes boss," came the unified reply.

"Now go and get showered. I'll see you all tomorrow so don't be thinking of crying off with any bad heads or hangovers."

Judd could hardly believe it. He was going to join the professionals in the spectacular arena of the West End. It was at times like these Judd wished he had a proper father whom he could give a call and share his excitement with. Surely any dad would be proud of what he was achieving right now?

As the players left the field Marlon Howell approached Judd. "You did well today, kid".

"Wow, thanks Marlon."

"You are from Birmingham I believe?"

"Yes."

"Like I say, you did well but don't get any big ideas just yet. The soft southerners at this club can only just about accept one Brummie taking the limelight and you still have a long way to go. Today was just a kick about and the boys went easy on you youngsters. You will have harder days than today if you are going to make it."

"I won't take anything for granted, Marlon."

"Make sure you don't," and with that Marlon sprinted ahead.

Judd felt slightly dejected by Marlon's comments. Was Marlon feeling a little put out, warning Judd off from trying to take his crown? Or was he simply offering some sound advice, trying to ensure that Judd remained grounded? Didn't Marlon realise that Judd looked up to him? Howell was an England international and Judd could tell that in today's training session, Marlon and the other professionals were not altogether taking the game seriously, whereas Judd and his youthful counterparts were playing out of their skin in an attempt to impress. Marlon Howell certainly had nothing to worry about.

It had been decided that the senior players would take Judd and the other youngsters to a bar near Covent Garden. It was not too many years ago that the area had been swarming with New Romantics, including the likes of Steve Strange, Boy George and members of Spandau Ballet.

So far the boss's instructions had been followed accordingly. Judd and the other youngsters were drinking soft drinks, Judd getting hydrated on orange juice, whilst even some of the more serious senior professionals were laying off the hard stuff.

"Hey, isn't that Andrew Ridgeley over there?" Enquired Levi Rutherford, a good friend of Judd's.

"Could be," answered Theo MacArthur. "You can spot the odd celebrity out and about in this part of the city but I think Mr. Ridgeley spends most of his time in Monaco these days."

Both Levi and Theo were products of Jamaican parents, although they differed considerably in their appearance and build. Levi was very slight-framed and although he was yet to finish growing it didn't appear that he would ever reach much beyond 5ft 6ins. What he lacked in height he more than made up for in pace and his little legs were a perfect size for securing the ball at his tricky feet. Levi made it look like the football stayed with him almost by a magnetic connection.

Theo on the other hand was well over 6 feet tall and built like an athlete should be. His rippling muscles were carved beautifully beneath his dark skin. Theo regularly played in the centre of defence for the first team and although very competitive, and at times even aggressive on the field of play, he was a perfect gentleman and a model professional for the likes of Judd and Levi to learn from.

Marlon Howell was drinking beer. "What time are we taking these young girls to the show then, Theo?" The reference to young girls disrespectfully being aimed at Judd, Levi and the other youth players.

"Well we haven't got any tickets yet so I think we can let them choose their own show. They all start in about half an hour or so."

"If we haven't got tickets then perhaps we can choose a show for them. Isn't it our duty to show them a bit of culture? We can teach these young lads a few things about the meaning of life."

"I know the sort of place you're thinking of Marlon. I don't think the boss would be too impressed. He is trusting us to look after these kids and they are under 18 remember."

"Oh don't be such a spoilsport Theo; don't you think these lads would enjoy a night in a titty bar?"

Judd and Levi looked at one another, their eyes alight with excitement. Neither of them had had a great deal of experience with the opposite sex, let alone being able to watch a lady, or even ladies, taking off their clothes right in front of their very eyes.

"No Marlon, the boss wouldn't like it."

"The boss goes there himself sometimes, I bet you any money when we get there tonight he is sat in the front row perving away."

"He would not want us to take the young boys there; he said a few soft drinks and a show."

"Exactly a *show*. Can't you read between the lines Theo, he was obviously hinting at us to take them to a proper show. You know what I mean?"

"I think you are calling this wrong, Marlon."

"Let's ask the boys what they would prefer then. An evening watching Mary Poppins or an evening having their eyes pop out."

Judd and Levi didn't need to give an answer; the look on their faces said it all.

Marlon had managed to convince the entire party of footballers to attend the strip club. Theo had reluctantly agreed to come along in the hope that he could at least try and limit the amount of trouble the young boys could find themselves in. His first commitment to this was to go to the bar for the first round of drinks, ensuring that all of the younger players were to drink fruit juices or cola.

Judd, Levi and the other apprentices felt like they had died and gone to heaven. So far they had been witness to no less than three diverse performances, though each one ultimately climaxed with the same end result – the revelation of every inch of a woman's body.

The first stripper used a chair as part of her act, bending suggestively across and around it; the second one using large fans teasing the audience with a scintillating routine of "now you see me, now you don't" and the third bizarrely shedding a safari outfit whilst having a live python wrapped around her neck.

In-between the ladies' performances, the audience were

entertained by a comedian-cum-compere called Dave, who had a gravelly cockney accent and a list of blue jokes as long as a football pitch. During one of Dave's stories, Marlon leaned over to Judd and Levi and said "You know boys, being a footballer can get you plenty of perks. Do you like the look of any of these ladies tonight?"

"Well sure," replied Levi. "Who wouldn't?"

"Well like I say, there are certain perks to being a footballer and this particular joint has a number of additional rooms where we can sample a little extra something if you know what I mean." Marlon tapped the side of his nose to emphasise his point.

"That's enough now Marlon," said Theo. "These boys have had enough entertainment for one night now leave it out. I'm serious."

Marlon could see that Theo was serious and wisely decided to withdraw from the conversation.

Dave finished his joke and he waited for the laughter to die down before continuing to address the audience. "Now gentlemen, soon we have a real treat for you. Our next performance will be from a new girl we have just had the pleasure of recruiting to the club. I know you will make her feel very welcome. Gentlemen, please put your hands together for...Cherry."

A young girl walked out amongst the applause and wolf-whistles, wearing a long sequined silver dress, complemented by a pair of white gloves that hugged her arms almost all the way up to her shoulders. She was clearly the most attractive performer that had entered the stage tonight, but there was a slight hesitance and awkwardness as she took centre stage, underlining the fact that perhaps she wasn't used to this sort of thing.

As the spotlight reached her pretty face it wasn't altogether obvious at first, possibly due to the heavy makeup that had been applied in sharp contrast to what this girl would usually wear, but it soon became clear that this girl wasn't really called Cherry at all. It was Bonnie from the ticket office.

Amongst the wolf-whistles and hand-clapping, Judd actually began to squirm a little. He had imagined, and even yearned, to see Bonnie Glass naked on many occasions. But not like this. He had no claim on Bonnie, he knew that, and although he had chatted with her many times, he was never sure if she would ever take him seriously as a potential boyfriend. But one thing was for sure, he was not going to let these testerone-fuelled footballers see her in the nip!

Judd needn't have worried. Bonnie, aka Cherry, had only managed to remove a single glove when she glanced into the audience and received an unexpected surprise when she spotted the footballers whom she knew from her every day job. She had already been unsure of this additional career path but suddenly she felt ashamed and humiliated. Bursting into tears she ran from the stage forcing Dave to return somewhat prematurely.

Amidst stunned silences and hissing, Dave offered his apologies cracking a quick gag about first night nerves and quickly introduced a more seasoned stripper onto the stage which fortunately began to satisfy the punters once again.

The footballers were a mixture of shock and high spirits. "Blimey that was Bonnie wasn't it?" they said to one another.

Before tonight's events, Theo had recognised that Judd had liked Bonnie and he had also spotted that the young footballer wasn't laughing or gossiping like many of his team mates.

"Okay lads, I think we have had enough entertainment for one night. What do you say we move on now? You know what the gaffer said, he wants us all at training tomorrow with a clear head, and I don't think there is any need to mention this to Bonnie either. Is that clear?"

Theo was always a voice of reason and everyone showed respect whenever the big man spoke. The laughing ceased and everyone agreed to get up from their seats and vacate the premises. Once outside and after the briefest of debates, everyone agreed it was a good time to end the evening and go home. Everyone except Marlon Howell that was.

"Come on lads, the night is young; let's go to a club or something."

"You carry on Marlon," said Theo. "The night has come to a natural end for most of us."

"Okay, I'll party on my own if I have to, but I'm sure I can find someone else to party with. In fact I may go back into the strip club."

"Erm, I'd like to stick around too," said Judd.

"You want to see if Bonnie's okay don't you? You've been trying for weeks to get into her knickers and now you know that she is a stripper you want a private showing of your own don't you young Stone, you randy little sod."

"Leave the kid alone, Howell."

"Are you going to make me, Theo?"

"If I have to."

Marlon Howell looked into the hard stare of Theo MacArthur and wisely decided not to react. Instead he spun on his inebriated heels and headed off on his own.

"Are you okay, Judd?"

"Yes thanks, Theo."

"Come on lads, it's time to go home. There's a taxi rank not far from here."

"I'll catch up with you lads."

"I'm not sure, Judd."

"I'll be fine, Theo. I just need a few minutes, that's all."

"Ok. Be careful."

"I'll be fine, Theo."

The young Judd Stone stood alone not really sure what to do next as raindrops enveloped him in the cold air of the night. He just knew he couldn't leave Bonnie alone at the moment but what should he do? Go back into the club after her? His dilemma was solved when Bonnie suddenly appeared from the club.

She spotted Judd and froze in her tracks. Judd could see that Bonnie's eye make up had suffered the effects of her crying, as black streaks masked her high cheek bones. To Judd she still looked beautiful.

"Judd, why are you here? Oh, I get it you've discovered that I'm working in a gentlemens' club and decided to hang around, as it must mean I'm easy right?"

"Not at all Bonnie. I just wanted to make sure that you are alright."

"Well clearly I'm not; I'm humiliated, and as I didn't even finish my erm... act... I haven't even been paid for the humiliation. At least I quit before they could sack me." Bonnie dropped her head. "What must you think of me, Judd?"

"I think you are lovely, Bonnie. I always have and I always will. Whatever happened tonight has no bearing on my feelings for you." Judd hoped that the dim street lights was enough to prevent Bonnie from seeing him blush.

Bonnie walked over to Judd and stroked his cheek. "You are so sweet, Judd. Thanks for waiting for me, it was very kind of you."

"Why did you do it Bonnie? Why did you want to be a stripper?"

"I wanted the money and I thought I wanted the attention. I don't get paid a lot by the football club believe it or not and I thought I would like men looking at me. I don't have much in the way of brains but I've noticed how men look at me and I thought I liked it, but I now know that stripping is not for me. A bit of flirting with the footballers is one thing but taking your clothes off to a group of strangers is another. At least I didn't actually get to strip off, this being my first night. Now I know I never will."

"We all make mistakes Bonnie, but I can see why you considered doing it. You are gorgeous. You would have made a great stripper but I'm glad that you have packed it in before it really got going."

Bonnie smiled at Judd's clumsy attempt at complimenting her. "Thanks for cheering me up Judd, and thanks for waiting for me. It's nice to see a friendly face. I bet all the others had a right good laugh didn't they? I don't know how I'm going to face them tomorrow?"

"No-one is laughing at you Bonnie," said Judd. "Come on, shall we go to a club or something to help you forget about things."

"I think I just want to go home, Judd. I'm sorry."

"That's fine Bonnie, another time perhaps?" Judd began to redden again.

"Perhaps." Bonnie smiled that beautiful smile of hers again. "You can escort me home if you like?"

"It would be an honour."

Bonnie linked Judd's arm and they made their way to the taxi rank.

During the taxi journey the two youngsters discussed all sorts of things. Judd informed Bonnie of his upbringing in Birmingham and Bonnie told Judd what it was like growing up in the east end of London as one of seven children. She explained how she loved her siblings but it had been a necessity to get her own place and she was pleased with her small home in Whitechapel which gave her a little piece of independence. However, the rent could be very challenging hence her ill-fated calculation to work as a stripper.

Judd was also surprised of Bonnie's dislike for Marlon Howell.

"I thought all the birds loved Howell?"

"Not me. I know he is regarded as the pin-up boy but he gives me the creeps. You see Judd, a guy like Howell can only ever love one person – and that's himself. I hate the way he looks at me as if he thinks I'm one of the women who should just fall at his feet. I know most women do just that but not this one."

"He was my hero not so long ago. They say that you

should never meet your heroes don't they? I really wanted to be like him but I must admit since joining the club I am seeing him in a very different light."

"You don't need to be like anyone else Judd, you are fine as yourself and tonight I've learned that you are wise beyond your years. I also saw you training today and you can be just as good as Marlon Howell, better even you mark my words…if you just pull up on the right driver, that will be fine."

The taxi driver brought the London cab to a halt and Judd could hear the diesel engine purring as Bonnie leaned forward and pecked him on the cheek.

"You know Judd, why don't you come in and have a coffee as they say?"

As Judd felt the butterflies in his stomach fly at record breaking speed he found himself surprisingly hesitant. "Bonnie, I really, really like you and that is why I'm not sure that it would be a good idea to come in."

"Well that doesn't seem to make a whole of sense."

"It's just, well you know. You may be feeling a bit vulnerable after the evening's events and I wouldn't want you to feel an obligation to ask me in."

Bonnie frowned as Judd clumsily continued.

"I can't believe I'm saying this. I've fancied you for so long. It's just I really respect you Bonnie. If after a good night's sleep you want to pick up where we have left off I'll be more than happy. I just want you to be sure about us Bonnie."

"Judd, you are a perfect gentleman and like I said, wise beyond your years; more's the pity for me tonight I guess. You are so sweet. Okay, I'll see you at the club tomorrow."

"You sure will and I hope I'm not going to regret this decision. Don't worry about the fare; I'll sort out the payment when I get to the Rileys'." The Rileys were the elderly couple who allowed Judd to stay at their house as part of the club's efforts to provide a home for their apprentices who originate from outside the London area.

Bonnie opened the door which instantly invited in a cold vapour to swamp the cab, but Judd was soon oblivious to the temperature as Bonnie moved towards him and they engaged in a very passionate kiss. The auburn-haired beauty eventually pulled away and left the vehicle. She tasted so good that Judd was very tempted to resist being a gentleman, but it just felt right not to rush things with such a sweet girl like Bonnie. He wanted everything to be perfect with her.

As the taxi manoeuvred away from the kerbside, Bonnie fumbled in her handbag for her front door key.

"Got it," she said to herself and gave a sweet sigh and smile as she reminisced about her kiss with Judd. She never really realised it until tonight, but she actually quite liked him. Judd's age had been the natural barrier but after tonight she almost felt like she had known him all her life. She realised that she felt very comfortable in his company. She swung open the creaky gate and made her way up the short path to her front door, the darkness of the night concealing how much it was in need of a lick of paint.

Bonnie's small terraced house also possessed a side-entry that was concealed by some slightly overgrown privet and bushes.

Suddenly a voice appeared unexpectedly from the darkness of the entry giving Bonnie a fright. "About time too. It's a bit cold out here, I need to get warm." The voice belonged to Marlon Howell.

The next morning's training session was a little subdued. Judd couldn't concentrate on his game and found himself continuously looking over towards the sideline searching for Bonnie. He couldn't help but notice that she hadn't been watching today. This led him to believe that in the cold light of day she must have decided not pursue their relationship and this feeling of dejection told heavily on his performance. Marlon Howell by contrast had a clear adrenalin rush and was even playing in a very over-zealous and aggressive manner for a training match with his colleagues.

Fortunately not much had been said amongst the guys about Bonnie and the unearthing of her somewhat surprising career path. Theo's influence seemed to have been enough to quash the smutty talk, but Judd was surprised at how even Howell wasn't talking about the unexpected discovery at the strip club.

The end of the day's training session couldn't have come any sooner for Judd, and once showered he went in search of Bonnie, only to discover that she had phoned in to say she was too ill to attend work today. Judd concluded that Bonnie must have cried off concerned about what the boys may say to her. He decided to head over to her house to inform her that all was okay and not much was being said about the incident at all.

Judd opened the creaky gate which led to Bonnie's home and noticed the rust caked on the hinges. Then he noticed the flaking paint on her door before knocking on it. As he waited for a reply he thought how he could perhaps impress Bonnie by offering to complete a bit of maintenance on the property.

Enough seconds passed to prompt Judd to knock again.

"Go away," came the voice from behind the wooden door.

"It's me, Judd."

"Go away; I don't want to see anyone."

"Are you crying, Bonnie?"

"Please, Judd. I just want to be alone."

By this point Judd was feeling concerned. "Bonnie, have I done something to offend you?"

"No Judd, not you. Please, I'm okay but just leave me alone."

"Well someone has clearly upset you, and I'm sorry Bonnie, but you sure don't sound okay."

"Please, go away, you don't need to concern yourself

with this. It's not fair on you."

"Concern myself with what?"

"Just go away Judd, please. I'm err not feeling very well."

"No one said anything today about the strip club if that's what you are worried about. That's why I came round, to reassure you. There is no need to be worried. Not even Marlon said much."

Judd heard Bonnie's sobs increase at the mention of the footballer's name.

"It's Marlon isn't it? What has he done?"

"Please Judd; I just want to forget it. Who would believe me anyway?"

"Believe what exactly?

Just then Judd heard the bolt of the door open and he was greeted by the tear-stained face of the woman he considered to be so beautiful and special. Her lip and left eye were both badly swollen.

"Oh Judd, I'm so sorry," and with those words she flung herself into his arms and sobbed uncontrollably.

"What is it, Bonnie? What's wrong?"

Bonnie seemed to reluctantly break away from Judd, she obviously felt a sense of safety being snuggled into his chest. "You had better come in," she said.

Once inside Bonnie closed the door behind them.

"What is it, Bonnie? You look so upset."

"When I got home last night, Howell was waiting for me. He started to tease me about the strip club and demanded that I give him a private show. He wasn't very happy when I refused and I told him to sling his hook and leave me alone."

Judd didn't have to be Einstein to work out what had happened here last night. If only he hadn't insisted on playing the 'gentleman' he could have protected Bonnie from the monster. He felt a sudden overwhelming sense of responsibility for what had happened to Bonnie, yet he also felt an overwhelming sense of vengeance.

"It will be okay Bonnie, I promise. Once I see Howell it will all be over."

"No Judd, think of your career in the team."

"To hell with my career."

"Judd, what's up, buddy? You look well vexed," asked Levi recognising instantly the look of thunder on his friend's face. Levi had never seen his friend look so angry before.

"Where's Howell?"

"He's in the canteen finishing off his meal. Why?"

But Judd never replied. Instead he simply clenched his fists and headed towards the canteen. When he rapidly arrived there he squinted his eyes with menace in order to search the dining tables for Howell, and soon located him shovelling a spoonful of desert into his mouth, quickly followed by a sip of coffee.

Howell was sitting with a cluster of senior players and as Judd marched towards them they couldn't believe that they were witnessing the unprecedented sight of an apprentice entering their eating area.

"Stone, what do you wan—" but before Howell could finish his question, Judd had punched him square in the face resulting in the star striker vacating his chair and hitting the deck. Howell's cockiness had deserted him just as quickly as he had fallen to the floor and he looked petrified as he stared up at Judd's angry face.

"You think you are untouchable don't you, Howell? Even I thought you were someone special but not anymore you dirty fucking rapist. You're going to pay for what you did to Bonnie." And with that Judd kicked Howell hard in the stomach forcing the wind out of him.

Finding it difficult to speak, Howell managed enough words to try and convince Judd to halt the attack. "Please Stone, she asked for it. She begged me to have it away with her; it was purely with her consent."

"You lying poisonous prick," said Judd as he kicked Howell in the ribs causing everyone to hear a cracking sound travel across the room.

The other players could hardly believe what was happening before their eyes. It was clear that the young boy was extremely angry and he had called Howell a rapist. The combination of curiosity and shock prevented them from intervening.

Howell screamed in pain before managing to speak once more. "If you touch me again Stone, that's your career finished in this team. Think about it kid, don't throw it all away for some slapper. We saw her at a strip club remember. She begged me for it, all women do. I'm Marlon Howell for Christ's sake. Leave me alone now and we will say no more about it, I won't tell the boss."

But all Judd wanted to do was to make this pathetic excuse for a human being pay for what he had done to poor Bonnie.

"You make me laugh bragging about the women you screw, how many of them were willing participants or more rape victims, Howell? To think I looked up to you like some sort of role model, and now look at you, you couldn't fight your way out of a paper bag you dirty fucking rapist. You're scum, Howell." And with those words Judd jumped on Howell and beat and punched his face until he was bloody, unconscious and within an inch of his life.

It took three senior players to eventually pull the raging Judd Stone off the footballing rapist and their intervention had managed to save Judd from being placed on a murder charge. As a result of the attack, the star striker spent a full week in hospital, missing two football matches, but the press were merely informed that Howell had suffered an injury during a training session.

Soon Howell returned to normal duties having survived Judd's beating and crucially for him the judicial system. The boss had believed Howell's version of events that Bonnie Glass had been a willing participant in any sexual encounter.

Bonnie had not had the confidence to go to the police in spite of Judd's encouragement, she always maintained that like the boss, the police would believe Howell and she would end up looking humiliated and branded a vindictive liar.

She also had fears of how the press would portray her and she made Judd promise to never involve them. She told Judd that he should just be pleased that Howell had received a damn good beating from him and that at least had served as a significant kind of retribution.

Bonnie was sacked from her job at the club and Judd was told to thank himself lucky that he also was only being relieved of his duties. The boss had told him he was fortunate that he hadn't been subjected to a charge for GBH.

Word soon got around the football circuit that a promising young footballer by the name of Judd Stone could not be trusted; his temperament did not suit that of a professional footballer. So Judd Stone's football career was over before it had started. Bonnie Glass committed suicide three months later.

Judd wasn't going to make the same mistake twice with Sab.

Even though she had been under careful police surveillance, a luxury of protection that poor Bonnie had never had, Judd had felt the years of guilt nagging at his psyche and he simply couldn't hold back and keep Sab in danger any longer. Every punch that he had laid on Banks' face was symbolic of the guilt that he still felt for allowing Bonnie to be subjected to the rape by Marlon Howell. Each telling blow had been as much for Bonnie as it had been for Sab, but the reality remained that no matter how many times, or how hard he had hit either Gareth Banks or Marlon Howell, it would never truly eradicate the guilt, responsibility and anguish he would always feel.

CHAPTER 18

"Take a seat Mr. Banks," offered DCI Chamberlain.

"Thank you," said Gareth Banks as he sat down.

"But don't assume that we are here to make you feel comfortable, you nasty little prick," spat Judd.

"What is this? Good cop, bad cop?"

"No. Bad cop, bad cop," sneered Judd.

"We gave you your right to make a single phone call, did you arrange for legal representation?" asked William.

"I don't need any. I have not done anything wrong."

"So let me get this clear, you are happy to proceed with this interview without a brief?" enquired William.

"Yeah, like I said, I've done nothing wrong."

"Ok, as you wish." William began to put the formal process of the interview in motion. "This interview is being recorded on both audio tape and video which can be monitored remotely. The time is twenty-three hours and nine minutes pm. I am Detective Chief Inspector William Chamberlain; other officers present are Detective Inspector Judd Stone. DI Stone would you please make your identity known for the benefit of the tape." Judd obliged with the request. "The suspect being interviewed is Gareth Banks who has stated that the interview can proceed without the presence of any legal representation on his part, for the purposes of the tape would you confirm this please, Mr. Banks."

"That is correct."

"And for the purposes of the tape do you confirm that you are indeed Gareth Banks."

"That's what my medical card says."

"Please simply state your name, Mr. Banks."

"My name is Gareth Banks," said the suspect in a slow and sarcastic tone.

Judd then picked up the line of questioning. "So you like knives, Mr. Banks?"

"I used to be a chef. Like most people who take a pride in their work they like to admire the tools of their trade. Do you not like your truncheon, DI Stone?"

"Ok, so using your own theory then, Mr. Banks, I would suggest that knives could also be the tools of the trade for a prolific serial killer, wouldn't you agree? Nevertheless, let's remain with the occupation of being a chef for the time being. So where have you worked in this line of business?"

"A few places around London. I don't think any of the restaurants exist any more?"

"Would you describe yourself as somewhat of a fantasist, Mr. Banks?"

"Why do you ask that?"

"I'm not sure that you ever were a chef. It's a bit convenient that the restaurants where you worked now cease to be accessible, denying us the opportunity to verify your story."

"Are you calling me a liar, DI Stone?"

Judd moved forward staring intensely at Banks. "I think that will be proven in good time, but for the record - yes. I'm calling you a fucking liar."

William decided to intervene as he saw the anger begin to engulf Judd's face. "So you were simply admiring the knives in the flat because you were once a chef?"

"Yes."

"Did you not realise that your handling of the knives could cause the young lady in your presence to feel threatened?"

"You mean that stooge you deployed? She was a policewoman no doubt."

"You thought that she was a prostitute. Do you visit prostitutes regularly?"

"No comment."

"Don't start that 'no comment' bollocks with us," said Judd.

"I have rights."

"So did the women that you decided to fucking kill."

"Where were you on the night of February 27th 2011?" asked William Chamberlain.

"I can't remember?"

"Where were you on the night of March 3rd 2011?"

"I can't remember?"

"Where were you on the night of March 7th 2011?"

"I can't remember?"

"That wasn't that long ago," said William

"I'm sorry. I can't remember?"

"I think you can remember but you have no alibi do you? You have no alibi because you are a sad and lonely little prick who has no-one in his life to provide an alibi for you," spat Judd.

"No comment."

"I also suggest that you have no alibi because you were responsible for the murders of Cassie Parker, Olive Jenas and Kez Raven."

"No comment."

William took over from Judd once more. "When you believed DS Mistry to be a prostitute, what was it you meant when you stated that you needed to 'deliver her from evil'?"

"That I would pray for her?"

"So why did you agree to meet Enigma the prostitute if

you don't approve of such lifestyles?"

"No comment."

Judd took over. "You wanted to meet her to kill her didn't you, because that's what you do? You meet prostitutes and then kill them in order to deliver them from evil. That's correct isn't it?"

"No comment."

William then produced the disturbing photographs of the three victims and placed them in front of Banks, including the same ones that had been shown to Hudson-Pigott. Whereas Hudson-Pigott was clearly horrified at the pictures, Banks showed no emotion.

"These poor girls were butchered and strategically placed in a very curious position, seemingly like Christ on a crucifix, and I would suggest by someone who has a fascination with knives."

Banks admired the handiwork that had evidently been inflicted on the three victims. When he eventually moved his attention away from the photos, he waited a moment and closed his eyes, to absorb the wonderful symbolism that had been inflicted on the poor girls. He opened his eyes only to reveal the same frustrating phrase again of "No comment."

"You know that we have detectives all over your flat like a rash at the moment? They're going over it with a fine-tooth comb and we only have to find one scrap of evidence to link you to these killings and bingo, we've got you by the bollocks."

"You know you really should learn to control your temper DI Stone. You enjoy hitting people far too easily."

"Don't change the subject. Besides, you resisted arrest."

"You know that's not true."

"No comment," jeered Judd.

"DI Stone is not on trial here, Mr. Banks."

"And neither am I. I haven't been charged have I?"

"It's just a matter of time, Banks. Now I'll ask you

again. Where did you work as a chef? Go on name just one place."

"The Ritz."

Judd fell about laughing. "The Ritz. Okay we will check that one out."

"Please do."

"So do prostitutes disgust you, Gareth?"

"No comment."

"Do they disgust you enough to kill them?"

"No comment."

"Why did you fetch the knife from the kitchen?"

The suspect just folded his arms. "No comment."

"You are really beginning to piss me off. Do you know that if you persistently say 'no comment' then you are not fulfilling your opportunity to explain yourself? It makes you appear as guilty as sin." The last word *sin* was said in a sarcastic tone that was not lost on Banks.

"No comment."

Judd leapt up from his seat and grabbed the back of Banks' head, forcing him to look downwards. "Look at these photos you prick, don't you feel anything at seeing them? Seeing young girls with their whole life ahead of them degraded by having knives shoved all over them like a fucking pin cushion, and having their pretty young faces slit from ear to ear. Well, what do you have to say about the state of these poor girls?"

Judd allowed Banks to free his head from his grasp then after a pause the suspect gave a smirk before finally speaking.

"No comment."

The rage in Judd was uncontrollable. The suspect had pushed all his buttons and Judd stood up from his chair again. Sensing what was about to happen, William stared up at the camera and concentrated as hard as he could, knowing that time was short. The intensity of the situation had caused his powers to work tenfold, and in the observation room, Sab and DI Scarrow were unable to view anything on the monitors as to them they curiously went blank. Judd punched Banks hard in the face causing him to fall off his chair, at the same time the audio machine fell off the table causing the tape to eject and spill onto the floor.

Judd moved towards Banks, contemplating whether to continue his assault. Banks began to speak very quietly, barely audible but loud enough for Judd to hear in his close proximity. "They deserved it the whores. They deserved it all. Shame your tape isn't on isn't it? I did it. They don't deserve to be on this Earth. God created the world in 7 days, but not for these Mary Magdalene type women to walk upon it and poison our existence. I did it. I killed them. It simply had to be done."

"I knew you did it you scum. Quickly, William set the tape machine back up." Judd had forgotten that William was unable to physically perform the task of retrieving the machine and reconfiguring it again. Judd of course was also unaware that by William protecting him from any video evidence being available of assaulting a suspect in police custody, he had now prevented the confession being captured on the video equipment too, although the whisper in Banks' voice would most likely have camouflaged the confession anyhow. The DCI simply watched on helplessly as Judd continued to assault the suspect, his admittance of killing the three girls incensing Judd somewhat – but thankfully the assault not being captured on anything tangible.

Judd indulged in a flurry of kicks as the suspect lay on the floor. "Confess you prick, confess into the tape. I'll give you no fucking comment."

Just then a large-framed lady walked into the interview room, wearing a grey suit, and a hairstyle that was cut unnecessarily short which did nothing to complement her harsh, yet bulging features. Both Judd and William recognised her as the unwelcoming battleaxe Miss. Harriet Flockhart, a defence lawyer whom they had come across many times before. She spoke in a cut glass accent.

"How dare you strike my client, Detective Inspector. I'll have your balls in a sling for this."

Banks began to cough blood from his mouth but still had the audacity to speak, "Oh didn't I tell you that I called my brief? You really shouldn't have started without her you know."

"You crafty little bastard," said William. "You lied to us."

Judd spoke next, "Interview fucking suspended."

CHAPTER 19

"My client is not answering any further questions until he has seen a doctor for the injuries that he has sustained by Detective Inspector Stone."

"He'll live, which is more than can be said for the three women that he butchered."

"Allegedly butchered, Detective Inspector Stone, and I strongly suggest that whatever has been discussed in the absence of my presence must be treated as null and void."

"He agreed to being interviewed without his brief."

"No doubt persuaded to co-operate via your violent tactics, Detective Inspector. And please be rest assured that I will be making an official complaint regarding your behaviour."

"Your client foolishly leant back and fell off his chair. I was simply attempting to help him get up, that's all."

"Save it for the official enquiry, Detective Inspector Stone."

"Perhaps you should be more concerned with your own client's predicament than mine. He confessed to killing three women."

"Do you have a written statement? No, I thought not and I would strongly contest that you illegally persuaded him to declare such a confession anyway with your bully-boy tactics. The way I see it Detective Inspector, you actually have very little evidence to charge my client with any crime at all, let alone the murders of three women. May I also remind you that you only have 72 hours in total to hold my client without charge, and the clock has already been ticking?"

William decided to step in to try and diffuse the situation to some degree. "Look Miss Flockhart, we want to follow the correct procedures so I suggest that DI Stone and I leave you alone for a reasonable period of time to allow you to acquaint yourself with Mr. Banks. I'll ensure that your client sees a doctor for his regrettable injuries before any further questioning proceeds.

"It looks as though the tape became damaged when Mr. Banks fell off his chair, so I am happy for the interview to begin again, but this time entirely in your presence. Does that sound reasonable, Miss Flockhart?"

The hard-nosed Miss Flockhart paused for thought and William was convinced that she wouldn't compromise, but after an age she said, "That is acceptable DCI Chamberlain."

"Very good. Now I'll arrange for some coffee for you both and we will return to question Mr. Banks in due course."

"Very well."

William used his crutches as support to lift himself up from the chair and signalled to Judd with a nod of his head to follow him out of the door.

They entered the observation room where DS Mistry and the weasel DI Scarrow had been watching the interview on the monitor screens. DSI Ben Francis had also wanted to observe but he had been called away at the last minute by the Chief Constable to assist with a firearms raid and had reluctantly made a judgment call to delegate authority to Scarrow, not wishing a DS to have to shoulder the responsibility with something so important. It had probably been fortuitous that Francis had not been able to view the unconventional tactics used by Judd Stone during the interview. William hoped that his telepathic intervention had been deployed in enough time to prevent Judd from being recorded so that a retrospective viewing could not take place either. Judd closed the door behind him; his face was full of rage.

"That fucking prick confessed to killing those girls, William."

"I know but we have no statement or record of it on the audio tape. What about the video, Sab?"

"Bad news I'm afraid, Guv. I've just tried to check the video and for some reason the recording stopped working at that crucial moment."

Judd looked down-hearted but became philosophical. "I'm not convinced that the video would have picked up his confession anyway, as he was on the floor at the time and he was making sure that he spoke quietly. You know, even when he was in that position he was pushing my buttons the manipulative little shit."

"That damn video system has always been dodgy," said William, feeling a sense of relief that Judd's assault on Banks wasn't on record. It had been a split second decision to protect his friend versus the probably inaudible confession of a lowlife. He was sure that he had made the right choice.

"That video system was working fine," butted in Scarrow. William just shrugged innocently. Everyone else ignored the scumbag DI.

"You heard what Banks said didn't you, William?"

"Yes, I heard him, but it's not enough, Judd. You know that. It's our word against his. At least we know we have the right man in custody, we just need some tangible evidence to eventually secure a conviction."

"That stuck-up bitch Flockhart is right of course, we only have 72 hours to hold him and the clock is ticking all the time."

"And that's why the bastard was going down the 'no comment' avenue," said William. "He knows we have no hard evidence on him, and he knows as things currently stand, it's up to us to prove he did this and not for him to prove he didn't."

"I know," sighed Judd, running his hand through his hair. "He is prepared to just keep on answering 'no comment' and then he can walk free as the sands of time run dry. It's my fault. I went in too soon when he had Sab. I just couldn't let him harm her, William."

"For what it's worth Judd, I'm glad that you intervened when you did. Believe me," offered Sab.

William released a hand from his crutch and gently held the arm of his friend. "It's okay Judd; I didn't want Sab harmed either. It was too risky once you and I lost that camera. Don't worry, we'll get him.

"I suggest that you and Sab get over to his flat while the battleaxe familiarises herself with the piece of filth. See what you can uncover, there must be something there to nail his arse. I'll start digging around on his history; I'll check out this claim of his that he worked as a chef at the Ritz, though I'm convinced I'll draw a blank regarding that one. I'll also see what else I can dig up on him.

"I'll also try and smooth things over the best I can with Francis and Haddock about you inflicting injuries on our suspect. I'll plead the usual - resisting arrest, self-defence and so forth, but at least I can throw in that you were protecting Sab to explain one of the beatings."

"Cheers William. It's just that weasel, you know you can see he is evil and…"

"I know, he brought it all back what happened all those years ago. I understand, Judd."

"Come on Sab, let's go and turn his flat upside down. We can excuse the other detectives from the scene."

William smiled, "Good lad. We'll compare notes later before we grill that monster again."

CHAPTER 20

"So what are we looking for, Guv?"

Judd had his back to Sab, as he looked out of a wooden-framed window which showed distinct signs of rot and a distant history of when it had last been painted. "Anything that links that bastard to the killings. One problem we have is that we are not going to find a murder weapon. His weapons of choice have been to use the knives that belonged to the victims, a tactic I presume not only to protect himself from supplying us with evidence, but also because the sick bastard interpreted it as some sort of poetic justice that their own knives should be used to take their lives. And as we discovered when he was with you, he wears gloves to commit the act in order to prevent any fingerprints being left on the knives."

"Forensics are checking out the gloves that he wore when he was with me though, right? You know, in case they can connect the gloves to the other victims."

"I think our man more than likely uses a fresh pair of gloves for each killing. I bet he burned the soiled gloves and blood-stained clothes after each slaughter. Come over here and take a look out of this window."

Judd held back the curtain to reveal a communal yard

for the apartment block where Banks lived, which was in fact a converted Georgian house which since the 1980s had been a total of 6 flats. At the rear of the yard was a metal bin that showed the scorch marks of a succession of fires where Judd suspected that Banks had burned his potentially incriminating clothes.

"We'll be lucky to get anything DNA wise to link him to the murders, Sab. I reckon he used that vessel that we see before us to burn all traces of clothing and we are pretty sure that he never had sex with the prostitutes before killing them either, so that also rules out any DNA from bodily fluids.

"If he was planning to have sex with you Sab, when you transformed into Enigma, it looks like it would have been the first time with a victim. Ironically, if you had been his fourth victim we may have obtained some DNA, though I was never going to let him get that chance."

"Glad to hear it. I actually think he was getting me stripped just to humiliate me and thinking about it, when he said he was going to *perform* I think he was referring to butchering not intercourse. Anyway, come on then Guv, let's start searching. We may have our work cut out considering how Banks has covered his tracks so well but we should never give up hope. You and DCI Chamberlain have always taught me one thing at least."

"What's that?"

"To expect the unexpected."

DCI William Chamberlain sat at his desk, searching the internet to try and establish some sort of historical picture of the man held in custody, well aware that the clock was constantly working against him and his team. His brain was aching trying to figure out a way to discover just who this suspect really was. William realised they needed to build a much more substantial case against Banks, and pretty quickly too, as currently they didn't have enough evidence to connect him to committing the three murders.

In the cold light of day what exactly did they have on this lowlife? He had terrorised Sab, but William was savvy enough to realise that his defence could easily articulate that this had purely been a build up to a sexual game. Or Banks could easily expand on his claim that he simply engaged in a harmless discussion about knives as he wished to share the details of being a chef by profession. William and Judd couldn't even book him for soliciting at the moment as no money had changed hands for sex. And after all, Banks hadn't actually harmed Sab had he? Judd had made sure of that.

William had contacted his colleagues in the London Met to establish if their records could throw any light on a violent man who perhaps fitted the bill of Banks. After all, Banks had stated that he originated from London and his accent cemented that claim. But astonishingly, the Met could not discover anything that linked this man to their crime records. Even Banks's fingerprints drew a blank on the national database which signalled that he was most likely a first time criminal. This was most unusual to not even have any history of minor offences, but it seemed that Banks had entered the crime world in the most significant way possible – instantly becoming a serial killer!

The Ritz Hotel investigation had proved less than productive. Data protection laws had been quoted when William had tried to enquire about the history of chefs that they had employed.

William had tasked a couple of DC's to liaise with the authorities to establish evidence of who had paid income tax and national insurance whilst working as a chef at The Ritz over the past 5 years. William knew that this would be a lengthy process – eating into time he didn't have. Deep down he felt it was just a process of elimination anyway, he fully expected that Gareth Banks would not be traced on the records of employment history at The Ritz.

William knew that he had to start thinking more laterally. What had triggered this psycho to do what he had done? Why depict the victims as a crucifixion? Why choose prostitutes to murder in this way? The answers must be out there somewhere.

Banks had claimed to Eddie Goode and his hooligan contingent to being the son of an East End gangster. Had both that claim and the one about being a chef at arguably the best hotel in London, simply been fabrications by Banks, as an attempt to make a marked impression on his peers? They had to be inventions by Banks didn't they? Banks had to be a fantasist. The Met had confirmed that of the most notorious gangsters of London known to them, none of them had a son named Gareth Banks.

So why be so extreme? Why inflate his father to appear as a gangster? Then the penny dropped for William. His old man must have actually been something quite different to a gangster. Something totally opposite? Our man Banks wanted to make his father something he wasn't? So if he was the opposite to a gangster what was he? A policeman perhaps? William got back on the phone to the Met.

"DCI Henry speaking."

"Sid. Hi it's Bill again."

"Got another theory on your psycho?"

"Yeah, get onto your Human Resources department. How many of your coppers have a son in their twenties?"

"Guv, take a look at this?"

"What have you found, Sab?"

Sab simply pointed to the inside of an open wardrobe door. It had a variety of news clippings meticulously positioned in chronological order about each of the murders of the 3 victims. In fact they had been placed in such a way as to present the shape of a cross.

"Well, well, well. If he isn't our man he certainly has an unhealthy interest in these particular murders."

"Exactly."

"I also found this Bible in his underwear drawer."

"In his underwear drawer! That makes sense actually.

He sees the Bible as a way of neutralising his underwear."

"Why?" asked Sab.

"Think about it. Our man Banks is killing prostitutes. He obviously finds them disgusting and in his mind he may well find the concept of sex disgusting for some reason. His underwear goes next to his genitals so he sees the Bible as a way of neutralising them. Our nut happens to be a religious nut who has to neutralise his nuts!"

"Look, I also found these." Sab lifted up three necklaces, one was silver with a charm, one was made from heavy gold and one was costume jewellery in the shape of large beads coloured by shades of lilac and lavender. Judd guessed that the latter once belonged to Cassie Parker, recalling the colour scheme of her apartment.

"Trophies. Serial killers often take trophies from their victims to remind them of their perceived acts of wonder. I remember hearing about John Wayne Gacy, the serial killer who liked to dress up as a clown. He was just one particular serial killer who collected trophies from his victims."

"I also found this?"

"A birth certificate. Well done, Sab. Let's take a look."

Sab handed Judd the slightly dog-eared parchment.

"This isn't for Gareth Banks."

"No it's for a Gareth Hibbett. Our man is using the pseudonym Banks."

"Good work, Sab. Really good. I'll let William know."

CHAPTER 21

"Are you sitting comfortably, Mr. Banks?" began DCI Chamberlain.

"Yes, thank you."

"Then I shall begin."

William signalled to Sab and Scarrow, who were behind the single-viewing mirrored window, to begin recording the conversation, whilst Judd operated the recording machine on the table. William proceeded with the standard introductions ensuring both his and Judd's identities were recorded.

"For the benefit of the tape could you confirm that you are Mr. Gareth Banks?"

"Yes I can."

"Oh, really. We'll come back to that one later, Gareth," sneered Judd.

"And for the benefit of the tape Miss. Flockhart, would you please make your presence known and state your capacity here today."

"My name is Miss. Harriet Flockhart and I am the defending lawyer representing Mr. Gareth Banks."

"Thank you Miss Flockhart."

"So Mr. Banks, would you say you are a man who is at

times a little economical with the truth?" continued Judd, his tone drenched in sarcasm.

"No?"

"So your name is not Gareth Hibbett?"

Banks flinched. "No, it's Gareth Banks."

Judd placed the dog-eared birth certificate onto the table.

"So this birth certificate in your flat doesn't belong to you?"

"Yes it does?"

"Would you please read out the identity of the child's name please?"

"Gareth Hibbett."

"My client changed his name by deed poll from Gareth Hibbett to Gareth Banks. He has not lied to you and he has not committed any crime."

"Very well, Miss Flockhart, a fair point well made. I can't help but wonder though what possesses someone to want to change their name. I mean, why would anyone wish to leave their identity behind so to speak?" Judd shifted his eyes firmly onto Banks. "What forced you to take such action then, Gareth?"

"No comment."

"Oh I see, we are back to that bollocks again are we?" retorted Judd. "I think we've got you scared haven't we, Gareth?"

"Not a chance. The only thing I'm scared of is flying."

"Perhaps I can shed some light on the matter for you, Mr. Hibbett, oh sorry, Mr. Banks," said William taking charge of the interview. "I think I know what has happened here, but please do correct me if I go off track. You see, when you look at that birth certificate the father's name hasn't been declared. Your mother's name is of course, Penelope Hibbett, so you took on your mother's name and not you father's whose name as I said is omitted from the birth certificate. Perhaps your mother was a certain type of woman; you know the sort I mean don't you? I think it is highly possible that she didn't actually know who your father was."

William and Judd noticed a pang of anger appear in the eyes of their suspect.

"No comment."

"That's okay; I'll continue to fill in the blanks for you shall I? You see, you are somewhat of a fantasist Mr. Banks, I'm sure of it. You live your life in a kind of... how can I put it, a parallel universe. You live by the law of opposites."

"No comment."

"Perhaps I should elaborate further; there appears to be a need to explain things more fully. Oh and once again I reiterate, do feel free to join in the conversation Mr. Banks if you need to correct me on anything.

"Now, your first anomaly was this claim to work at the Ritz Hotel. The Ritz is perhaps the most luxurious hotel restaurant that any chef could wish to work for. And I did discover that a Mr. Gareth Banks did indeed train to be a chef at the College of Food and Domestic Arts, right here in Birmingham in fact, which would help explain your familiarity with our good city. It's a good college but probably not one that would produce someone capable of working at the Ritz hotel? Not impossible, but not likely either.

"It's funny, but no income tax records could be matched to a Mr. Gareth Banks ever working at The Ritz, and I'm sure that you would agree that a hotel of that calibre would most certainly have its wage structure in order. However, the authorities did discover a Mr. Gareth Banks working at a two star hotel named The Camden Oasis, situated just outside of Camden Town, which is at least two tube journeys away from the Ritz Hotel. I would suggest that The Camden Oasis is perhaps the *opposite* kind of hotel to that of the Ritz, especially as it has a history of problems with environmental health in its kitchens. Oh yes, some of the relevant authorities have been very co-operative today with sharing their records."

"My client informing you that he worked at the Ritz is not a crime, Detective Chief Inspector."

"Wasting police time is though," retorted Judd on William's behalf.

Judd found great satisfaction in watching the confident and smug Miss Flockhart squirm with embarrassment at his well-executed one liner.

William continued. "And wasting police time is going to be the least of Mr. Banks' worries."

Banks then momentarily wavered from his 'no comment' strategy. "I told you that I was a chef and that's why I was interested in certain knives. I did not want to harm that girl whom you entrapped me with. I was telling the truth about my interest in knives, they are an instrument of my craft."

"Oh, I don't doubt that Mr. Banks, I think I understand what your craft is. And we may have to agree to disagree regarding the reasons for your fascination with knives, until it is proven otherwise that is, which I assure you is going to happen. Please allow me to continue with my analysis of your past. You see, with this life of opposites that I believe you engage in I delved further. I suspected that your father wasn't really a gangster from the East End of London as you had claimed during your brief spell as a football hooligan, so I thought what is the opposite of a gangster? At first I thought okay, a policeman. Perhaps your old man had actually been a policeman, but I checked with my pals in the Metropolitan Police and they couldn't locate a match."

Banks gave a smug smile, which would soon be wiped from his face.

"So then I thought okay, what else could be the opposite of a gangster and I thought how about a man of the cloth."

Judd and William noticed the shift in Banks' expression.

"And do you know what, I found out that in the Borough of London there was indeed a vicar from the Church of England named David Banks. Bingo I thought, but then discovered that his only son, who was indeed called Gareth, tragically died in a car accident some 8 years ago. It was a very upsetting phone call that I had with Reverend Banks when he revealed this information to me. So I knew then that you weren't his son. But I still suspected that a man of the cloth had to be your dad, and I thought well, you know in the Church of England the man of the cloth is allowed to produce a family so what's the issue? A vicar can have a family with his wife. If you were a product of a vicar the only issue would be if you were a love-child. The result of a seedy affair perhaps? Hardly a reason in itself to turn you into a murdering monster though. But thinking your dad could have been a vicar was a bark up the wrong tree.

"Then I received a call from Detective Inspector Stone to inform me that Detective Sergeant Mistry had discovered your birth certificate. I straight away asked who the father was and of course it was not disclosed on the certificate. Which got me thinking. Why would the father's name be omitted? I had already suspected your dad could be a man of the cloth so I thought; of course…he must have been a priest. And a priest has to remain celibate does he not? In other words he is not allowed to father a child in any circumstances. Your dad was a priest wasn't he Gareth? And that is why your mom could not place his name on the birth certificate?"

"You can't prove that."

"Maybe I can and maybe I can't, but it is not your father who is on trial here. Your mother on the other hand was on trial on more than one occasion for prostitution according to our records. Found guilty time after time she was; how did it feel Gareth to know your mom was nothing better than a good time hooker?"

"Watch your mouth, Chamberlain."

"Get back in your box, Banks," snapped Judd. "We've worked it all out." Judd then began to turn to William and the two detectives began to have a conversation amongst themselves, ignoring the other two people in the room.

"So William, we know he is not the son of an East End gangster so could he really be the son of a priest?"

"Well if Banks wanted to portray his father as being the opposite of a priest, short of stating that his dad was Jack the Ripper or Charles Manson, I guess being an East End gangster is the next best thing?"

"Indeed, but how can Banks then make himself appear to be even more worthy than his real father, if we are to keep with this theme of contrary interpretation?"

"Yes, this is important to him to be able to achieve. He needs to prove to himself that he is a much more worthy man than his father. The situation with his father has haunted him terribly throughout his life. But he has to be the opposite of his real father, the priest, and he needs to be even more evil than the fictitious father who he has created as being a gangster."

"That's right. So what can he be?"

"He has to become a serial killer."

"Of course, it all fits now."

William abruptly returned his focus towards Banks. "When DI Stone informed me that your birth name was Hibbett, I researched that name and discovered through Reverend Banks that a young offender called Gareth Hibbett was caught defacing churches. There was no particular bias in your targets as it seems that you were happy to deface both C of E and Catholic churches, but fortunately for you neither church wished to press charges hence the reason why I was unable to locate you on any criminal database.

"The agreement was that you would help out with maintenance of the graveyards and surrounding gardens at the homes of the less than fortunate community, in exchange for not going to the police. I'm sure they believed that their strategy of forgiveness was more productive than sending a young man to prison, but you still allowed your hatred of the church to fester even after their acts of kindness. It appears that their misplaced notion to forgive you simply let you off the hook for your psychosis to manifest and build.

"And it seemed opportune for you at some point to take the name of Banks to rid yourself of the name Hibbett. The real Gareth Banks had been raised in a very loving and secure family – not quite the same childhood as yours. In fact quite the opposite. And you taking on the role of serial killer with the name Gareth Banks appealed to you for some warped reason."

"My dad was the liar; he was a phony. He was not a priest he was a charlatan. I know how to do God's work. Not him or people like him."

"Remain calm Gareth; they still have no direct connection to the murders. All this past experience with churches and your change of name is irrelevant. Remember why they wanted you here," said a concerned Miss Flockhart.

"We are beginning to establish motive, Miss Flockhart," sneered Judd.

William continued, "You say that you are doing God's work but you really just want the company of someone. You know that a prostitute will sit and talk to you, unlike most people who come across you in your life. You know this as you heard your own mother do it on many occasions from the haven of the one wall that separated you as she entertained her male friends.

"Then while you are sitting with these kind women you hear daddy's voice telling you that you are engaging in a sin with sinful creatures, so you kill them to wipe away the disgust you begin to feel about yourself.

"You kill and do acts of violence because you never had the balls to kill your dad; he died naturally and not at your hand like you wanted. You wanted that taste of revenge so badly but you failed, so for each 'Chelsea Smile' that you place on your victims it represents each and every time your dad beat you and laughed at you. For each hooker you slaughter it's another knife driven into your daddy's heart. You loved your mother but hated what she was, and what was she? A hooker. You hated the way she had to be a hooker just to keep a roof over your head and to put food in your mouth because your dad, the priest, wouldn't pay her any legalised maintenance. How could he? A priest is not allowed to father a child; however I did discover that a certain Parish in London had some unusual miscellaneous entries in its accounts for money that was taken from the funds. I suspect that was to pay for your mother's services and not for her little brat. It is all such a mess isn't it Gareth? And the only way out of this mess is to kill prostitutes as you see this as a way of cleansing your mom from the job that she had to do. The job that you hated so much. And it is up to you to single-handedly ensure that no one else does this job of prostitution. You are ridding the world of sin by killing prostitutes one by one."

Judd then stepped in unable to resist twisting the metaphorical knife. "Poor, sad little Gareth never having any mates in life. A total loser so he has to pay prostitutes to talk to him and pretend he is the son of an East End gangster to try and get some mates. Sad, pathetic little Gareth."

The teasing was too much for Gareth It all too clearly took him back to those days in the playground whilst growing up in the capital when he was bullied, and even back then he had tried to convince the other kids that his dad was an East End gangster. That's why the other kids never saw his dad around like the other dads as he was out doing gangster work. The pretence worked for a short while and the bullying stopped, but kids get wise to lies very quickly, and once rumbled they simply bullied the weaker-built Gareth even more.

Judd Stone was pushing those same buttons now that those playground bullies had pushed all those years ago. "God damn you Stone, you will rot in hell." Gareth leapt from his seat and attempted to grab Judd, but Judd easily deflected the suspect's assault and pushed Banks' head to the desk, holding it firmly in place before turning to Miss. Flockhart. "As you can see Miss Flockhart, Mr. Banks frequently loses his temper and I simply have to restrain him within the means of the law."

For once Miss Flockhart was at a loss for words.

Eventually Judd released him. "Quite a temper you have, Gareth. I think you hear the voices of your dad and you lose that nasty temper of yours and kill poor innocent girls don't you?"

"No comment," spat Gareth.

"You have a very unhealthy interest in the three killings thus far Mr. Banks and I suggest that is because you are responsible for those killings. At your flat, DS Mistry and I found newspaper clippings of the murders placed in the shape of a cross How do you explain that?"

"No comment."

"And we found three necklaces which we are having checked out right now as a formality to confirm that they belonged to each of the three victims. Do you wish to explain how they came into your possession?"

"No comment."

"You can 'no comment' all you want you little prick. We have enough shit on you to build a complete and convincing profile of why you carried out these murders. There is simply no one else in the frame and we are going to put you away for a very long time to stop you hurting any more innocent girls. Gareth Banks, Gareth Hibbett or whatever your fucking name is we are charging you with the murders of Cassie Parker, Olive Jenas and Kerry Raven."

With time running out, William knew that Judd had little option but to charge Gareth with the murders, he just hoped that they really did have enough evidence on him. At least they had a confession of a sort when Gareth had said that he was simply "Doing God's work." The only way they were now going to get any more of a confession from Banks was to let Judd beat the shit out of him and that was not an option that William could allow. Unfortunately.

CHAPTER 22

"My, you are getting a big boy these days," said Gareth's mom as she playfully ruffled his golden locks. "I can't believe that you're nearly eight now, you look much older."

Gareth simply took his mother's words as yet another example of the lies that she regularly fed him. Her intentions were good, it broke her heart that her son wasn't as popular as the other kids and she simply wanted her son to feel better about himself. The reality was that Gareth was the smallest and weakest kid in the class by far which made him an easy target for bullying, even from some of the younger kids at the school.

Gareth had temporarily managed to stop the bullying and had even earned himself a period of respect when he had informed the other boys that the only reason that his dad didn't feature much at the school gates was because he was an East End gangster. Gareth regularly span yarns about how his dad was always busy indulging in dangerous and criminal activity. His favourite tale, which always resulted in leaving his peers open-mouthed, was when he told of a particularly desired approach to punishment by his dad, in drowning people in the River Thames for not towing the line. It wasn't too difficult a story to believe when told with the sort of vigour executed by Gareth, this was after all the East End of London and even boys the age of Gareth had grown up with the knowledge of the notorious Kray twins and the like, with their legacy still chillingly evident in the local culture.

But just as he seemed to be gaining some respect from his classmates, disaster struck for Gareth, when ironically the son of a true East End gangster was transferred into Gareth's school after being expelled from another one. Derek Holloway took great pleasure in putting the record straight about Gareth's misinformation and as a result the bullying got worse for Gareth with Derek usually leading the way. Gareth became terrified at the prospect of attending school and his skill at inventing stories manifested into tricking his mother into believing that he had woke with a belly ache or some other illness, resulting in him not attending school on most days. His mom, always a soft touch for her only child, often took the boy's words at face value no matter how contrived they became.

Gareth hated his mom's line of work and she naïvely believed that the young Gareth didn't understand what was going on in the next room, but covering his ears with his hands to drown out the noises of his mother's activities was still a better prospect than having his head flushed down the toilet again and again back at school.

In later years when Gareth moved to Birmingham, he deployed the same story that his dad was a gangster in an attempt to win friends. After all it had worked once before, albeit as a momentary solution, but Gareth drew inspiration from the one and only time in his life that he had managed to gain some quality admiration from other individuals. And what was the alternative? Informing people that his dad had been a priest? Surely that could never be a good idea in attempting to gain some street credibility? Gareth had also witnessed only too well how having a gangster for a father had enabled Derek Holloway to have all the reverence and friendship he ever needed. When Gareth became involved with a group of Birmingham based football hooligans, he was amazed at how his story had demanded him immediate respect with some of the group. In London there was a saturated market of gangsters, but in Birmingham, Gareth kidded himself that he was an important big fish in a small pond. For all his insecurities Gareth will always be a true narcissist.

With all the males that came and went from their home, his mother tried to offer an explanation to her son that the men simply visited her in a professional capacity. They were suppliers who provided her with goods to sell so she could earn some cash for them both. The young Gareth had been forced to decipher much too early in his young life that the only goods for sale had been his mom, as he crudely heard the movement of the bed and other telling noises through the thin walls. One method Gareth used to disguise what his mother was doing, was to turn up the volume on the black and white TV to try and drown out the disgusting liaison that was occurring.

The flat was dank and disorganised – a symbol of his mother's fragile state of mind. In spite of his mother's line of work and the fact that she got paid for it, it never seemed to secure a wealthy upbringing for Gareth and he hated the way his mom sold herself for obvious pittance. Some of the cash had been spent on various drugs over the years, as his mother attempted to free her own mind of her depression and low self-esteem. In later years when Gareth discovered that other women could secure a life of luxury by entertaining men he would ensure that they would never be allowed to lead the affluent lifestyle that his mother never could.

Just as his mother had finished ruffling his hair the doorbell rang. The boy's heart sank as he realised that once again he was about to lose his mother's attention to one of the men who would call at the flat.

"Mommy has just got to answer the door, Gareth. When I have finished with this err, supplier perhaps I can take you for a walk around the park. Would you like that, Gareth?"

Gareth simply shrugged never allowing himself to build up any hopes. His mom was so scatter-brained she rarely delivered her promises to him.

From where Gareth was positioned on the flaking PVC sofa, he could look down the hallway to see his mom answer the door. Gareth tensed as he watched the man whom he feared most of all the men who came visiting step over the threshold. Gareth knew that this particular client had a different relationship with his mom than the others. He had overheard them discussing how they actually "loved each other".

But this man always dressed from head to toe in black clothing, except for the white rectangle that was visible at his throat. He was a priest and a priest was not allowed to fall in love as he had chosen to devote his life, without distraction, to serving God. Yet this priest had often told his lover that one day he would leave the church to be with her, but in reality it never happened. Sadly, Gareth's mom had always believed that it would.

Gareth had reason to strongly believe that this man was his father. Heaven knows the priest reminded him often enough when he beat him, spitting out the words that he was "a constant reminder to the sins he had committed with this sinful woman."

One day, before the reality of his mom's situation had become evident to Gareth; he saw the man in the priest's clothes and naturally smiled at him only to be struck hard across the face as the priest said "I'll wipe that smile off your face once and for all. Every time I see your face I see God judging me for my sin." Gareth was confused for a long time and the priest's actions disturbed the little boy, making him feel magnitudes of guilt with no particular reasoning. When a child is led to believe that they have done something wrong, but they are not empowered to correct that wrong, or even understand that wrong, it breaks the child's spirit. On occasions like this Gareth's mom would cry and beg for the priest not to beat the child, but her words were always in vain.

Gareth's mother was weak by nature and she was never able to find the courage to split from the priest even though he beat her son. Besides, by falling in love with a priest she foolishly believed that she was cleansing away any sin from her that she may have been attracting in her line of work. She always hoped that the three of them could set up a happy home one day, but she was only dreaming in reality, which became all too evident when the priest died of an unexpected heart attack on the church altar whilst giving mass one Sunday morning. His secrets of having a son and a lover dying with him.

All of this shaped the troubled and disturbed mind of Gareth to permanently have both God and violence in his life. He could not live without the two elements existing hand in hand. Later, he would seek out prostitutes as it made him feel close to his mother, but then would believe that his very association with them made him just as disgusting as his father, so he would have to kill them and place them in the style of a crucifixion. The crucifixion symbolised forgiveness and sacrifice. They needed forgiveness just like his mother had needed forgiveness, and they needed to sacrifice their lives to prevent him and other men from being just like his father. This fuelled his warped belief that he was God's true instrument on Earth, not like his father who had been a hypocrite in all that he preached and claimed to stand for. His father was a charlatan and a fraud but through Gareth, God's work could be done, cleansing the world of sin.

To Gareth, these girls had to die to justify his own reason for living.

PART II
BIGGER THAN JESUS

CHAPTER 23

Many months following his arrest, Gareth Banks walked away from court a free man.

It had taken all of DCI William Chamberlain's years of experience to convince the Crown Prosecution Service to place Banks on trial, but just as he had feared there simply wasn't enough DNA evidence to convict Banks of being the murderer.

The forensics team had worked more than admirably. They had produced evidence that was close to miracles in fact, establishing strands of hair and finger prints at all three crime scenes, but Gareth had freely admitted to 'visiting' the three ladies in question at one time or another as he liked to talk through his troubles with them. Gareth explained to the jury how he paid the kind girls for their time, but they simply listened to him talk. Their services to him were of a counselling nature and not a sexual one, and with the absence of any sexual DNA being supplied by Gareth the jury opted to believe him.

The jury had even begun to feel sorry for this pathetic loner, choosing to see him as a victim of life instead as someone who was capable of killing these three women. He admitted to stealing their necklaces when they weren't looking and declared that he was ashamed of this act, but he stated to the courtroom that he simply wanted a reminder of the three lovely girls who had listened to his troubles and he had always planned to return them one day. Banks even managed to break down in tears, regretful that he would never have the opportunity to return their jewellery or speak with them again because someone had taken these three lovely girls away from him.

Crucially, there was none of Gareth's DNA on the weapons or actually on the three victims. The prosecution claimed that he had wore gloves to carry out the murders and then burnt his clothes, but frankly there was no concrete evidence to support this very plausible yet unproven theory. Significantly at the time of his arrest, Gareth hadn't had the Rohypnol about his person, which could have potentially linked him to all three murders. The fact that he had lost it en route to seeing Enigma was something that had ironically helped Gareth Banks escape prison.

When questioned about his claim to be "simply doing God's work" as Banks had quoted in the interviews with Chamberlain and Stone, the jury once again believed Banks' version of events. The story he shared with the jury was that whilst talking to the girls he was simply trying to educate them to consider a life away from prostitution. He felt that he was simply introducing the girls to the positive aspects of his religious beliefs, trying to show them the right path as demonstrated by the word of the Lord, and he even claimed that the three girls were responding to his advice. One female juror was even gullible enough to wipe a tear from her eye as Gareth explained how he informed the girls of his own mother's mistakes at being a prostitute and how she had tragically been unable to free herself from her cyclical life of debt and abuse at the hands of men.

Those individuals known as the 'accused' in murder cases do not usually opt to take the stand, but Banks played a blinder, connecting with the jury ensuring that they empathised with the difficult life that he had lived. His award winning performance had the jury almost eating out of his hand.

The judge had also pointed out to the jury that it was very difficult to give the suspect a fair trial on the basis of the media footage that had escalated since his arrest. Judd and William had understood how the unusual details of the case could be exploited by the tabloids and the excessive investigative journalism that was an unfortunate part of British culture. Both the detectives had worked hard to protect the information from being known anywhere else except in the court room; however their efforts had seemed to be in vain. The media had even given the serial killer a label, *The Crucifier*, which pulled in sensational as opposed to helpful interest.

They suspected that the leak could only have been from Lionel Scarrow – who else would have sunk so low? Even though Scarrow was most likely convinced that Judd and William had got the right man, the little weasel would have gained far more satisfaction getting one over on them than imprisoning a serial killer of three women.

Frustratingly, the judge had agreed with Miss Flockhart's opinion of police entrapment the night that Gareth had held a knife in front of Sabita Mistry aka Enigma. Banks' fascination with knives and so on was deemed inadmissible evidence. The jury never had an opportunity to consider the evidence from Banks' night of capture.

What the jury did learn of was the police brutality inflicted by DI Judd Stone on the accused, and therefore any evidence that Gareth had shared at that time could only be construed as being unsafe, as would be any forthcoming conviction.

Lionel Scarrow had even astonishingly taken the stand to give evidence against the 'notoriously bad-tempered DI Judd Stone'. It was accepted that Scarrow had been called by the defence team so he had no choice but to give evidence, but even so, what had led them to believe that he would make such a good witness for them?

Furthermore, the defence contingent led by Miss Flockhart had built a case against Judd and explained how 'this unorthodox and atheist policeman had found it necessary and amusing to harass a man of Christian faith'. The defence had simply painted Banks as being as well-behaved as a boy scout, who had admirably found substance in his faith as a means to deal with his troubled childhood. They told how Banks had even helped out at his local church, performing maintenance work on a voluntary basis – which Judd and William knew had actually been implemented because Banks had been discovered defacing and damaging church property and stealing from churches in his grudge against his father. Nevertheless, it was Judd who had been made to look more like the criminal.

In short, the jury had decided by a majority verdict that Gareth Banks could not be convicted for the murders of Cassie Parker, Olive Jenas and Kez Raven. The jury would not accept that he had slain these women beyond all reasonable doubt.

On the steps outside of Birmingham Crown Court, Banks stood victorious with his arms aloft as members of the press swarmed him in a bid to capture his views on walking from court a free man.

"Ladies and Gentlemen of the press, I have always stated my innocence in these murders and I have indeed had my day in court as they say."

"It must be a relief for you Mr. Banks, to finally be able to put the trial behind you and start to get on with your life again?" asked one eager and assertive female reporter.

"I take small comfort from being able to clear my name, because of course there remains a killer out there somewhere responsible for the slayings of those three poor women. I hope that the police can refocus and get their act together to catch whoever is responsible for these tragic murders."

"Do you have any criticism of the police, Mr. Banks?"

"Only in that they have arrested and put to trial an innocent man."

"Bollocks Banks, you know we had the right man but that stupid jury believed all your bullshit." Suddenly the majority of the reporters moved to the small assembly led by DI Judd Stone who had vented the words, closely followed by DS Sab Mistry and DCI William Chamberlain who was just about keeping pace on his crutches.

"Detective Inspector Stone, do you believe that the police handled this case correctly?" asked a notoriously abrupt reporter from one of the national television channels.

"We did all that we could under the circumstances."

"The judge appeared to criticise the handling of the case by the detectives involved, particularly by you. Do you have any regrets about how the case was handled?"

"Your line of questioning seems to suggest that we screwed up. Well if indeed we did screw up, if that is what the underlying factor is here, it still equates to one thing – we had the right man in Gareth Banks didn't we? We simply failed to secure a conviction; but we all know he did it. We all know that we had caught the man you and your lot chose to dub The Crucifier, so turn your attentions to that piece of scum standing there and not me."

"May I remind you that my client was acquitted, DI Stone?"

"I'm well aware of the mockery of justice that has occurred here today Miss Flockhart, but you know as well as I do that Gareth Banks is not an innocent man. I don't know how people like you sleep at night."

"I sleep very well thank you Detective Inspector, perhaps you should concentrate on your own failings rather than mine. And perhaps you would like to comment on the accusations of police brutality levelled towards you DI Stone, in the presence of these members of the press?"

"No comment."

"Oh the irony," sang Gareth Banks.

Judd tensed and William Chamberlain placed a crutch across his DI's path sensing that any second now the press would have a field day with Judd giving them an explicit display of police brutality if they hung around long enough. "Easy Judd, don't take the bait."

Judd relaxed his posture.

"Miss Flockhart," spoke William. "May I congratulate you on the success of defending your client - for now. Justice will prevail eventually. I look forward to sparring with you again some time, professionally speaking of course."

"Professionally speaking of course. It's a shame that your DI doesn't spar metaphorically as opposed to literally."

"Well I grant you that DI Stone is perhaps a little less patient than I am but I assure you that our passion for justice is equally as acute. DI Stone simply chooses to channel his frustrations in a much more transparent manner and he tends to specialise in exercising justice of a more poetic nature. As I said, justice will prevail sooner or later and I suggest that to prevent an example of the former you get that little shit out of here because I do not know how much longer I can hold DI Stone back from dishing out some of his poetic justice."

Miss Flockhart was lost for words. She turned on her heels and thought it best to lead Gareth Banks away for his own safety, balancing the necessity to do so against what would be a valuable public display of Judd Stone's violence. The press fortunately chose to follow them leaving William, Judd and Sab alone to contemplate their tragic defeat in court.

"How will justice prevail, William? What further

evidence can we find on that piece of shit? We can't retrial him without fresh evidence otherwise it will just be double jeopardy, and we struggled to find anything tangible on him this time around, hence the bastard walking free from court."

"Then we will just have to find more evidence," spoke an optimistic Sab.

"Don't worry Judd; we'll get him, I know we will. I'll make sure of it. There is more than one way to skin a cat you know. To get even with someone can take a long time, sometimes a lifetime. You have just got to keep the faith and look for the opportunities when they arise, and I think one has just presented itself."

Judd and Sab looked at one another blankly. They didn't realise that William was not solely referring to Banks when getting even with someone after a very long time; he was also referring to those who had been responsible for hurting his sister.

William began to chuckle to himself which confused Judd and Sab even more as he replayed the well known phrase over and over in his mind: *Kill two birds with one stone.*

It became apparent to William, that if Banks truly believes that he is destined to kill people due to his warped logic of carrying out God's work, then he could also look to kill those who do not truly carry out God's work; those he would consider to be imposters or pretenders. It would play right into Gareth Banks' devastating perception regarding certain opposite entities in life. For example it wouldn't take much to inflame his opinion of priests considering his feelings towards his father being a charlatan. In fact, anyone who he considered to be only 'playing' at carrying out God's work could easily upset the narcissistic Gareth Banks. Therefore, surely Banks could also quite easily have a dislike for cult leaders too.

The little shit just didn't realise it yet.

CHAPTER 24

"Come in gentlemen and shut the door behind you," spoke a calm but clearly serious Detective Superintendent Ben Francis. In spite of his strong annoyance, his natural sense of goodness broke to the surface as he felt the urge to assist William Chamberlain into a chair. Francis resisted recognising the Detective Chief Inspector feeling patronised when anyone attempted to intervene and help him regardless of their good intentions. The more-than-proud William Chamberlain strictly considered that the MS was *his* illness to cope with and didn't much care for busybodies or do-gooders who wanted to get involved. Recently Francis had noticed the acute demise in William's condition and sympathised with his physical disabilities, but William's ability to do his job had never been in question – until today that was. But if it was illness clouding William's judgment what excuse did Judd Stone have? Ben Francis' concerns regarding William Chamberlain's police work were more around his misplaced loyalty in backing this loose cannon, rather than for any mistakes that he had personally made on the Gareth Banks case.

"Now that you are seated comfortably gentlemen, I will

come straight to the point. Obviously the Chief Constable and I are bitterly disappointed at Banks being able to walk away a free man."

"It was that weaker than weak jury, sir. They bought Banks' soft soap story about a difficult childhood and he convinced them that he could never commit a murder," offered Judd.

"But if forensics had been tighter he could have been Mother Teresa and we would still have proven it was him. It was him wasn't it?"

"Yes sir, off the record he admitted as much. He is our killer for definite," said William.

"Stone, I can't help thinking that a lot of this lies at your door. You are too ready with your fists. You are a good copper but this rage you have inside you clouds your judgment. It allows you to make mistakes. What were you thinking of beating a suspect to a pulp? Around here we do things by the book, Stone. There are rules and protocols to follow, have we learned nothing from the miscarriages of justice in the seventies and eighties when people have since been able to walk away from imprisonment due to unsafe convictions regardless of their guilt? We are professionals not savages Stone, the days of beating confessions out of people are long gone no matter how tempting it may be."

"Sometimes rules need to be broken to get a result, sir."

"Not on my watch, Detective Inspector," shouted Ben Francis slamming his desk and ironically uncharacteristically displaying the very type of rage that he was criticising Judd for.

"I apologise sir. I did not mean to appear either flippant or disrespectful."

Ben Francis took a few seconds to compose himself.

"Look Judd, I bent over backwards to protect your arse with the Chief Constable and the inquiry by the Police Complaints Authority. I came up with all sorts of bullshit making out that Banks had been resisting arrest and at one point I even found myself suggesting that Banks had simply fell off his chair. Fortunately, because my own reputation is strikingly contrasting to yours Stone, I was believed, more fool me aye? Why should I put my neck on the line for you, Judd? Why should I bring my own integrity into disrepute? Go on answer me."

Judd could not offer a response.

"I've decided that you need time away from, shall we say, these more dramatic duties. Both of you that is. William, I'm concerned for your health as much as anything."

William was visibly annoyed. "Are you suggesting that I can't do my job any more, sir?"

"Not exactly William, but you are not superman and you do not possess superhuman powers. Your health will demise if we put you under too much pressure; I don't want that on my conscience. I have a duty of care as well as having to address areas of failed discipline. Perhaps I delegated too much responsibility to you for Operation Dakota; I should have taken a more hands on approach."

"Now listen here, sir. My health will only demise if you pull me off these so called 'more dramatic duties'. If I become a pen pusher I'll die within a month. To be frank sir, I find your attitude very offensive and bordering on discrimination. And another thing, are you forgetting that we were faced with a very unusual serial killer, the type which Birmingham and District CID has never experienced before? This is a man who displays his victims as if they have been crucified, and slits their mouths in the style of a ghastly smile whilst leaving behind no telling forensic evidence. Yet despite all this we still got the right man."

Ben Francis thought hard for a moment. Perhaps William was right, who was he to play God and tell him what he could or could not do, and perhaps to suggest that his illness was affecting his job was an act of discrimination."

"Okay William, I apologise. I only have your best interests at heart believe me. You can remain on your current duties but I will assign Scarrow to you. I have no wrestling with my conscience reining Stone in for a while."

William was enraged at this decision and screamed out the single word "NO". As he shouted, the photo of Ben Francis shaking hands with the Chief Constable on the day he became promoted to Detective Superintendent fell from its position on the wall onto the floor, causing the covering glass in the frame to smash. It seemed a coincidence that William's venom had coincided with the frame falling to the floor, but it had been no accident. In spite of what he had said moments earlier, the Superintendent didn't realise that his DCI actually did possess superhuman powers of a sort, and it was the power of his mind, acutely fuelled by his anger, that had caused the frame to fall.

"I wouldn't trust that low-life Scarrow to cover my arse if his life depended on it. He is a snake in the grass. He is the copper you should be kicking out not Judd. He testified against us in court for fuck's sake. He is much more instrumental in making Banks walk free than any of us. Judd is a good copper; he would literally sacrifice his life for this force, would any of us do that? Scarrow certainly wouldn't. Judd wears his heart on his sleeve. Judd is passionate about getting justice sir, that's all."

Somewhat taken aback by William's fervent outburst, Ben Francis couldn't help but be affected by the incident and after a short period of reflection he spoke again. "Okay, but Stone listen to me. You are in the last chance saloon, do you understand me?"

"Yes sir, I won't let you down. I will convict the killer and avenge the deaths of those three women if it's the last thing I do. I swear on my life that I will."

"Yes he will sir. I'll make sure of it."

"Very well. I must need my head seeing to. Now both

of you get out of my sight."

CHAPTER 25

24 years earlier

Tilda couldn't believe that her plan had actually worked. So far at least.

The Adonijah Truthsters, as they had labelled themselves, by enlarge lived off the land that they farmed and harvested in the remote camp that they had set up in the Appalachian Mountains, on the borders of Central Alabama and Mississippi. In spite of their self-sufficiency, it was required on occasion to send *disciples* into the nearby towns, or even into Birmingham, Alabama itself, to stock up on necessary supplies for the camp to feed and function. Such items that would be required were cleaning products, toiletries, clothing and a limited amount of food produce that could not be farmed. Today, Tilda had been chosen to accompany a handful of disciples into Birmingham, Alabama to fetch such supplies. Included in the assembly were the man who had recruited her, Jaden, and the closest person that Tilda could call a friend, Rowena.

The majority of the disciples travelled to the city in the back of an open truck, whilst Jaden sat behind the steering wheel allowing Tilda and Rowena to travel in the cabin alongside him. Jaden had always taken a shine to Tilda, referring to her as "his special one", something that made Rowena jealous. Rowena would have preferred to have been the subject of Jaden's affections; but little did she know that ironically, Tilda would also have preferred Rowena to be the focus of Jaden's attention instead of her. These days, Jaden simply made Tilda's skin crawl, but she had learned to hide it well.

Once the vehicle had been parked up following the long drive, the citizens of Birmingham, Alabama looked curiously at the mountain folk as they climbed out of the back of the truck in their unfashionable clothes and detached expressions on their faces. There was an obvious aura about them that signified that they were a unit that belonged to one another, but not to society in general.

The disciples were each tasked by Jaden to attend various locations of the vicinity to obtain the necessary items, and for once he allowed Tilda out of his sight. He instructed her and Rowena to go to the grocery store. Meanwhile he was simply going to sit in the truck and leisurely wait for the disciples to return.

As Tilda and Rowena ambled in the beaming Alabama sunshine towards the grocery store, it crossed Tilda's mind to simply make a run for it. Although not too much alike in reality, the sounds and actions of this Birmingham at the moment reminded her so much of the Birmingham that she had been forced to leave behind, and she ached to be back home with her big brother and once familiar surroundings. But she knew if she ran she wouldn't get far. Rowena, although her closest ally in the cult, was still completely brainwashed and believed fully in the Adonijah Truthsters and their warped mission. The Adonijah Truthsters were to be the only survivors come judgment day because they had the new Messiah amongst them in the form of their leader Eli Zane, often actually referred to by members of the cult as Adonijah. Eli was supported by his two deputies of the cult, Boris and of course, Jaden.

If Tilda tried to escape, then Rowena would run back to Jaden and he would easily track her down in the truck and capture her – or perhaps worse. She knew that potential defectors had been killed before. Eli, or Adonijah, had often said that anyone was free to leave the Truthsters whenever they felt the need, but Tilda knew that in reality that would never be allowed. So when the two girls walked past the street tables outside the bar, and she heard that familiar accent being spoken, she at first thought that she must have imagined it. Her mind must have been playing tricks on her in this beating sun, as she daydreamed about halcyon days in the West Midlands.

But then she heard it again. She hadn't been mistaken. She heard that distinct pronunciation of the vowels of the English language, spoken the only way that people of the West Midlands ever could.

She turned to see a couple, possibly in their late twenties, sitting at a table. The man was drinking a bottle of beer and the lady was allowing a cup of coffee to cool. They both had kind faces and the lady smiled at Tilda.

"Excuse me, but I couldn't help but notice your accent," said Tilda. "Are you from the West Midlands in England by any chance."

"Yes love, we're from Pelsall, which is part of Walsall. Our accent is very conspicuous around these parts I guess. We're on our honeymoon. I'm now Mrs. Zoe Cavendish." Zoe flashed a huge rock on her wedding finger, the engagement ring actually outshining the wedding band she was aiming to show Tilda. "And this is Mr. Rod Cavendish, my husband of five days. Are you from our area back home then, love?"

"Well, yes kind of. I'm a Brummie."

"Oh, not too far at all then. What brings you here; you are a long way from home? Is your friend also from Birmingham?"

"Birmingham, Alabama ma'am, not England," said

Rowena frostily. "Come on Tilda, we need to go shopping. You know you don't want Jaden catching you speaking with people outside of the Truthsters."

"The Truthsters?" said Rod curiously in-between sips of his bottle of beer. "Are they like some sort of American Football team or something?"

Rowena grabbed hold of Tilda's arm and pulled her away from the couple.

"I'm sorry, I really need to go," said Tilda. "It was nice meeting you."

"Ok honey. Take care of yourself." As the two girls walked away towards the grocery store at the end of the street, Zoe turned to her new husband. "I'm worried about that kid, Rod. Something doesn't seem right."

CHAPTER 26

Once inside the store, Tilda looked along the aisles and caught a glimpse of what she needed.

"Rowena, you go ahead and get the cleaning products. I really need to go to the bathroom."

"Sure thing, I'll meet you at the checkout if you haven't caught up with me by then."

"Okay Rowena, I won't be long."

Having been to the store a couple of times before, Tilda knew that the toilet facilities were at the rear of the establishment. It was only after discreetly raiding the stationary aisle en route that she quickly made her way towards the bathroom.

Tilda knew that she didn't have much time so she had quickly assessed the items on display and managed to pick out a pen, a note pad and a pack of envelopes. She had glanced up at the ceiling and was confident that there had been no CCTV camera focussed upon her. Looking around her for prying eyes, Tilda had swiftly grabbed the items and made her way to the bathroom. Seconds later she had seen the sign that read *please do not take unpaid items into the bathroom*, but by then she had already shoved them into her cloth bag, hopefully undetected.

But Tilda hadn't spotted the lady with the slicked-back hair who had been watching her every move.

Once inside the toilet cubicle, Tilda removed the notepad and pen from her bag and began to scribe a very brief message, realising that time wasn't on her side. Once satisfied she removed the cellophane covering from the envelopes, ripped the page she had scribed upon from the notepad and placed it inside one of the envelopes. Then she secured the contents by licking the gummed seal and wrote an address very quickly on the front.

With all the anxiety of the situation, Tilda then had to use the bathroom for its usual intention, before clawing back some time by uncharacteristically refraining from washing her hands.

Once outside of the bathroom, Tilda raced down the full length of the store and managed to catch up with Rowena at the checkout.

"Hey Tilda, you took your time."

"Oh, you know what it's like. When nature calls you just gotta go."

Rowena just smiled at her friend.

"Here Rowena, let me help you with some of those items."

"Thanks."

Before long the two girls were placing the items from the shopping basket onto the conveyor belt and consequently packing them into carrier bags.

The cashier was a skinny youth with a red-checked shirt which he wore open, with a black T-shirt underneath sporting a design that was not easy on the eye and impossible to immediately decipher, but Tilda thought she spotted a human skull in there somewhere. He had long hair with huge ginger sideburns and chewed gum in an extremely exaggerated manner. Although he was sitting behind the cash till, the top of his jeans were on view and they carried an unnecessary amount of chains dangling from the belt loops. His sleeves were rolled to just below his elbows, and the exposed parts of his arms were covered in tattoos that were once again too difficult to make sense of. Tilda sensed that in the mind of this dude, he was simply biding his time as a grocery store cashier until the inevitable discovery was made of whatever rock band he played in, prior to obvious world domination. At this moment in time Tilda would gladly trade places with him.

"That'll be forty-three dollars and thirteen cents for you crazy chicks," said the cashier in his southern-state drawl.

Not impressed, Rowena simply tutted as she pulled out a credit card from her purse. It was one of a variety of credit cards that the Adonijah Truthsters had in their possession that were either stolen or fraudulently applied for, this one being one of the latter.

With this particular store not yet having the chip and pin facility, the cashier simply swiped the card and asked for Rowena to sign the slip of paper that had been generated accordingly.

"Well thank you, Miss. T.M Baskerville. You have a fine day now with your fine and dandy name."

"Thank you," replied Rowena and somewhat paranoid wondered if the cashier had somehow sensed that the name had been a false one. She and Tilda gathered the shopping and were just about to vacate the check-out when they were halted by a new voice, this one belonging to a female.

"Not so fast. You two young ladies can hold on right there for a cotton-pickin' moment."

CHAPTER 27

"There is nothing wrong with that credit card," blurted out an anxious Rowena.

"Nobody said that there is ma'am. I'm more interested in what you're pretty little friend has got hiding in her bag."

"N...nothing Miss," stated Tilda.

"Is that right, cutie? Are you sure that you have not forgotten to pay for anything?" said the lady with the slicked-back pony-tailed hair. Tilda couldn't help but notice how tall and elegant the lady looked. The cashier was also having a good time undressing her with his eyes as well, leching at her beautifully proportioned curves in the tight-fitting camel-coloured trousers and cheesecloth blouse that was unbuttoned perhaps one or two buttons too many.

"I think we have us a shoplifter here, Chuck," said the lady turning to the cashier who hoped that she hadn't noticed his leching as her eyes met his.

"Oh, right. Okay, yeah," he stammered.

"Oh yeah. Who says?" protested Rowena.

"Me, that's who. Sheri Jackson, the store detective of this establishment and soon to be your worst fucking nightmare if you continue that tone of voice with me young lady." Turning to Tilda she instructed, "Open your bag little lady, I have reason to believe that you have something in there that you sure as hell ain't paid for."

Tilda looked at Rowena, and her friend's expression had a mixture of confusion and anger at this unwanted attention being drawn to them. Eli had always been explicit in teaching his flock not to involve those who didn't understand their quest. "What have you done, Tilda?"

"I swear, I haven't done anything wrong," protested Tilda innocently.

"I'll be the judge of that," snarled Sheri. "Now come on, don't be shy. Show me the contents of your bag."

Tilda placed her bag upside down and let the entire contents drop onto the conveyor belt. She shook the bag while it was turned over to emphasise that it was now empty, and then she even handed it to Sheri who looked inside and frantically inspected it as if it possessed some sort of secret compartment. It was clearly empty.

The selection of Tilda's contents that had been spilled onto the conveyor belt included a small round compact mirror with a slight crack in the corner indicating that it was clearly a few years old, and a small sprig of bluets tied in a bundle with a lace ribbon. Bluets are a four-petalled blue and white flower which grows on the Appalachian Mountains and are also known by the name 'innocence.' The flowers were one of the few things that Tilda had been fond of during her time in the states. There was also a selection of other different coloured ribbons, a dog-eared photo of Tilda cuddling a boy clearly slightly older and taller than her with an obvious family resemblance, a small sewing kit and an opened box of sanitary towels that were not stocked at this store.

Exasperated, Sheri handed the empty bag back to Tilda. "My apologies ma'am, I seem to have made a mistake."

"That's okay, no harm done," said Tilda, not as smugly as she might have as she placed her things back into her bag.

"You pretty little things have a nice day now," offered Sheri as the two girls left the store.

A few hours later when Sheri herself would need to the use the bathroom she would discover the notepad, pen and opened pack of envelopes placed behind the toilet brush.

As Tilda and Rowena made their way back to the truck where Jaden was waiting for them, Tilda was glad to see that Rod and Zoe were still sitting at the same table as earlier. Rod had clearly got himself another bottle of beer and Zoe was now munching on a sandwich. As the two girls got nearer to the newly-wed couple, Tilda allowed Rowena to walk ahead slightly and she hoped that no-one noticed her place her own hand up her skirt and pull the envelope she had prepared earlier from the rear of her panties. Tilda saw that Zoe had noticed her and the fellow west midlander gave a warm but concerned smile towards Tilda.

"Are you okay, love?" asked Zoe, as she placed her sandwich down on the plate.

"She's fine," answered Rowena on Tilda's behalf.

Tilda flung herself at Zoe and began to hug her. "Oh, it's so nice to see someone from England. I'm really glad that I have met you."

Rod momentarily refrained from sinking his beer and looked on curiously, thinking that this act of camaraderie from Tilda was a little excessive. Even Zoe was a little taken aback.

"It's been lovely to meet you too."

As Tilda broke away from her clinch with Zoe, she discreetly handed her the envelope shielding the activity from Rowena with her body. Zoe looked puzzled and Tilda placed her finger to her lips signalling for her to keep quiet.

Zoe understood and swiftly placed the envelope under the napkin that was placed on her knees.

"Come on Tilda, we need to get back to Jaden," said Rowena, oblivious to what had just happened.

"I'm coming. Bye, Zoe and Rod. It really was nice to meet you."

"You too honey. Look after yourself," said Zoe

"Yeah, nice to have met you," said Rod.

Still refraining from eating her sandwich, events overtaking the moment, Zoe watched Tilda and Rowena enter the cabin of the truck while a handful of other dowdy looking individuals climbed in the back. Not long after, the truck pulled away to return to the mountains.

"I hope that girl's gonna be okay?" she said to Rod.

"Yeah, I wonder what she was doing all the way out here with that bunch of weirdos."

"She gave me something," said Zoe as she pulled the envelope from under her napkin.

"Open it. What does it say?"

"I can't, it's not for me."

"Who's it for?"

Zoe read out the address to her husband. "William Chamberlain, Birmingham and District Police, Birmingham, West Midlands."

CHAPTER 28

The young Detective Sergeant William Chamberlain had thanked the newly-wed couple from Pelsall with all his heart when they handed him the envelope. He instantly recognised that the handwriting belonged to that of his missing little sister, Tilda. This at least proved what he had always hoped for – she was still alive.

He had almost tracked down Tilda in Cornwall a couple of years earlier but had agonisingly just missed the prize. When Tilda had left home in the hope of becoming a singer, William had quickly begun to realise that he had allowed his sister to join a religious cult. Initially naïve to such elements of society, when his sister failed to make contact, William knew something was amiss. His sister was a very shy and sensitive girl, she had promised to keep in touch and she would have acutely felt the need to. For Tilda to travel away from the family she loved so dear, and the familiar surroundings of Birmingham, West Midlands would have been a quantum leap for her.

Amazingly, Tilda's spontaneous plan in Birmingham, Alabama had worked. Following receipt of the note that she prayed would find her brother, DS William Chamberlain was now standing on a ridge in the heart of the Appalachian Mountains where Central Alabama begins to border with the state of Mississippi. At his side was Chief Bill Chambers of Birmingham Alabama Police Department and an array of armed US police officers. They were looking down on a deserted farm house and accompanying ranch that had been usurped by the Adonijah Truthsters. Dotted around the surrounding farmland were sprinklings of tents.

Chief Bill Chambers had offered the desperate young police sergeant from England a tremendous amount of assistance ever since William had contacted him following the note received from Tilda. In-between the serious parts of their conversations, they had found amusement at the similarities between the two men such as the familiarity of their names, their professions and their home cities sharing the same name of Birmingham, albeit being thousands of miles apart.

There were two distinct differences between Chief Bill Chambers and DS William Chamberlain though – their skin colour and their outlook on religion. Bill Chambers was a black man with a devout Evangelical faith, his faith being the driving force of his desire to bring to justice the charlatans of the Adonijah Truthsters who took the Lord's name in vain on a daily basis. Ironically, along with the obvious drive of simply wanting to rescue his sister, William's constant disillusionment with his own faith helped drive his commitment to eradicating the sick cult that his sister had got herself mixed up in.

Chief Chambers had been able to educate William regarding the origins of the Adonijah Truthsters. They had been founded by a bunch of dysfunctional Baptists (although clearly, their subsequent recruits to the cult did not have to belong to any initial faith, just as long as they were susceptible enough to being converted to the Truthsters' beliefs). These dysfunctional Baptists believed that the new messiah would eventually evolve from the biblical King David. According to the book of Samuel,

King David's empire had seemingly been handed to his son Solomon, but after the deaths of his elder brothers Amnon and Absalom it had indeed been Adonijah who would be the natural heir to the throne. However, it was Solomon, a younger brother, who was preferred to his older brother.

Adonijah made a bizarre attempt to "reclaim" his throne by trying to marry David's concubine but he was seized and put to death. According to the belief of the Truthsters', Adonijah had been cheated out of becoming the rightful King, and with Eli's *guidance* they viewed conventional organised religions as declaring false idols to being the heads of their respective faiths. For instance, they did not recognise the authority of the Pope as being the leader of the Catholic Church. Therefore, 2000 years or so later according to the Adonijah Truthsters, Eli Zane was believed to be the new messiah. A prophet sent by God to right the wrong experienced by Adonijah, to avenge his suffering and to bring a selection of chosen people into his fold for when judgment day arrives.

The followers believed Eli to be the one true leader, with the one true voice of God and to subsequently activate God's intentions. Eli would *choose* the members of his flock with the help of Boris and Jaden, his two most loyal disciples – why have one St Peter when he could have two? They would prey upon the vulnerable victims of society, people who appeared void of a purpose in life, and the three men were skilled in offering the Adonijah Truthsters as the only viable path forward.

Tilda would have been targeted for her innocent vulnerability, acutely affected by the bullying she had received during her schooldays. Initially she would have jumped at the chance of having a group of friends to belong to.

Other recruits would have been persuaded to fund the cult with their life savings and by selling off assets to ensure the cult's survival in its isolation from the rest of the world.

The cult interpreted the Bible as fact but their interpretation would only be based on how Eli interpreted it, which would be extremely distorted and beneficial to him. His manipulation was enough to convince his followers that the Bible tells us that the end of the world is nigh. They believed that the truth about God had been lost when Christ had been crucified and related false teachings had subsequently snowballed for the following centuries. They believed that since the crucifixion, the only way to access the truth was through the prophetic books of the Bible, in particular Revelation, and in all of this they believed that it pointed to Eli Zane to be the man to lead the way.

And now that Chief Bill Chambers had proof that the Adonijah Truthsters were keeping a girl against her will in the form of Tilda's note, he believed that he could at last arrest the slippery threesome of Eli, Boris and Jaden with kidnap, if nothing else.

Although on very unfamiliar territory, William felt a greater sense of imminent success standing amongst his American counterparts. The disappointment of the failed Cornwall siege had been very hard to stomach and William had been concerned that he had missed his one golden opportunity of rescuing his sister.

In Cornwall, The Adonijah Truthsters had set up camp on a deserted farm not far from Bodmin Moor, but somehow their intelligence had been stronger than both the police forces of Birmingham and District, and Devon and Cornwall, because when William entered the farm they had already vacated the premises and fled the country. It was not until William had received Tilda's note that he had any clue where the cult had subsequently settled.

The Adonijah Truthsters were made up of various followers, but not all had declared to their friends and family left behind that they had joined the cult, or indeed where their whereabouts were. William had suspected that the Southern States of America was the most likely destination once they had fled England, knowing that several of their members were from this part of the world. But locating exactly where the cult had settled had been like searching for the proverbial needle in a haystack – until he had received Tilda's note.

When William had contacted Chief Bill Chambers he had expected an unhelpful response, after all why would a decorated Chief of Police across the pond be interested on the thoughts of an English Detective Sergeant accusing his fellow countrymen of kidnap and false imprisonment? Besides, Tilda had initially joined the cult under her own free will so where was the tangible act of a crime? However, Chief Chambers could not have been more helpful, and his ability to take William seriously demonstrated to William part of the reasoning why this man was such a respected and decorated Chief of Police.

Unfortunately the response had not been as helpful by the Devon and Cornwall Police Department who had not been keen to admit that a cult existence could be happening on their patch. William had always suspected that the Adonijah Truthsters had been tipped off by a member of the Devon and Cornwall Police Force allowing their escape, thus resulting in moving the problem elsewhere.

Before the planning of today's siege in the Appalachian Mountains, Bill Chambers had informed William further of the cult leaders and the cult itself – as much as he knew anyway. Eli and Boris had both derived from Mississippi whilst Jaden had originated from Tennessee. Although they appeared to be practicing a cult, in truth it seemed that Eli was adept at appearing to just stay within the boundaries of the law, and Bill was constantly frustrated at not being able to blow the operation apart. But now through Tilda's note he had reason to intervene. William had initially worried about the strength of the note in his quest to gain US police support, but in actual fact it had proved very powerful in ensuring that the Adonijah Truthsters could be raided. The note appeared to suggest a case of false imprisonment and that was good enough for Bill Chambers to act.

Chief Bill Chambers had decided that any attempt to simply approach the camp in order to negotiate Tilda's release by her own free will would prove futile, and in addition he did not wish to place her in any danger. Instead, since William had contacted him two months previously, the police chief had deployed two of his finest undercover detectives into the cult in order to build up a level of intelligence on Eli Zane and the Adonijah Truthsters. In reality, due to the restrictions in the camp of communicating with the outside world, it had been difficult for Detectives Dirk Jolsen and Kris Peebles to keep Chambers regularly informed. Nevertheless, Chambers' meticulous approach, which was initially frustrating to William who was keen to simply get amongst the cult and free his sister from their clutches, had been justified, as the two detectives had managed to inform the Chief of Police of the alarming amount of weaponry the cult had placed about the residence to fight off any challenge to their existence. Initially the police hadn't suspected that the cult would have such a significant amount of arms, but thankfully learning of this information enabled them to plan accordingly. It would have been much easier to obtain arms in the southern states of America than it would have been during the cult's time in Cornwall, hence the probable option not to stand and fight in England two years earlier.

The primary channel of communication chosen by the undercover detectives had been to take Tilda's lead in leaving written notes at the grocery store in Birmingham, Alabama, for another undercover detective to collect who was temporarily employed at the store. Fortunately for William, the notes had also informed them that Tilda was in good health in spite of everything.

The use of mobile phones had been deemed too dangerous. If the detectives had been caught with a mobile phone in their possession it would have at the very least been confiscated by Eli, but more importantly it would most likely have blown their cover of being integrated cult members.

The detectives had pretended to be homeless people disillusioned with their life, which had fooled Jaden into recruiting them one day whilst in Birmingham, Alabama. The smug Jaden had mistakenly believed that their recruitment had been as easy as taking candy from a baby. He had no concept that they could have ever been from the law.

William felt the sun beat down hard on his face, escalating his already sweaty brow due to the intensity of the situation. Bill Chambers was slightly more relaxed, but it was impossible for the heat of the sun or the situation to be lost on him. "Okay, William, as you can see I'm not taking any chances here. Jolsen and Peebles are to leave for town today as a matter of routine and they will bring Tilda with them. When they reach this part of the road I envisage we will intervene with their journey and successfully get Tilda out of the truck while we seize whoever else is in the vehicle. Then we will carefully proceed to ambush the remaining residents who have stayed put at the establishment.

"We need to tread carefully due to the amount of weapons they have at hand and I am sure they will put up a fight to protect their community, but the more bodies we seize from the truck the more people we manage to get out alive. This is a delicate operation and I'm not ruling out casualties on their side. If we do get Eli, Boris and Jaden out alive we can charge them for false imprisonment of Tilda at the very least, but I'm convinced that we can uncover a lot more than that. I'm sure that many of their weapons are illegal for starters and I will ask to see the correct documentation if we get that opportunity, but my boys have been told to shoot without hesitation if necessary.

"I'm declining to undergo the siege during the hours of darkness as I want Tilda safely out of the residence before we go in with any type of attack, and of late she has been included in these trips into town so that's ideal. She is the one person I know who is totally innocent in all of this so I don't want her coming to any harm. Are there any questions, William?"

"No thanks Bill. I'm just grateful for your cooperation in saving my sister."

"Let's not count our chickens just yet, William. As I said, this is a very delicate operation but one that cannot be allowed to fester forever. Now is as good a time as any to take the bull by the horns and blow this damn cult apart."

William nodded in acknowledgement.

Meanwhile, down in the Adonijah Truthsters' residence, Eli was sitting in his favourite armchair in the centre of the main living room. He used the armchair as if it were a throne. Much of the group were sitting on the floor before or around him, hanging on his every parasitic word. However, Eli had witnessed Peebles and Jolsen whisper to Tilda and felt a gut instinct to enquire as to where they were going.

"We're just off to Birmingham to fetch some supplies, Eli," offered Peebles.

"You two are always fetching the supplies, why are you always so keen?" enquired Eli in his deep voice and typically long drawn out delivery. It was the kind of voice that could make the devil himself shudder and had the ability to deliver the most banal of words to appear like rolling thunder.

"We just want to do our bit for the Truthsters, Eli?" offered Jolsen this time.

Eli slowly ran his hand over his chin that housed a couple of day's growth, purposefully making his most basic actions appear important. "Why is she going?"

Eli had noticed Jolsen link Tilda's arm and the body language and chemistry between the three people fuelled the usual paranoia and suspicions he encountered on a daily basis.

"It is my time of the month Eli. I need some women's supplies," spoke Tilda meekly.

"Women's supplies? Do we have none already in the house? You shouldn't even be needing 'em now girl. I'm growing tired of you Tilda, why haven't you ever caught and bore me a child like the other girls? It must be the devil's work keeping you from bearing me a child – or perhaps you are spawned from the devil yourself and that is why you never catch?" Taking Eli's words into consideration, Tilda suddenly felt that she owed the devil a mountain of gratitude.

Eli exaggerated his hand movement once more over his stubbly chin. "Okay, okay. I accept that a man shouldn't ask for women's things so Susie, you go with Kris. Tilda you come and sit with me and we will pray together to see if the Lord will allow you to bear me a child one day. Dirk, you stay too. It ain't healthy how you and Kris are always joined at the hip. Are you a couple of fags or something?" Eli laughed at his own joke, but then his warped religious beliefs turned his persona serious once again at the blink of an eye. "I hope you are not fags. That would not be the Lord's way."

"We are not fags," offered Dirk evenly, biting his tongue at the blatant display of homophobia. "Please allow Tilda to come with me. She was going to help me choose some fish and nourishing food for our supper tonight. We felt like throwing a bit of a party in your name Eli, as a way of thanking you for your guidance."

The flattery was not lost on Eli who ran his hand over his chin once more in an exaggerated movement as an actor in a film might do. After an unnecessary pause he spoke again. "I need Tilda to pray with me. Dirk and Susie you go and fetch the supplies. Susie has a fine taste for food and wine. You can take a few of the others with you too if you're to collect a large amount of items. Kris, we're gonna need some wood chopping for the fire if we're gonna have us a party tonight. A big strong lad like you is ideal to prepare for that kind of thing; there is no need for you to go to the stores."

Kris and Dirk shot each other a worried look. Things were not going to plan but they had to at least make the trip, even without Tilda, to avoid suspicion. Hopefully Dirk could sort something out once the chief and others intercepted the truck, but the reality now would possibly be for his friends in the force to have to storm the ranch in order to get Tilda out. That was not the option that anybody wanted. And neither Kris nor Dirk underestimated the delicacy of the situation.

Eli's booming and masterful voice spoke again. "Boris, I want you to go too."

Boris smiled and simply nodded.

"Here they come," exclaimed Bill Chambers peering through the lenses of his powerful binoculars.

"May I?" enquired William. Bill gladly passed the binoculars to his English friend.

"Take your places, boys. I want as many of them taken alive and we only shoot if absolutely necessary. Is that clear?"

"Yes sir," answered the gathering of armed officers to their police chief.

"We need to ensure that Tilda is delivered safely to us, and we don't want any friendly-fire winding up in Kris and Dirk either."

Concealed by foliage, the gathering of US police officers and the English Detective Sergeant watched from the ridge. The road bent just before them and the parked police vehicles were obscured from the view of the ascending truck. The lawmen's advantageous view point was positioned little over a mile away from the Adonijah Truthsters' ranch.

As the truck approached nearer, William desperately searched the faces of the cult followers hoping to hit upon his sister, but frustratingly he was unable to spot her. There appeared to be two or three individuals shielded from view due to their seating position in the rear of the vehicle, but he somehow had a feeling that Tilda wasn't one of them.

"I don't think Tilda is on the truck, Bill."

"Are you sure? I know Dirk and Kris would have tried their damndest to make sure she was on there. Something must have gone wrong."

Bill noticed the fear in the Englishman's eyes.

"Let's not panic, William. I still want to seize the occupants of the truck. They won't be expecting an ambush so I don't envisage much of fight from them, and then we can work out how they can lead us to Tilda." Bill placed a hand of support on his friend's shoulder. "Try not to worry William, we will get Tilda out safely." Both men realised that in all honesty this would be much easier said than done.

Even though Boris had accompanied Dirk on the trip into town, along with several other devout Adonijah Truthsters, Dirk had at least managed to negotiate to drive. As he approached the bend in the road he knew that his comrades would be waiting for their surprise attack. He picked up as much speed as the old pick up truck would allow.

"Hey, what's the rush big fella?" spoke Boris, a little confused. But not allowing any time to supply an answer, Dirk turned the corner at high speed then violently slammed the brakes on to bring the truck to a jolting halt. The cult members who sat in the back of the open truck all banged into one another like a set of stacked dominoes. In the cabin area sat Dirk and Boris, the latter smarting a slight cut on his forehead after becoming intimate with the dashboard.

Dirk's emergency stop had proved successful. By the time the Adonijah Truthsters had composed themselves the truck was surrounded by armed officers and the occupants obediently placed their hands in the air showing no resistance.

All except Boris that was, who slammed his door into the armed cop that was pointing a gun at him through the window. It gave Boris enough time to climb out of the vehicle and pull a gun from his pocket aiming it at the terrified officer who squirmed on the floor. But before Boris could fire the trigger his bulk of a frame was jumping like a catfish on a pole as he became riddled in a hail of bullets. Boris was the only casualty of the siege and the big man took many hits to the body before keeling over and eventually dying. The sound of the shots that rang out into the blistering sky had not escaped the residents down at the ranch, including Eli.

He gave a self-assured smile before he spoke in that chilling voice of his. "It looks like we have company."

The armed officers had handcuffed their prisoners and secured them within the police vehicles. The activity had allowed enough time for Eli to set up defence of his territory and the remaining Adonijah Truthsters became strategically placed around the ranch complete with weaponry.

Dirk had informed Bill Chambers that there were at least twenty-five to thirty members remaining at the ranch and although the seizing of the truck had gone seamlessly well, the penetration of the dwelling would not be so easy. These people would be prepared to defend their territory and their leader Eli Zane until their death.

Bill Chambers had already seen two of his officers gunned down as they moved downhill towards the ranch, but the lawmen had managed to gain a strong footing, yet were unable to advance any further locked in a position of stalemate with the Adonijah Truthsters. Chambers didn't want any more deaths if he could help it and he was forever mindful of what predicament Tilda may be in.

In actual fact, Tilda was still in the living room with Eli as he had instructed, postponing his orders for her to pray with him. Even at this eventful and uncertain time, the lechful Eli still had the wherewithal to stroke Tilda's hair.

"Do you feel frightened, Tilda?" asked Eli.

"Yes." Tilda knew that Eli referred to the gunfire and uncertain future of the ranch, but in actual fact, Tilda was more scared of Eli and she wondered if he somehow knew that this siege had been caused by her note being passed onto her brother in England. Surely he couldn't know could he? This was the level of fear that Eli was able to generate in Tilda.

"Don't be frightened. This is God's way, a test of our little set up here. What God will do is identify the true Adonijah Truthsters and shelter them. Therefore I am not scared, and if you truly believe in me Tilda, you will be saved also. You do believe in me don't you, Tilda?"

"But of course," Tilda hoped that she was a good liar.

"Well there you are then. You have nothing to fear."

Suddenly, Kris entered the room holding an axe. "Leave her be, Eli."

"Kris, why aren't you chopping wood like I told you to? Actually, more's to the point, why aren't you defending the ranch with the others?"

"Why aren't you?" Eli was somewhat taken aback at Kris's counter. "Do you dare to question me, boy?"

"Yeah, too right I fucking dare to question you. If this ranch is so important to you, why are you not out there defending it alongside all those gullible suckers?"

Eli reflected for a moment. "Things are now beginning to make sense. You and that friend of yours Dirk are responsible for this aren't you? I always sensed that you weren't really committed to the Adonijah Truthsters." Eli began to laugh hysterically like a madman.

"Perhaps you won't laugh so loud once I drive this axe into your skull. You are just an everyday psycho Eli, you are not a prophet. I don't quite know how you manage to convince anyone otherwise, but your farcical reign ends today." Kris began to run at Eli causing the phony to uncharacteristically fear for his life. Eli placed his hands over his face as some sort of pathetic attempt to protect himself from the axe that was about to meet his head. But as Kris raised the axe above his own head he suddenly froze as a gunshot could be heard from behind him.

"Rowena, what have you done?" screamed Tilda.

Rowena was standing in the doorway of the living room shaking as she held a smoking gun with both hands.

"I had to kill him; he was going to kill Eli."

Now realising that Rowena had saved his life, Eli began to laugh hysterically once more. "You see, even with an axe aimed at my head I have been forsaken. I am safe. I am alive. I cannot die until my time is chosen by God."

Tilda began to sob into her hands.

Eli began to stroke Tilda's hair once more. "Seeing your friend Rowena kill a man is not an easy thing Tilda, I know, but like she said he was going to kill me. What else could she do?"

The anger and frustration inside became too much for Tilda. Suddenly she felt as though she had nothing to lose by confronting this wicked charlatan, and before she realised what she was doing, all the frustration and pain that had been welling inside her poured out like a fountain of venom. "Don't you dare touch me. I don't want you to ever touch me again. I wish Kris had sunk that axe into your crazy skull and then this farce would all be over. Without you these misguided sheep that follow you would all be free."

Eli was stunned. "My child, the Devil has entered inside of you. You are speaking with a forked tongue."

"You are the one closer to the Devil than I am, Eli.

You are the evil one. You are a monst–" but before Tilda could say anything more, Eli's hand struck her hard across the face silencing her immediately.

"Rowena, please will you fetch me my whisky and glass. I need to calm my nerves while I decide what to do with this possessed child." Rowena obediently brought over the whisky and glass and poured Eli a drink while he hugged a copy of the Bible close to his chest. He took the glass from her with his free hand and sank the whisky quickly. "Another please, Rowena."

Before Rowena could pour another glass, Tilda sprang up and grabbed the bottle out of her hand. Then she began to act dazed and confused.

"What has come over me? Please allow me to pour your next drink Eli, it would be an honour. I think you are correct, the Devil has entered me. Please forgive me, Eli."

Eli looked confused and signalled for Rowena to allow Tilda to pour him a drink. After all what harm could it do?

As Tilda handed the glass of whisky towards his outstretched hand she flung the drink into his face causing his eyes to burn. She swiftly followed the act up by smashing the now empty glass across his head stunning him slightly and producing an instant flow of blood and swelling.

"Evil bitch. Seize her Rowena."

But Rowena didn't know what to do as she saw her friend run towards the door. Tilda turned to her misguided friend, "Come with me Rowena, this is probably your only chance."

"I c…can't. I belong with Eli and the Adonijah Truthsters."

"Then may God truly be with you Rowena," and with that Tilda slammed the door behind her. Rowena realised that she could have once more pulled the gun from her apron to shoot at her friend but could not find the inclination to do so following their years of bonding.

Once outside the door, Tilda noticed the series of

strategically placed candles burning in the hallway. Eli had insisted that lighted candles would be an ever-present feature designed to keep evil spirits away from the house. Tilda realised that she still had the bottle of whisky with her and it was almost full. She noticed a large rug a few feet in front of her and dragged it to the door that she had just closed behind her, adrenaline allowing her to overcome its weight. She doused the rug in whisky and spilled the candles onto it. She smiled as she watched the flames quickly take hold and rapidly begin to lick at the door.

As she turned her line of sight met the window and she was astonished to see a police car crash through the wooden gate to the ranch ploughing down four members of the Adonijah Truthsters as it hurtled towards the house. She could just about make out the driver of the vehicle and it caused her to gasp. There was no mistake. It was her brother, William.

Moments earlier an astonished Bill Chambers had been shouting at William to come back as he helplessly watched the English policeman climb into the police car, take the wheel and start the engine. It had been a helpless plea.

"I'm tired of waiting Bill," shouted William from the already open window of the vehicle. The tyres spun with dramatic momentum and the vehicle kicked into life as William placed the accelerator pedal to the floor.

"Shit," was all Bill Chambers could say as he helplessly watched the car head towards the ranch, leaving a trail of dust behind it created by the speeding tyres as it careered down the sun-dried, dusty road. "God damn it. Come on guys, some of us need to follow him. We can utilise this old truck of theirs, I'll take the wheel. Palmer, Murray, Wright, Dougan, Cook, Thompson and Stowell, you all jump in the back and have your guns at the ready, the rest of you hold your positions and fire down on those sons of bitches whenever you see fit. Thanks to our English counterpart we need to firmly take the bull by the horns now, okay?"

"Yes sir," came the unanimous and positive reply. Within thirty seconds Bill Chambers and his collection of armed police were making their way down the dusty track in the Adonijah Truthsters' truck.

The hail of bullets that was peppering the police car being driven at high speed by William Chamberlain did nothing to deter his quest. William was like a man possessed; his entire focus was getting into that ranch and getting his sister out of it. Any associated consequences that could be caused by his haste had paled into insignificance.

As he approached the wooden gate he didn't contemplate reducing his speed, and he saw the terrified look in the eyes of the gathering of Adonijah Truthsters who had failed to secure the ranch from the out of control police car. William simply crashed through the gate taking the four hillbillies with him.

As he brought the car to a halt, expecting to be approached by other Adonijah Truthsters, William soon realised that his drastic and daring actions had been the correct approach as he saw the front door to the farmhouse fly open and a young woman in her early twenties run towards him. William couldn't believe it as he stepped out of the car. His heart filled with an unrivalled feeling of joy and relief and tears welled in his eyes as he could see that the young woman was his sister, Tilda. The last time he had seen her she had been a teenager.

The momentum of her passionate run towards him nearly knocked him over as she embraced her brother, holding him as tight as a bear would, and never wanting to let go. She buried her face into his large chest and sobbed tears of joy and relief. She hadn't felt this secure for so many years. "Oh William, it's you. It's really you."

"You bet it is kid. Come on sis, as much as I want to hug you, you need to get in the car. I want to get you out of this godforsaken place."

As Tilda finally let go and climbed into the back of the police car, William noticed that a fire was rapidly taking hold of the farmhouse and in-between the sounds of crackling timber he could hear screams coming from the property. He hoped the screams were coming from the bastards who had been responsible for imprisoning his sister the last few years.

Suddenly a bullet whizzed past his face and he turned to see a couple of angry looking Adonijah Truthsters running towards him, but then shots rang out from elsewhere and he saw the two assailants drop like a sack of potatoes. Not long after, the truck pulled up alongside William, and Bill Chambers got out. He slapped his English friend affectionately on the arm. "Go on William, get your sister out of here; we'll finish things off here."

"Bill, I can't thank you enough. Please understand that you have a friend for life and I'll let Tilda know how much you helped me."

"We'll stay in touch friend, no worries. Now go on, get your English ass outta here before I bust ya for loitering with intent and obstructing police business."

William Chamberlain climbed back behind the steering wheel and drove away from the ranch that had imprisoned his sister. With the farmhouse being made of timber, Bill Chambers and his officers were soon forced to leave the site as the fire dramatically took hold of the property.

In the moments that unfolded, Bill Chambers and his police department had either shot dead resisting cult members or secured those that were more sensible and surrendered peacefully. A handful died in the fire, a mixture of trapped individuals and those who chose to perish believing it to be God's way of taking them to the Promised Land – dying for their cause. In his wisdom, Chief Bill Chambers opted never to investigate the actual source of the fire, documenting its cause as a likely accident caused during the drama of the siege. He guessed differently.

Some 2 miles south of the ranch from a mountainous viewpoint, a small gathering of people were looking down on the burning farmhouse.

Eli turned to Jaden and Rowena, "We are the chosen ones, and God has forsaken us. We have been spared to continue with our pursuit of the truth."

"Amen," answered the gathering.

CHAPTER 29

The year 1993

In the months and even years to come, Tilda gradually revealed to her brother the atrocities that had been exercised by Eli Zane and the hardcore element of the Adonijah Truthsters, including of course his hench men, Jaden Rivers and Boris Gray. Not only did Tilda painfully reveal the abuse that had been inflicted on her, she also informed William shocking information regarding many other victims, including the murders of a number of once dedicated disciples who grew wise and dared to question Eli's motives.

Tilda had been left considerably scarred by her lengthy ordeal; she would wake in the night with vivid nightmares reliving the awful life that she still found difficult to accept that she had managed to escape from. Deep within Tilda laid an embedded root of fear which enabled Eli, Jaden and perhaps even the deceased Boris to possess some type of invisible hold over her. She never felt safe and found it hard to understand that the probability of meeting any of the Adonijah Truthsters again was extremely unlikely.

Unfortunately, Tilda informed her brother that she

would never testify against any of them as she was too scared of what they might do to her. No matter how William tried to assure her that she was now safe with him and totally protected from their clutches he could never quite convince her.

William wanted those responsible for his sister's torment to pay dearly, but in addition to recognising his sister's reluctance in testifying, where were they now anyway?

Perhaps they had even perished in the fire, which would negate the need to track the monsters down in any event of wanting to bring them to justice.

Although relieved to have his sister close to him once again, it would break William's heart to watch her experience acute bouts of depression and post-traumatic stress, with hours upon hours of tears rolling down her face. Tilda had remained very withdrawn from society for some time, and rarely entered into conversation even with William, but after several months of being back in Birmingham, England, she eventually began to confide in William of the disturbing things that she had been exposed to. For example, she explained how an active approach of breeding took place in the cult in an attempt to keep Eli's bloodline present, should the Devil ever appear and take him from them. The stories Tilda told her brother was fascinating. Highly disturbing, but fascinating.

Tilda was able to augment, and add to, the information which Chief Bill Chambers had managed to uncover about the Adonijah Truthsters. Eli, Boris and Jaden, like many of the cult members, were dysfunctional Baptists. They called themselves the Adonijah Truthsters as they believed Eli Zane to be the new messiah who was yet to claim his rightful place, and therefore ensuring that through him, Adonijah would at last be able to also claim his rightful place.

When the second coming would arrive, and the Adonijah Truthsters firmly believed that the end of the world was upon us, they, and only they, would be saved with Eli Zane being the only surviving leader of all mankind. Gone would be all other religious leaders, presidents, kings and queens and so on. They believed that 2012 would be the destined time for the world to end, with everyone being departed from this world except them. With Eli Zane a.k.a Adonijah surely leading them from Armageddon.

In 1967, Israel occupied the city of Jerusalem through the 6 days war for the first time in 2000 years. The Adonijah Truthsters interpreted this as the fulfillment of the prophecy that said "Jerusalem will be taken down by the gentiles until the time of the gentiles be fulfilled." In many writings a Biblical generation is said to consist of a 40 year period, therefore the second coming, led by Eli Zane, would equate to being 2007 following that crucial intervention of 1967. However, it is believed by many, and not only by the Adonijah Truthsters, that the current calendar is actually calculated incorrectly by 5 years either side of the year zero. Therefore, if Jesus Christ was in reality born at a different time by 5 years, then 2012 becomes the year of the second coming for the Adonijah Truthsters and not 2007 – and of course they had already lived through 2002.

It troubled William that such interpretations could fester in the midst of such dangerous minds and it troubled him even more to see his sister in such a broken and fragile state. But at least she was home. Unable to entirely be sure that Eli and Jaden had died in the fire, William made a promise to himself that while he had breath in his body, and if he ever discovered that they were indeed alive, then both Eli Zane and Jaden Rivers would indeed pay dearly for what they had done to his sister. If they perhaps believed that they were destined to meet Boris in the afterlife as part of their warped plan he vowed never to disappoint them.

Those initial conversations William had with Tilda had

been very strange. William in all honesty didn't quite know what to say to his sister or how to approach subsequent conversations with her. She had clearly been affected by the years of captivity and William learned how she had literally been detached from the outside world.

They found some common ground when they discussed topics such as music. Tilda always liked to talk about music, in fact one of the most engaging conversations William had had with Tilda since her resettlement was breaking the news to her that her beloved Wham! had parted company in 1986, something she never knew such was the isolation that she had encountered from the outside world. When she had been "captured" in 1983, like most teenage girls, Tilda had been besotted with George and Andrew and was now disappointed to learn they had split up. William was able to provide Tilda with the entire Wham! back catalogue in order for her to catch up with their musical achievements, and he informed her how they had been the first western group to play in China. Shutting herself away in her bedroom, listening to Wham's up-beat music was one form of therapy that helped Tilda get through her darkest memories.

And at least since her escape from the Adonijah Truthsters, Tilda was now able to tap into the incredible ongoing success of the *Faith* album and George Michael's solo career to make up for her lost years of the mid eighties.

Ironically, William had taken some small comfort that Tilda's exclusion from the outside world had at least protected her from the tragedies that had plagued her home country prior to her rescue. In particular, 1987 had been an unpleasant year in many respects. Putting music and therefore the release of Michael's album *Faith* aside, incidents outside of the music world were laced with disaster. On 6 March, 193 passengers and crew were killed at sea when the cruise liner, *Herald of Free Enterprise* sank on its voyage from Dover to Zeebrugge. Then on 19 August in Hungerford, Berkshire, a 27 year old unemployed labourer named Michael Ryan, indulged himself in a killing spree with two semi-automatic rifles and a hand gun, shooting 16 people dead and wounding 15 more, before eventually turning the gun on himself. One of the 16 victims had been Ryan's own mother. The exact motive of this tragedy is still unknown. And in November of the same year, tragedy struck the transport industry once again when 31 people were killed in London due to a fire at Kings Cross train station.

The world of football had also experienced its share of poignant tragedies as the disease of football violence continued to dominate the media. In 1987, Judd Stone had watched on TV the incredible footage of a Wolves fan falling through the roof of Scarborough's primitive football stand as the Wolves' supporters had more than made their presence known at the north coastal town. Before that incident, in 1985, an innocent boy had been tragically killed when Birmingham City and Leeds United supporters had clashed at Birmingham's stadium St Andrews, prompting the 1986 report which investigated the atrocities of football violence, to liken the Blues and Leeds clash to that of the "Battle of Agincourt." Unfortunately, during this period of time, football hooliganism seemed a necessary pastime for many teenage boys to get involved in, and not much later Judd Stone found himself becoming involved in this world.

Tilda would eventually learn of all of these disasters, especially as they hadn't happened too long before her escape and they remained raw on the minds of the British people, but fortunately 1988 provided her with some noticeable musical headlines which helped bring her slowly back to living in the normal world again. Music became her salvation in many ways as she was able to lose herself in the rich and positive vibes.

Whilst the 'feel-good' Stock, Aitken and Waterman juggernaut was taking the charts by storm, The Beatles were entered into the Rock and Roll Hall of Fame, Michael Jackson purchased his Neverland Ranch whilst releasing the long time awaited follow up album to *Thriller*, named *Bad*, and sixties singer Sonny Bono became the Mayor of Palm Springs once more signalling the existence of showbiz influencing American politics. After all, at that time Hollywood Film Star Ronald Reagan was still occupying the White House. Reagan's reign finally came to an end in 1989, something that Tilda was able to witness.

But now, a small number of years since her rescue, with Tilda beginning to reclaim her life once again, a most amazing turn of events happened.

At this time, Tilda was living with William in his semi-detached property in Erdington. Like most families in the United Kingdom, the order of the evening was to sit on the sofa with their tea (known as dinner in most parts of the UK but not in Birmingham) resting on their laps whilst they watched the evening news, a fact so expertly interpreted in that very English songsmith Clifford T Ward's song "Watching the TV News". In these times there was no instant access at our fingertips to understand what was happening around the world. There was no dedicated news channel in Britain and the internet was still a distant reality.

"Can we turn the radio off sis, so we can watch the news?" said William as he handed his sister a plate of double egg and chips. It was a rare treat for Tilda to have her tea cooked for her, one of the natural progressions that had occurred whilst Tilda had lived with her brother was that she tended to cook and clean, she seen it as one way of repaying her brother for his amazing support.

"Oh Wills, I wouldn't mind but there is never any good news reported. I would have thought that you encounter enough pain and suffering at work considering what you have to see. Why on Earth do you want to watch such matters on the box?"

"It's tradition, sis," and with that, William turned off the radio bringing the opening piano filled bars of Julian Lennon's "Saltwater" to an abrupt end, slightly annoying Tilda as she liked the song very much. William turned on the TV and didn't need to switch channel as it was already on BBC1.

After only a few tastes of their meal, the siblings could hardly believe what unfolded on the screen.

It was February 1993 and the news reports were reporting on an American cult who had set up residence at a ranch named the Mount Carmel center in Waco, Texas. The cult was known as the Branch Davidians and their leader was an individual called David Koresh whose real name was apparently Vernon Howell. The footage showed helicopters hovering over the ranch and cattle trucks full of armed agents being sent in to confront Koresh. The reporter was articulating information of a gun fight between the agents and the Davidians which had resulted in four ATF officers and six Davidians being killed. Tilda couldn't believe this was happening; it was as if she was experiencing a case of déjà vu. Here was another cult in America at war with the American authorities. Tears filled her eyes as she relived her own ordeal and she watched the consequences of another misguided religious cult unfold before her.

When William and Bill Chambers' men had rescued Tilda, the Adonijah Truthsters' demise had been swift and relatively low key, but in contrast the "Waco" siege had become prime time viewing, falling under the radar of the media spotlight. Along with the rest of the world, Tilda and William tuned into the proceedings of the Waco siege and were gripped for the next 51 days, watching the amazing events unfold as the FBI took control of operations from the ATF.

It became apparent that some children and adults were allowed to leave the ranch but most Davidians decided to stay and defend their church with Koresh seemingly having the same influence as Eli Zane had in the Adonijah Truthsters. The standoff made for gripping television, no-one quite knowing how this stalemate was ever going to reach a conclusion. Fortunately the events at the Appalachian Mountains in smashing apart the Adonijah Truthsters had been relatively short-lived. Tilda would have hated to have been involved in a siege like this one. Negotiations frequently stalled between Koresh and the 25 FBI negotiators, and eventually the FBI decided that their only option was to conduct another raid, which unfortunately amounted to a blood bath.

On April 19, 1993, the Chamberlain siblings and the rest of the world learnt how the US government had sent Bradley tanks into the Davidians' dwelling and CS gas was also deployed to try and bring the situation to a close. As in the Adonijah Truthsters' siege a fire started, the origins shrouded in mystery. People the world over were gripped to their screens as flames engulfed the ranch in Waco, Texas. For Tilda, the parallels were uncanny. Koresh was killed within a total of Seventy-six people, including, two pregnant women and more than 20 children. Tilda and William found no comfort in learning that twenty-four of the victims were British.

As the months passed more and more details emerged about Koresh and the Davidians. Like Eli Zane, Koresh had believed that the messiah would descend from King David hence his name change to David. Koresh had informed his followers that a battle with the government would lead to the end of the world. His prophecy fell true for him personally and for many Davidians, but obviously not for the end of the world as a whole. Yet again a doomsday cult had failed to deliver or realise its promised prophecy.

And Tilda realised that she was a survivor of such a cult – someone who had lived through the ordeal, seen what their purpose was and come through the other side - in reality a rare specimen. With the Branch Davidians, the

Adonijah Truthsters and whatever other cults were out there, the events of watching the ranch going up in flames seemed to signal something to Tilda and stirred something deep within her soul. Suddenly she understood what her vocation should be. She was in a unique position where she could make a difference. She had the knowledge to raise awareness of cults and try and counter their onslaught and evident destruction to society. Just how she was going to do this she wasn't yet quite sure, but her destiny was absolute.

CHAPTER 30

Not for the first time recently, Detective Inspector Judd Stone walked away from the casino having lost more money than he had won. By quitting while he was *not* ahead ironically meant that Judd managed to convince himself that he wasn't a gambling addict, which was probably true, but nonetheless it was fair to say that the hours and money that he chose to spend at such establishments bordered on being an unhealthy obsession.

Not overly concerned with his lack of success - he had certainly had worse nights - Judd found himself in bed by midnight. Slightly inebriated with alcohol he was able to fall into a deep sleep pretty much as soon as his head hit the pillow, but was awoken just over half an hour later when the phone which was connected to his landline began to ring. Slightly disorientated and not sure if the unwelcoming sound was part of a dream; Judd answered the phone on the fourth ring.

"Hello," he answered somewhat groggily.

"Detective Inspector Stone, I do hope that I haven't woken you?" the slight time delay in the caller's response allowed Judd to realise that the incoming call was from a mobile phone.

"Who is this?" Judd didn't immediately recognise the sinister voice at the end of the line.

"Well now, how best should I answer that one, Detective Inspector? I believe that it would be inappropriate to refer to myself as being a friend of yours, I mean I'm not one to hold grudges myself, but I fear in the primitive way in which you view the world, Detective Inspector Stone, I don't believe that you would allow me the same courtesy. Yes, I am quite sure that you still harbor a grudge against me."

Suddenly Stone was wide awake. "Banks. Is that you, you piece of filth?"

"I think you have just proved my point Detective Inspector, and there was me simply calling you up for a friendly chat. I had hoped we could perhaps bury the hatchet."

"The only place I'd bury a hatchet is in your fucked-up head, Banks."

"I see those anger management classes are coming on a treat, DI Stone."

"What do you want?"

"I just thought you may be interested to know where I am at the moment, or at least who I am with."

"Why would I give a fuck?"

"Oh, I think you would."

"Ok, where and who?"

"Well, I'm in a lovely part of Edgbaston actually. I'll leave the exact location for you to work out; after all I need to leave something for you to test your detective skills on. We both know you need the practice."

"I don't think that I do actually. We got the right psycho last time, and you know it."

Ignoring Judd's remark, Banks continued with his mockery. "I'm currently nestled on a very cosy bed indeed while a very nice young lady is in the next room slipping into something much more comfortable for me; she seems such an accommodating young lady."

Knowing that Banks was within one mile of a vulnerable female was enough to make Judd's nerves jangle, but assuming that Banks was telling the truth, his concerns dramatically increased to know he was in such close range to a potential victim.

"Where in Edgbaston are you then, you freak?"

Judd knew Edgbaston quite well; it was one of those Birmingham districts that possessed diverse and contrasting pockets of communities. A large proportion of the district was classed as an inner-city area, housing some of the most poverty-stricken members of society, and Judd had often been involved in tackling both gun and drug crime in the area. The lower-budget end of the prostitution market was prevalent in parts of the region as well, whilst other areas of Edgbaston were extremely affluent with high-end residency being plentiful amongst millionaires, such as surgeons and lawyers living in large-sized Georgian properties nestled within leafy litter-free streets.

Edgbaston was also home to the county cricket ground of Warwickshire, often hosting England international matches. Other notable places included a range of private hospitals, the high-achieving University of Birmingham and the impressive Botanical Gardens which was almost like a magical world hidden beneath the Birmingham skyline.

Edgbaston possessed no factories or warehouses making much of it idyllic. Edgbaston can even claim to enthuse the greatest examples of literature, for instance the towers of Perrett's Folly and the Waterworks were the inspiration for the two towers in JRR Tolkien's Lord of the Rings. Yet sadly in the shadow of all of this richness and cultural splendour remain the drug pushers and an illicit way of life for some of Edgbaston's society.

So when Banks had revealed to Judd that he was in 'a lovely part of Edgbaston' was he being literal or sarcastic?

"So DI Stone, you are interested to know where I am.

Well I'm willing to give you a little clue, seeing as we know each other of old. I'm near Five Ways."

Judd racked his brain. Five Ways didn't exactly narrow things down. Five Ways was the area of Edgbaston so called because of the 5 major roads which broke away from the significantly-sized traffic island. The area was swarming with pubs, clubs, restaurants, cinemas, offices and even a bowling alley. "Are you on the Hagley Road or Broad Street?"

"You are so predictable DI Stone, suggesting locations that are so obvious. Perhaps you should concentrate more on *who* I am with and not *where* I am, although this area does remind me a little of old London town."

Old London Town? He must be referring to the Georgian properties that create the gateway towards Harborne, as they mimic the way many London districts are constructed.

"I am with a very interesting lady indeed. I'm with someone who leads a double life Detective Inspector; imagine that, me with someone who leads a double life." Banks broke into a short burst of self-satisfying and somewhat manic laughter.

"You would know all about double lives wouldn't you, Banks?"

"Moi? You know Detective Inspector you have me all wrong. I was proven innocent remember?"

"No, you were unable to be proven guilty that's all. I'm warning you, you had better not hurt whoever you are with."

"You know, she smiles a lot Detective Inspector, this girl in the next room I'm waiting for. Perhaps when she returns I should ensure that she keeps a permanent smile upon her pretty boat-race. What do you think?"

Judd recalled the chilling image of Cassie Parker with the *Chelsea Smile* that had been inflicted across her once beautiful face.

"You know what, Banks? I think I know where you are and it isn't such a big area. I'm coming to get you now you piece of shit. I'll find you and I'll make you regret making this call."

"You won't find me while you keep thinking of *where* I am DI Stone as opposed to *who* I am with. The location is incidental not significant. You really should be thinking of the location as being perhaps a red *herring*."

Judd knew he may not have much time to save this poor girl and he needed to think fast, but how was he meant to work out who Banks was referring to?

"What's so special about this girl then, Banks?"

"Oh, she's special."

"Come on you lunatic, who is she?"

Banks began to break into song, "You shall have a fishy on a little dishy."

"Why are you singing? Are you where the Birmingham Hard Rock café once stood?"

Banks laughed. "I'm hardly singing hard rock, Stone."

Judd tried to process the clues. *Red herring? Fishy on a little dishy?* "Shit, you are not with who I think you are - are you?"

"It depends if you have worked it out, DI Stone? You could call it an *arresting* development."

"Oh my God, you are."

"Let's just say Mommy wouldn't be very pleased if she knew how her daughter makes most of her money."

"She's the Chief Constable's daughter, Banks. If you harm a hair on her head how on Earth do you think you could get away with it?"

"Well I've got away with worse before now according to you, Detective Inspector. I have to say that Agatha Haddock's daughter's flat is very nice you know, it wouldn't come cheap, but then again she does seem to work all hours."

Flat, thought Judd instinctively. That did narrow it down. Banks had made a rare mistake in letting information slip as flats in the Georgian area of Edgbaston were very few.

"If you touch her Banks, I can promise you, you will not get away with it."

"I find it so ironic, Detective Inspector. Agatha Haddock's daughter being a lady of the night. Who'd have thought it? You see she leads a double life. Oh, the shame on her strait-laced mother if it ever got out. Perhaps I should teach her a lesson; you know bring it to her attention where she is going wrong in life. What do you think? Just think of the scandal for her poor mother. I can see the headlines now in tomorrow's newspaper 'CHIEF CONSTABLE'S DAUGHTER WORKS AS A HIGH-CLASS HOOKER'. I reckon I'd be doing the Chief Constable a favour if I were to show her daughter the error of her ways."

"Leave her alone, Banks."

"Let me think, will I leave her alone? Will I teach her lesson? I mean Detective Inspector, whatever I choose to do who will believe you anyway? I've been cleared in a court of law once of being a murderer, haven't I?"

"Don't you touch her Banks, I mean it." The desperation in Judd's voice was amusing the taunting serial killer.

"Oh, I think she's coming back from the bathroom. Nice speaking with you Detective Inspector, we should do it again some time. Ciao."

The phone line went dead.

Judd had heard Haddock mention her daughter Tabitha on a number of occasions. She lived local to the area as she worked for a local high-end and prestigious Health and Spa Club in Birmingham city centre. It seems, however, that she actually has two jobs!

Realising she was in imminent danger, Judd knew he had to somehow locate the address of Tabitha Haddock. He phoned the Health and Spa club, fully explained who he was and explained to the poor girl working on reception called Roxy that this was a serious matter and Tabitha's life was in danger. The shocked receptionist willingly gave

Judd, Tabitha's address and understood Judd's instruction not to tell anyone as it could jeopardise the operation. Fortunately he had no need to inform the receptionist of her colleague's additional occupation.

For some reason, Judd felt it necessary not to bring Tabitha's lack of safety to the attention of his own colleagues, despite how dangerous that decision could prove to be. Why was this? Was it because he didn't want the Chief Constable to discover how her daughter contributed to earning her wages? Was it because he agreed with Banks and feared that no-one would believe him anyway that the serial-killer was about to kill again? Or did he think it a waste of valuable minutes to stop and phone into the station?

Regardless of his reasons, which Judd didn't exactly have time to analyse, he was intent in rescuing that girl single-handedly, not least because he knew that to react in the moment would most likely be the best use of time.

Unsuspectingly he had also clearly taken Banks' bait.

Judd's flat was in Sutton Coldfield If he drove as fast as he could along the A38M Expressway, he estimated that he could make it to Edgbaston within 15 minutes. Still enough time he realised for Banks to kill the girl.

As the engine kicked into life, the opening scream of John Lennon's 'What You Got' cried out as the car's music player also came alive. Judd had left the CD *Walls and Bridges* in position. Although the scream was spookily appropriate for how Judd was feeling, Judd chose to kill the car stereo not wishing to have any distractions - not even from the voice of his musical idol.

Fortunately traffic was fairly light, and Judd soon reached Five Ways Island at the top of Broad Street passing the cluster of bars, eateries, night clubs and cinema. Luckily the UK premiere of animation film The Lorax, complete with red carpet treatment for its main star Danny DeVito had not been tonight, for the swarms of adoring crowds would surely have heavily compromised

Judd's quest. Moments later, courtesy of Roxy, Judd was screeching his car to a halt at Tabitha's property, a huge and once single Georgian residence now converted into four luxurious apartments.

Judd didn't bother to shut his car door behind him and ran at the communal entrance door which fortunately wasn't as secure as it might have been. Judd proceeded to kick it through which took a total of three attempts. The next door he kicked in was flat 1, taking only a single kick to dislodge the lock, Tabitha's flat being conveniently positioned on the ground floor and to his immediate left.

Judd quickly found his way to the bedroom where to his relief he was greeted by a very startled girl who was very much alive. In spite of the serious consequences of the situation, the fact Tabitha was wearing a skimpy black negligee was not lost on Judd, who quickly acknowledged that she must have taken her father's looks for she bore no resemblance to her repulsive looking mother.

"Please, don't hurt me. I have money."

"Where is he? Where's Banks?"

Looking confused but still afraid, Tabitha answered the question. "There was a young man here, he seemed very nice. Nice but a bit weird really."

"Oh, he's weird alright."

Tabitha began to relax slightly. "So you don't want to rob me, you want the man who was here? I'm afraid he has gone. I returned from the bathroom and that was it, he had left! Perhaps he was a bit nervous." Content that Judd was not a robber and noticing his attractiveness albeit in a slightly dishevelled way, Tabitha concluded that perhaps the night could still be salvaged. "You seem awful tense mister, perhaps I can help you out a little, you know, come to some arrangement."

As tempting a sight Tabitha was, Judd pulled out his badge remembering whose daughter he was with. "I'm Detective Inspector Judd Stone; I'm not here for anything like that. I thought that man was going to kill you. You've had a very lucky escape Tabitha."

Discovering that Judd was a member of the police should have made Tabitha feel safer, but instead a new panic shot into her mind. "Oh shit, you are not going to arrest me are you?"

Judd simply offered what he hoped was a reassuring smile.

Tabitha paused trying to take in the whole situation, and when she succeeded to some degree she continued to speak. "Wait, he was going to kill me? OMG. That is really scary. But if you arrest me my mom will kill me, let alone that guy."

"It's okay Tabitha, you are safe now and I'm not interested in arresting you. No crime has been committed here by you tonight. It really is okay now." Judd took the young girl in his arms as she began to weep with the realisation of it all. Judd fully resisted any testosterone-fuelled urges that may have been bubbling beneath his surface, and simply wanted to comfort Tabitha in her moment of realisation and shock.

Just then the dim light of the room was contrasted by a series of flashes originating from behind where the couple were embracing one another. Judd turned, momentarily releasing the girl whose scantily-clad attributes were once again on show.

"Who the hell are you guys?" Judd could see two men with cameras before him and another three individuals fighting to get through the doorway. He soon answered his own question in his mind. These were the press.

The first victor to make it through the doorway began to speak. "DI Stone, we had a tip off that you were here with the daughter of a very distinguished member of society, in shall we say a less than legal situation. Would you like to comment?"

"Yes, print any of this I'll kick you so hard in the balls you'll be choking on them."

"Thanks for the quote, Detective Inspector Stone."

CHAPTER 31

"Judd, are you ok?"

Judd swayed as he stood in his lounge, bottle of Bourbon Whiskey in one hand and the phone receiver in the other.

"I'm cool thanks, mate. Now I've been suspended I have all the time in the world to drink until my heart's content."

In-between the slurred words of his friend, William could make out the melody of 'I Am The Walrus' in the background of Judd's flat. "Drinking's not the answer, Judd."

"It helps me," slurred Judd, his words slightly inaudible. "It helps to blot away the memories and the fact that I'm a useless piece of shit that couldn't organise a piss up in a brewery... Ha, ha piss up in a brewery, no pun intended."

William was concerned for his friend who had taken his suspension very hard. Once he had been linked to "entertaining" Chief Constable Haddock's daughter in addition to failing an alcohol breathalyser test, it had been a step too far for Judd's superiors. Judd's accounts of events hadn't been listened to; instead there would be time to explain his side of things through the internal enquiry process.

William realised that he needed to give Judd a purpose to keep him on the straight and narrow.

"I need you sober, Judd."

"Why?"

"Because whether you are suspended or not, one day we are going to expose Banks for what he really is. So whatever I need you to do you do it. No-one needs to know do they?"

"I guess not."

"So get cleaned up, we've got work to do."

Although in reality, William didn't quite yet know what he needed Judd to do.

CHAPTER 32

When Charles Milles Manson was released from Terminal Island Penitentiary on 21st March 1967 after an unremarkable 'career' of pimping and petty crime, he already had two sons from the same amount of failed marriages. Then, once he had established his hippie commune known as *The Family*, who eventually became mass murderers, one of his disciples had also given birth to another of his sons on 1st April 1968.

The identical twin boys of Nancy Arcadia had been born little under three months earlier on 15th January 1968.

In April 1967, Nancy of San Francisco had been an impressionable 19 year old, totally lost in the liberating world of 'flower power' and not for a second considering what she should aim for in life as a career. Nancy did however manage to earn enough money to survive from day to day, including being able to maintain her stock of influential music records, by working part time at the local grocery store.

One balmy, spring Saturday night, Nancy Arcadia went to a party being thrown at the house of a girlfriend whose parents were on vacation, and a mysterious but captivating looking fellow had also managed to attend the party. During this time of free love and relaxed attitudes to life by the younger generations, it was not uncommon for folk to hook up with like-minded people they had never met before. Nancy had been to plenty of social gatherings where she had engaged in conversations with complete strangers who were simply indulging in a common outlook whilst sharing a joint or two of marijuana.

However, Nancy wasn't actually that successful in exercising the activity of free love. Although she was not a virgin, her sexual exploits were minimal and she was often perceived as the proverbial 'wallflower' who sat on the side smoking marijuana and getting lost in the music of the day like The Beach Boys, The Beatles and a relatively new band called The Doors, the latter's music seemingly intricately linked with the effects of drug-fuelled hallucinations. As she tripped alone, attentively listening to the lyrics, other members of the party would do so whilst shedding their clothes and indulging in free lovemaking.

At this particular party, the music for the most part was being supplied by the charismatic little man who sang songs of love whilst strumming away at his acoustic guitar. When he finally stopped playing to his captivated and enchanted audience, out of all the females in the room it was Nancy whom he approached. He was without doubt very charming, which unfortunately enabled him to be very manipulative if he so desired, especially to a sweet and relatively naïve girl who was usually unlucky in love such as Nancy Arcadia.

As he spoke, Nancy hung onto his every word. She looked into his eyes and for a moment she thought she observed a distinct element of madness - or could it just have been the marijuana he had been smoking giving that glazed-over impression? Mad or not, his eyes still had a certain magnetic quality and they hypnotically drew Nancy in who found herself to be simply helpless.

He told her his name was Charlie and commented on

her beautiful long-flowing red hair. Before long they went upstairs and had sex. When he was ready to go again, at Charlie's insistence, others joined the lovemaking session. Charlie even began to orchestrate the movements and watched on eagerly as at least three, or was it four different men took their turn with Nancy, who was so caught up in the moment high on marijuana; she uncharacteristically became a willing participant.

Nancy never saw Charlie again after that night. Not in the flesh anyhow. It was not until the dreadful murders in Hollywood occurred two years later, including that of movie star Sharon Tate, that she saw Charlie on television accused of conspiring, or some were suggesting actually ordering, the murders that had shocked the wealthy community of Los Angeles and beyond.

When she witnessed the horror revelation on her TV screen, Nancy was confused. She thought Charlie had been like her, someone who dug love and peace. Wasn't that what their one night of passion had all been about?

She had never tried to track Charlie down after the birth of the twins, she didn't know how to. She didn't know where he was and convinced that he was destined to become a famous musician she thought she would either one day be able to locate his whereabouts, or stick with the decision not to tell him about his twin sons so not to hold back his career.

It was true that Nancy could not be completely sure that the twins were Charlie's. After all she had sex with a string of men that night, but she had always believed, or until this moment hoped, that they were the product of the charismatic musician whom she had briefly acquainted. When Nancy learned of the gruesome murders she was relieved that she had never revealed the possible identity of the father of her twins to anybody at all, not even to her parents and especially not to Charles Manson.

Sadly as the years progressed, Nancy became only too aware of the likely gene pool that her two sons had inherited. It seemed that the boys both had their father's eyes, their stare projecting an air of madness and detachment from the real world. There was a vacancy in those eyes that sent shivers down people's spines, yet they were dark, mystical and enticing, offering an excitement and attractiveness that could not be measured. The boys had seemed to inherit Manson's dark hair too avoiding the colouring of their mother's red hair, though in certain light a slight red tinge could be observed through their hair, which they would forever choose to wear long.

Eventually, Nancy did break her vow of silence on who the possible father of her twins were– to them. It was a mistake.

The twins, Harry (christened Harrison) and Jim-Ray (a hyphened name christened after Morrison and Manzarek of The Doors) had always given their mother a difficult time. They were unruly at school; they damaged neighbours' property and progressed to joy-riding stolen cars. Nancy had always tried to defend her sons, forever using the excuse that the boys behaved the way they did due to the absence of a father, although deep-down once she knew who Manson really was, she realised that the absence of their probable father could only be a good thing for them. The fact that she was a single mother in seventies California attracted little empathy from her judgmental community.

One day the twins badly overstepped the mark by sexually assaulting a local girl in broad daylight.

"It was just a bit of fun, Mom," protested Jim-Ray, totally oblivious to the seriousness of his and his brother's actions. "I just stuck my hand up her skirt while Harry squeezed her titties, it was no big deal."

"It was a big deal for that poor girl. You can't go around taking what isn't yours and that includes touching a girl without her consent. You are very lucky that she is not pressing charges. Her very angry daddy has been to see me and I have promised him that I will punish you both, I have told him that you didn't realise the seriousness of the situation and that you will both go and apologise to her. The fact that you are both still juveniles has just about saved your skin."

"Punish us, Mother? How will you do that then?" jeered Jim-Ray.

"I haven't decided yet."

"That's because you can't punish us. You don't possess the capability. You can't control us you pathetic woman. You are just a joke."

"Don't speak to me like that Jim-Ray, I am your mother. Show me some respect."

"Ha, respect you. Don't make me laugh. You are known as the neighbourhood whore Mom, did you know that? Me and Harry are the only kids around these parts without a daddy."

"Well if you think I am not up to punishing you, perhaps I should have let Emily-Lou's daddy teach you both a lesson after all. It took all my effort and persuasion to stop him bashing your heads together, and do you know what? You would have both deserved it."

"Bring it on, we'll gladly enjoy taking the sanctimonious piece of shit apart limb by limb, and then Jim-Ray and me can properly see to his daughter right in front of his eyes as he lies there fighting for his life."

"Ha, ha. Good one Bro," cackled Jim-Ray appreciative of his brother's support.

"You disgust me. Both of you do. You are your father's boys all right." And that error of judgment expressed by Nancy, who had been pushed to the limit by her wicked sons became the defining moment. There and then Nancy went ahead and told them exactly who their father was. She didn't need any DNA test; this latest incident coupled with the demonic look in their eyes convinced her they had to be Manson's offspring. For 14 years she had protected them from the truth. They had nagged and nagged her over the years to tell them who their father was, but she had somehow always managed to avoid it. But something snapped in her on this occasion. They were her sons and yes she loved them, but increasingly there was a part of her who was becoming to realise that her two sons could not escape the accident of their likely fatherhood and she desperately worried for their future. And the future of others.

After telling her twin sons that Charles Milles Manson was their father, even though in truth she didn't really know for sure, she went ahead and dropped another bombshell that proved to be a catastrophic error of judgment on her part.

"You know what you two? I'm going to call the cops myself." They were the last words Nancy Arcadia ever spoke.

Jim-Ray and Harrison Arcadia spent 10 years in a secure unit for the murder of their mother. Being juveniles, and with the powers-that-be determining that the murder had not been pre-meditated, this pitiful sentence was all that they were required to serve. Once released they tried to follow in their 'father's' footsteps and set out to attract a following like Charles had done with his Family, but they failed miserably. Jim-Ray and Harry unquestionably had the essence of evil within them, but they lacked the charisma and powers of manipulation that Charles Manson once enjoyed.

They eventually left California and made their way to England, feeling they needed a new place to begin a new life in an English speaking country. They felt that California had let both of them down and had also let down the person who they believed to be their father. It was part of their narcissistic make-up to believe that California owed then something, when the reality of course was that California owed them nothing.

Although kept apart, the identical twins had instinctively spent all of their imprisoned life doing the same things, reading and studying the Bible and educating themselves about Charles Manson and his Family through associated literature. They, like members of the original Manson Family, believed that Charles Manson had literally been Jesus Christ 2000 years ago, so in turn they believed themselves to simply be the sons of Jesus Christ, and most importantly therefore belonged to the bloodline of Jesus Christ, which naturally should bring them inherent privileges and respect in life. The fact that Manson had fathered a child named Valentine Michael, to Family member Mary Brunner, was irrelevant to the psychotic twins - as was the two Charles Manson juniors born before Valentine.

Even though Harrison and Jim-Ray were detained separately, their connection as identical twins enabled them to choose the same paths behind bars unbeknown to one another until they were reunited once more on the outside. They believed whole-heartedly what their mother had told them regarding the origins of their father, and seeing the revelation as something to embrace, they interpreted all of Manson's warped beliefs in the same way that he had done.

Now existing in the civilian world once again, both boys had nowhere to belong, and after failing to convince the world that they were the bloodline of Jesus Christ due to a distinct lack of manipulative skills, their aspirations to form their own cult could never transpire. Therefore, until they could convince the world of their identity and importance, they felt that joining the Adonijah Truthsters, a cult they had stumbled upon, was the most obvious temporary solution.

The twins' time in England had been a life of petty crime and living in and out of hostels. By now, the Adonijah Truthsters had welcomed some unknown survivors of the Waco siege into their fold, increasing the cult membership as an addition to the little known Adonijah Truthster survivors of Alabama. Because Eli

Zane and Jaden Rivers had survived, the cult members believed that they must be the real deal, i.e. the true leaders to follow as chosen by God. After all, Zane and Rivers were the only leaders ever to survive a doomsday prophecy siege.

However, in Harry and Jim-Ray's minds they believed that Eli Zane was not the actual new messiah, but instead he was a catalyst, a temporary vessel sent by God to continue their daddy's work whilst he was unable to do so from his constant prison cell. They believed that on some rightful day, which was not yet evident (the twins believed that some sort of self-explanatory sign would appear when the time was right), Eli Zane would hand over the reins to them as the blood line of Charles Manson, and therefore also of Jesus Christ, to lead the followers into the Promised Land.

The twins believed Eli Zane had been sent by God to act as a channel for Charles Manson's desired actions, incidentally something they had yet to share with Eli. Eli of course would have dismissed this claim – in his mind his work was instructed by God and it had nothing to do with Charles Manson. Eli was the new messiah and no one else could possibly claim that honour, with able assistance in the form of Jaden as his true equivalent of St Peter. In contrast, the twins didn't recognise Jaden as anything special.

For now, the wayward twins simply needed to belong to something with a sense of purpose, even if that purpose was warped. From the studies they engaged in surrounding their father, they knew that Manson had once stated that his employment was that of an Evangelist on a credit card application. This cemented their belief that they were safe to belong to this cult as the Adonijah Truthsters too were Evangelists, preaching the Gospel (as they interpreted it anyhow), until such time the twins' turn to hold the reins was both presented and accepted.

On this particular day, Harry and Jim-Ray had ventured out from the Adonijah Truthsters camp and were in the city of Liverpool, England.

The two of them had decided to kill a bit of time soaking in the character of the docks before activating their true motive for being in the city. The fact that they were able to do this, and incorporate their deadly intentions as part of a day out, highlighted their psychopathic tendencies.

As they rested on the black metal railings overlooking the River Mersey, Jim-Ray turned to Harry. "I was led to believe that it always rained in Liverpool, but today is a splendid sunny day. Look how the rays glisten off the water, Harry."

"The sun always shines on the righteous my dear brother; it is a sign that God is in appreciation of why we have arrived in Liverpool today."

"Amen, to that brother." Harry and Jim-Ray gave each other a high-five.

Harry turned away from the murky water to face the famous Liver Building. Favourably studying the Liver birds that perched above the structure he made a matter-of-fact announcement. "And I feel that now is the time to carry out our important work."

"Yes, I feel it is time too, Harry. Those who threaten the true course of the revolution must be removed from the path and cast aside."

"Amen, to that Jim-Ray. This woman we have come to seek out was little more than a conspirator, planted in the camp by Satan himself no doubt, in an attempt to prevent Eli from doing Daddy's work until the time is right when we are truly recognised as the prophets to lead the chosen ones into the Promised Land."

"Indeed, brother. Does she not realise even now that because Eli survived Satan's wrath it is clear that he is the vessel chosen to represent the new messiah on this Earth?"

"Absolutely, and Daddy was party to the whole cause. Whilst trapped in his prison cell he asked God for a catalyst to carry on his work and God chose Eli as a channel and as a custodian of the correct path for the chosen few when the end of days begins. And then we as his bloodline will claim our rightful place and be recognised as the ultimate chosen representative of God.

"We will of course thank Eli, and even Jaden for the good work they have done in caretaking Daddy's vision, but have no fear brother, we will be recognised when the time is right. And God will choose the time, he knows when to intervene and he knows when to begin the end of days. He is simply waiting for the perfect moment to gain maximum impact. The world has to be ready to understand that Jesus Christ has a bloodline through us.

"And remember Daddy was saved from the death penalty. The Lord orchestrated this so that California would abolish the death penalty just as Daddy was facing trial. This can be no coincidence. When Daddy needed assistance, God intervened. God can intervene whenever he needs to assist his master plan, and for now he has chosen that you and I brother take the form of Appollyon the exterminating angel from Revelation: Chapter 9. Sometimes extermination has to happen in order to win a war that is justified."

"Amen, to that brother. Daddy also recognised himself as being Appollyon when he ordered the killings in the hills of Hollywood. Let us waste time no more, follow me to the car as we go on our mission, a mission chosen by God to exterminate Tilda Blake."

Along the suburban roads of Liverpool, Harry sat behind the wheel of the car that had been stolen a few days earlier. The twins nodded away manically to the music coming from the Beatles CD commonly referred to as the 'White Album'.

"Just listen to the lyrics to this song 'Helter Skelter',

Harry. It is as relevant today as it was in Daddy's time. The world is still aching for a social uprising and a revolution, and we can be the individuals to make that happen by rising from that bottomless pit as stated in Revelation 9: Verse 11. We have the key to unlock it all, Brother."

"Yeah, I know what you mean. Daddy being in jail is in the bottomless pit, and you and I are at the bottomless pit of society, with no-one yet prepared to believe who we really are and why we exist. And now we find ourselves in Liverpool, home of The Beatles: the locusts, the four angels of Revelation 9, with their hair of women and their breast-plate guitars. We could not be in a better place to avenge what Tilda did to Eli or to continue Daddy's message. And she lives not far from Menlove Avenue where John Lennon lived as a child and a young man. It all fits together so neatly."

"It is God's way."

"Amen, to that. God guided Tilda Blake to Liverpool, the home of the locusts who sent Daddy messages through their songs, as the most significant place for her to meet her end. Her execution which will take place in such a significant location will be the beginning of the world having to take notice of Harrison and Jim-Ray Manson."

Soon the twisted and disillusioned twin brothers, who had now abandoned their mother's surname of Arcadia, in favour of the convicted felon whom they believed to be their father, were parking up at the middle-class suburban home of Luther and Tilda Blake.

Tilda had met Luther Blake at the University of Liverpool. Since her ordeal at the hands of the Adonijah Truthsters, Tilda had needed to surround herself with the hustle and bustle of city life in contrast to the rural locations where the cult had set up home. If she ever found herself to be alone in quiet surroundings, Tilda would always feel a great sense of vulnerability. Her home town of Birmingham was busy enough, as was London and many other English cities of course, but as part of coming to terms with her ordeal at the hands of the cult she had studied a range of Theology and Religious Studies, achieving qualifications within somewhat of a specialised field. Subsequently she had been offered an attractive post at the University of Liverpool as a Specialised Lecturer. So Liverpool, full of culture and vibrancy became her adopted home.

As a form of personal therapy aligned to a genuine willingness to help others, Tilda needed to try and make some sense as to what made religious cults tick. Furthermore she felt it was her duty to use her own experiences to educate vulnerable people and prevent them from entering anything that remotely resembled a cult. She was the active founder of a charity which supported families and victims of cult experiences. Her university lectures included significant elements about cults in addition to simple multi-faith awareness. Her efforts also gave Tilda a sense that her awful experiences had not simply been in vain as she became the vehicle to help others. Her valuable work also off-set her reluctance to testify against the cult leaders, if they were still alive that was, or could ever be found.

Tilda had established countless facts and consistent patterns about religious cults, many that ran parallel to one another, such as the manipulative leader of the sects usually being someone claiming to be the new messiah. No better examples perhaps than Charles Manson, David Koresh and Eli Zane.

Tilda would speak in her lectures about how many self-proclaimed messiahs would promote intercourse with their female followers, establishing the belief that their seed could cleanse the females of sin, a familiar pattern that she had personally been a victim of.

When Tilda had finally escaped the Adonijah Truthsters she discovered that a medical condition prevented her from ever having children, a painful realisation in one sense, but a blessing in the other that she had never been able to fall pregnant to Eli Zane and bear his child.

During her lectures, Tilda would educate her students regarding other 'messiahs' who practiced the 'cleansing solution', including Jeffery Lundgren and Sun Myung Moon. Moon told his Moonies that because Eve had fornicated with the Devil in the Garden of Eden, all children, and therefore all generations thereafter, must be a product of sin. As Moon convinced his followers that he was the new Messiah, he was able to 'cleanse' them with his seed.

Jim Jones was another example of a manipulative cult leader who claimed to be the Messiah. Jones ensured that his financial position was more than secure by persuading his followers to hand over to him their life savings and ready cash. Eli Zane also adopted much of this approach when he could, in order to secure finances. Jones created Jonestown in the country of Guyana, with the explanation that his followers, who were known as the Peoples Temple, could go about their business without fear of ridicule. The fact that this isolated the Peoples Temple from 'normal' society and even trapped most of them from taking an alternative path was immaterial it seemed. And when the media 'intruded' into Jonestown it was discovered that many people did indeed wish to leave as they no longer believed in Jones and his warped vision. At this revelation Jones ordered a shooting to take place at the air strip, killing 5 people, then following this atrocity 900 of his followers went on to commit suicide, many with cyanide. Jones himself took a quicker way out with a gun shot to his head.

And of course in addition to all of these notorious cult leaders and their misguided followers, Charles Manson and his Family were a regular and fascinating hot topic in Tilda's lectures. Students were fascinated at how Manson could possibly interpret the lyrics of The Beatles as an inclination to eradicate others, with his belief that his actions were propheted through the book of Revelation.

Certain patterns in all of these cults were constant. And all these 'wannabe' Messiahs were narcissistic and pathological liars. Astonishingly they always seemed to conveniently forget a key fundamental commandment: Thou shalt not kill.

So helping and informing others was how Tilda had chosen to channel all the emotions that had affected her since her time in The Adonijah Truthsters. When she had watched the flames engulf the Davidians' Mount Carmel Center at Waco, Texas on her big brother's TV screen in 1993, she made a commitment that she would have to turn her experience into something positive.

As Head of the Theology Department at the University of Liverpool, Luther Blake had interviewed Tilda for her post and instantly took a liking to the warm, yet shy Tilda Chamberlain. A highly perceptive man, he was intrigued by the younger woman and could sense that there was something hidden deep within her soul that troubled her. Luther, who was ten years Tilda's senior, was a gentle and patient man with smooth cocoa- coloured skin, grey flecked hair and strong personal values. He was the perfect lifelong partner that Tilda needed after her unsettling time with the cult. A qualified therapist as well as a professor in Theology and Religious Studies, Luther could be Tilda's confidante and tower of strength with an immeasurable sense of understanding. Once they had got together, Luther would willingly spend hours cradling and reassuring Tilda during the tearful nights when she woke in a cold sweat or whenever she experienced an anxiety attack. Luther was a man that Tilda could trust with her life, which was exactly the type of man she needed following the dramatic abuse she encountered following her initial trust in the Adonijah Truthsters.

Luther Blake answered the front door a few seconds after hearing the door bell ring to be greeted by identical looking men wearing pin-striped suits and pony-tailed dark hair. He didn't immediately open the porch door as he peered cautiously at the two strangers through the plain glass. Forever in an astute frame of mind, something informed Luther that these two men didn't normally wear such formal and smart clothing. Something in the way the suits hung from them didn't strike him as the type of attire that they felt natural in, and he couldn't help but be wary of these two individuals.

"Can I help you?" spoke Luther through the glass, as politely as ever.

The twins were a little put out that Luther had answered the door, with their impulsive naivety they had expected to find Tilda, which would have enabled them to carry out their wicked deed as quickly as possible.

"Mr. Blake, I believe it is us who can help you actually. Or to be more precise I think we can help your wife. Is she home at all?"

"What do you want with my wife? And may I ask who you are?" Luther's deliverance was still polite but a little sterner in tone.

Harry flashed up a fake ID through the glass which was too quick for Luther to fully digest, but nevertheless it just about seemed genuine enough.

"It's a little difficult sir, but my brother and I work for the Football Pools Company and we have some terrific news for your wife. We have a duty to abide by customer confidentiality but I'm sure that you can perhaps work it out why we are here?"

"Are you telling me my wife has won the pools?"

"Err, you place me in an embarrassing situation Mr Blake, but like I say I'm sure that you can work it out for yourself as to why we are here?"

"The Football Pools Company is based here in Liverpool, yet you have Californian accents."

"How very observant of you, Mr. Blake," spoke Harry. "My brother and I are huge Beatles fans so we made a pact that one day we would come and live in Liverpool. We have some experience in the movie business back in Hollywood, so fortunately the pools company employed us as ideal ambassadors for their cause."

"Yeah, they think we provide an element of show business for when we break the good news to the winners," offered Jim-Ray.

"To be honest with you Mr. Blake, It embarrasses us really. I mean my brother and I only appeared in a handful of unsuccessful movies, but it was enough to get us the job. Actually Mr. Blake, speaking of movie stars, you yourself possess more than a passing resemblance to a certain Morgan Freeman, I'm sure it has been said to you before."

Luther found himself smiling. Still not entirely sure if he was doing the right thing, Luther decided to open the porch door. "Perhaps you should step inside. I could make you a pot of tea while you wait for Tilda, she shouldn't be too long. She has only popped into the city centre for a spot of shopping. She particularly likes to go down by the docks."

Jim-Ray and Harry entered the house and closed the door behind them as quickly as they could. "It is lovely down by the docks. My brother and I have just been down there ourselves as a matter of fact, before coming here."

"Your first time, huh?"

"Yes, sir," answered Jim-Ray.

"How long have you worked for the pools company?"

"Four years or more," answered Harry.

"Yet today was your first time visiting the Liverpool docks?"

The twins looked at one another, sensing they had been rumbled by the old man.

"Will you leave my house, please?" said Luther. "Come to think of it I'm not sure that Tilda even does the Pools. It's the Lottery that she does."

Jim-Ray began to speak with a sudden amount of venom. "You're a typical fat cat of society aren't you, Mr

Blake? Looking down your nose at those less established as you in society, yet as soon as you thought there was some cash coming your way you were willing to let us into your house. Well more fool you. Get that kettle on while we wait for Tilda, she is the one we have come to see after all."

With the three men still standing in the Blake's hallway, Luther reached down to the hall phone and picked up the receiver. "I'm calling the police."

"I don't think so Mr. Blake," spat Harry as he struck Luther hard across the face with the back of his hand.

Luther looked stunned. "Who are you people?"

But the twins didn't answer; instead Jim-Ray pulled a knife from the inside pocket of his jacket and thrust it into Luther's stomach before the older man had time to try and prevent the attack. However, still holding the receiver of the phone in his hand, Luther cracked it across Jim-Ray's head causing an instant cut and swelling, but then Harry revealed a blade and was too quick for Luther as he shoved it into the professor's neck. The 5ft 2 inch twins then continued with an appalling frenzy as they stabbed the poor man over and over again. At least Luther had lost consciousness at the fourth stab wound and was oblivious to the twenty or so others that followed.

The twisted twins finally stopped the slaughter and they looked at one another with their demonic eyes, clearly satisfied with the horrific assault that they had inflicted on Luther Blake. Their pin-stripe suits and white shirts were drenched in Luther Blake's blood. Jim-Ray callously stuck his finger in one of the many open wounds and began to write words on the flock wallpaper of the hallway, just above Luther's lifeless body.

After scrawling the words he wanted to, Jim-Ray spoke excitedly. "I think this is the sign we have been waiting for Harry. We were inadvertently presented with a black man today and we were meant to kill him. If we kill Tilda as well we will have killed a mixed-married couple, this will undoubtedly start a race war as Daddy has always predicted. The blacks will blame the whites and the whites will blame the blacks. A third of mankind will be wiped out just as Daddy said. Dear brother we don't hold the key we *are* the key. Daddy is still the king in his bottomless pit and we are his key to finally unlock his vision."

Harry nodded in complete acknowledgement. Twisted minds think alike.

"Let us find the kitchen and the kettle Jim-Ray. I think we have earned that cup of fine English Tea."

Not long after, Jim-Ray and Harry, who were sitting in the living room on a now ruined, blood-soaked sofa drinking a cup of tea, heard the porch door open, followed by the sound of a key turning in the front door. When they heard the loud scream it confirmed to them that Tilda Blake had entered the house and discovered the body of her dead husband.

Shocked and stunned, Tilda placed her hand to her mouth, hardly able to digest what had happened to her husband. "This can't be real," she whispered.

Then she glanced above Luther's head to see that two words had been scribed on the wall in her husband's blood. They ambiguously read 'PIGS' and 'RISE'. Due to her knowledge of cults, Tilda instantly realised that these words were the same references as those made in the Family killings of the 1960s, and in spite of her shock she began to try and reason why her husband had been slain in this manner.

Luther was a black man, so were the killers trying to start a race war just like Manson had tried to instigate all those years ago? Albeit Manson's actions had been to order the killing of affluent white people in the belief that this would cause the blacks to rise up against the white people. Therefore was this act on Luther a kind of warped reverse psychology?

Was it a copycat killing of some kind?

Was it revenge by someone with intent to hurt her as they didn't approve of the awareness that she raised about religious cults?

As she wrestled for some kind of logic to her husband's killing, two identical looking men appeared in the hallway standing at 5ft 2 inches tall with demonic eyes. Tilda couldn't believe it. It was as if two Charles Mansons were standing right in front of her.

"Hello Tilda. Eli sends his love."

Tilda turned on her heels, ran out of the house and up the drive to her car. She had been unable to park on her drive as the twins' stolen car had been blocking her driveway, an intervention by the evil twins that ironically could yet prove to save Tilda's life. Fortunately she had parked in front of the twins' car and therefore had a head start on them. She turned the key in the ignition, fired the engine and sped away from the awful scene. The twins entered their car like a couple of manic cackling hyenas and were soon not too far behind the terrified Tilda Blake.

As she sped out of her street and along the subsequent road network, Tilda was soon driving along Menlove Avenue. On the opposite side of the dual carriageway she could see that the National Trust owned minibus had pulled up outside Mendips, the childhood home of John Lennon, to allow pilgrims of the Beatles to enter the house.

Tears streamed down Tilda's face, and she had to physically wipe them from her eyes in order to clear her vision as she sped down Menlove Avenue, with the evil twins in hot pursuit.

The twins were once again playing 'Helter Skelter' from the Beatles' white album in the car, as they chased their proposed victim with an insane focus.

"Come on Harry, you need to catch this bitch. It is God's wish. We have to kill her and then we can claim our thrones from Eli and Jaden. When they hear what we have done they will have no choice but to recognise our worth."

"I'm going as fast as I can. But what if Eli and Jaden won't see things as we do?"

"Simple. We will kill them both. Nothing can stand in our way now Brother. It is our time and the followers will know that we have been sent to lead them. Our true position will be realised."

Driving at an extreme pace, Tilda found herself with Calderstones Park at her left, and she prayed that a child would not run out in front of her, knowing that she would not have any chance of stopping in time. She shot over the junction with Yew Tree Road and Beaconsfield Road, narrowly missing a taxi which sounded its horn, but she hoped that her risky manoeuvre may halt the twins' pursuit of her. However, Tilda's heart sank as she gazed in her rear view mirror and she realised that they were still hot on her tail, in fact they were now gaining on her. Not long after, they got so close that they managed to bang into Tilda's rear bumper on a couple of occasions, but fortunately Tilda had managed to maintain control of her vehicle.

The twins were oblivious to the fact that they had not long passed Strawberry Field on Beaconsfield Road, the Salvation Army Orphanage made famous in the Beatles' song, and the two cars continued down the A562 road towards the city centre. Tilda had done this same journey only a couple of hours or so earlier, not knowing that she would be following the same journey in such intense circumstances later in the day.

Soon Tilda found herself approaching another junction, the very busy junction with Queens Drive, and she could see the tree emerging which sat in the middle of the traffic roundabout. Fortunately the traffic was flowing from her lane across the roundabout and she got as close as she could to the car in front. As it happened that car had taken a gamble and had pulled out quite discourteously from the junction, with Tilda appearing even more reckless as the oncoming Vauxhall that pipped its horn miraculously just missed the rear of Tilda's car. However the Vauxhall didn't altogether survive impact.

The twins had intensely continued with their chase and hadn't bothered to check the flow of traffic, and their car hit the rear of the Vauxhall causing it to spin around with the twins being taken completely by surprise.

Then worse was to come - for them.

With the speed of the incident, an on-coming lorry was unable to avoid the twins vehicle and it hit them side on with such a momentum that they careered into the tree that sat in the middle of the roundabout. The twins had neglected to put on their seat belts and had been flung through the windscreen with both landing belly down on the bonnet of the car. Their torsos were pierced with shards of glass and mangled metal. Their faces fell into a position that faced one another and their demonic eyes seemed to create an eerie lifeless stare at his twin.

Tilda could see that the twins were no longer following her and had sensed that they must have crashed, though she didn't dare to stop until she reached Penny Lane and she pulled over at the bus terminus. She killed the engine and burst into tears. After a few minutes she managed to compose herself to reach for her mobile phone and selected 'William' from the list of stored contacts.

After three rings her brother answered. "Sis, how are you?"

"William, something terrible has happened."

William could clearly recognise that his sister was in an acute state of distress and desperately tried to calm her.

"What's wrong, Tilda?"

"They're back. The Adonijah Truthsters, they're back."

By this time a crowd had gathered around the wrecked scene of the twins' car as it lay mangled with the tree.

Due to the car hitting the tree with such impact, coupled with the truck crushing it even further, the Beatles CD had popped out from the player like a piece of toast from a toaster. The radio kicked in and miraculously it was still working. A song by the rock group Kasabian was playing.

Linda Kasabian had been the one member of the family who had testified against Charles Manson. She had been instrumental in ensuring that the cult leader would spend the rest of his life behind bars.

CHAPTER 33

"Eli. Harry and Jim-Ray have been killed in an auto wreck," said Rowena.

Eli Zane didn't even flinch at the news. "Then that must be God's way. I was never convinced that those two were on the same path as us anyway."

"They were looking for Tilda."

"I've been looking for that bitch for over 20 years for what she did to us. If they failed to kill her then I am even more convinced that they were never meant to be on the same path as us. It is by my hand and my hand alone that she must die. It would have made life far easier if the two little freaks had told us exactly where they had been looking for her. What were they playing at hiding that kind of information from me?"

"We may never know."

"And that's a fact."

CHAPTER 34

William was extremely angry at the death of Luther Blake. He had always been fond of his brother-in-law, realising that he had been acutely instrumental in encouraging his sister to believe that her life was worth living again.

Chief Bill Chambers, William's friend across the Atlantic Ocean, had kept him informed about the investigation into the Adonijah Truthsters in the months and years that followed Tilda's dramatic rescue. Frustratingly there was very little unearthing of new information. This led the Birmingham Alabama Police Department to conclude that it was most likely that Eli and Jaden had died in the fire, although they could never be sure. The array of charred teeth and bones that had been recovered from the intense fire had eventually proved not to have belonged to the two twisted individuals. This had always left a nagging doubt in William's mind that the evil pair who had subjected his sister to years of abuse could indeed still be alive.

Now he was convinced that they were.

The stolen car that was now almost beyond recognition following its collision with the tree on Queens Drive, Liverpool, had been traced to a carpet salesman from

Kidderminster. Accompanied by a junior detective, William visited the salesman to inform him that his car could never be returned. Firstly because it was beyond use, and secondly because it had been used in connection with a murder in Liverpool.

The salesman was clearly distressed to learn that his car had been used in a murder, and William was content that he had no knowledge of the attack on Luther Blake, the theft of his car making him simply an unfortunate victim of circumstance.

With the car being stolen in Kidderminster, at least William was pleased of one thing: if Eli and Jaden were behind the murder, then the location of the car theft suggested they were not too far away. Kidderminster is situated approximately 30 km west of Birmingham.

By murdering Luther Blake and subsequently killing themselves in the stolen car, the evil twins had inadvertently provided the best lead in finding Eli and Jaden in years. Unfortunately, it had been an extreme price to pay for Tilda's husband.

Technically, due to the location of Luther Blake's slaying, the murder investigation was being conducted by Merseyside Police. The Senior Investigating Officer, Detective Chief Inspector Michael Froggatt was not convinced that the murder of Luther Blake was a result of some vengeful American religious cult.

Froggatt listened to William's story about the Adonijah Truthsters with some interest and promised William that he would keep an open mind during the investigation, but he was convinced that Blake's murder was more likely connected to a far simpler explanation. He admitted that motive had not yet been established but he would be foolish to rule out a race killing. Furthermore tensions on the streets of Liverpool were becoming apparent as the public themselves were beginning to perceive this same theory.

Froggatt accepted that Luther Blake could have been

targeted because of the work that he and Tilda undertook regarding cults, and he recognised the style of killings being similar to that of Charles Manson's Family with the scrawling of words in blood on the wall, but for the moment Froggatt was interpreting the unprovoked murder to being a copycat killing by two warped nuts, who wished to glorify the Manson killings of California in the 1960s. Froggatt failed to see any connection with the Adonijah Truthsters. He wasn't convinced that Tilda had been the initial target, and for him it seemed more likely that it was indeed Luther Blake whom the killers wanted dead.

The fact that Tilda had not recognised Harry or Jim-Ray from her time in the Adonijah Truthsters, added weight to the theory that she had never been the twins' intended target. And although she recognised that the two men had an uncanny resemblance to a certain Charles Manson, Merseyside Police simply interpreted this as coincidence and not significant to their enquiries.

So officially it was Merseyside Police who was investigating the murder of Luther Blake, and DCI Froggatt promised to keep William informed of 'developments'. In contrast, William Chamberlain was keen to conduct his own unofficial investigation regarding the killing of his sister's husband.

Firmly believing that the Adonijah Truthsters were behind the killing, logic told William that if Eli or Jaden were near Kidderminster, then they would most likely keep within their philosophy of setting up a way of life in a secluded rural location in order to function under the radar. Their most likely settlement of a sheltered and isolated existence would be in either the Severn Valley or perhaps the Clent Hills region. But as these areas incorporated many villages and towns such as Bridgnorth, Bewdley, Highley, Arley and possibly even as far north as Ironbridge and as far south as Malvern, identifying their exact location within these locations would prove to be a challenging prospect.

Doing things unofficially meant that in effect the only resource William could throw at his investigation were his loyal team of Sab Mistry and the suspended Judd Stone – how unofficial could it get! Judd and Sab worked tirelessly and as discreetly as they could to try and come up with something tangible for William. As Judd had time on his hands due to his suspension, this perhaps proved a blessing to enable him to delve into the unofficial investigation. Following conversations with local estate agents across the vast geographical area, a shortlist of rural house buyers was compiled which could prove key to locating the cult leaders. It would be unlikely that Zane and Rivers would use their own names on any telling paperwork.

A cluster of properties that were investigated early on seemed promising at first glance, in particular a small number of dwellings that had been purchased around the Clent Hills area. They seemed an intriguing choice, the site of their erection being linked to the legend of St. Kenelm who was murdered on a hunting trip at the north eastern slopes of Clent Hill in 821 AD. St. Kenelm's Church in the parish of Romsley actually marks the site of his murder and the unofficial team felt that the site could have been chosen as some sort of symbolic significance. But after interviewing the residents of these homes it became clear that they were not linked to anything sinister and the notion of setting up the cult on these premises was just a romantic interlude. Besides, the Clent Hills was so popular with tourists it would prove difficult for the Adonijah Truthsters to remain hidden in such a vicinity. Turning the attention away from estate agents and primarily from the Clent Hills, solicitors were targeted next.

And one line of enquiry revealed one particular property to stand out like a sore thumb.

CHAPTER 35

To their surprise, both Judd and Sab discovered that they liked Gilbert Mutch.

Several solicitors in the Severn Valley area had not been half as co-operative as Gilbert had, stating uncompromisingly that "time was money" even when it came to helping the police with their enquiries. The fact that Judd and Sab were not exactly following official lines of enquiry, and Judd was even suspended from active duty, made the balancing act of teasing out information all the more challenging.

Gilbert Mutch, a Bridgnorth based solicitor with a ginger handlebar moustache and comb over hair that struggled to camouflage his freckled bald head, was in contrast very helpful and seemed almost eager to share his knowledge with the detectives. Gilbert had obviously been in the game for a number of years and his blue pinstripe suit was more than a little tired looking. Judd and Sab assumed that it had once been a perfect fit for the solicitor, the fact it was now so ill-fitting gave the impression that it had grown with him as a loyal companion through the years of his career.

Gilbert Mutch worked very much as a one-man band,

apart from his single employee of Mrs. Powell who typed letters and attempted to keep on-top of the paperwork. As Sab looked about Mutch's office, the décor suggested to her that not much in the way of refurbishment had ever taken place since the days of Gilbert's great-grandfather who had founded the family business. Rows of dated filing cabinets compromised the little available wall space of the office, registering with Sab that it was unlikely that any active file retention policy was being exercised here.

Admittedly Mrs. Powell was beavering away on a computer as opposed to an ancient typewriter, but it was unlikely to be utilising an up-to-date operating system. The loyal secretary who was admirably working way past her expected retirement age, signifying the contentment she had experienced working for this family business over many years, was sitting at a large oak desk that had been built in the days when such items had been designed to last for years.

The office of Mutch Solicitors sat midway within a series of converted terraced cottages that were now used for commercial use including charity shops, a shoe shop and even restaurants for fine Indian and Chinese cuisine respectively, but it was only the solicitors' office that could boast to being there for any significant length of time.

Gilbert ran his podgy fingers through his ginger-coloured flapping fringe with a nervousness that was not usually associated with the conduct of a solicitor. Acutely aware of client confidentiality, Gilbert balanced that notion with a desire to help the desperate looking detectives, and he openly shared with Judd and Sab his recollection of about ten years previously when an eccentric and reclusive lady whom the business represented had died. The lady had never married or had children and he had experienced great difficulty tracing an heir to the lady's large estate which was situated in a secluded setting between Highley and Bewdley in Worcestershire. The dogged solicitor informed Judd and Sab that he eventually tracked down the rightful heir, a woman, in California of all places.

"California! Nice work if you can get it," said Sab.

"You would think so wouldn't you, Detective Sergeant, and I did manage to factor in a few Californian sights, but the work side of the trip wasn't a very pleasant experience in all honesty."

"Why was that Mr. Mutch?" Enquired Judd.

"Not long before her death, I had a few conversations with Miss Baxter, the lady whom I represented, and she was very reluctant to provide me with any details of an heir. She had never married nor had children, so I naturally enquired if there were any other family members whom the estate could be handed too. She was a stubborn old soul at the best of times, and for many of our conversations she declined to provide me with a name until one day she surprisingly relented. I'm afraid Miss Baxter could never have been described as a charitable lady, and for some reason it finally dawned on her that it may be best to at least keep the estate within the family rather than to simply hand it over to the authorities with an element of uncertainty. She spoke of her late brother's daughter who was originally from Bridgnorth herself but had decided to leave for the USA with her mother under somewhat of a cloud. This niece was the only available heir as far as she was concerned. By making further enquiries I discovered that her sister-in-law had died since moving to the States."

"Why did they head to the States?" enquired Judd further.

"She never told me. It was not something that she elaborated on, and I didn't feel it was my place to press Miss Baxter for an explanation, but she did reveal that her brother more or less died of a broken heart once his wife had abandoned him taking the child with her. Miss Baxter reasoned that the niece was perhaps not to blame for the disappearance, being guided by the mother no doubt, so I think on reflection she felt that the estate should go to her brother's daughter.

"Anyway, I tracked the niece to a rural dwelling in sunny California to inform her of the news following the death of her aunt. She was indifferent to her aunt's passing but seemed pleased to inherit the property. She told me how the inheritance must be God's wishes and I had been sent from God to give her this news. I don't go in for that kind of thing myself but if that's what she believed so whole-heartedly I didn't attempt to question her beliefs. Engaging in polite conversation I enquired as to why she came to the USA and her mood changed dramatically. She became quite hostile and was very cagey indeed about her reasons for moving to the States, but she agreed to fly back to England to have a look at the estate she had inherited from her spinster aunt. I returned alone. I didn't particularly want to travel with her so I made my excuses and hooked up with her again at my office before accompanying her to the property."

Just then Mrs. Powell placed a tray displaying a fine Wedgwood tea service onto the solicitor's desk, complete with steaming teapot, sugar bowl, plate of assorted biscuits and jug of milk.

"I for one can express the uncomfortable aura that the lady projected," said the loyal employee. "When she came to the office to meet Mr. Mutch, she gave me a cold stare and she always seemed to display a perpetual mocking smile. Exactly what she was mocking and laughing at all the time is anybody's guess. They say that the eyes are the window to the soul but when I looked into that cold stare I couldn't see anything behind them. She seemed somehow detached emotionally, if you know what I mean?"

"It's true," confirmed Gilbert. "It was as if her soul had been removed from within her."

"In a way Mr. Mutch, she did kind of have her soul taken away from her. I suspect that you are confirming to us that this woman was part of a group of people whom we are very interested in, and brain washing, soul cleansing or whatever the practice is called that they do is unfortunately what they do best." Judd momentarily broke his speech to reach for the sugar bowl. "Please continue with your story, you are being most helpful. And thank you for the tea and biscuits, Mrs. Powell."

"You are welcome, Detective Inspector."

Gilbert Mutch watched in some bewilderment as the Detective Inspector placed four sugar cubes in his tea before stirring it and placing it to his lips.

"It gives him the energy to solve crimes," offered Sab as half an explanation.

Gilbert smiled before continuing. "The woman was most odd. She kept things very close to her chest but there were a few things that intrigued me. Although she was originally from these parts her memory of the area was quite poor, as if it had almost been erased, though I concede she was quite young when her mother took her across the Atlantic.

"Another was her interpretation of the name of our area. 'Severn Valley,' she said to me. 'I like that; it reminds me of Death Valley in California.'

"And when I commented to her that she had inherited such a large estate for one person to live in, she informed me that she would not be living alone. She said that she would be sharing the property with some very interesting people, the kind of people that I would never understand and should never attempt to. I don't quite know why but her words sent shudders through me, it felt like a threat almost. Needless to say she didn't choose to keep me as her solicitor once the paperwork had been finalised, even though I know her aunt would have preferred her to. In spite of that I have always remembered the job ever since, almost above all others, and I can assure you I have served many clients, Detective Inspector."

"Believe me, Gilbert; I think that you had a narrow escape. You are lucky that they didn't want to recruit you."

"Recruit me for what?"

"To join their religious cult."

Gilbert was clearly taken aback. "Religious cult! Blimey, I never guessed but that does make sense come to think of it. I made the mistake a couple of years later to look in on Miss Baxter's niece on the off chance; I just felt a sense of responsibility having represented her aunt for so long. But as I drove up that long drive I began to come over all sweaty and sensed that it was a bad idea. Nevertheless, I knocked on the door and two very scary looking gentlemen answered informing me that the lady was not at home and even if she were she would not want to see me. Even though they were quite small in stature, they unnerved me even more than she ever could; their eyes were almost demonic like, really insane looking. I quickly made my excuses and left as fast as I could, which was the correct decision as one of the men began to chase me but I managed to get in the car and drive away. I dread to think what he would have done if he had caught me. I should have gone to you chaps really, but decided against it."

"Were they perhaps brothers, Mr. Mutch? Twins even?" asked Judd.

"Yes, an evil looking pair of twins at that. They were identical so twice the amount of evil was projected."

"Harry and Jim-Ray," said Sab. Judd nodded in agreement.

"Don't worry Mr. Mutch; they won't be bothering anyone again. Can you tell us anything else?"

"Let me think. Miss Baxter's niece was very badly scarred on her hands and I suspect further up her arms but she wore long sleeves to shield any inflictions. I concluded that she must have experienced some sort of accident that involved fire."

"Where exactly is this property, Mr. Mutch? I think we need to go and make some enquiries there."

"It is in an ideal location for a secluded property; very remotely situated. Your initial approach towards the property is by going along the remote B4555 road. The area is isolated somewhat by a considerable stretch of the river Severn which has deep fast-flowing channels and deceiving currents. The house is surrounded by extensive hills of woodland. Due to the soft sandstone banks of the river, it is difficult to build bridges that can bear heavy loads, another sound feature if you wish to hide yourself away. The only public access across the river is here at Bridgnorth and another one at Bewdley, resulting in the fact that there is no way for road traffic to cross the river for some 16 miles. Most travellers choose the busier A442 as the preferred route along the river instead of the B4555, but the property itself remains isolated and inconspicuous to many."

"It appears that Miss Baxter inadvertently gave her niece and her associates the most perfect hideaway for their warped cause," said Judd. "What was the name of this niece, Mr. Mutch?"

"I never forget a name, Detective Inspector. Her name was Rowena. Rowena Baxter."

CHAPTER 36

The unmarked Peugeot was parked at the foot of the long driveway that led to the property inherited by Rowena Baxter. It was also extremely likely that within the estate, the Adonijah Truthsters, including their leader Eli Zane and his deputy Jaden Rivers, would be found there too.

Judd was in the driver's seat and William occupied the passenger seat, while Sab sat in the rear of the car.

"Are you sure that you are up to this, William? Sab and I could have handled it."

"I've waited near on 30 years to get even with these snakes for what they did to my sister. Wild horses wouldn't hold me back now. I need to look into their eyes."

"Okay let's do it," said Judd as he revved the car to manoeuvre it towards the property.

Judd's concern for his friend was due to the recent decline in his health caused by the Multiple Sclerosis; not least the rapid downward spiral of the big man's dexterity. This was no more evident than when William attempted to get out of the car once they had reached the house. Still fiercely independent, William refused the offers from his two companions to assist him out of the passenger seat, instead choosing to take several attempts to stand upright with only the help of his two crutches for support. William's walking was becoming more laboured and he staggered unsteadily behind Judd and Sab as the detectives approached the door.

It was Judd who rang the vintage doorbell and the huge chimes sang out into the still air. Not too long after, a lady answered. Judd pitched her age at being not much older than him and believed she had the potential to be quite a looker if she had bothered to apply some make-up. Her hair was cut short in a non-descript style with small flecks of grey breaking through and her clothing was faded and dowdy.

"Can I help you?" she said frostily.

The three detectives flashed their badges in perfect unison; Judd had failed to hand his in in spite of his suspension. Although William was stood at the rear of the trio he couldn't hold back on taking the lead.

"I am Detective Chief Inspector Chamberlain of B.A.D CID and I am accompanied by my two colleagues Detective Inspector Stone and Detective Sergeant Mistry. We are here to ask some questions about the murder of Luther Blake."

The woman made an exaggerated attempt at appearing to think of the name. "Luther Blake, Luther Blake. I can't say I know of that name."

"He was murdered in his own home in Liverpool; surely you will at least have heard about it on the news?" enquired Sab.

"We have no television sets in this house, Detective Sergeant. TV only serves to corrupt the mind, so I'm afraid I have not heard of this murder on any news." She then turned her conversation towards William. "Liverpool is some distance from here Detective Chief Inspector, it sounds an awful business but how can I possibly help with the killing of the poor man?"

"We have reason to believe that the killers recently lived at this house with you," answered William.

"So you already know who the killers are? Can't you simply ask them as to the reasons for their actions?"

"They are both dead Miss Baxter, though I suspect that you already knew that. Are you amusing yourself with this little charade you are playing? You are Miss Rowena Baxter I presume?"

"Yes, I am Rowena Baxter, but I can assure you that I have no knowledge of a murder and I am not in the habit of harbouring criminals in my home."

"Oh, is that right," snapped William. "Well let's put the murdering scum to one side for a second shall we? Do you not have people living with you who kidnap people and keep people against their will?"

"No-one lives here with me against their will. Look at me. How could I force people to stay here? I'm not exactly blessed with brawn."

"But probably very well blessed in the art of manipulation. Anyway, what about Eli Zane and Jaden Rivers, are they living here with you? I believe that they are very adept at keeping people against their will. Or perhaps the world has been saved from their monstrous activities because they perished in the fire over in the States. Fingers crossed."

Rowena was a little taken aback at how much the detective inspector seemed to know. How did he know about Eli and Jaden for instance? Then when she thought a little more deeply about his name it began to explain things.

"Chamberlain. Detective Chief Inspector Chamberlain."

"You recognise my name I take it? My sister is Tilda Chamberlain, well was."

"Was? Is Tilda dead?"

"No, though I suspect you and your loony contingent would prefer it if she were. She is known as Tilda Blake these days."

"Oh, I see. So Luther Blake was perhaps her husband?

Poor Tilda, she was my friend."

"Some friend you turned out to be. And stop pretending that you know nothing about the murder of Mr. Blake." William's rising anger was acutely evident.

"I swear to you DCI Chamberlain, I know nothing of Mr. Blake's murder."

"Why don't you swear on the Bible?" said William testily.

"How dare you, Detective Chief Inspector. The Bible is very precious to me; I don't use it as an instrument to satisfy the wild accusations of the ignorant. God knows my innocence and he shall judge me and all of us accordingly when he chooses the day of reckoning." Judd and Sab couldn't help but notice how William's emotions were beginning to cloud his judgment. He was becoming too angry, too personal and was in danger of losing any productive engagement with Rowena to gain any critical evidence. Although it was clear she was not exactly intending to co-operate.

"What kind of a set up do you exactly have here, Miss Baxter?" enquired Sab.

"I have some friends who live with me and we simply like to keep ourselves to ourselves. We study the teachings of the Lord, harvest our own land, and to be frank with you we don't do much else. We commit no crimes here and I resent the implications that we do?"

"Perhaps we could come in and talk things over, Miss Baxter. Perhaps we could even meet some of your friends as well?" Judd, for once traded places with William as the more level-headed copper.

"As this murder occurred in Liverpool, I suspect that it is the Merseyside police who are investigating the crime, and therefore you have simply come along today primarily because of my once connection with Tilda."

"Do you have anything to hide, Miss Baxter?" asked Judd evenly.

"You would not understand either us, or our way of

life, Detective Inspector Stone, so forgive me but I prefer not to allow you into the house. Whatever we do here it is for God and it is only God who can judge us."

"Funny, I would have thought that a house of God would be welcome to all?" said Sab.

"In the circumstances, and due to what I perceive as your intentions, I must insist that no police are passing through my door without a proper search warrant."

The clever bitch had played her trump card. They had hoped to get further than this by bluffing, but they did not have a warrant as it was indeed the Merseyside police who were conducting the investigation.

"We thought that you may have been a little bit more co-operative with us Rowena, and your lack of co-operation will not go unnoticed in the long run. We know that the killers of Luther Blake lived here; we just need to tie up a few loose threads. We will achieve that with or without your help. And I know that you must be keeping people here against their free-will just like you did with my sister, and if Zane and Rivers are in there then you are harbouring kidnappers and rapists so pray all you want, your crazy and warped little empire is about to crumble. You have not heard the last of this." William turned away and staggered back to the car, his emotional state at odds with his physical capability.

Of course, William had never expected Rowena to admit to harbouring Harry, Jim-Ray, Eli or Jaden but he was content that he had achieved one key thing. He had found the Adonijah Truthsters.

He had tracked down the bastards who had taken his little sister and he had looked at least one of them in the eye. It was now just a matter of time before justice could be realised for both Tilda and Luther.

"I'll pray for you Detective Chief Inspector Chamberlain; I can see that you are not a well man."

"Don't bother," retorted William.

"And please give my love to Tilda; tell her she is

welcome here any time."

"William, don't bite," whispered Judd and he held up a hand to halt her words, coupled with an icy Judd Stone stare, which was enough to silence Rowena. She had made her point anyway.

The three detectives entered the car and drove away from the property. Once Rowena was back in her house she was greeted by the two men that mattered the most to her.

"Well done Rowena, you serve us well," said Eli. Jaden simply smiled.

CHAPTER 37

Detective Chief Inspector William Chamberlain answered the phone at his desk cutting short the fifth ring. His grip on the receiver was not as tight as he would have liked.

"Hello, Chamberlain."

"William, Michael Froggatt here."

"Michael thanks for agreeing to take a look at those psychos as part of your investigation. Is there any news for me?"

"Well, I sent a total of five officers armed with an official warrant down to that spooky house, but as the knife used to kill Mr. Blake was found in the mangled car with the dead twins it was always going to be difficult to unearth something in the Severn Valley area. I mean, if Rowena and her cronies had even admitted to knowing Harry and Jim-Ray, which they didn't by the way, it still wouldn't prove that they had any knowledge of the murder. I bent the rules a little to get a warrant as a personal favour to you William, although I was intrigued to at least try and join some dots myself based on the information that you had given me."

"I appreciate it Michael. Bear with me a moment, I'm just gonna have to put you on the loud speaker. The receiver is making my arm ache. Damned MS."

"No problem."

"Okay, I'm back with you Michael. Can you hear me?"

"Loud and clear."

"What about Zane and Rivers?"

"Alive and well, and their paperwork checks out for residing in the UK."

"So the bastards are here. They have people everywhere committed to helping them with their sick cause. That's why the paperwork stands up."

"No obvious evidence I'm afraid."

"Did you find any arsenal there?"

"Not a dicky bird. I sent five of my best officers William, and they couldn't find anything that compromised the position of those living there, including anything that linked them to Harry and Jim-Ray. Eric Dovedale, a DI that works for me suspected that the place had been set up as if they were expecting our visit; he could sense they were hiding something but at the end of the day that kind of hunch doesn't stand up in a court of law. If they are involved in anything they've covered their arses pretty well."

"Did you speak to Mutch? Show him a photo of those identical dead goons and he will be able to tell you that he remembers seeing them on the premises."

"A bit of a problem there too, William. My boys went to do just that and found Mutch hanging by a rope in his office. His secretary was beside herself; we couldn't console the poor thing."

"Mutch is dead? Don't you find that a bit of a coincidence?"

"Yes I do, but that is all it is at this stage. It definitely looks like suicide; no foul play is evident at all."

"Did he leave a suicide note?"

"Not that we could find, but it still proves nothing, William. It could even have been a sex game gone wrong. It happens. Perhaps he entertained women in his office, it went tits-up - no pun intended, and off she scarpered."

"No way, not Mutch. The way Sab described him he was asexual if anything. I don't buy it, Michael. Those warped bastards had something to do with his death. They wanted to stop him talking."

"Mrs. Powell did inform us that the business was suffering of late, and Mr. Mutch had some acute financial difficulties. We've checked that out and it rings true. We simply can't connect his death to the people you call The Adonijah Truthsters I'm afraid."

"I know they were responsible somehow. I get the picture though, Michael. Thanks for your efforts."

"William, I'm sorry but I just can't make anything stick. At least you know that the two scumbags who killed your brother-in-law are dead; perhaps you should accept that justice has already been done albeit in a different way."

"For Luther maybe, but not for my sister. There are some individuals who still need to pay for what they have done to her."

"I hear you big fella, but unless Tilda testifies we are simply pissing in the wind relying on a lot of dead wood from a long time ago. I can't say I blame her either; it certainly wouldn't be easy for her. And even if she does testify, the CPS in this country would find it hard to take the case. I'm not saying I don't believe you or your sister William, but in reality it could just amount to being her word against theirs and from what I understand, in the beginning at least, she agreed to hook up with them of her own free will. I can assure you William, my officers asked some very searching questions but we found no evidence of anyone being held against their will at present. If we had we could have built a case around that to help you. On the contrary, everyone seemed content to be living in that house, which I have to say checks out to being legal and all above board."

William fought to hide his frustration. "Okay, thanks again Michael."

"No worries William, I'll keep an open mind and if I am able to offer you any crumbs in the future I will. I'll keep you posted on any developments."

"Okay, appreciate it, bye."

"Bye."

William killed the loud speaker with a heavy heart, but he hardly had time to digest his disappointment when the phone rang again.

William activated the loud speaker once more.

"Hi William. Bill calling here from across the pond."

"Bill, how are you doing? It's good to hear from you. Is retirement keeping you busy?"

"I'm doing a lot of gardening these days, in-between being a bank for my 11 grandkids that is, but I've also made time to try and indulge myself in my favourite hobby of studying The Adonijah Truthsters."

"I could sure do with something to nail those scumbags, Bill."

"It still pains me, William that they managed to escape to the UK right under my nose without me bringing them to justice in the States. I've tried to move to extraditing them back over here, but all I can pin on them is some minor fraud activity that ain't exactly creating an appetite to drag them through the US justice system. My successor, Chief Quentin Jenson ain't too concerned about them, as far as he is concerned as long as they are off his patch they can do whatever they damn well please. And that's his attitude even if Zane is alive somewhere else. He is a real unco-operative asshole; he conveniently forgets that I lost good men to those crazy people."

"Don't beat yourself up Bill; we all thought there were no survivors from that fire. Besides, now they're on my turf I have them firmly in my sights. They won't get away again."

"How's it going with this Froggatt guy? I could always fly over and have a word with him, try and educate him on the history of these weirdos."

"Thanks Bill, though I have informed him as much as I can without sounding like a paranoid lunatic. He keeps a pretty open mind but these Adonijah Truthsters cover their tracks pretty well and he is the type of cop who does everything by the book. He can't make anything stick. He did confirm one crucial thing though. Zane is alive and living at that old house."

"Wow that's something at least. A bittersweet experience for you perhaps though, William?"

"A little. He deserves to be dead just like those crazy twins. I kind of figured he must still be alive though. And what's more, a key witness who could have placed Luther's killers as belonging to the cult has wound up dead. Suspected suicide but I'm convinced that the cult is behind it."

"Yeah, I'd be damned sure they are too. What about your man Stone, he does things a little more unorthodox doesn't he? Can't he come up with something?"

William refrained from informing his friend that Judd was currently suspended from duty. "He's helping me Bill. He's a good guy alright, but even his powers of persuasion are hitting a brick wall."

"I did run some checks on those twins, William and you ain't gonna believe this."

"Try me."

"They spent time in a penitentiary for killing their momma, and they used to boast that they were the sons of Charles Manson no less, though their birth certificate never said as much, so they could be fantasists. But it still weaves into this crazy underworld of religious cults."

"There was some evidence at the murder scene which was typical of the Californian killings by Manson's Family, so if they weren't his sons they were at least copy cats and was tuned into all this cult culture. Tilda is an expert in cults these days and together we have pieced that the current Adonijah Truthsters are made up of surviving original members but have also taken in survivors of the

Waco siege, and now it would seem the illegitimate sons of Charles Manson."

"Making The Adonijah Truthsters the definitive super cult led by the only surviving one true prophet of God - Eli Zane, even outshining David Koresh."

"That's about it. While Manson's behind bars he is a largely forgotten leader even for his boys it seems."

"Who are now dead. Perhaps the Lord found a way to punish Luther's killers when they ended up wrapped around that tree in Liverpool."

"Maybe, but there are still Zane and Rivers to take care of."

"Oh yeah, Jaden Rivers. Eli's St Peter. Is he alive too?"

"Yep."

"And this bunch of loonies still interprets 2012 as the being the year of Armageddon?"

"Yeah, as far as I can gather they would still think that. Not because of that Mayan Calendar thing that everyone's talking about, but because Jerusalem fell to Israel in 1967 to fulfill some sort of end of days prophecy."

"Oh yeah, that 40 year biblical generation thing. Wait that would mean 2007, we have already survived Armageddon. Shouldn't someone tell these demented creeps?"

"No Bill, not if the true birth year of Jesus Christ was apparently 5 BC or is it AD. Anyway, the Christian calendar is out by five years they reckon, whoever *they* is."

"Oh yeah I forgot. Most Baptists think that actually, I should have known that. I guess I just love Christmas too much."

"You and me both, my old pal."

"William, it was good to speak with you my friend, I'm sorry I can't be of more help."

"Bill, you are a dear friend, it's good just to talk to you. Don't leave it so long next time."

"Okay buddy. Good luck with nailing those psychos."

"I think I need to start getting imaginative. While there

is still breath in my body those two evil morons Eli Zane and Jaden Rivers will suffer somehow. That's a promise. Bye Bill."

"Bye, William."

CHAPTER 38

"Those dumb cops couldn't prove a thing, Eli."

"Well we have the Lord protecting us, Jaden. He won't let anyone get in our way, not even the law. And we were tested by integrating those two Manson boys into our flock, but the Lord has removed them as they were not meant to be forsaken come the day of reckoning."

"So they have not died a martyr's death, Eli?"

"Not to my mind, Jaden. All they have done is exposed us to the police and caused us problems. I believe the Lord removed them from us as their path was different, especially as they failed to get to Tilda. What was the use in killing her husband? That was just an act of evil, and they used trademarks of the 1960s Californian killings that their daddy ordered, like scribing messages in blood. That's not our way, Jaden. No, those boys are no longer needed in the Adonijah Truthsters."

"I agree. Tilda has to die and that solicitor fella had to die. It was fortunate that we were able to hide the gun in a priest hole. I didn't have to even fire it as it happens, but due to the gun laws in England, it would have roused suspicion with those cops for sure if they had come across it."

Eli laughed. "Yeah, that misguided religion which is so widely accepted by the masses helped us conceal our weapon, a weapon that was used to protect our journey. It does have a certain irony that it is now safely placed where catholic priests used to hide in this old house."

"It was so easy to get that Mutch to hang himself; I just pointed the gun at him and told him to stand in the noose. Those dumb cops didn't work out that I simply kicked his chair away from under him. And it was quite amusing watching his scrawny little legs desperately trying to connect with something that simply wasn't there. The manic mid-air peddling soon became nervy jerks as the life drained away from him and his eyes began to bulge. "

"And this is what must happen, Jaden. Anyone who tries to compromise our existence must die. Those who are not part of our flock will all die on the day of reckoning anyway, but if need be we shall cast them aside on the way. For it is only us that can survive the end of days. Only us."

"Amen to that, Eli."

"Amen."

PART III
CRIPPLED INSIDE

CHAPTER 39

It had been almost nine years since Judd received the news that rocked his world. Even now his stomach churns when he thinks of the time he received the unbelievable words from William. No-one else had had the balls to break it to Judd, but then again who could have been better placed to have delivered such compellingly tragic information?

At any given time when his mind allows, which is always whenever he is in his own company, Judd can still vividly relive the feeling of nausea coupled with an instantaneous drying of the mouth as his friend's implausible words barely seemed to register.

William had tears in his eyes as he explained the circumstances to his friend. Judd's pregnant wife Frankie had been killed and the chief suspect was Delroy Whitton, a known villain who had earlier been released from jail after serving a fraction of his sentence due to that old adage of 'good behaviour'. Judd had almost single-handedly taken this piece of useless scum off the streets. The wannabe gangsta had been found guilty for serious drug offences, including supplying school kids, and after his stretch Delroy had hunted down Frankie and stabbed her to death, simply as an act of vengeance towards the cop that had put him away.

As it happened Delroy never got sent down for Frankie's murder. In fact he didn't even make it to trial. Unbeknown to everyone except Judd and William, Delroy paid for his crime in the form of torture and an eventual slow death. After all, Judd had put the scumbag away once; he didn't want to risk him ever being allowed to walk the streets of Birmingham again.

Whitton's eternal resting place became the foundations of a hotel that was being built in Birmingham's city centre.

It seemed that Whitton had been trying to tell Judd something in his final few breaths of life, but the words had been too incoherent, such was the demise in the villain's physical state. Perhaps it had been an apology? If it had been an apology it wouldn't have sufficed anyhow and Judd was content that vengeance had been realised in the only suitable way possible.

Most people suspected that Judd must have had something to do with Whitton's disappearance, and few could ever blame him, but Lionel Scarrow had typically wanted to press the matter. However, Scarrow has never been able to find any compelling evidence against Judd. Judd made it explicit that Delroy Whitton would have had a list of enemies as long as Spaghetti Junction queuing up to get revenge on the double crossing scumbag, so there was little point in squarely pointing the finger at him alone, regardless of his motive. It hadn't pleased Scarrow, after initial investigations had drawn a blank in the disappearance of Delroy Whitton, when Ben Francis ordered his officers not to waste a large amount of police resource on any sort of ongoing investigation, and he was happy for the case to remain unsolved. After all, it seemed the streets of Birmingham were one piece of filth less to have to deal with.

Judd had never especially been good at showing his emotions and his one regret was that he had never told Frankie how much he truly loved her. She would often turn to him and say "I love you, Judd," and he would have simply replied "Yeah, me too. Love, love me do." But he had never been the instigator of showing such verbal affection and by nonchalantly disguising his message within a Beatle song title he somehow diminished a possible escalation of uncomfortable soppiness.

Instead of promising to himself that he wouldn't make the same mistake twice if another partner was ever to come his way, Judd instead made a pact to simply never fall in love again. In his mind nobody could ever hold a torch to his beloved Frankie anyway, so why bother to get emotionally involved with someone?

The sweet and beautiful Frankie would indeed always prove to be a tough act to follow, but Judd seemed hell bent on never allowing himself to be happy again. Since the loss of his wife and unborn child, he had never even contemplated having a serious relationship.

Judd blamed himself for four tragedies that had occurred in his lifetime. On four occasions he had not been there at the crucial moment that women had needed him: the slaying of Frankie, the rape of Bonnie, the drug-fuelled death of his birth mother and the killing of his foster mother Evelyn by a drunk-driver. Due to this overwhelming feeling of responsibility, Judd had rushed to protect both Sab and Tabitha at the hands of Banks. Additionally, Judd believed that he had also let down the victims of Gareth Banks as long as the serial killer walked free. His perpetual guilt rested heavy on his shoulders and heart.

In terms of having a serious relationship, Judd simply felt that it was easier, and wiser, to not have any women rely on him for he was sure to let them down.

Judd completed the short walk from his American fridge to his leather sofa losing the metal top off his bottle of pilsner along the way. The open-planned layout of his home always enabled him to approach the sofa in the same way; he simply flung himself from behind it and over its upright backrest. It was far simpler than taking the effort to walk round to the front of the sofa to sit down in a more contemporary fashion.

He took a swig of his beer and took a moment of reflection. It was never good for him to be in a position to reflect, it was better if his mind could be kept busy. For during his times of reflection his demons would take hold and torture him, which inevitably shifted his mood from relaxation to depression. This would most often begin the cycle of an initial relaxing beer turning into a skinful to try and blot out the pain.

Judd pressed the remote control to fire his flat-screen television into life, which in truth was a little too large in relation to the room. The TV was typically already set on the sports channel. Judd's leisure time was usually filled by either viewing the sports channel or listening to a Lennon album.

Swigging his beer again, Judd was exposed to some mundane lower-league football transfer news which hardly registered as his mind wandered to more torturing things.

Judd was lonely. He realised this, but he convinced himself once again that being alone was how it was meant to be. Any woman he had ever come into any significant contact with had wound up dead, and the most disturbing of all had been his beloved Frankie. Why had he not arrived home sooner to be with her? He knew Whitton was being released, should he have guessed that Whitton would hunt her down and try to kill her to get to him? If only he had been there the tragedy would never have unfolded.

Instead of coming home that fateful day, Judd had chosen to attend the bookmakers and place £100 on that last race at Cheltenham racecourse, convinced he would actually come home to his pregnant wife and make her happy with the news that he had produced a nice little earner. But as he watched the race on the bookies' TV screen he also watched his money drain away, as it had done each day that week in the same bookies. Judd hadn't placed his £100 on an each way bet and the horse he backed agonisingly finished second, resulting in him winning nothing.

That last race had allowed just enough time for Whitton to kill Frankie and the child inside her.

Judd swigged at the bottle of beer once again. A wry smile came across his lips as he recalled the justice he inflicted on Whitton once he had caught up with him. He at least had some comfort knowing that he had avenged Frankie's death in suitable fashion. However, he would of course trade anything to have Frankie and his child in his life instead.

Judd began to contemplate just what had he actually done with his life?

Ok, he had made it to the rank of Detective Inspector in Birmingham and District CID, indeed a worthy career position, yet in his mind his latest flaw had been the clear failing of three young women. Three young women who would have expected him to bring their killer to justice, but that killer continues to walk the Earth a free man.

And before Judd found a career in the police force he was nothing better than a football hooligan, perversely finding pleasure in beating the living daylights out of someone simply for supporting a different football team. A period in his life Judd was less than proud of.

Yet when he had operated undercover to fight alongside Eddie Goode he had tasted what it was like to be in that environment again. And he had enjoyed it. Judd felt ashamed, football was meant to be a spectacle for enjoyment, like the days when he would accompany William to a match to sit in the disabled enclosure, simply to watch the entertainment unfold before him on the football pitch. Football should never be an excuse for grown men to beat the crap out of one another.

Continuing with his self-analysis, Judd recognised that

he had indeed been a football hooligan and he had also been a gambler. In fact he was still the latter, partaking regularly in card games such as on the night Cassie Parker had been murdered. He also enjoyed a substantial flutter on horse and dog racing, football betting and he felt extremely at home inside a casino.

Keeping with the theme of gambling, Judd evaluated that he was a loser in life. If he gambled with money he would lose, if he gambled with women he would lose. He was simply a loser.

Judd's brain snapped into auto-pilot, searching for a way to alleviate the self-negativity. Then he thought again about his time watching football with William. Dear William, his only constant in life. The magnificent man had Multiple Sclerosis. Unlike Judd, William found himself in an undesirable situation due to absolutely nothing of his own doing, and he handled it all with such dignity. William was constantly determined not to allow the MS to take control of his life, despite the daily battles that the illness chose to introduce. In contrast, Judd had a choice to stop gambling. It was often said that gambling was an illness, an addiction, but Judd refused to compare his self-inflicted situation to that which William was confronted with day after day.

And then suddenly the way out of all his troubles hit Judd like a bolt of lightning. And it wasn't rocket science either. He really did need to get his act together. Only he had the power to turn his life around, and if he just thought about someone else for a change instead of wallowing in his own self-pity he could actually be of some use. Above all he realised he owed it to his friend. William had no choice in his inflictions but Judd did. And there may be a time soon when his friend would have to rely on his support, and if Judd was to going to provide any type of decent support he needed his head-space to be right. William had supported him for so long, better than any older brother or even father could have done. The physical decline he had witnessed in William suggested to Judd that their roles may need to be reversed any time soon. He would need to support William and William would no longer be in a position to support him.

William, being William, would of course be fiercely independent until his last ounce of strength would fail him, but Judd knew he had to be there for his friend once that day came. It was time to stop feeling sorry for himself and to stop being so selfish. The gambling he would try and stop. The drinking he could make less excessive.

But to stop feeling guilty about the women he perceived that he had let down would not be quite so easy.

William was having yet another bad day. The messages from his brain to his limbs were once again not fully connecting. The diazepam helped his muscle spasms a little, but they had become more regular and intense of late. William received regular physiotherapy to try and teach other muscles to compensate those that couldn't function like they used to, but the unfortunate reality was clear. His physical condition was steadily deteriorating.

William had moved from the house in Erdington he once shared with Tilda, to an apartment on the ground level. Tackling stairs was now a real problem for him, but the apartment had not yet been fully converted to a standard required for disabled people, William being far too proud to live in such a dwelling. He also viewed it as a personal achievement that so far he had been able to fight off the threat of a wheelchair.

William's strong-mindedness ensured that he would never fully admit defeat to the Multiple Sclerosis no matter how much it hacked away at his physical capabilities. Curiously he had noticed that his telekinetic powers were continuing to become increasingly more acute as his MS gradually took hold of him.

William had just finished eating a boiled egg, the final events of the cooking procedure being carried out solely by the power of his mind. Conventionally he had just about managed to fill the pan with water, drop the egg in and bring the pan to the boil by switching on the hob. However, ten minutes later with the threat of the pan boiling dry, William frustratingly found himself being been unable to get out of his chair, and even if he had got to his feet he would have struggled to lift the weight of the boiling water off the hob. So instead he used the power of his mind to switch off the gas and levitate the egg out of the boiling water, like a mini UFO gliding through the air, and onto a nearby plate. The plate was then manoeuvred across the room onto William's lap where he stared intensely at the egg for a number of seconds until the shell simply broke away. William was then able to feed himself using his hands – just.

Some thirty minutes later, William discovered that with a struggle he was finally able to stand from his chair. He walked unsteadily and slowly to the large window that looked out onto the road and leant heavily on the window ledge that took the brunt of his whole weight. William's apartment block formed part of Cavernshow Place in the centre of Sutton Coldfield and stood opposite a Public House. His view of the road was that of a hill that descended to the gateway to the shopping area, and looking north acted as the cut-through to the local swimming baths and leisure centre, as well as one of several entrances to Sutton Park. Judd's apartment was actually in the same block as William's but sat two flights above, such was the extent of their friendship to be in such close proximity to one another. Unbeknown to William, Judd had actually mirrored his movements and was also looking nonchalantly from his window. Anyone looking up from the road or pavement would have smiled at the mirrored images of the two men standing a floor apart.

Judd took a swig of his beer; William scratched his nose which had begun to itch. Both men noticed a young woman begin to ascend the hill with the unenvied task of pushing a pushchair up the steep incline. The buggy was the type that accommodated two children and it was likely that the occupants were twins (a much sweeter pairing one would presume than Harrison and Jim-Ray). The lady had a third child with her, who was a little older than her siblings, and was eating an ice cream with one hand whilst carrying a bag under the other. Both Judd and William assumed that the mother was taking her eldest daughter, who appeared no more than about seven years old to the swimming baths. The girl was a pretty little thing with brown pigtails bouncing in time with her playful gait. She was wearing a pair of funky Aztec patterned leggings and a T-shirt sporting a doe-eyed puppy dog whose head was purposefully depicted as being a much larger than its body to enhance the cute factor. Judd smiled at the innocence that oozed from the girl and once again found himself contemplating what his life could have been like if his unborn child had not been so cruelly taken away from him.

Suddenly, and in spite of the substantial double-glazing windows of the apartments, a combination of noises could be heard from outside. Both Judd and William watched in horror as they saw a pick-up truck zooming down the hill at far too great a speed than was necessary, creating a sound of jangling and crashing metal. The truck's inhabitants had obviously had a successful day of collecting unwanted household scrap metal.

One of the twins added to the stress levels of the young mother when he threw its bottle onto the pavement causing it to roll down the hill. The mother secured the buggy by applying its brake and then hurried to retrieve the bottle from rolling all the way into town, whilst instructing her eldest daughter to keep still until she returned. "Heidi, don't move."

From his higher viewing position, Judd could see that the hoard of metal, which included broken washing machines, bicycles and other jagged unwanted items, had not been secured to the maximum safety level possible, and as the truck careered down the hill he saw Heidi standing still and as good as gold, just like her mother had told her too. Obliviously she was licking away merrily at her ice cream cone. Judd's stomach churned as he feared that something awful was about to happen.

The Cup public house, as it was known at that time later to give way to a Mediterranean restaurant, curiously sat on a large triangular traffic roundabout at the foot of the hill. The triangular area separated the two possible travel paths of traffic, and the truck driver belatedly realised that if he was going to clear the kerb of the island he was going to have to apply some significant pressure to his brakes – and quickly. The driver panicked and as he slammed his brakes on causing a large pane of glass, which was being housed by an old style metal window frame, to come hurtling over the top of the truck.

Judd could see that the pane of glass had broken free from the frame and was heading straight for Heidi, with the distinct certainty of slicing the pretty little girl into two.

On impulse, Judd helplessly cried out the words "Look out," but he knew that his words would serve no effect as the girl would be unable to hear them, and in any case would not have had time to react to his warning.

The truck driver and his mate both sat open-mouthed as they saw the glass fly towards the girl and they feared the worst. Heidi's mother, who had successfully retrieved the toddler's bottle, simply froze to the spot screaming hysterically as she realised what was destined for her daughter.

Once Heidi realised what was happening she dropped her ice cream, that in itself a sign of the seriousness of the situation in a young child's mind, and the terrified girl began to scream as she saw the glass come flying towards her at an almighty speed. She closed her eyes in an impulsive, split-second attempt to blot out the danger.

The glass was inches from the little girl's throat when suddenly, as if my magic or some kind of divine intervention, the glass simply shattered into tiny pieces right in front of her, and the tiny shards of glass fell to the pavement, not a single one harming a hair on young Heidi's head.

"How the f-?" Judd said to himself, astonished but thankful at what he had just witnessed. The two scrap metal merchants both breathed a huge sigh of relief and Heidi's mother ran and gathered her daughter in her arms, barely unable to conceive that she hadn't suffered any injury. "It's a miracle," she exclaimed.

William was simply laid flat out on the floor of his apartment, totally exhausted at his greatest ever demonstration of telekinesis to date.

CHAPTER 40

William found himself returning briefly to his childhood as he attempted to make shapes from the clouds that were swirling and transpiring in the blue sky above. He was able to take some comfort that his eyesight wasn't deteriorating anywhere near as acutely as his other body parts were. He had established the cotton wool forms of a dog's head and a dolphin whilst gazing out of the passenger window of Judd's car, before finally turning to speak to his friend. "Thanks again for taking me to my appointment with the neurologist, Judd."

"What are friends for, William?"

"I'm sure you have better things to do with your time than ferrying me around. To be honest I don't really see the point of attending these appointments. It's not as if the fella can ever do anything for me. He just gives me an update on the 'hows' and 'whys' as to my symptoms getting worse. He never has any good news for me. In fact thinking about it, it is *me* who tells *him* that my symptoms are getting worse and then he just makes a note of it and attempts to tell me why."

"I think he means well mate, and it is important that the medics monitor your progress."

"Progress? Are you taking the piss, Judd?"

"Sorry, wrong choice of word, it's just a turn of phrase that's all. I just want to be positive for you, William."

"I'm sorry for snapping, Judd; it just becomes so frustrating when putting one foot in front of the other and almost every little movement starts to become a chore. Your brain tells you to do something and your damn body goes and does something else entirely different."

Judd had noticed recently how William's speech could break or become slightly slurred, but the younger of the two friends chose not to draw attention to his observations. "I don't claim to understand, mate, but I'm sure it can't be easy for you."

"Knowing you are always there for me helps, Judd; I wish I could repay you in some way?"

"Repay me? For what? William I owe my whole life to you. You helped me secure a profession in the police force when most employers wouldn't have even entertained giving me a job; you helped me get on my feet again, twice, when I lost my mom and Frankie. I'll always be there for you. You know what? You just being my mate and the big brother I never had is enough repayment for me."

"Don't let Sab hear you talk like this, she'll think you've gone soft."

Judd laughed.

"It's not just the MS that frustrates me, Judd. It still riles me that that slippery murdering scumbag Banks was able to walk free from court, and I hate the fact that the kidnappers of my sister are also walking free. Is it something to do with me, Judd? Have I lost my skills as a good copper, you know because of the MS?"

"Listen, your brain may play tricks on your limbs these days mate, but you're still as sharp as ever when it comes to being a detective. You're second to none in my book. We were just unlucky with Banks, and the cult thing is unfortunately out of your hands as it stands. Merseyside are running the show where they are concerned."

"I guess so; it's just hard to take. I know that Zane and Rivers have blood on their hands and not just for Luther and Mutch either. I'll think of something though, I'll make them all pay one day. That's Eli, Jaden and Banks."

"I don't doubt it William, we just need to be patient. The solution will present itself one day."

A natural pause followed between the two friends until Judd relieved the silence. "Traffic is slow to the QE today." The QE was the name used by citizens of Birmingham for the prestigious Queen Elizabeth Hospital which specialised in many things, neurology being just one of them.

Judd's car was stuck in a line of traffic alongside the Alexandra Theatre in Birmingham city centre. The most logical route to the hospital would be to cross the roundabout where the Chinese Pagoda statue stood and then join the A38 as it became the Bristol Road.

"If I swing a right at the island I can go the back way, and then I'll still get you there in time I reckon, William."

"Whatever you say, you're the driver."

As Judd drove unconsciously competently, he allowed his mind to wander, and even though he had attempted to be philosophical to his friend about the lack of luck being evident regarding Gareth Banks, his usual feelings of anger began to surface. It didn't help matters that Judd's detour to the hospital had taken him in the vicinity of Tabitha Haddock's residence to remind him of how Gareth Banks had enjoyed a warped sense of entertainment at his expense.

"You know William; it does bother me too when I think of the murderer of those poor women walking free. How on Earth did he get away with the awful things that he did to them? The bastard slit their mouths, disfigured their beautiful faces and then stuck knives in them to portray them as a crucifixion. I'll never forget that dickhead smile he had as he left the court a free man. And then to add insult to injury he has the audacity to mess with my head. He phoned me and taunted me, the cheeky bastard. I really thought he was going to kill Tabitha Haddock that night you know."

"The danger is Judd, is that he will kill again. He is just biding his time I'm sure of it. He has got away with murder at least three times to our knowledge; he can't help but want to kill again."

"Well somehow I want to get to him before he does. I've often thought about giving him the same justice I gave to Whitton."

"Very apt but too risky, Judd. Both the media and internal affairs would be over you like a rash with that one. Remember he walked from court a free man, they would point the finger at you straight away, Judd. The appetite wasn't there to find out what happened to Whitton, putting Lionel Scarrow to one side that is, it would be a different scenario with Banks. The public think that *he* was the victim for Christ's sake."

"I know; it really frustrates me."

"Listen, Judd. I know you feel that you let those poor girls down. I feel that too to a certain degree, but I know that the enormity of the situation has magnified this hobby you persist to have of beating yourself up. Unnecessarily I should add."

"Please don't psycho analyse me, William. The facts are plain to see aren't they? I let down Bonnie; I let down my mom – both of them, Frankie and now the three victims of Banks. The guilt eats away at me each and every day."

"Judd, no one knows you better than me. You are a great friend and a fantastic copper with a heart of gold under that tough guy exterior. What you are not is psychic. How could you have known that Evelyn was going to be knocked down by a car? If you let her down then didn't I too? How could you have possibly known that Bonnie was going to be raped? How could you have known that Whitton would show when he did to kill Frankie? And how on earth could you have known where and when

Banks was going to strike? We didn't even know who the killer was until after his third murder. You have to stop torturing yourself buddy, you really do."

"A heart of gold you reckon? What have I ever done with my life, William? I was a football hooligan, nothing better than a common thug. I took pleasure from kicking the living daylights out of someone and why? Because they dared to support a different football team to me. It's pathetic."

"That was a long time ago, Judd. We all make mistakes. Look at you now; you attend the football matches with me for all the right reasons. I don't think you would accompany me to watch a game in the disabled section if you were still up for the ruck."

"I only go with you to the match because as your carer I get in for free." Judd allowed himself a smile as he joked with his friend. However, his mood soon turned sombre again. "The thing is William, I thought I was over it, but when I went undercover with Eddie Goode and his cronies and I got involved in that fight with the Welsh lads down by Millennium Point, I got that taste again. I swear I was enjoying that fight as if I had never been away from the whole damn football hooligan environment."

"A victim of circumstance, Judd, that's all. What were you supposed to do, stand there while you got your head caved in? You were placed in a situation where you had to defend yourself."

"Was I meant to enjoy it though?"

"Winning at anything is usually a good feeling, Judd, and if you won that fight you are bound to feel better than losing it."

"Maybe. Do you really think Banks will kill again?"

"It is very rare for a serial killer to stop once he has started. He may get cocky, and when he does he will make a mistake and we shall be there waiting for him."

"Amen to that, William."

"My mouth feels a bit dry with all this talking; the

medication can do it to me. Would you mind stopping when you can for a bottle of cola?"

"Sure thing, we have time. I could do with some chewing gum anyway."

Not long after, Judd was able to bump his car up onto the kerb in front of a newsagent. The road was quiet so he was easily able to get out of the car with no fear of oncoming traffic. William stayed in the car and was beginning to notice how we was experiencing particular difficulty in moving his legs. The position of his legs during the car journey was also causing his muscles to cramp.

Judd was at the fridge choosing the cola, and marvelled at the mechanism that enabled a second bottle to slide into place where he had just taken a bottle from. Judd had heard how this was the idea that inspired the owner of the Toyota car business to introduce lean engineering into his business. The Japanese realised that the same concept could be used on a production line, where a gearbox for example, could instantly appear to replace the one that was now being installed. Judd's trail of thought about the wonder of Japanese motor car engineering was interrupted by a disagreement occurring at the shop counter.

"I saw you place something in your pocket."

"I saw you place something in your pocket," repeated a youth in an exaggerated mock Indian accent designed to humiliate the shop owner. His two friends found his disrespectful impression hilarious.

"I need you to pay for what you have placed in your pocket please?" said the shop keeper nervously.

Judd was concealed from the three thugs but he could see that the shop keeper was naturally a gentle sort, and although he was quite rightly standing his ground there was a distinct anxiety on his face.

"Why don't you search me then if you think I've got something? Come on I'd like to see you try?"

"That won't be necessary, if you don't want to pay for

what you have taken then at least please leave my shop and please don't come back here again."

"Ha, ha. I think he's trying to bar us lads." The thug switched to a more menacing tone. "Listen to me very carefully. I have told you that I have not lifted anything and I don't like being made out to be a liar. Now you have two choices, you can either search me or you can try and throw me out of your shop."

When the shopkeeper merely gulped and was obviously not prepared to carry out either request the yob raised his voice. "Well come on then tough guy, what is it to be?"

Just then Judd made his presence known by nonchalantly approaching the counter, placing the bottle of cola down and taking a pack of peppermint gum from the shelf before also placing that down on the counter.

"I think that is something like £1.93 sir, here is 2 quid. You can keep the change."

"Thank you sir," replied the shop keeper, a little relieved at Judd's presence.

"'Ere mate, can't you see that there is a queue here?"

Judd turned slowly to the surly youth and as Judd looked him squarely in the face he certainly wasn't impressed at his features that perfectly matched his bad attitude. His nose was very wide, covered in freckles and his hair was spiked in the main part but he had had two lines purposely shaved away to make a deliberate pattern appear. Judd noticed that there was another patch of hair missing on the other side of his head which had been caused by an ageing wound of some description. He stood a couple of inches shorter than Judd but he was built quite stockily.

Judd allowed himself to break the yob's stare momentarily in order to weigh up his two mates. One was black and one was mixed-race. They were both wearing baseball caps, so unlike their 'white trash' friend, Judd was unable to make out their hairstyles. They were both as ugly as each other, the black guy was skinny, with his clothes hanging off him, but the mixed-race guy was quite athletic looking.

"A queue you say? That's very interesting, because from what I could make out you weren't planning to buy anything. Now I understand that you have something that belongs to this nice shop owner. I'm not going to search you before you ask, just as you requested this gentleman to do. Not because I am afraid but because I don't want to dirty my hands, so instead I'm going to give *you* a choice. Now listen very carefully to this one time offer that I am going to give to you. By the time I have counted to five you will have either paid the gentleman the money for the goods that you have concealed, or you will have returned them to him and quietly walked away from the shop. You do not want to even contemplate the alternative action if you don't comply my friend. Your time starts now, 1."

"You've got some balls you know talking to me like that."

"2."

"Come on Treds, just give it back. This dude ain't worth it," said the skinny black guy.

"3…4"

"Okay, here," and with that Treds, obviously a street-name of some description, took a single can of cider from his jacket pocket and slammed it on the counter. Treds then turned to Judd. "This isn't over, mister."

"Whatever," sighed Judd, and with that the three goons left the shop.

"Thank you, sir," said the shop owner, relieved that the situation was seemingly over. "Do you want a bag for your goods?"

"No thanks. I can carry the bottle and just stick the gum in my pocket. I'm allowed to once it is paid for. Have they done this type of thing before?"

"Thankfully no, I haven't seen them in here before."

"Well if they come back don't hesitate to phone the police. I see you have CCTV installed so that's a good thing, but perhaps a baseball bat under the counter wouldn't go amiss?"

"I'm not a violent man, sir."

Judd smiled. "I get that. You'll be alright now mate."

"Thanks again."

"No problem."

When Judd stepped outside the shop the three troublemakers were waiting for him.

"Do you want something? A photo perhaps?" enquired Judd sarcastically.

"Yeah I want you," answered Treds and with that he pushed Judd in the chest.

"You don't want to do this boys, believe me."

"Are you fucking chicken or something? You are all mouth ain't you?"

"Well the odds are stacked a little unfairly; I mean there are three of you and only one of me."

Treds laughed. "Tough."

"Okay, I did warn you, you see I think that you guys need more than three of you for this to be a fair contest, but never mind aye. Some people just can't be told," and with that Judd placed his bottle of cola on the pavement, stood back up and promptly punched Treds in the face causing him to instantly stagger.

To be fair, Judd had seen other men hit the deck from one of his punches, but Treds had a bit of resilience about him and he flung himself at Judd, pushing him up against the shop window. The shop window was toughened, and although shook with the impact it fortunately didn't give way. Judd could see the other two goons move towards him so he initially got rid of Treds by kneeing him in the groin and then smashing him in the face once more, but this allowed enough time for the skinny black guy to throw a kick which connected with the side of Judd's leg, but it would take much more than that to topple Judd Stone.

Judd's adrenaline prevented him from feeling any significant pain from the kick and he was able to land a punch on the mixed-race chap before he got too close. The skinny guy had retreated ensuring that he was no longer in reach after striking his kick and shouted encouragement to his friend, "Go on Don, give it to him."

"Don't worry Slick, I intend to." Don was the best fighter of the three and he and Judd were exchanging blows, but Judd was clearly having the better of the fight. Judd noticed Slick approaching him again and he was able to smash him in the face halting his onslaught, but this allowed Don to earn a couple of extra slugs.

Judd fought back hard as rage surged through him and in three telling punches later Don had been knocked unconscious.

By this time Treds had made another attempt to get to Judd, but Judd simply gave him a one-two combination that obviously hurt the thug. Then Judd turned his attention to Slick and a flurry of punches soon had him pinned against the bright red letter box. Judd punched Slick repeatedly in the chest and the cracking of his skinny ribs sang into the cold air.

All this time William was watching from the car, helplessly unable to physically intervene and help his friend. William was desperate to get out of the car and assist in preventing the attack but his legs simply would not move. In truth he could see that Judd was more than adequately handling the episode without his help, but as Judd was busy hospitalising Slick, William witnessed Treds get up from the floor and pull something from his pocket. There was no mistake it was a knife.

The low sun reflected on the steel of the blade. Judd, emerged in the onslaught of Slick, didn't realise Treds was creeping up behind him armed with a knife. And by now Don was groggy but awake and crawling along the floor to make a grab for Judd's legs, but he still had some distance to go.

William managed to open the car door but looked on helplessly as Treds got nearer and nearer to Judd and the knife became closer into view. Any second now Judd was going to feel a knife enter his back.

William stared hard at the knife, focusing all his energy away from trying to move his legs and instead on the lethal weapon. Suddenly Treds was in disbelief as the knife seemed to gain a life of its own and freed itself from his grip.

William concentrated harder and harder and suddenly the knife flew up in the air, turned to face Treds and sliced the thug across the face before moving down his body and finding a final resting place deep in his thigh.

His face a bloody mess, Treds fell to the floor screaming. "I've been stabbed, I've been stabbed."

Judd turned away from Slick, who was relieved to be allowed to slide unchallenged down the smoothness of the letter box gripping his excruciatingly painful ribs. Don halted his attempt to reach Judd and all three men were compelled to look towards Treds to enquire what had caused his screams.

"How the fuck has that happened? This guy was nowhere near him," said a breathless Slick from a sitting position.

"Treds, you've stabbed yourself you dummy," said Don now getting to his feet.

"Okay guys," said Judd. "We can either continue to trade punches while your friend here bleeds to death or you can get him to a hospital."

The two men took position and then staggered towards their bleeding friend supplying Judd with his answer.

William, content that his intervention had been successful, slumped back in his seat and closed the car door.

Judd picked up the bottle of cola, got into the car and handed it to his friend.

"One bottle of cola mate, now I need to get you to the hospital, and those guys need to get that lowlife to a hospital too. It was thoughtless of me really not to mention that I was going there wasn't it? Is it too unkind of me not to give them a lift?" Judd gave a mischievous smile.

"I don't think they would expect you to under the circumstances, Judd."

"Perhaps you are right. What a stupid kid stabbing himself like that."

William glanced out of the car window and said nothing.

CHAPTER 41

Judd looked out of the window of his apartment and wasn't surprised to discover that it was raining. Again.

The rain had managed to hold off somewhat miraculously for the Olympic Games hosted in London, but by the end of 2012, the rainfall had been so eventful in Britain that the year would enter British weather history as one of the wettest on record.

Turning away from the depressing sight of the weather, Judd pointed the remote control at the TV causing the screen to flash into life.

Not long after, Judd had typically once again selected to view the sports news channel as he settled down onto his sofa.

The sports news was still full of the success of the London Olympics, both in terms of Great Britain's hosting of the tournament, and the surpassing achievements of the British athletes which were suitably aligned to the triumphant event.

Magnificently *Team GB*, as the athletes quickly became affectionaly known - complete with Stella McCartney designer sportswear, far exceeded expectations winning 65 medals in total, 18 more than the previous impressive and again unexpected achievement in Beijing in 2008. To have performed so well and to have accomplished what they had done on home soil had made the achievements of Team GB that little bit more extra special.

Overall Team GB finished an impressive third on the Medals table, behind athletic heavyweights USA and China. Of those 65 British medals, 19 were Bronze, 17 were silver and a whopping 29 were Gold - including an astonishing 8 in cycling events alone, where Team GB dominated on the road or in the velodrome thanks to some amazing performances including Bradley Wiggins, Victoria Pendleton, Laura Trott and Chris Hoy. In addition 4 golds were achieved in athletics and rowing respectively, with Jessica Ennis and Mo Farah particularly impressing in the former, and a further 3 gold medals were each achieved in the boxing ring and the equestrian.

Team GB and everything associated with the London Olympics had certainly played a huge part in making 2012 a memorable year. British success also exploded at the Paralympics, and Judd was able to make the short trip to Aldridge to see the main post box painted a gold colour in contrast to its usual red. This had been done in recognition of Ellie Simmonds' achievement of a Gold medal, the phenomenal paralympic swimmer who originated from the West Midlands town.

Another local success connected to the Olympics was having the Jamaican team hang out at Birmingham's Alexander Stadium to train for the event. Champion sprinter Usain Bolt and his sprinting buddy Yohan Blake loved Birmingham and the welcoming Brummies so much that they tweeted a massive thank you across the social network.

Largely due to the euphoria of the London Olympics, the unprecedented step of entering a Great British football team took place for both men and women teams. Football across Great Britain has always presented itself in individual form i.e. England, Scotland, Wales and

Northern Ireland, and in spite of the success of the Olympics many found it difficult to get into the mindset to be able to fully get behind a Great British soccer team.

Judd Stone, and much of the English nation, simply didn't share the same amount of dejection and disappointment at Team GB losing to South Korea in the Quarter Finals on penalties, as he did for the England football team, who also went out of the Quarter Finals on penalties to Italy in their respective competition the European Championships. It seems that the familiar curse of the penalty shoot-out to decide soccer matches for footballers of English origin was even to plague the Olympic Team. The England football team have certainly fell foul to this obstacle on a number of heartbreaking high-profile occasions, as Judd Stone and countless others Englanders knew only too well as they watched the realistic dream of achievement agonisingly slip away before their very eyes.

Although the London Olympics was undoubtedly a fantastic success inspiring many British people to become involved in 'unfashionable' sports, by enlarge football remains the primary national sport for the people of Great Britain. Yet football was never going to be considered a major player in the Olympics. It was the athletics, boxing, cycling, martial arts and swimming pool events that would draw most interest. In contrast, the England Football team being the sole British representative at the European Championships had a golden opportunity to further increase that 'British feel-good factor' of 2012, as had been achieved by the Olympics and the Queen's Diamond Jubilee celebrations. How? By winning the damn thing – an expectation that still ran high since 1966 when England had last won a major competition – the World Cup Finals - the only British team to ever do so. Alas, disappointingly in 2012 for the England football team it was not to be.

And it was this disappointment of English football that fuelled the sudden 'Breaking News' Story that would dominate the rest of the day's sports news.

Judd looked with interest at the pretty face of the sports news presenter on his TV screen as she revealed the details... *"We have some breaking news to report. It has just been confirmed by the Football Association that the current England football manager has resigned. The full details are still unknown at this early stage, but in an initial statement released only minutes ago, the main reasons being attributed to the decision is due to the lack of success that the England Football team has been able to achieve in relation to the success and achievements of Team GB and the London Olympics itself. The FA and now former manager are bitterly disappointed that in comparison to so many Olympic medals and related achievements being celebrated by the nation, the England football team have failed to reach the same high level of accomplishment and expectation in 2012 at the European Football Championships, particularly as this has also been the year of the Queen's Diamond Jubilee. In short, the England football team has failed to tap into the feel good factor of the nation. Therefore, the England team temporarily find themselves without a manager, however, the FA also go on to announce that they don't believe that the vacancy will be available for too long as they are keen to put an end to this situation and are already in talks to appoint a new manager."*

The pretty presenter paused for a moment and placed her index finger to her earpiece to signify that she was receiving some additional information. "...*Well these are quite extraordinary events occurring in the world of English football today... now I'm hearing that apparently the FA are indeed in talks as we speak with a possible successor and they are confident that a new manager will be appointed by the end of the week, if not today."*

As the presenter continued with the remarkable breaking story, a photo of the likely successor to become England manager was projected behind her. Judd couldn't believe it as he saw the photo of a well-known face appear, his blonde hair now thinning a little in comparison to the perm he once sported decades ago.

Judd stared bewilderingly at the photo of a man he

loathed with all his being, and whom he still felt shouldn't even be given air to breathe, let alone be given the England manager's job.

The presenter continued… *"It appears that the new appointment would be someone whom the majority of England fans would approve of, the people's choice so to speak. The man in question is a man who has had significant success of playing for England during his playing career and has also reached high accolades as both a player and manager for a selection of London and Midlands based clubs during his career. Yes, the imminent appointment of the England manager looks set to be Mr. Marlon Howell.*

CHAPTER 42

The elegant looking lady had never been to Sutton Coldfield before. Directed by the disembodied voice of her satellite navigation system, she had not long driven past her intended destination, but she had progressed further having spotted directions to the multi-storey car park of the Gracechurch Shopping Centre which should be ideal for parking her car.

Following her intended business in Sutton Coldfield today, she decided that she wouldn't mind indulging in a spot of retail therapy, and she recognised that the shopping centre was conveniently compact in scope and was home to some of her favourite stores such as House of Fraser and Marks and Spencers.

Once securing her Aston Martin car in the parking space, the outlay of the car park actually allowed her to walk through the M and S store as a route to her destination. Resisting the urge to browse there and then in the store, within five minutes or so she was at the gates of the impressive looking apartment block.

She fully expected to have to speak through the intercom to gain entry, though she anticipated that this could prove to be very difficult as she doubted that she was going to be made welcome by the man she was hoping to meet. It would most likely take some significant persuasion in order to gain entry, but fortunately there was a young couple entering the vicinity just before her, and they allowed her to follow them into the building unchallenged which negated the need to use the intercom.

She thought their actions quite foolish really, how could they be sure that they hadn't just let in a bogus salesman or worse still a suicide bomber? Apartment blocks such as this tended to have strict protocol not to allow unknown tailgaters into the building. But the couple, although clearly more interested in their playful flirting and one another, still had enough presence of mind to take a look at the lady behind them and they recognised how she oozed respectability with her expensive looking hair style, clothes and jewellery. Her face was immaculately and tastefully decorated in high-end make up, and it seemed a natural activity to allow her to enter the building.

Seconds later she was ringing the door bell of the apartment she had driven all this way to visit.

Using the power of his mind, without any involvement of his hands whatsoever, William Chamberlain had managed to glide his glass of milk within centimetres from his lips when the ring at the doorbell broke his concentration causing the glass to fall and spill milk over the glossy-finish of his dining table. Fortunately the glass didn't break.

Feeling irritated, he eventually managed to stand and stagger to his door using a zimmerframe, actually wondering if it would be worth the effort, as the person who had rung the bell could easily have left after assuming that no one was home considering the length of time it had taken him. But the visitor knew about William's Multiple Sclerosis and had prepared herself to wait patiently. Besides, she had heard the crash of the glass drop even through the sound barrier of the door, so she knew someone was in.

Eventually, William opened the door.

"Can I help you?" He said panting slightly.

"Hello. William, I presume? I am Crystal Stance, from the English Branch of the Institute of Noetic Science. We have spoken on the phone a few times. I do hope that I am not disturbing you? I heard a noise. Are you all right, Mr. Chamberlain?"

"I dropped a glass but there is no use crying over spilt milk as they say."

"Oh dear. Please, allow me to clean it up for you."

"To clean up the milk you are assuming that I am going to allow you to come in. I thought that I had made myself clear the last time you phoned me. I distinctly remember informing you that I had changed my mind about getting involved with you people."

"Please, Mr. Chamberlain; I have had a very long drive to get here which I hope gives you some idea of the importance I place in speaking with you. What you have told me so far is very intriguing. We could learn a lot from you and the intention is to try and understand what is happening so that we can put our findings to good use."

William thought hard for a moment. Crystal seemed very sincere, and to be honest he hadn't disliked her when they had spoken on the telephone. Seeing her in the flesh wasn't an altogether unpleasant experience either he discovered. He just wasn't fully convinced of what her true intentions were. He had suffered enough poking and prodding at various hospitals and neurological appointments over the years, he didn't want to start allowing himself to be experimented on now for some mumbo-jumbo organisation.

"You have 15 minutes and that includes the time it takes to clean up my milk and to make yourself a drink. I have tea or coffee."

"Thank you, Mr. Chamberlain. You are a perfect gentleman."

William allowed himself a smile as Crystal entered his

home, gently closing the door behind her. "Flattery won't help you in whatever your quest is Ms. Stance."

"Mrs. Stance, but please call me Crystal."

Unexpectedly, William instantly felt his heart sink when he discovered Crystal was married.

"Mrs. Stance. Married then?"

"Widowed actually. My husband died about five years ago, a heart attack which occurred right out of the blue."

"I'm sorry to hear that, Crystal."

"Thank you. I have some comfort knowing that he is happy where he is."

"How do you know? Sorry that was insensitive of me. Please sit down."

"I'll clean your spilt milk up first; the clock is ticking after all. Is there a cloth I can use? And I know he is happy because he has told me so."

"Told you?"

"Yes. It is very difficult for me to receive a reading for myself, but he managed to let me know on just that one occasion. It was enough to reassure me and let me know he was at peace."

"You are a medium?"

"Well this dress is a size 16, does that equate to a medium or large?"

William laughed. He liked this woman but he wasn't altogether convinced with what she was telling him. In spite of his own ability to perform acts of telekinesis, his mind remained relatively closed to matters such as mediums and psychics, his cynicism fuelled by his many years on the police force where the natural instinct is to be mistrusting of everything and everyone.

"There is a cloth on the side in the kitchen, you can use that and put the kettle on for yourself while you are in there."

"Thank you William, though I'll pass on the drink if I only have 15 minutes of your time. I can hopefully use the small window of time I have more constructively." Crystal guessed that there would be a couple of coffee bars in the shopping precinct on her way back to the car any how.

"As you wish."

Crystal found the cloth and efficiently cleaned up the milk. Her seemingly down to Earth nature impressed William; although she clearly wasn't short of money, Crystal hadn't given a second thought to getting splashes of milk on her expensive designer dress.

They finally both sat down, William on his orthopaedic chair and Crystal on the adjacent sofa.

"So Crystal, you claim to be a psychic? I won't be caught out by describing you as a medium again. Actually, are mediums and psychics two different things?"

Crystal couldn't help but notice that William's voice failed at times, but it was possible to hold a conversation with him. "Slightly different I suppose, but actually I have traits of both. I am able to contact people who have passed over and I am able to predict certain events that will occur. I get flashes of images, sometimes quite intrusively, some make sense and some don't, and before you ask no I can't predict next week's winning lottery numbers, it doesn't quite work like that."

"So why is someone who claims to have contact with the spirit world working in the field of science? I thought that spirituality and science held opposing theories on things."

"Well I believe that I am certainly more spiritual than scientific."

"Then why do you study science?"

"If something can be disproven or proven by science then fine, I accept that. But anything that can't be disproven or proven by science clearly opens the door to the spiritual world. There does not have to be a scientific explanation for everything. I'm content when science can only suggest that something must be spiritual."

"A good point well made. So you believe that the power of the mind for example can lend itself to a spiritual existence rather than a scientific one?"

"Science versus spirituality, it is the age old argument, William. But we get so hung up on terminology it can make us distort the truth. For example the word 'experiment'. Using the word experiment we tend to think of a scientific episode with a Bunsen burner or nuclear energy perhaps, however what about conducting an experiment in order to prove a spiritual theory?"

"How do you mean?

Crystal recognised that William was an intelligent man and she admired how he refused to allow the breaks and croaks in his voice to prevent him from having the appetite and passion to engage in inquisitive conversation. "When our organisation was initially set up by Astronauts in California, the early experiments centred around exploring the power of the human mind and its capabilities. It was discovered that when focussed correctly the human mind had the ability to tangibly interfere and manipulate physical mass. From the information that you have revealed to me over the phone, you should have no difficulty in understanding this concept."

"As I sit here before you today, I know better than most what the human mind can and can't do, but to understand it is an entirely different matter."

"Mr. Chamberlain, I'm much more interested in talking about you. We have had some very interesting conversations over the phone, and the information that you have provided me with regarding your experiences has compelled me to come and meet with you."

"And if you recall I told you at the end of our last conversation that I regretted getting in touch with you. I should have kept what I can do to myself."

"But why are you so afraid of sharing this amazing knowledge of your abilities?"

"Well for one reason, at the moment I am still considered to be a very creditable police detective. If the lads at the nick knew I'd been phoning you, claiming to move things with my mind, I'd be a laughing stock. They would think the MS had finally affected my faculties."

"People often mock what they do not understand, but I can assure you that I can promise strict confidentiality."

"I'm sorry; I consider it too risky I'm afraid. There are always leaks in any organisation, no matter how water-tight they may think they are. Most people have their price and there is always some rat willing to release information for their own personal gain. I've come across it many times during my police career, very rarely is anyone infallible. History tells us that there have been leaks right at the very top of anything that you wish to name, so I don't buy this confidentiality thing. Everyone has their price."

Crystal seemed genuinely offended at William's words, interpreting them as being directed at her. "Not me Mr Chamberlain, I can assure you that I don't have a price."

William felt himself redden. "I didn't mean you personally Crystal, just someone at your organisation. It happens."

Crystal quickly slipped back to her usual calmer demeanour. "And would it be so terrible if the world did know what you could do? You have informed me that you can move objects with your mind, and switch on lights, television sets or radios. This is remarkable evidence."

"Evidence for whose benefit, Crystal? What do you suggest I do, go on TV and give some sort of magical display of my abilities like a second-rate cabaret performer?"

"No of course not. Look William, it is already a proven phenomenon, regardless of what many ignorant people may think, that the human mind has the power when focussed correctly to interfere with and manipulate physical mass. I have already told you that at the very birth of our organisation in California such experiments were conducted to prove that this can happen. What makes your case so intriguing is the fact that whilst your Multiple Sclerosis is affecting your physical abilities, the power of your mind over matter is increasing; I want to learn and understand more about why this can happen. Just think William, if we could understand how your brain is making this happen and reverse the techniques, we may be able to discover a way to make the messages to your limbs improve."

"What find a cure for MS? That is a bold aspiration."

"But surely not impossible. Once the greatest minds on Earth believed that the world was flat and if we were to sail to the edge we would surely fall off, but eventually it was proven that we are a revolving sphere. All movements to discovering the truth can initially appear ridiculous."

"Let me tell you a little bit about MS. It is caused as a result of damage to myelin, which is a protective sheath that surrounds the nerve fibres of the central nervous system. It is this damage to the myelin that interferes with messages that the brain sends to parts of the body, therefore the concept of using the mind to move limbs becomes impossible for a sufferer of MS. If I could do it Crystal, believe me I would."

"I'm sorry William, I do not wish to claim that I can necessarily find a cure for MS, but in spite of the messages from your brain not reaching parts of your body, you are still able to significantly project some form of mind control outside of your existence and I would like to understand why. You have a very fascinating brain."

"Nice of you to say so, I suppose. But ok, answer me this. Are my actions something scientific or something spiritual?"

"That's what I would like to try and discover. Maybe they are both? Tell me, have you ever worried about something that you were sure was destined to happen but the awful event never actually materialised in spite of its probability? It's difficult to prove, but I believe it is the energy generated from those thoughts that prevents the fear from becoming a reality."

William thought for a moment and it was true that he

had known certain events not to turn out as bad as he once feared, but he just put it down to luck rather than any kind of intervention from energy.

"Well Crystal, there are some things in my life that create a whole lot of energy and they have not materialised as they should."

"Explain further please."

"I know that a serial killer is walking free. I know that there is a religious cult existing not too far from these parts that have murderous blood on their hands. Believe me, I have generated much energy to try and bring them to justice but to no avail."

"The point is it has to be positive energy, William. I am sure it is very difficult not to be angry when you see injustices in your line of work, but the studies also show how anger is not generally an emotion that can gain a positive outcome."

"But when I am angry I am able to move things. I prevented my colleague from being killed recently by using the power of my mind, and at the time I was very angry."

"A bit like the Incredible Hulk? I Hope you are not going to turn green and all scary on me, William?"

William allowed himself a smile.

"Seriously William, you must have discovered some way of channelling your anger to move objects, something I would like to discover more about, but your anger does not appear to be working as a force to make things happen on a spiritual level, like positive mind energy could. Even pop stars are questioning these things now?"

"How do you mean?"

"George Michael nearly died in 2011 due to an acute strain of pneumonia with complications, and he knew that he had many fans wishing him to get well and even those who were not ordinarily of a religious persuasion began to pray for him. Mr. Michael received the best medical care he could have wished for; he fell ill in Austria which ensured that he was fortunately able to benefit from the wonderful specialist medical assistance that is available there. Now what's interesting is that George Michael literally asks the question in song: was it science that saved him or the positive collective force of his fans praying for him? He sang the song at the Olympic closing ceremony you may recall?"

"A unified mass of positive energy caused by a whole bunch of people hoping he gets well?"

"Exactly. Mass meditation, mass prayer or any positive force of collective mind energy can make things happen. I'm convinced of it."

"Interesting. So not necessarily an answer from God?"

"I would never rule it out but not necessarily."

William began to reflect on the conversation that he had just had with Crystal. He liked her and much of what she had said actually made sense to him, but he knew that he remained angry for the injustices experienced over the years and he felt he had every right to remain angry. Anger was not an emotion that he wanted to compromise. William was determined to get even with Gareth Banks, Eli Zane and Jaden Rivers. He was confident that these powers that he possessed in his mind could be used to bring all three of these lunatics to justice, he just hadn't figured out a way how to yet.

What if he allowed Crystal to study him? Allowed her to place wires and electrodes all over his head and body to understand how his brain worked? Could she really stumble upon a way to assist the symptoms of MS or even eradicate them? He felt it unlikely and he feared that her getting to know how his brain operated would more likely hinder his plans rather than help him. She would never condone acts of violence or revenge, she was too damn nice. If she were to tap into his psyche she could damage any hope he had of putting his powers to the demise of these individuals.

Crystal Stance appeared to be a lovely woman, but that signalled that she was a do-gooder and she wouldn't allow his mind to be put to the use he intended it to. If he allowed her to get too close she would surely prevent things from happening. What if she blocked his energy to seek revenge? What if she began to understand what he wanted to achieve? It was a risk he was not willing to take.

He looked up at Crystal and stared straight into her eyes. They were beautiful eyes; the colour of sapphires complemented by tastefully applied eye shadow. True there were a few wrinkles and a slight bagginess under her eyes whispering a sign of her age, but she was still a very attractive woman.

However in spite of all this, William knew what he had to do. He focussed hard. Even more than when he had intervened in the fight that Judd had experienced. Soon she was under his spell.

Without another word, Crystal got up from the sofa, walked out of William's flat, walked through the parade of shops and totally ignored the usual pull of her favourite stores.

People stared at her; the woman seemed to be in some sort of a trance.

She continued obliviously to the pay station in the car park, entered her ticket, opened her purse and sorted the exact change of £2.10 to pay the car parking fee. She collected her ticket, collected her car and drove away from Sutton Coldfield.

An hour later she woke out of her trance as she travelled along the M40 towards her North London home.

How did I get here? She thought. Then she smiled after her initial bewilderment. *Controlling other people's minds? Performing acts beyond the power of hypnosis it seems? Mr. Chamberlain you are indeed a very interesting specimen.*

CHAPTER 43

"I got here as quickly as I could."

"Big fuss about nothing, Judd," croaked William, his voice noticeably shaky and only just achieving audibility. "I shouldn't even be here."

"We all need to accept a little help sometimes, Boss" said Sab, who had arrived at the hospital approximately twenty minutes earlier than Judd.

"What happened?" enquired Judd.

"He fell. Hurt his back and hip. We are waiting for the results of the x-rays."

"I am here you know, I can speak for myself," said William churlishly.

"Yeah, we know, but I knew I'd get a proper answer from Sab. You never admit when you need help, you deceiving stubborn old git."

"Well, I phoned Sab didn't I?"

"And then chastised me for phoning for an ambulance!"

"Sab did the right thing," said Judd. "Are you in any pain, William?"

"A little."

"A lot you mean. Hey, if the regular medication isn't

helping, William, I could always sneak you in some of the exotic substances that have been brought in during the recent drug raids."

"Don't tempt me. Not for the pain but to blot out yours and Sab's bloody do-gooding. Anyway, the only drug I need right now is caffeine."

"That's a good idea. Judd, will you help me carry the coffee back?"

"Going off to talk about me are you?"

"Don't flatter yourself, big guy," said Judd. "Sab hasn't got three hands you fool."

William just grunted.

Once out of William's earshot, Sab sparked up the conversation with Judd. "Seriously Judd, I am worried about him. As long as he is not hurt too badly I think the fall may have been a blessing in disguise."

"How do you mean?"

"The hospital staff had a discreet chat with me, and they can't understand how he is managing to cope living on his own. They suggested it may be a good idea to keep him in here for a few days in order to assess his needs in greater detail."

"You know how independent he is, Sab. It breaks my heart seeing him the way he is sometimes, but as long as he has some independence half the battle is won in his eyes. Sometimes to get around at home he has to abandon his zimmerframe and crawl around on all fours, you have to admire him really."

"I know what you mean but he could be putting himself in danger when left alone. What are the chances of getting him to agree to stay here just for a few days do you reckon?"

"Honestly? You'd have more chance of raising the Titanic."

"I thought as much. Oh well, at least he will be in for the night; they need to be certain of his x-rays and the impact of his injuries."

"They won't discharge him if it isn't safe to do so, Sab. Try not to worry."

It broke Sab's heart watching William drink his coffee. He even struggled to hold the specially designed mug. Nevertheless he managed, and Sab understood that William needed to be allowed to do things for himself; if his independence was taken away from him the man would consider himself to be finished. The irony was of course that if she and Judd had not been present, William would have coped a lot better by using the power of his mind to manoeuvre the cup to his lips. While they were with him he had to cope a lot more conventionally for appearances sake.

"Haven't you two got anything better to do than spend a night in a hospital with me?"

"I'm at least staying until they provide us with the results of the x-rays," said Sab firmly. "Besides, all I was going to do was watch the open and closing Olympic ceremonies again, I'm so glad I recorded them. I can't believe how good they were."

"George Michael played didn't he?"

"At the closing ceremony yes, he looked really well considering his illness last year. I didn't realise you were a George Michael fan, Guv?"

"I'm not particularly, but my sister Tilda will have watched his performance over and over again. She has loved George Michael since the days of Wham! So how come he has recovered so well? Was it science that saved him? He had the best treatment available apparently, in Austria."

"I haven't thought about it, but yeah, I guess him falling ill in Austria was quite fortunate considering the science and medication that was available to him out there."

"Not the power of prayer then? He had a lot of folk praying for him, you know?"

"Well, I guess that could have helped also. Who knows?"

"Yeah, who knows," smiled William, his sergeant totally oblivious to his gauging interest. In his mind, William had debated the concept of science versus spirituality since the seed had been sown at his meeting with Crystal Stance.

"I preferred the opening ceremony I think," said Judd. "Anything that involves the Beatles has got to be good and Macca performed 'Hey Jude' which always gets a crowd going."

"Are you forgetting the 'Imagine' sequence in the closing ceremony where those kids made John Lennon's face appear?"

"Oh yes, shame on me for forgetting that, Sab. I guess I just homed in on the live acts. It saddens me that Lennon couldn't appear in person. It is a shame that the world has been robbed of his talent, I mean he wasn't even part of Live Aid and stuff since the mid eighties."

"Would he have played the jubilee concert this year?" enquired Sab, warming to the discussion of music. She knew Judd was a big Beatles fan and in particular his admiration for Lennon.

"It's hard to say. Would Lennon have mellowed in his old age? He sent back his MBE remember and he was always pretty anti-establishment and outspoken. Would we have ever seen Sir John Lennon like we have seen Sir Paul McCartney, who of course did play at the jubilee concert? Even if Lennon had been offered a knighthood would he have accepted it? If George Harrison was still alive would the Beatles have reformed for the patriotic events of 2012? I'd like to think they would have, but perhaps for some strange reason unknown to me it was meant to be this way. It's hard to understand why though."

The conversation was interrupted when a nurse appeared through the doorway. Judd noticed how her uniform clung to her stunning figure like a second skin.

She was of mixed-race and had gorgeous chocolate-coloured eyes. Her hair was shiny and all at once, Judd totally understood the reference to a *dusky jewel* in the Doors' song.

"I'm pleased to inform you, Mr. Chamberlain, that your x-ray results do not show any signs of serious damage. You'll feel a bit sore for a few days but no bones are broken."

"Well that's a relief," said Sab.

"See, I told you there was nothing wrong," snapped William.

"It is wise to keep you in for observation, Mr. Chamberlain, at least for tonight. The neurologist would like a chat with you in the morning, just to touch base with how your MS is affecting you. The fact that it most likely led to your fall causes us some concern."

"I just lost my footing that's all, it could happen to anyone."

The nurse smiled the warmest of smiles, which wasn't lost on Judd even though it wasn't directed at him. "Of course Mr. Chamberlain, still you may as well use the time to rest over the next few hours or so. Let us spoil you; I'm sure you deserve it."

"Come on then Sab," said Judd. "That's our cue to leave and grab a bottle of red whilst we watch the ceremonies all over again. We'll leave grumpy alone now we know he'll live and is being well looked after."

"That sounds like a good idea, Judd. Is it okay with you, William? Will you be okay?"

"Sab, I insist you leave. You kids have fun while you can. I'll be out of here soon enough to crack the whip at you two again."

The nurse named Brooke smiled her warm smile once more. Judd and Sab bid farewell to their boss, and a few minutes later, William was alone in his hospital room.

What he hadn't let on to his two friends was how scared he was. His lack of mobility had caused him to fall and his limbs were gradually losing their dexterity. He had always remained positive about his condition but for the first time he felt a little vulnerable. He knew that he could use the powers of his mind to move things, to assist him with eating and drinking, but a fall could come from nowhere. He was also concerned of the perception back at the station; would the fall and his physical difficulties be interpreted that he couldn't do his job effectively anymore? He felt very exposed.

Suddenly he was no longer alone as a figure entered the room.

The sight of the figure unnerved him, so much so he attempted to move but his limbs and bones failed to respond due to a combination of the soreness caused by his fall, the acute state of his MS, and perhaps a form of paralysis caused by fear.

At first William couldn't see the intruder's face. The intruder was wearing a hoodie with the string pulled tight to conceal his features. In spite of this, the wearing of the tightly pulled hood simply confirmed to William who the intruder was and a pang of terror shot through his gut. In fact he was beginning to feel quite nauseous.

The intruder closed the door gently behind him, and although William felt very much alone and very much trapped, William refrained from pressing the button to call for a nurse.

His pride wouldn't allow a nurse to come to his aid in such a circumstance, but in the main he did not want a nurse to have to be subjected to the piece of evil scum that stood before him. William knew this man was capable of doing terrible things, and in particular to women.

The intruder slithered forward before freezing like a statue. He seemed content to simply stand still for now, his little beady eyes now visible through the hood that clung to his bony face.

William decided to speak first, refusing to be intimidated in spite of his lack of physical ability.

"What do you want, Banks?" croaked William, his voice failing slightly.

Without breaking his stance, the statue spoke. "Speak up William, I didn't quite get that."

William didn't oblige, so Banks continued.

"I thought I'd come and see you in hospital. I'm quite a considerate guy in reality you see. You and that psycho Stone had me all wrong you know."

"It's not Judd that is the psycho. It's you."

"Tut, tut, tut. Now that's not very nice. I've come all this way to see you in hospital and you insult me?"

"You've only come in the hope to finish me off." William struggled to get the words out and spoke them with a cough.

"Well, well, well, I guess they will make a detective of you yet William, unlike that idiot Stone, there is no hope for him. Except your little detective work will sadly never see the light of day, how ironic is that William? You are quite correct, I have come to finish you off, but there is no rush. I wanted to laugh at you first.

"Seeing you so helpless in hospital is very amusing, but don't worry, I will soon put you out of your misery. The way we do when we attempt to rescue a bird following an attack by a cat, but ultimately we have to resign ourselves to smashing it to smithereens with a shovel to avoid an otherwise long and painful death. Or when we stamp on a spider that has had all of his eight legs pulled off. I love doing that, what is there left for it to do once it is just lying there like a useless raisin?

"In truth though William, I am a little disappointed; my entertainment is not quite complete. I was hoping that you would have a plethora of tubes coming out of your fat body, or you'd be attached to a heart machine or something. That way I could simply walk over and cut a tube or unplug the machine, you know like they sometimes do in the movies. It would have been fun watching you agonisingly slip away as you gasp for breath like a salmon flapping on the river bank desperate to get back into the water. So what I'll have to do is resort to this, my Plan B, which of course you know is usually my plan A."

William's stomach churned as he saw Banks unveil a knife from his hoodie pocket. The blade gleamed as the lights of the ceiling caught its reflection in the silvery metal.

Banks began to prowl closer to William's hospital bed.

William needed to think quickly or he was going to be sliced open by this psycho.

"If you are going to kill me at least have the audacity to remove your hoodie so I can clearly look into your eyes as you do the act. Or are you too much of a coward to do so?"

Banks hesitated for a moment and then began to laugh. "Not the last request I thought you would ask for, but okay if that's what you want. I'm not an unreasonable man and I note there are no CCTV cameras in this particular room." Banks slowly released the cord from his hood and allowed it to fall behind his head, revealing his blonde hair that was cut shorter than William recalled, yet still had the look of sweat and flattening that occurred when someone removed an item of headwear after a period of time.

Banks moved closer to the bed and stood over William, taking his time, toying with his victim, allowing the blade to move slowly over William's body without yet touching flesh.

By indulging himself Banks failed to connect with William's eyes.

"Another request if I may?"

Banks became agitated and held the blade straight at William's throat.

"Quickly."

"Tell me why you killed those three girls."

"They were a mockery of the word of the Lord Jesus Christ. Selling their bodies like they did showed they were helpless sinners. They were a symbol of evil. I had to save them. They were just like my mother; she gave herself so freely to that imposter, that man of the cloth. He portrayed himself as a symbol of our God in Heaven, yet he was a charlatan. He was not fit to represent God."

William knew his time was short and he desperately needed Banks to look into his eyes, maybe just a couple of seconds would do it and then he could get the maniac to shove his own knife into himself.

But then William's genius made an appearance, just as it had done so many times before when solving those seemingly helpless crime cases in the past.

The words Banks had said so disrespectfully about Judd had angered William. What Banks had done to those poor girls had angered him too. The parallels of what Banks had done to his victims and what Zane and Rivers had done to Tilda angered him. Suddenly he wasn't afraid anymore, and he instantly thought of a way to use this piece of scum that stood before him in order to serve his own purpose.

Getting him to turn the knife on himself was not the answer.

"I agree Gareth, imposters to God should be punished and I know of two very significant imposters to God."

Banks looked genuinely intrigued, but puzzled. "What are you talking about Chamberlain? I will slit your throat in an instant if you are going to mess me about."

William knew that he probably only had one chance to get this right. "Well look into my eyes then you fucking coward," whispered William.

Banks obliged. William could sense that the psychopath was going to drive the knife into his heart at the same time, but in a split second their eyes locked and it was just long enough. William had him in control.

"Gareth Banks, you will do exactly as I say, do you understand me?"

Banks nodded obediently before speaking in a monotone.

"Imposters to God. Imposters to the Lord. They need to be punished…"

William was struggling to project his words but he was determined to give Banks the instructions that would make everything alright.

He was convinced he could pull it off; he had already proved to himself that he could control minds, just like he had when he engineered Crystal Stance to leave his flat. But could he achieve what he intended on such a grand scale?

He was going to try.

Through Gareth Banks, William was going to ensure that Eli Zane and Jaden Rivers were going to pay for what they had done to his sister.

And what's more he would ensure that his dear friend, Detective Inspector Judd Stone would come up smelling of roses. He was sure of it.

And he would ensure that this piece of scum who stood before him would finally be brought to justice.

William managed a smile as he ordered his instructions to the helpless killer.

"…There are two clear imposters to God and they make a mockery of the word of his son, the Lord Jesus Christ. Here is what you must do…"

CHAPTER 44

Earlier that day

The two men had met before.

Never as friends exactly, but as a partnership of shared interests.

A wide grin spread across the wide unattractive face before the disproportioned mouth released its words, "He is a sitting duck, I tell you. You can get to him easily."

"I'd rather get Stone," said Banks.

"But that is an altogether more difficult proposition. The man is as crazy as you are, besides there are better ways to hurt Stone, and I achieved that some years back when I informed a certain Mr. Delroy Whitton of the whereabouts of Stone's late wife Frankie.

"Whitton killed her, breaking poor Stone's heart forever. Keeping him afloat in a life of torment is so satisfying. You see with a man like Stone, it is better to let him live and instead hurt the ones he loves. It's much more fun and William Chamberlain falls right into that category. Stone loves that fat waste of space like a big brother, and taking him out of the picture will serve nicely to apply some further mental torture to the Neanderthal.

It's perfect."

"Makes sense I suppose. Obviously Chamberlain isn't on my Christmas card list and I would like my revenge for the part he played in trying to put me away. Sabita Mistry remains accountable for her sinful actions too."

"She can keep until another day. You have bigger fish to fry and today you need to focus on getting to Chamberlain. He is ready and waiting for you in a hospital bed. It'll be so easy for you. Besides, the way his health is these days you'd be doing the fat old dog a favour, you can put him out of his misery."

"And it would mess with Stone's head wouldn't it?" grinned Banks.

"Look, you know how amusing it can be to tease Stone. I gave you Haddock's daughter on a plate but for once you resisted the kill. You soon worked out that you could have more fun using her as an asset to get at Stone. His emotions and anger are so charged you can play him like a fiddle. Just wind him up and watch him go. It can be truly hilarious at times."

"So in which ward exactly will I find DCI Chamberlain?"

CHAPTER 45

A hypnotist is trained to specialise in the ability to influence how people think. Intelligence agencies the world over have created extensive programmes in attempts to perfect mind control. Going back as far as 1950s USA, heavy experimentation with mind control took place. Vehicles such as hallucinogenic drugs were used, such as LSD, and long before the Beatles and other rock stars of the 1960s made it fashionable. Researchers have since claimed to have uncovered evidence that states not much later programmes were put in place to formulate individuals to perform like robots - in order to kill.

William Chamberlain had never trained as a hypnotist and in spite of his police work had never even flirted with mind control techniques. Yet as his Multiple Sclerosis took hold of him, somehow he increasingly possessed the natural ability to control the minds of others, an extension of the powers of his own mind escalating from his telekinetic powers. If only they knew he would be the envy of every orchestrator of brainwashing programmes that have ever existed.

"This is the place, pull up just a little past the opening to the drive so that your car is sheltered by the foliage of the trees. Keep the meter running for as long as it takes."

"Sure thing."

The taxi driver named Clint had attempted to drum up conversation with the creepy little guy he had picked up at Kidderminster Train Station early that morning, but Gareth Banks had remained aloof throughout the journey, only speaking when necessary which was to supply the address of where they were destined and the occasional offer of a direction.

Clint had been in the taxi business for quite some time yet he struggled to recall when he had picked up such an intimidating passenger. The address that he had been directed too didn't exactly fill his heart with joy either. Clint detected something eerie about the property, as if it held many secrets. Still, at least it seemed his unfriendly punter was going to pay him well for the fare.

Banks vacated the car and in a trance-like state walked up the driveway of the big old house. There were people about him cultivating the land and engaging in various modes of work, which allowed a couple of men to approach him blocking his path before he could reach the door.

"What do you want here, stranger?"

"I want to join your family. I want to join the Adonijah Truthsters. I believe that the end of the world is upon us and I realise that to be saved I need to be a part of your family and follow the direction of the prophet known as Eli Zane. I have no place in the outside world; instead I need to be a part of your world."

The two men looked at one another, slightly cynical of the stranger's words. How could they be sure that he was being genuine? But any recruitment to the group was not their decision, and if there was the slightest glimmer that someone was in need surely they shouldn't turn him away.

"Follow us, we will take you to meet Eli and he can decide if you should join us."

"Thank you."

The front door was unlocked, a necessary requirement considering the amount of Adonijah Truthsters who needed to enter or vacate the house throughout the day. On entering the house the two men led Banks into the second room on the left, where a large man was sitting in a large chair, reading a Bible.

"Excuse us Eli, we have a visitor. This man says he wants to join the Adonijah Truthsters and he believes that you are the chosen one to lead us."

"Is that so," rolled the deep voice of the American. Eli weighed up the stranger who stood before him. His eyes appeared a little glazed but he had no real reason to doubt the stranger's intentions. He had come alone after all and it was difficult for a man like Eli to be unresponsive to having his ego boosted.

"Well come in friend, let's talk." Eli placed a book mark into his Bible and placed it on the table next to him, indicating that Gareth could have his full attention.

"Do you need us to stay with you, Eli?" enquired one of the men.

"Not at all Dave, go and inform Jaden that we have a visitor. I think he would like to meet him."

Jaden. The second imposter.

A slight uneasiness registered with Eli in that the Adonijah Truthsters were usually recruited by Jaden homing in on the vulnerable members of society, but here was a stranger who had come of his own free will and who seemed to understand their purpose.

One reason for Eli not to feel threatened by the stranger however, was that he always kept a pistol close by, and it hadn't gone unnoticed by Banks that the Bible had been placed next to it in easy reach of the cult leader.

"Please take a seat. What is your name?"

Banks sat down in a seat directly opposite Eli.

"My name is Gareth; it is a privilege to meet you, Eli. I know that the end of the world is upon us and you are the only true prophet to lead us through the valley of death."

"Amen to that, Gareth. I'm just a little intrigued how you know so much about me and what our purpose is here at the Adonijah Truthsters."

Gareth leaned forward, his glazed eyes connecting with Eli's. "I was told by God, Eli. God came to me in the night and told me to follow you. I am young and strong, I can help you on the land, and I could be a great asset to you."

Eli ran his hand over his chin, contemplating what Gareth had said to him. The man seemed to deliver his words in a very even pattern, almost robotic, but still he seemed genuine. And with Eli's ego forever readily poised for massaging, of course it made perfect sense that God would guide followers to him.

"Please Eli, may I read a passage to you from your Bible. It would give me enormous satisfaction."

Eli thought about the request. It was his Bible and nobody else ever usually read from it. But why not?

"Okay Gareth, I look forward to hearing you read."

Eli reached out to his right, taking the book from the table in his right hand and leaving the gun resting nearby. Gareth had calculated that with his right hand occupied, Eli would be unable to reach for the gun with his left hand with any amount of ease, preventing Eli from being able to defend himself in time.

With a broad smile across his wide face, Eli offered the Bible towards Gareth. "Here you go, son."

It was enough time for Gareth Banks to make his move. The outstretched hand holding the Bible had no time to react as Gareth pulled a knife from the inside of his boot and stuck it straight into Eli's throat spearing his Adam's apple like a skewer. Eli's grin was replaced by an expression of desperation as blood spilled from his mouth. He dropped the Bible and his instant reaction was to bring both hands to his throat. The evil man who had spoken so many words in his life, providing false interpretation and direction from the Bible, manipulating his words to deceive his susceptible followers was finally silenced. He could speak no more. He offered an inaudible gurgle before slumping in his chair.

Banks knew that the big man had remained alive just long enough to hear his message. "Tilda sends her love." The big man's eyes widened at these words just before he took his final breath.

Banks looked at the big man with no flicker of emotion. He wiped his nose with his sleeve before picking up the gun and putting it in his pocket. This was a bonus; he hadn't expected to come across a gun. Now he had an extra means of attack to assist him in addition to his expert use of the knife.

Staring at the warm corpse with the frozen look of wide-eyed terror perfectly captured on his victim's face, Banks decided that there was one final act required in order to make his mission regarding Eli Zane complete. He pulled a knife from his other boot and slit the sides of the cult leader's mouth.

Banks had given Eli Zane a *Chelsea Smile*.

The slaying of Eli Zane had been accomplished.

There are two imposters. One down, one to go.

Gareth Banks turned his back on his dead victim with the intention of leaving the room when a figure appeared in the doorway. The man instantly noticed Eli's dead body with a knife sticking from his throat and an insane bloody grin spread across his face. The bloody scene seemed like a surreal film set.

"What have you done? Do you *know* what you have done?"

"Yes, I know. Jaden Rivers, I presume?"

In a fit of rage, Jaden threw himself at the stranger who had killed his mentor grabbing him around the neck. He pressed hard and Gareth was close to losing consciousness. Although he had the gun, Gareth still had a knife in his hand and as he was falling to the floor, ironically only being held aloft by the grip on his throat by Jaden, he managed to drive his weapon of choice into Jaden's leg.

Reactively, Jaden released his grip as he reached for the wound in his leg. The knife was still in Banks' hand and he went to stab Jaden a second time, but Jaden sensed what was about to happen and turned his back on Banks to make for the door. The injury to Jaden's leg prevented him from excelling to the speed required and Banks' knife settled sweetly into the middle of Jaden's back causing him to fall like a pack of cards.

Banks could hear activity and voices in the hallway and he decided it was time to leave. He left the knife sticking out of Jaden's back and as he reached the doorway he turned and took one final look at Jaden. He was groaning but moving. Not his legs however, they seemed to have no movement at all, but the cult member was sliding his torso across the floor using the power of his arms, leaving a slippery trail of blood behind him. He looked up at Banks; agonising pain etched across his face, but at the same time strong elements of desperation and determination to *chase* after his attacker.

Jaden Rivers was still alive.

Banks pulled the gun from his pocket and cocked the barrel aiming it at Jaden, determined to finish off the second imposter. Banks fired his shot.

But something unlikely happened. Jaden could be forgiven for believing it to be a miracle. Somehow, Banks had missed his target.

Hearing the gunshot, cult members began to rush towards the room. Banks realised that even with his weaponry he would be outnumbered, and he made a run out of the house and down the driveway.

Some had given chase to Gareth whilst others had ran into the room to somehow deal with the massacre that greeted them. Even as he reached the end of the long driveway, Banks could hear a woman shriek, "Call an ambulance. He is still alive. Jaden is still alive."

Banks was pleased to see that the taxi was still waiting for him and he flung himself onto the back seat and ordered Clint to drive away at high speed.

As the taxi sped away from the scene, Banks looked out of the rear window to see that a hoard of Adonijah Truthsters had been hot on his heels, and even a couple of the younger ones had continued to run in an attempt to reach the taxi. Inevitably the vehicle pulled away leaving Banks' pursuers helplessly stranded.

Clint was a little shaken at having his taxi chased like that and shared his thoughts with Gareth. "Blimey mate, looks like you've upset a few people in there. Where are we off to now? I don't want any more trouble."

At first Gareth Banks didn't reply to the taxi driver. The killer's mind was whirring; he was getting recollections of visiting William Chamberlain in hospital. Had Chamberlain now agreed that he had been right to kill those prostitutes last year? He was getting visions of his father, the fake priest. He knew he needed to kill two imposters to God.

Banks was confused.

The grip on his throat from Jaden had blocked some levels of oxygen reaching his brain and interfered with the mind control imposed on him by William.

And his own psychotic mind that needed no help from anyone to fester was beginning to kick in.

The mind of Gareth Banks became a spiral of confusion, compliance and deathly intent.

Two imposters. I've killed Eli Zane. Jaden Rivers is alive. Two imposters? One more must die. There exists a higher level of substantial imposters than Jaden Rivers. Rivers is not an outright leader, he was always in Zane's shadow. He was not the second one meant to die. I must cleanse the Earth of the second imposter. I must cleanse.

"Take me to Birmingham New Street Train Station, and make it quick."

CHAPTER 46

Judd Stone discovered that he had just enough time to catch a glimpse of the back end of a Mercedes Benz as it speeded away from the hysterical group of people at the foot of the Adonijah Truthsters' driveway. He had no way of recognising that it had been a taxi but he sensed that whoever was inside the vehicle must have had something to do with the chaos unfolding before him.

And whatever it was that William had wanted him to witness he was too late.

William had allowed the killer almost a night's sleep before he was to carry out the mission to execute Eli Zane and Jaden Rivers. Banks had woken early that morning like a programmed robot, his mind focussed entirely on reaching the house in the picturesque setting of the SevernValley in order to carry out his mission.

Judd, by contrast had enjoyed an enjoyable evening at Sab's place, so good in fact that he had needed to crash on her sofa for the night as the red wine had flowed a little too freely as they watched the highlights of the Olympic ceremonies. Fortunately for the world outside of Sab's home, the local population had been spared the drunken pair's repeated tuneless phrase of "na-na-na-na-na-na-na" as Sir Paul McCartney expertly orchestrated the Olympic audience to the mammoth amount of closing bars to "Hey Jude." Although both the worse for liquor, Sab and Judd managed to obediently respond to Macca's instructions: "Now all the ladies sing," directed the deep and playful Liverpudlian tone of Sir Paul's voice signalling for Sab's participation, followed by "Now all the boys in the house," indicating Judd's turn, and finally "All together now" which enabled both Sab and Judd to reunite in singing with a considerable amount of gusto.

With his head banging due to the levels of alcohol consumed, Judd didn't appreciate the call from William to his mobile phone early that Saturday morning, informing him that it would be in his best interests to get over to the Adonijah Truthsters' house. Regardless of his annoyance, Judd chose not to respond negatively to his friend as William explained that something major was going to go down at the dwelling of the cult and he needed to be there. However, he needed to be careful.

Besides, William had ended the call pretty quickly allowing Judd no time to enquire about his friend's cryptic message, but whatever he was meant to witness the time he took to line his stomach with luke-warm eggs, toast, orange juice and paracetamol, kindly left in clear view by Sab who had somehow admirably managed to raise herself and attend the station for her shift, was enough to compromise the timing of his appearance at the Adonijah Truthsters' house.

Judd Stone was someone who required background noise as he undertook everyday activity and this was often accomplished by firing into life a TV set. As he finished his breakfast, Judd had been sidetracked further by the news programme that was elaborating on the findings of the recent Hillsborough Report where 96 Liverpool football fans had lost their lives on 15 April 1989 whilst waiting for the FA Cup semi-final to take place between Liverpool and Nottingham Forest.

It pained Judd to discover that the original enquiry, undertaken by some of his now retired colleagues, had incorrectly supported South Yorkshire Police's accounts of the victims being killed by Liverpool football hooligans. 2012 was proving to be quite an eventful year and in September the truth finally surfaced regarding the tragedy, when it was publicly revealed that police officers had changed their statements to cover up their own failings.

Judd was himself a copper, who didn't always do things by the book, but even he was ashamed to be a policeman today. He understood how important it was, especially for the families of the victims, that the Liverpool fans had finally been exonerated. It was now clear that football hooliganism had played no part in the tragedy and society were at long last better informed of what had really happened on that awful day in 1989.

Judd stepped out of his car, flashed his police badge at the frenzied crowd and enquired what was happening to no one in particular, his head still pounding a little as the paracetamol struggled to ease his hangover. Although Judd was suspended from duty he hadn't surrendered his badge like in the American cop movies – quite an oversight by B.A.D CID that they hadn't asked for it.

A frantic female member of the Adonijah Truthsters screamed back at him, "Our leader, our leader Eli Zane has been killed, it is terrible. The Devil himself has just visited us and taken our leader from us."

Now it crossed Judd's mind for a moment that if someone had arrived and killed their leader Eli Zane, the most obvious suspect would be Detective Chief Inspector William Chamberlain, but Judd also realised that that was extremely unlikely as his friend was recuperating in a hospital bed. "What did this, erm, Devil look like?"

The Adonijah Truthster called Dave stepped forward. The sight of Judd's police badge coupled with the enormity of the situation had uncharacteristically forced the Adonijah Truthsters to open up to the outside world. "I saw him clearly. He was small and scrawny, had fair hair and he spoke with what sounded like a London accent."

"Did you get his name?"

"No, I had never seen him before today."

Judd's mind was whirring, the killer's description sounded just like Gareth Banks. But Judd was struggling to join the dots here. Why would Gareth Banks want to kill a cult leader, and considering the early morning phone call how would William know it was about to happen? His thoughts were halted when an ambulance appeared.

Judd was the first to greet the ambulance crew showing his badge once more.

"I think you are too late. I understand the victim is dead."

"No, we have one further casualty in our brother, Jaden. He has been hurt but God has intervened and saved him. Please follow me." Dave led Judd and the paramedics inside the house.

When Judd saw the bloody corpse of Eli Zane complete with a *Chelsea smile* it confirmed to him that this had indeed been the work of Gareth Banks. He stood staring at the lifeless form, painful memories flooding back to him of when he had first set eyes on Cassie Parker, the poor girl robbed of a young life by Banks, pinned to the wall with a selection of knives in the style of a crucifix, and her beautiful face displaying that same carved-out grin of a Chelsea smile. Judd felt no such sorrowful feelings for Eli, but his confusion was escalating.

Judd turned to see the paramedics working on Jaden, who despite his obvious injuries was still alive and it looked as though with their help he was perhaps going to make it. They attentively dressed his wounds and applied oxygen. Within 15 minutes Jaden was inside the ambulance with the sounds of sirens signalling his departure to the A&E department of the nearest hospital. Rowena had accompanied him in the ambulance.

Dave turned to Judd. "Please, will you find whoever did this? I will pray for God to assist you in your quest."

Judd thought for a moment. He wasn't altogether concerned at catching the killer of the cult leader. Judd was well aware of the abysmal techniques of recruitment and manipulation Eli Zane had demonstrated over the years, and he sensed that the world, and even the Adonijah Truthsters, was a damn sight better off without him. But nevertheless a crime had been committed here, a serious one, and if it had been by Gareth Banks, Judd now had an opportunity to catch that scumbag once again. Perhaps the Lord did move in mysterious ways after all?

Judd placed a hand on Dave's arm. "Don't worry. I'll catch him."

"Thank you. May God's love be with you."

CHAPTER 47

Judd had very quickly experienced a stroke of luck. The taxi driver who had taken Banks to Birmingham New Street Train Station had become spooked by his passenger's odd behaviour and had sensed something terrible must have happened at the house in the Severn Valley. Chillingly Banks had also encouraged Clint to "Keep watching the news; I'm going to be in it."

Once he was safely void of Banks' company, Clint informed the police of his concerns about the strange passenger who he had just dropped off. Fortunately, Sab had overheard some officers who were discussing the crime log and she speedily informed Judd, who promptly made his way to New Street station.

At present only Judd, Sab and of course William knew the identity of the killer – Gareth Banks. Judd had decided that there was no time to include any other police; he would let them conduct their own enquiries and conclusions and allow them to get tangled in the semantics of B.A.D and West Mercia forces working out who would take ownership. Besides, Judd quickly decided if he were to try and convince his colleagues that Banks was their man it could prove counterproductive, compromising valuable time, whilst they would surely only surmise he had some sort of grudge against the man who had walked free from the previous attempt to have him convicted for the Crucifier killings.

Judd's credibility wasn't altogether intact either due to his current suspension, so realistically who would believe him? He doubted they would even believe Sab, but he was grateful to his loyal DS that even throughout his suspension she had still looked to him for guidance and direction. No, it was better to work with Sab in order to catch Banks. So Sab discreetly beavered away at her desk and computer at B.A.D HQ, and Judd maintained contact with her via his mobile phone.

In any case he wanted the prize of catching Banks.

He was owed it.

Ironically, and somewhat typically breaking the law himself, Judd held his phone to his ear as he manoeuvred his car into a short stay parking space at Birmingham New Street station, knowing perfectly well that it would not be parked for a short stay in reality, and amazed at the fact that a vacant space was even able to present itself. This was Birmingham New Street Station before its magnificent transformation into Grand Central which was revealed in 2015, and the parking facilities in 2012 at the entrance where the impressive huge digital eye now looks across at the Bull Ring were less than desirable.

"Banks has been stupid enough to use his credit card to purchase his train ticket, Judd. He is on the train to London Euston."

"Good work, Sab." Judd was pleased with the ease of

tracking Banks down but this only fed his confusion. Why had a meticulous serial killer like Banks, one who had cheated the judicial system and covered his tracks so carefully on previous occasions, all of a sudden be foolish enough to buy a train ticket on a traceable credit card?

It was still unclear how William knew that Banks was going to go and kill Eli, and wasn't that a gratifying coincidence for William? The one man that William wanted dead above any other was Eli Zane, and how was it to be that Banks had done the slaying? Banks certainly wouldn't do William any favours?

And why was Banks now heading towards London? He originated from London so was he simply returning to his home town to keep a low profile after the killing? He had obviously attempted to kill Jaden as well as Eli, but why? Was he heading to London to kill again? What was the significance of killing Eli Zane this time around instead of prostitutes? Why would he wish to kill a cult leader?

Judd pondered these thoughts as he ran into the train station. Looking up at the timetable screens, and then at his watch, he could see that a train was due to leave for London Euston in less than 3 minutes from platform 2.

Fortunately, flashing his badge was enough to allow him through the turnstiles unchallenged and he successfully entered carriage D of the train that was already nestled at the platform ready for imminent departure.

Managing to find a couple of unoccupied seats, which was even more miraculous than finding his parking space, Judd sat alone to gather his thoughts. Judd knew he still had to work out exactly where Banks was destined for once he got to London, which would be at least an hour and a half ahead of this train journey if not more with

Banks having a head-start on him.

London? Why London?

Would Banks really be returning to London as a means to hideout and lie low? London was the capital of England, the country's largest and busiest city, with eyes everywhere. London was indeed an unlikely place to lie low, and besides, Banks had originally fled London, destined to start a new life for himself in the Midlands. The capital city had not appeared to have been a happy place for Banks, so again, Judd found it difficult to fathom why the killer would see London as a place of solitude.

Judd racked his brain. Where was Banks going to? What was he doing? What was happening in that warped mind of his?

Then Judd thought about the traceable train ticket on the credit card. This was an uncharacteristic schoolboy error on Banks' part.

Or perhaps he had become complacent? He had literally got away with the Crucifier murders, so did he believe that he was invincible and he simply could not be caught?

Banks was certainly arrogant enough.

Or was he toying with Judd, giving just enough information away to taunt him? After all, simply by buying a train ticket to London didn't prove that he had killed anyone.

Serial killers had a habit of tormenting their pursuers, no better example than that of Jack the Ripper, who terrorised Victorian London with some of the most grotesque murders that have ever been committed. Jack had enjoyed sending letters of a boastful and mocking nature to the SIO, Inspector George Abberline. The

Ripper had even been malicious enough to send body parts belonging to the victims to the suffering Inspector. Jack the Ripper had killed prostitutes, just like Banks had done – could this be the reason for Banks to be heading to London? Was he heading to Whitechapel for some warped and connected reason?

Then Judd really allowed his imagination to run wild as he tried to make some sense of it all.

Had Banks purposely left a trail because he had been programmed to do so for some reason? If he had been programmed it would explain the uncharacteristic errors of Banks not covering his tracks. Had Banks become a victim of mind control? A patsy like Lee Harvey Oswald? The term 'patsy' for potential 'stitched-up' killers had come from the mouth of Oswald himself - the man identified as killing JFK. And after all, hadn't Banks chillingly told Clint the taxi driver to "Keep watching the news; I'm going to be in it?" It was almost as if Banks wanted to get caught. Who was he planning to kill next? Somebody famous?

Being a huge Beatles fan, Judd was familiar with the intricacies of the killing of John Lennon – his favourite Beatle. There was still a school of thought that John Lennon had been assassinated because of his anti-establishment activity and support of various protests, and fundamentally because people listened to him. He had more influence over the masses of his generation than anyone in power could have ever had.

Many believe that Lennon's killer, Mark David Chapman, wasn't simply a 'lone nut' or a misguided Lennon fan that 'chose' to kill his one time idol. Such investigators who indulge in uncovering alternative reasons for Lennon's death in their evidence have leant on the fact that the 'patsy' curiously made no attempt to escape from his horrific crime, despite the possibility of escaping into Central Park. Instead he calmly, and perhaps conveniently, waited for the police to come and collect him as he clutched his copy of *The Catcher in the Rye.*

If Judd had been a New York cop that day he doubts Chapman would have made it to trial. His unconventional approach to policing would have seen to that, and if faced with the killer of his idol, Judd knows that he couldn't have held back. Patsy or lone nut!

Then there were those, the majority in actual fact that believed Chapman to be a narcissistic individual who worked alone and wanted to kill Lennon in order to gain his own fame. Judd himself had never entirely been sure which route had led Chapman to kill Lennon, and now he was having similar contrasting thoughts about Banks. Was Banks purely a narcissist working alone and therefore not a patsy? That would make sense, but persistently, Judd kept coming back to the same thing – ordinarily it was not in Banks' nature to want to get caught.

The train started up and pulled away from Birmingham City centre. With Judd trying desperately to fathom out what Banks was up to, it compromised him from looking out of the carriage window and noticing the battleground near Millennium Point where he had inadvertently helped Eddie and Hank defeat the Welsh football hooligans.

Judd closed his eyes as he attempted to focus his mind.

William had always said to him, in order to catch a killer you need to think like a killer. So all Judd needed to do was work out exactly what this psycho was up to.

But it sure wasn't going to be easy.

CHAPTER 48

"Sarge, Reception has just called. There is someone here to see you. A Mrs. Stance," said Detective Alfie Winston, a considerably young detective who had served his initial years as a constable in West Mercia Police before making detective in B.A.D CID. Sab had often figured that young Alfie had a bit of a crush on her. Whenever he was around her his face would blush and his mannerisms would become quite animated, such as running his hands through his hair or clumsily waving his arms about.

"She will have to wait; I'm doing something very important at the moment."

"She asked to speak with DI Stone first. She seems to be quite upset and states that she has some news about the killing of that bloke from the religious cult."

"Hasn't DI Singh been assigned to liaise with the other police forces regarding that case?"

"She wanted to speak with you Sarge. She was quite insistent."

Sab took a deep breath taking a moment to decide what was best. She needed to be available for Judd, but curiosity got the better of her. Besides, it sounded as if this Mrs Stance may be able to offer some information which could help them. "Okay Alfie, I'm on my way."

When Sab entered the reception area of B.A.D HQ, the desk sergeant nodded towards a well-presented and not unattractive lady pacing around in a clearly agitated manner.

"Mrs. Stance? My name is Detective Sergeant Sabita Mistry. I understand that you wish to speak with me."

"Detective Sergeant Mistry, thank you so much for meeting me. Is there somewhere we can go that is more private, not everyone would necessarily understand what I have to say?"

"I have an interview room right here, please step inside." Sab opened the door and showed Crystal Stance a seat, but the agitated lady chose to stand.

Sab closed the door and decided to also remain on her feet. "What is this all about then, Mrs. Stance?"

"What I am about to tell you, you may find difficult to believe. I need you to keep your mind open Detective Sergeant Mistry, more open than you have ever had it open before. And please be prepared to accept the unacceptable and believe that the impossible can become possible. I fear we do not have much time."

Judd's mind continued to whirr as he passed through the stations and landmarks along the train journey. He hadn't batted an eyelid at the LG Arena and National Exhibition Centre complex where he had witnessed many concerts under the metal spider frame that held the arena in place. Nor did he notice the various fleets of aeroplanes stacked up at Birmingham International Airport. Once he had passed through Coventry and Rugby train stations, the train raced through the countryside, the hypnotic sound of the track guiding his mind to work overtime.

Judd began to try and understand what the significance of London could be for Gareth Banks. 2012 had been a great year to be British, and London had been the catalyst for the events that propelled the good feel factor for the nation, hosting both the Queens Jubilee and the London Olympics. Both had been generally accepted as being a great success. But were these two events somehow inspiring Banks to go and kill someone?

Banks had traditionally killed prostitutes but now he had just killed a religious cult leader, so who could he now be looking to slay next? And where was the link? Could Banks be going after someone high profile for some strange reason? If so, London was the most obvious location. It dawned on Judd just how possible it could be for a high profile figure to be targeted. The sadness and reality of this filled Judd with emotion every time he heard a Beatles' record. It still bothered him that John Lennon had been wastefully gunned down by Mark David Chapman, outside the singer's home that he shared with wife Yoko and son Sean, the Dakota Building in New York City. If a star of Lennon's magnitude could be reached in New York City, it was more than possible that a celebrity could be reached in London.

Keeping with the possibility of a high profile target being in Banks' sights, Judd began to search through his mind for likely victims. The film maker Danny Boyle had put on a fantastic opening ceremony for the London Olympics, although it had not escaped some levels of criticism. Some critics had viewed the ceremony as being something that the global audience could not always understand due to the Britishness of the event. A prime example being the inclusion of entertaining sessions regarding the National Health Service, definitely something to be celebrated in Britain agreed Judd, but he was also aware of certain elements of society who questioned the showcasing of such a thing in an Olympic ceremony. But was this enough for Banks or anyone to want to kill the film mogul? Judd doubted it. Besides, was Boyle even a resident of London? Judd wasn't sure.

Sir Paul McCartney had closed the Olympic opening ceremony in a year that was also of personal recognition for him; he had turned 70 years of age on the 18th June. Did Banks want to step into the shoes of Chapman and kill a Beatle? Being a huge Beatle fan, Judd certainly hoped not, as he tried to contemplate the enormity of the prospect. But it was certainly possible. Lennon had been murdered and an attempt to kill George Harrison had also occurred on 30 December 1999, when Mike Abram broke into the ex-Beatle's Oxfordshire home and stabbed him repeatedly in the chest. Fortunately, with the help of his wife Olivia who was armed with a lamp, Harrison managed to overpower his attacker and survived the attack.

Judd realised that Macca had a home in St John's Wood, north London. Killing Paul McCartney could only be for some sort of warped personal gain for Banks, there would be no obvious conspiracy theory of FBI involvement as in Lennon's case. It was common knowledge that files had been kept on Lennon and that he had his phone tapped in the first part of the 1970s. Lennon had been an activist for peace and several controversial causes around this time but chose to withdraw from the public eye, including musically, once his second son Sean had been born in 1975. Then just as he was making a musical comeback in his 40th year, with the potential to influence the public once again he was killed. Was this simply a coincidence?

A 70 year old McCartney by contrast was no real threat to anyone, so it was difficult to imagine Banks being programmed as a 'patsy' to kill Macca, or perhaps any other celebrity for that matter. In this day and age there didn't seem to be any famous face with the kind of 'dangerous' influence that Lennon was perceived to have had. Had Chapman even been a programmed 'patsy' or was the most recognised theory of him being a crazed fan simply the truth? And if Banks had been programmed to kill, who had been responsible for the mind control? Judd was of course ignorant to William's newly developed ability to "programme" killers. How could he have even considered looking a lot closer to home?

And then the words of his dear friend and mentor, William came back to him. "To catch a killer you have to think like a killer". This is what he had to do. Judd thought about Banks' known victims to date. Three prostitutes, each one displayed as a crucifixion. Plus Banks' tally of killings now included the leader of a religious cult. It seemed to Judd that the theme of the murders was religion somehow, and it appeared to be centred on Christianity. This opened the door to extreme fundamentalists being targets, such as Eli Zane and Jaden Rivers, but of course there was the more accepted side of Christian religion that existed in Catholicism and the Church of England for example. So Judd began to think of a link between such high profile individuals and religion.

Lord Coe and David Beckham had been two prominent figures in the Olympics, either could be a target to seek personal gain by a killer who wanted to usurp their fame – another of the more accepted theories for Chapman killing John Lennon, but neither would be considered to be people with obvious religious connections. Perhaps it was actually the exclusion of a religious aspect from the ceremonies that had offended Banks? This could once again bring Danny Boyle into consideration. And what about the athletes themselves? Were any of them particularly known for strong religious attributes?

Judd decided that in the short window of time he had, he needed to dismiss the Olympics and those connected with it as an inspiration for Banks to kill, as there seemed no obvious religious connection. He was now convinced that religion was the key to Banks' killing spree, the displaying of his first three victims as crucifixions and the slaying of a religious cult leader was too much of a coincidence. He hoped that his rationale was sound because in truth, only Banks could know what was in that warped mind of his and what his motives for killing were.

So that brought Judd to think about the other significant British event of 2012, the Queen's Jubilee. Again, Sir Paul McCartney had appeared at this event and the thought haunted him once again of another Beatle being cruelly taken from this world. Had Banks made some perverse connection with the songs of the White Album, or any other Beatles' songs for that matter, in the same way that they had fed the warped minds of Charles Manson and his Family? Then it hit him like a juggernaut. Mike Abram, George Harrison's attacker, had incredibly believed that George Harrison had been a devil and he had been sent on a mission by God to kill the ex-Beatle. Proof enough that a warped religious motive could instigate someone to try and kill a Beatle and that could quite easily fit the profile of Gareth Banks and any reasoning for progressing from killing prostitutes.

But as big as the Beatles undoubtedly were and still are, in 2012 the Jubilee concert itself was bigger than Sir Paul McCartney performing live, for it was the celebration of the Queen's jubilee. The true star of the occasion, the lady at the centre of it all, was indeed the Queen herself. The thought of a third Beatle being targeted overwhelmed him, but in the time he had to sum things up, and with the year being 2012, Judd shuddered as he seriously contemplated that Banks may be going after the British monarch for his next victim.

"You are telling me that William Chamberlain, one of my bosses, has amazing powers of the mind?" said an astounded Sab.

"I know it is difficult to believe, but William possesses the kind of capability of performing mind-over-matter that really excites us at the Institute of Noetic Science, and I can definitely confirm that he was able to hypnotise me. Not in the traditional sense, but more by controlling my mind. I left his flat in a complete trance. What worries me more are the disturbing visions that I am receiving."

"Go on," encouraged Sab, surprising Crystal at the Detective Sergeant's willingness to listen and to try and understand. Crystal had expected a much more difficult conversation to entail.

"Well, disturbingly I am having visions of William with a knife in his hand, and for some reason he is slashing people across their faces, causing terrible splits either side of their mouth. He seems to be doing it in either a church or within a crowd of people."

Sab at once recognised the infliction as a characteristic of Gareth Banks. The 'Chelsea Smile'. "In a crowd of people? At a football match perhaps?"

"Well yes, I guess that's a possibility. I don't know what any of this means, Detective Sergeant Mistry; I am simply informing you of what I am seeing. And I know William is in hospital so he cannot be physically doing this himself, but I believe I could be seeing visions of him because he is controlling someone's mind and therefore orchestrating them to carry out these acts of violence.

"I'm sorry Detective Sergeant; I know that DCI Chamberlain is a good man and someone that you personally respect and look up to, so I struggle to see why he could, or even would, want to orchestrate such behaviour. Maybe my vision is simply representing something else and not killings in the literal sense? This happens sometimes.

"I also received a vision of a man dripping with the very essence of evil, but this evil man has been killed in my vision. He was a man who has tortured and controlled people for many years, but in a very different way to how William can control minds."

Sab stared hard at Crystal Stance and the medium hoped that the Detective Sergeant didn't view her as being some sort of crazy woman. Then Sab spoke.

"Crystal we are going to the hospital. I think we need to speak to William and get to the bottom of this."

Judd broke into a deep sweat as he seriously considered that Banks was going to London to kill the Queen in her jubilee year? As the train speeded through Bushey station, Judd found the prospect a difficult one to envisage, but not an altogether impossible one. He needed some verification, some information to define if his unbelievable hunch was correct. Judd spotted a young oriental male, whom he took to be a student, taking advantage of the train's Wi-Fi connection. He went and sat next to the youth and showed him his police badge.

"Young man, my name is DCI Judd Stone and I am on important police business. I need to use your laptop. I have some serious googling to do."

"Of course, please be my guest." Judd was pleased to find that the youth not only spoke perfect English, but he had a similar accent to his own. Perhaps the future of the British monarchy now rested on the shoulders of two Brummies!

"Thank you." Judd closed down the social media site that the youth was browsing and typed into the search engine the words 'monarchy and religion'. There was a possibility of 200 plus sites having something to offer for this phrase. Judd entered the first hit. Scanning the information as quickly as possible, Judd was able to determine that the British Monarch held the accolade of being Defender of the Faith and supreme governor of the established Church of England. Motive perhaps for Banks? Did he have a problem with the Queen being supreme governor of the Church of England? What did Banks make of the monarch being a 'defender of the faith'? Did he view it as being incorrect that someone not of an obvious religious vocation should hold such power? Of course King Henry VIII had been more than influential in establishing the Church of England, but Judd searched his brain to think of when the position of being Defender of the Faith had ever caused controversy in modern times.

He couldn't think of a single incident.

Judd continued to read on. He discovered that the Archbishop of Canterbury and the bishops of the Church of England are appointed by the monarchy, but only on the advice of the Prime Minister. This suggested to Judd, that the leader of the government has more influence on the Christian faith of Great Britain than any Monarch does, even though the King or Queen holds all the titles! At this current time the Queen is nothing more than titular in the process, a process that in its entirety seems more a traditional and uncontroversial formality simply to elect the Archbishop of Canterbury. She is Defender of the Faith in name only and not active, but would Banks understand that the Queen is not even claiming to be a true head of the church? If he did understand, and if religion is his driver for killing and not some attempt at gaining a warped sense of fame, he would seemingly have little motive to target her.

Judd noticed the owner of the laptop peering over his shoulder. "Is your important police business something to do with the Queen?"

"Don't speak too loud son, but yes. I fear it may be," said Judd.

"Is she in danger?"

"Again, I fear she may be."

"Then perhaps it is a good thing that she is out of the country at the moment."

CHAPTER 49

When Sab and Crystal walked into the hospital room together, William was almost as surprised as when Gareth Banks had visited him.

"Hello Sab, Mrs. Stance."

"What's going on, William," demanded Sab. William was a little taken aback by the assertive tone in his Sergeant's voice.

"What do you mean?"

"Well let me put it this way; I'm certainly not going to look into your eyes when you answer me."

"You really shouldn't listen to what this woman tells you Sab, she is a little misguided with her opinions."

"Oh, is that so Detective Chief Inspector." This time William was taken aback at the assertiveness displayed by the medium, who had been such a gentle soul on their previous engagement. Her response actually shamed William into realising that he had attempted to make the woman appear nothing short of a liar, and she didn't really deserve that.

Crystal continued. "I'm pleased that you were able to amuse yourself with the unusual manner in which you were able to remove me from your home Detective Chief

Inspector Chamberlain, but believe it or not, that connection you made with my brain has caused me to experience some very disturbing visions involving you and I would like an explanation in order for them to stop."

William looked at the two women before him. They were two women he respected and he was disappointed that their expressions informed him of obvious concern. He hadn't meant for anyone else to become involved, and he presumed that these visions that Crystal was experiencing must have something to do with what he had instructed Banks to do.

"Sab, could you please confirm if there have been any significant crimes committed in the not too distant past please?"

"I'm sure that you won't be surprised to hear that Eli Zane has been murdered."

William couldn't help but smile. "Good, that will rid the Earth of one less monster. Has anyone else been murdered?"

"Are you expecting someone else to be murdered?"

"Of course not."

"You don't seem too surprised that Eli Zane is dead. He was found with a slit across his face, his mouth portrayed like some sort of crazy grin. A brutal infliction on the victim, similar to the prostitute murders that we investigated, wouldn't you say? This is something I am sure that you can recall, William. If you are wondering about Jaden Rivers, he was injured but he survived."

Both Sab and Crystal noticed the disturbance in William's face. "Survived? He was meant to be killed too. I mean…"

"How did you do it, Boss?"

"Do what exactly? Are you suggesting that I got out of my hospital bed and somehow managed to scramble my way to the Adonijah Truthsters' dwelling to kill Zane and then attempt to kill Rivers? I suppose my Multiple Sclerosis has miraculously cured itself, or perhaps I have been able to transport myself quite a distance like someone out of a science fiction movie?"

"You can control minds, William. I know that for a fact," said Crystal.

"And I believe what Crystal has told me, Guv. Talking of minds I've always kept mine open about these sorts of things. Now listen, Judd is on his way to London because of whatever it is you have been able to orchestrate, and who knows what danger he is being led into. So if you care about what happens to Judd, I suggest that you help us out a bit here and start to open up about things."

"Okay, okay. I never meant for Judd to be in any danger, quite the opposite. I'm trying to make him a hero and get his career back on track. If I tell you what you need to know please don't dob me into Haddock and Francis, Sab. You must believe me; I partly did this for Judd too."

"You know me better than that Boss, and besides, I think I may have a job convincing Haddock and Francis what is happening in reality, don't you? I'm not convinced that they would share the same open-mindedness as Crystal and me. Now is Judd in danger and is Banks involved? Has Banks gone to London to try and kill someone else?"

William sighed accepting that if Judd's life could be in danger it would be best to share his intentions with the two ladies before him. "Not long after you and Judd visited me I had another visitor."

"Banks."

"Yes, Banks. He was going to kill me, Sab, but I was able to cease an opportunity, turning my imminent death into something beneficial for all of us. For a split second, just before he was about to drive a knife into me, I managed to look into his eyes and I concentrated harder than I have ever concentrated before. My life depended on it after all, and I managed to enter that sick mind of his and gain some form of control. And as I stared into those evil eyes and manipulated his thoughts it came to me like some kind of divine intervention. I realised that if I could control his evil then I could gain revenge and justice. Not only for those poor girls that we know Banks killed, but also for my sister too, whose life has been permanently scarred by those cult lunatics.

"And I wanted Judd to be able to claim the prize after the way Banks had managed to make a mockery of justice and brought Judd's policing into question. Judd Stone is the best copper that force has ever had and he deserves his time in the sun. I thought that I had found a way to succeed, to change the destiny for all concerned to what it should be, and so whatever you two ladies may be thinking at this moment, I believe that the end justifies the means.

"I knew how Banks felt about imposters to God and how such individuals were at odds with his belief of the true meaning of God. Do you remember, Sab, his warped feelings towards his father the priest when we interviewed him? I knew I could convince him to view Eli and Jaden as being imposters just like he considered his own dad to be an imposter. Banks never understood how a man of the cloth could take an oath of celibacy and then go on to portray the weakness to father a child, even though the child was him. Knowing this tormented Banks, recognising that he was simply the product of wrong-doing in the eyes of God.

"In a split second I saw an opportunity and took it. I wanted two bad men dead and I stand by the righteousness of that decision. But now I fear that as Banks has only managed to kill one bad man he could be out to kill one good man in error."

"So you have made Banks your patsy? Your Lee Harvey Oswald or Sirhan Sirhan, the killers of the Kennedys?" said Sab.

"Yes, I guess I have. But there is a big difference in my intended targets. I sent Banks after evil men."

"Except he has only done half the job. Who could he

be after now?"

"Banks has fled to London you say?"

"Yes, that must be where his next victim is?"

"I'm sorry Sab, I haven't a clue."

CHAPTER 50

With the knowledge that Her Majesty was safely outside of London, Judd breathed a sigh of relief and instantly placed her as a lower priority on his mental list of high profile targets. But this relief was short lived as he pushed the Archbishop of Canterbury towards the top.

Judd tried to think logically about the situation. He wasn't familiar with any security being in place at Lambeth Palace, the residence of the Archbishop of Canterbury, but he figured that it wouldn't necessarily be the most robust. That would perhaps make it ideal for Gareth Banks to target his next victim.

As the train sped towards the capital, Judd looked out of the window and he noticed the archway of Wembley Stadium and for the first time today remembered that an England football match was to take place in the next few hours with a new manager at the helm - a certain Marlon Howell.

Now Judd had something else to curse Gareth Banks for. Even with Howell in charge, Judd would usually be spending his evening watching the match in the pub, or at the very least on his flat screen TV in his apartment, but here he was in earshot of the renowned stadium and he couldn't even go and see the match. Instead he was chasing a psychopathic serial killer across London before he had chance to murder a high-profile target.

As the Wembley Stadium archway faded from sight, Judd began to reflect on what he knew about previous high-profile murders. This inevitably led him to reflect once again on one of his all-time idols - John Lennon. The slaying of The Beatle had been such an unnecessary tragedy for the world to have had to suffer.

Then his thoughts rallied through all the previous well-known murders that he could recall, from Julius Caesar to Martin Luther King. From Abraham Lincoln to Sam Cooke. From Sharon Tate to Jill Dando. It occurred to him that basically any high-profile individual could be a potential target no matter how efficient their security may or may not be, including therefore the Archbishop of Canterbury. After all, someone as high-profile as JFK had been murdered in Dallas all those years ago whilst being totally surrounded by police and security. This could be because JFK's death was said to assist with the aspirations of several different groupings and many still believe that Lee Harvey Oswald had received a helping hand on 22nd November 1963. For instance, the President had been travelling in an open-topped Lincoln Lancer motor car which curiously slowed down after the first shot was fired, enabling Oswald, and possibly others, to have further clear shots at the President. So even if the Archbishop of Canterbury was being well protected, and Judd wasn't convinced that he was, could Banks be receiving a helping hand to reach him for some reason? Who else would benefit from the killing of the Archbishop of Canterbury? Judd didn't rightly know.

Other elements of the assassination of JFK have added weight to Oswald not acting alone on that tragic day. Did Oswald even fire a gun at all? Witnesses claim that four shots or more were fired; many recalling from the direction of the grassy knoll area, yet Oswald had been positioned several floors up in the Book Depository. This contradicted the claim by the authorities that 3 shots were fired from Oswald alone. And what was to happen too many of these witnesses in years to come? They were to die in unexpected circumstances: car crashes, suicides, cut throats and killing by gunfire all featured in their demise. All convenient coincidences perhaps?

Cut throats and gun fire! A realisation screamed inside Judd's brain. Banks was handy with a knife and now of course he had a gun in his possession.

Oswald had always claimed that he had been a 'patsy', a 'fall guy'. There is evidence to suggest that Oswald was even programmed or brainwashed to kill the president.

Apparently Oswald had once been a gay man but hypnosis had managed to turn him into a heterosexual and even a married man! A "Mind Control" scheme had reportedly been deployed in the USA, initially used to assist with interrogations, but one that rapidly spiralled to manufacture assassins of perceived threatening individuals, these assassins never having recollections of being instructed to carry out the crimes thus becoming 'patsies'"

Oswald would indeed have been an easy target to 'programme.' He had been a narcissist, very similar to Mark David Chapman the killer of John Lennon. Lennon, an outspoken activist for peace was worshipped by millions. His influence on society was incalculable and therefore a perceived threat to certain authorities. At the time of his murder, Lennon was a well-established American citizen following earlier residency complications, on the brink of a musical comeback, thus placing him once again in the limelight after 5 years of 'hibernation' raising his son Sean, baking bread and feeding the cats in his family home of The Dakota.

To allow Lennon the opportunity to connect with the masses again would surely have caused eruptions within the FBI who were commonly known to have had the ex-Beatle followed and bugged only a few years earlier. Hence many conspiracy theorists believe Chapman was also a programmed and brainwashed assassin used to silence Lennon.

Like Oswald, Chapman was a narcissist.

Like Oswald and Chapman, Banks was a narcissist.

So had Banks also been programmed to kill?

How little Judd realised that he was thinking along the right lines, but the source for the programming of course was not any authority. It just happened to be his best friend and mentor DCI William Chamberlain!

Just then Judd's interesting trail of thought was interrupted by the ringing of his mobile phone. As he answered the call, the oriental passenger sitting beside him listened with interest.

"Judd, it's Sab."

"Sab, I think our man is after someone of a high-profile nature."

"Well after speaking with William I tend to agree, but your best bet is to consider people with some kind of religious connection."

"Mmmm, I figured that likelihood too, and I have even considered musicians with some kind of religious connection." Judd paused as he felt the passenger's attention bearing down on him. "Give me a second, I'm just going to take the call in the toilet, this train has ears."

The student looked away sheepishly. As Judd got up from his seat he noticed that the student now had a current news story displayed on his laptop screen with today's date clearly displayed. It had photos of Sir Paul McCartney and his wife Nancy strolling through New York only hours earlier. Judd could rest easy that it looked unlikely that Banks' next target was a Beatle. He also knew that Ringo Starr lived in the USA. Judd walked away from his seat, taking several steps before pushing the button on the carriage door to release the doors. As the doors opened they produced that whooshing, vacuum-enabled sound. Once safely locked inside the toilet, Judd spoke as quietly as he could hoping that he wouldn't lose the signal. "Sab, if we are going with religion as a motive, I think that the most obvious target in London must be the Archbishop of Canterbury."

"It could be yes, but to be honest we don't know for sure. William reckons Banks is after someone whom he could perceive as being an imposter to God, hence the reason why Eli Zane was murdered. There is no bigger imposter than a cult leader."

"Unless you count someone who is at the head of an organised religion of course? Who knows how Banks interprets things in that sick brain of his, and the head of a church that was created some 1600 years or so after the death of Jesus Christ may offer some form of pretence to Banks."

"You could well be right Judd, and are they not in the process of changing the position of the Archbishop to another chap? I forget the name of the new fellow but I'm sure I heard he had been appointed recently."

"Yeah, come to think of it I heard that too. I think you are bang on the money, Sab, and it would make the timing good sense for Banks to achieve maximum effect. The target has to be the Archbishop of Canterbury. I'll head for Lambeth Palace and see if Banks is sniffing around there."

"Ok Judd, but I'll do some more digging just in case. William has, shall we say, been very helpful too."

"Good, William is the brains of our outfit, so I'm glad that the old git has been able to help even from his hospital bed."

"Oh, believe me; William has been more helpful than you could ever understand, Judd. I'll call you if I find out anything else that I think you should know."

"Before you go Sab, do you ever buy into any of that conspiracy theory stuff? It may sound crazy but I'm just contemplating if Banks has been programmed to kill. You know like Lee Harvey Oswald could have been when JFK was killed?"

"Oh, I sure do believe people can be programmed Guv, and so does William. If I brought you fully up to speed now I think you would have a hard time understanding. All you need to know Judd is that all things have been considered this end, and we are confident that religion is the key, so just keep that focus and you should end up tracking down Banks."

"Thanks, Sab. We'll speak soon."

Judd's call to Sab ended in symmetry to the train arriving at Euston station. He unlocked the toilet door which provided the similar piston, vacuum sound as the carriage door did and was pleased to discover that the exiting passengers were only just gathering in anticipation of the train ultimately coming to a halt, therefore his conversation with Sab was unlikely to have fallen on any unintentional ears. He noticed the oriental student towards the rear of the gathering passengers and Judd mouthed a silent "thank you" in recognition of the use of his laptop. The student gave a 'thumbs up' signal.

As soon as the train stopped and the external carriage doors opened, Judd caused a disturbance as he fought his way to the front but didn't have time to respond to the cursing passengers as he sprinted along the platform, through the terminal and its various booths, and on towards the pedestrian entrance of the station where he continued to move with pace down the left-hand side of the escalator in order to catch the underground tube.

Judd had a choice of two lines - Northern or Victoria. He followed the black markers for the Northern line and realised that this would get him to Embankment station. There he could switch to the Bakerloo line, where he could depart at Lambeth North station on the south of the Thames. Then a short run would take him to Lambeth Palace, the residence of the Archbishop of Canterbury. *Conspiracy theory or no conspiracy theory, religion still seemed the key and focus*, he told himself.

Judd flashed his badge to the attendant at the disabled terminal who obediently allowed him access by releasing the mini-doors, after Judd had explained that he would be assisting with important top-secret police business. Judd thought to himself that he should use this approach more often to gain access to various places, even if he wasn't necessarily on police business. Being currently suspended he strictly wasn't today either!

Judd sprinted down the stairs and felt the gust of wind sweeping through the walkway tunnel indicating that a tube had just pulled in. He glanced quickly at the map on the wall, refocused on the black line to indicate the Northern line, spotted the word *North* somewhere to validate his thoughts, ran through the tunnel and flung himself into the carriage just as the doors were closing. The tube began to pull away and Judd smiled at a pair of olive-skinned teenage girls whom he took to be as tourists. They didn't smile back.

The carriage was typically packed with people going about their business and as Judd turned to his right he was greeted by the sweaty armpit of a large man with glasses, which were clearly too big even for his rather rotund face. The man smiled at Judd. Judd didn't smile back.

He allowed his mind to think about the football match he was going to miss later today. Judd loved watching England games, although these days he needed to try and put to one side that the rapist and monster Marlon Howell was in charge. Nevertheless he briefly contemplated jumping on the Bakerloo line in the opposite direction once he reached Embankment station as that would take him to Wembley Central. He could walk up Wembley Way and try and grab a ticket from one of the inevitable touts to enable him to enjoy the game. Ticket touts were always at the ground early doors. However, his dream of seeing the match was brought to an abrupt halt when he heard the well-spoken female voice announce "This stop is Mornington Crescent."

Mornington Crescent! Judd hadn't got on the Bakerloo line in the opposite direction but he had got on the Northern Line in the opposite direction! In all the confusion of rushing onto the tube, Judd had embarked on the Northern Line as intended, but had headed northbound. He had needed to head southbound for Embankment.

The tube pulled away from Mornington Crescent and the same beautiful pre-recorded voice spoke once more. "This train terminates at High Barnet; your next stop will be Camden Town."

Judd had always loved Camden Town.

CHAPTER 51

Judd stepped out of Camden Town Underground Station viewing his mistake as perhaps a quirk of fate or some sort of divine guidance in order to find his suspect. Gareth Banks had once worked at the Camden Oasis Hotel; therefore perhaps the scumbag had come to Camden Town to lie low for a few days. Judd knew that serial killers preferred to operate in familiar territory. Perhaps Banks was even going to stay at the Camden Oasis; it made sense to Judd if the killer had chosen to do so. Before Mark David Chapman had targeted John Lennon at the Dakota Building, he had stayed in a New York hotel until executing the tragic event. If Banks was ultimately targeting the Archbishop of Canterbury, then although Camden Town was situated quite a way in relation to Lambeth, the Northern Underground line served as practically a direct route to the residence.

Besides, Judd loved Camden. In spite of the urgency of the situation, Judd wasn't going to rush his walk to the Camden Oasis Hotel; he was instead going to soak up the ambience of this diverse and bohemian part of London. Camden often reminded him of Moseley; a similar bohemian and diverse part of Birmingham, only Camden was on a much larger scale.

As he headed towards Camden's famous markets that sprawled considerably yet deceivingly beyond either side of the street, Judd noticed the huge Doc Marten boot that hung triumphantly as a symbol of the British SKA movement of the late seventies and early eighties. Other varying manic figures reached out at him from the walls above the shops, while tunes from yesteryear spilled out onto the pavement from the doorways.

Once Judd reached the edge of the market at Camden Lock, with the unique seating area of the Lambretta scooters overlooking the canal whilst the aroma of oriental and other Asian cuisine filled the air, he spotted a display of Amy Winehouse inspired clothing proudly announcing the tragic star as the 'Angel of Camden.' Amy had been one of Judd's more contemporary favourite artists and he remembered coming to Camden on a previous less intensive occasion and spotting her in the Hawley Arms pub enjoying herself with a small group of friends. The encounter was not long after Judd had purchased Amy's "Back to Black" album, an album that he rated as one of his all time favourites. Judd remembered Amy inadvertently making eye contact with him and the sultry singer giving him a passing smile, nothing too alarming but a connection nevertheless which Judd would always be thankful for. When the tragic news broke of her death, not altogether surprising yet equally surreal and sad, Judd felt compelled to return to Camden once again where he gathered with Sab and a number of other individuals outside her home in Camden Square, pleased that he could always treasure that small connection he had experienced with her. The crowd gathered around a cluster of lighted candles as they sang out Amy's music in her honour, and Judd realised that although he had experienced that minuscule connection, one of Amy's strengths was her ability to connect with the entire world through the transparent and honest lyrics of her songs.

Whether it was the subconscious calling of the 'Angel of Camden' guiding Judd into the arena of another world, or simply Judd's own desire to explore the hidden charms of this most unique of markets, Judd entered the winding open-aired corridors between the stalls.

Judd soon became completely lost in his sidetracked journey around the market, browsing various images of Winehouse, as well as Jimi Hendrix, The Beatles, Jim Morrison and Buddha, their faces being displayed upon posters and clothing.

Eventually Judd found himself at the final row of stalls with some of them erected in the style of wooden cabins. A couple of stalls offered both temporary and permanent tattoos, and Judd couldn't help but notice a pretty young thing having a dragon etched into her hip area. Other stalls offered candy, candles, dream-catchers, imitation designer bags and fish pedicures. These fish pedicures were fast becoming a rage across the British nation around the year 2012.

At this point the market opened up a little, offering a little more space from the congested rows of stalls, and Judd quickly snapped back into reality as if he had returned through his wardrobe into his bedroom leaving the magical world of Narnia behind him. He decided that he needed to concentrate on getting to The Camden Oasis Hotel as soon as possible. He was supposed to be preventing a murder happening after all, although the intended target still wasn't altogether clear.

As Judd hurried along the passageway, he was greeted by a group of over-excited males coming in the opposite direction.

"Eng-er-land, Eng-er-land, Eng-er-land," they chanted, recklessly and needlessly spilling garments and items onto the floor as they made their way aggressively through the crowd. Despite the football match being an evening kick-off, the capital city had typically been swarming with followers of English football from an early hour.

Judd considered them to be crossing the line of acceptable excitability as they unnecessarily disturbed the items of the stalls; however being a fan of the England national team who was known to get a little excited himself on occasion, Judd had decided not to intervene. Anyway, he simply didn't have time to interfere and they were clearly in a position to outnumber him.

But then against the odds, one of them seemed to recognise him.

"You look familiar, mate."

"Do I really?" responded Judd to the shaven-headed individual who had a scar down his left cheek and a distinctive crooked nose. He looked to be about the same age as Judd.

It seemed that Judd's accent was evident to the thug. "A Brummie are ya? Now I know where I know you from. You used to be in a crew back in the day. I remember you and your boys giving me a right kicking near New Street Train Station a few years back. I never forget a face even after this amount of time."

"I'm flattered you remember me but I'm in a bit of a hurry, and unlike you mate I grew out of all this bollocks a long time ago."

"I got this scar in that fight. Do you think I am just going to let you go now we meet again?"

"Well, yes I do actually. I mean, we are all united for England today are we not?"

"Not where you are concerned Brummie," and with that the thug pulled his head back with the intention of bringing it crashing down onto Judd.

Judd anticipated what was going to happen and managed to slip aside causing the thug to catch him on the shoulder with his head butt, still causing an amount of pain but nowhere as significant as if he had caught Judd as intended on the nose.

Judd retaliated by punching the thug in his left ear, causing him to lose his balance and topple, which allowed

Judd to follow up with a kick to the stomach sending the thug spilling amongst a rail of flowery dresses.

This inspired the rest of the gang to turn on Judd.

"Look guys there is no need for this, we are on the same side today. Come on let's have a sing-song "Eng-er-land, Eng-er-land, Eng-er-land."

Judd could see that he was failing to foster any kind of level ground with these representatives of one of the London clubs; Judd hadn't figured out yet which one. Before long he was being summoned to a few punches and kicks coming his way. All Judd could do was curl into a ball on the ground as he was hopelessly outnumbered by the thugs as they reigned blow after blow on him.

Judd could hear women scream and cries of "they'll kill him", and then all of a sudden the onslaught stopped as sudden as it had begun.

Once he was confident that the attack had stopped, Judd rolled out of his ball and was relieved to discover that apart from a few throbs here and there, he didn't actually feel that injured all things considered. He looked up to see that the thugs who had set upon him were now being otherwise distracted by them now having to defend themselves, and as it appeared not too successfully as blood sprayed from their respective mouths and noses.

Then Judd spotted a familiar face, which had the audacity to wink at Judd as he knocked one of the Londoner's to the ground. It was Eddie Goode. As Judd looked to the side of Eddie, he saw Hank kicking a man in the ribs as he was sprawled on the concrete floor.

Judd decided that there was only one thing that he could do in the circumstances.

He got up off the floor to help out.

Judd noticed that the yob with the scar who had started all this had managed to recover, and he stood up from the pile of dresses with some sprawled around him, giving the impression of him being a very masculine and ugly-looking transvestite. Judd decided to put the loser permanently out of the occasion by punching the already groggy thug square on the jaw, sending him back into the pile of dresses and into an instant slumber.

Judd turned to see an almighty brawl going on between a set of Londoners and a set of Brummies, and noticed that Eddie currently had to deal with two opponents. Although Eddie was coping quite admirably on his own, Judd decided one good turn deserved another and he intervened by grabbing one of the thugs by his hoodie and swinging him around, causing the thug to choke. The thug finally landed in the doorway of the fish pedicure booth, and Judd ran over and kicked him in the stomach, considerably forcing the wind out of him.

Judd's next move was to grab the yob and shove his shaven head into the fish tank. The little fish began to feast on his cauliflower ears, fleshly cheeks and nostrils as Judd forced his head under the water. The yob tried to fight against Judd's grip, his arms and legs kicking frantically, but Judd was too strong for him. Eventually, just as the thug began to lose consciousness, Judd yanked his soaked head from the tank, complete with little fish still nibbling at his features, and simply tossed him aside to cough and splutter up water from his lungs.

Judd merged with the remaining brawling bodies, trading punches with the cockneys, until the battered Londoners finally came to their senses and ran away. Those that could anyway.

"Eddie, I never thought I'd be so pleased to see you," said Judd catching his breath after all the brawling. "But thanks, I mean it."

"My pleasure. I couldn't let those cockney twats take out a Brummie boy now could I? Even if he is a copper."

The two men laughed as they slapped each other on the shoulders.

"Here for the game I take it, Eddie?"

"You bet. Howell was a good manager for our club so we wanted to travel down for the England game to give our support. We have plenty of time to indulge in the culture of the pubs of the capital before kick-off, although I don't relish paying London prices for a pint of beer. How about you?"

Judd chose not to share his opinion of Howell with Eddie. It would take too long and he had kept his promise to Bonnie inside him all these years not to make a public issue of what the monster had done to her. It ate away at Judd how the public's general perception of Marlon Howell was that he was some sort of hero, this opinion being so far removed from what it would be if they were to know what he was truly capable of. "As much as I would love to join you I'm on official business, well sort of, and believe it or not I'm looking for that idiot Gareth Banks."

"Yeah, I saw all that shit in the news. It seems he screwed you over the killings of those girls. What went wrong?"

"I can't go into it now but I think he is in London and he is once again the main suspect in a murder. I need to stop him before he kills again."

"He is in London you say? I'll keep an eye out for him, I never liked what he did to those girls and he shook Fleur up big time as you know."

"Well Eddie, I guess if you and the crew can keep an eye out for him until you get to the game I'd be grateful. Do us a favour though. Don't kill him, no matter how tempting it may be, just hold him for me. Let me know where you are and I'll come and get him. Do you still have my number?"

"Yeah, I've got your number. It's filed under PC Plod. Just want us to hold him do you? I get it. You want the satisfaction of doing him in yourself?"

"Something like that."

"Well like I said before Judd, you're no different to me. You like the ruck."

CHAPTER 52

"You know, Guv, you really shouldn't have discharged yourself from hospital like that. You can hardly move at the moment."

"Look Sab, if I got Judd into this mess I owe it to him to get him out of it."

Whilst at the hospital, Sab had indicated her desire to return to B.A.D HQ and continue researching on the computer in order to be in a better position to support Judd. She hoped to stumble upon anything that could help him. Whilst Sab could concentrate on the more practical kind of help, Crystal had expressed her desire to assist from a spiritual position; but she wanted to be near Sab should any telling visions appear. At this point, William had declared that he could assist from either position and it was difficult for either Sab or Crystal to disagree.

Sab had already raced ahead and fired up her computer, whilst Crystal manoeuvred William in his wheelchair before settling him at the side of Sab's desk. Even with all of the intensity of the situation, Sab couldn't help but notice that the two of them had the potential to make a nice couple. They really did look good together.

"Perhaps if I can interrogate Banks' credit card account

again, it could pinpoint us to his exact location."

"Oh, that's really clever, Sab. You could try and locate where he is spending with his card? You can actually do that?"

"Yes that's right Crystal," replied Sab. "I can't believe he has been so stupid as to leave a trail, I mean, if he had have purchased his train ticket by cash instead, we would never have even guessed he was heading to London."

"Remember his mind is very focussed on achieving his goal so he will not be as careful to cover his tracks as he has done with previous crimes. He is likely to make mistakes, as protecting himself has simply become secondary compared to the need to catch his prey," offered William like some wise old owl.

"Well then," said Sab. "Let me see if he has made any more mistakes."

"How many guests have checked in today?" asked Judd to the hotel receptionist, a taller-than-average and attractive woman of Eastern-European origin.

"We have had five check-ins in total."

"Did any of those happen to be a bloke on his own?"

"Only one, the others were couples or families."

"Was he a small guy with blonde hair?"

The receptionist searched her mind. "No, he was a tall man with dark hair, and dark skin colour too."

Judd doubted that Banks' powers of disguise could stretch to changing the colour of his skin, and he was convinced that if Banks had surfaced here he would have surely checked in alone.

"Has anyone checked in with the surname Banks or Hibbett?"

"I am not sure that I can share that information with you, sir. Our client's details are confidential."

Judd flashed his badge, remembering how often it succeeded in getting things done. "The information is very important, literally a matter of life and death."

It worked. The receptionist was a nervous type and Judd could tell that she wouldn't want anything untoward on her conscience. She took a moment to scan the computer and double-checked the signed paperwork of the guests who had checked in today. "I'm sorry sir, there is no-one with either of those names staying here."

"Okay, I guess it was a shot in the dark anyhow. Thanks for your assistance."

Judd walked out of the hotel and stood on the chipped concrete steps that led to the entrance, not really knowing what to do next. He allowed the door to shut behind him and putting his head in his hands he was temporarily at a loss. He suddenly felt foolish at even entertaining exploring Camden Town. What valuable time had he lost getting involved in a fight with football hooligans and soaking up the atmosphere of this bohemian location? Banks could already be at Lambeth Palace right this minute pointing a loaded gun at the Archbishop of Canterbury.

Just then his phone rang.

"Sab?"

"Hi Judd, how are you doing?"

"I think I've just sent myself on a wild goose chase around Camden Town when I should be on my way to Lambeth Palace. I figured that Banks may have returned to the Camden Oasis Hotel to lay low for a short time, but now that seems unlikely."

"I'm not sure that Lambeth Palace is his intended location after all, Judd. I've managed to trace another credit card transaction."

"Really?"

"Yeah, another train ticket but this time for the Eurostar."

"The Eurostar? For the life of me who could be his target in Europe, and most likely France I'd have thought? Have you checked out if there are any religious figures or celebrities expected to be around in France this weekend?"

"Yes I have, Judd. I'm still searching but no-one of any significance from what I can tell."

"Wait. Oh my God, we need to stay with the religious theme. We are on the right track, Sab."

"How can you be so sure?"

"Is there a time on his ticket do you know?"

"Yes, he is going from St Pancras at 15.30pm."

"Half-three. I have very little time but enough. I think his journey is to Verona and then on to Rome for his final destination. I remember when I interviewed Banks for the murders he told me he was scared of only one thing."

"What was that?"

"Flying."

"I don't follow, boss."

"Banks wants to be in Rome for Sunday, but he wouldn't fly there hence the need to travel today. So now who do you think is his most likely target, Sab?"

"OMG. It's numero uno."

"Yes indeed. I reckon he is going after the Pope in his own backyard. St Peter's Square, during Sunday Mass."

CHAPTER 53

So it seemed that Gareth Banks was to attempt to succeed with Pope Benedict XVI what Mehmet Ali Ağca had failed to achieve with Pope John Paul II.

To kill the Holy Father.

The first attempted assassination of Pope John Paul II had taken place on Wednesday, 13 May 1981, in St. Peter's Square at Vatican City, and it seemed likely that it was somewhere in this vicinity that Banks would attempt to kill the pope of 2012, even though the shielded vehicle affectionately known as the 'Pope Mobile', with all its security measures, had since been introduced to ferry the pontiff through the crowds.

Exactly why Pope John Paul II had been Agca's target remains somewhat of a mystery. Agca has changed his story as to his reasoning on various occasions, fuelling debate that the assassination attempt could have been either politically or religiously motivated. And just as with Oswald and the like, many also believed that others were involved in addition to Agca.

However, Judd was by this time convinced that Banks' intentions were purely self-motivated. He figured that to Banks, the Pope stood as a symbol of his father. His father the priest, who had lived a life as a phony, in particular through the sinful relationship with his mother. To Banks, his dad had been a deceitful charlatan, and therefore the Pope, this most righteous symbol of his father's faith simply had to pay the ultimate price.

Of course, Judd was not yet fully aware that the psychotic killer had received a helping hand by the ironic intervention of his friend and mentor William Chamberlain and his power to control minds. Albeit the intention of that intervention was now going slightly pear-shaped to say the least.

Judd figured that his only remaining option was to head to St Pancras Train Station, which was only a short underground journey away, and wait for Banks to show before the killer boarded the Eurostar to Verona.

As Judd briskly walked once more through Camden Town in order to reach the underground station, his mind whirred again about Banks and his ambitious target. Yes, Banks was a disturbed individual for sure, and yes if he had his sights on taking out a high-profile religious figurehead, then they don't come much bigger than the Pope. But if Banks was so intent on succeeding with his prey, why was he being so careless in leaving clues behind?

Did he want to be stopped on some kind of subconscious level as the target was too colossal to contemplate even for Banks?

Was he leaving clues because he was supposed to? Had he been programmed to assassinate the Pope and he was therefore destined to become the patsy? Judd thought about Lee Harvey Oswald, Mark David Chapman and Sirhan Sirhan. All of those assassins were believed to be the patsies according to certain conspiracy theories, and they had all conveniently been easily accessible to arrest and blame.

But the more Judd thought about it, the more it still made sense to him that Banks' target would have to be the Pope purely from his own perspective.

Banks had been scarred for life learning that his dad had been a priest, a man who was meant to devote his life to God and commit to a life of celibacy. Clearly by becoming Banks' father the priest hadn't executed his vows the way he was meant to. And if Banks viewed his biological father's role as a priest to be a phony existence, who had ultimately allowed this to happen? Who could be held responsible? Who stood at the head of the Catholic Church and was accountable for allowing priests to do things that they weren't meant to do? The Pope of course.

Perhaps Banks even struggled with the concept of the successor to St Peter being voted in to the role of Pope. How could a man who was simply appointed as Pope by a committee of other priests, cardinals or bishops correctly be the successor to St Peter, the true right hand man of Jesus? Did Banks view the whole elective system as a farce?

Banks viewed his dad as being a sign of immorality so did that equate to all priests being a sign of immorality? Banks surely must view the Pope as the head of all this wrong-doing yet he is not even necessarily the true successor to St Peter? So to Banks even the Pope is perhaps a charlatan and a phony.

Judd Stone suddenly felt like he was in a Dan Brown novel

For Banks to target the Pope now made more sense than targeting the Archbishop of Canterbury. The Archbishop was ranked third in the Christian leader rankings and as stated by Sab, the Pope was clearly considered "numero uno". The Archbishop was undoubtedly the principal leader of the Church of England, the symbolic head of the worldwide Anglican community, but crucially he is simply not a catholic as Banks' father was. The Pope is Bishop of Rome and leader of the Catholic Church, so it is only he who can be held accountable in a mind such as Banks'.

What puzzled Judd was the fact that the Pope had been

to the UK not too long ago in 2011, which included Oscott College in Birmingham, a place where young men commit to various theological studies in a quest to become priests themselves. The Pope had been at the college from 16 to 21 September. Why on Earth had Banks left it to a complicated trip to Rome to attempt to kill the head of the Catholic Church, when the Pope had conveniently been visiting on his doorstep?

The journey on the Northern Line back to Euston station, along with the short walk to St Pancras, would not eat significantly into the time remaining for Banks to catch his train to Verona, so Judd estimated that catching him was a definite possibility. All Judd had to do was spot him as he made his way into the luxurious train station. But still, Judd wished he knew precisely where Gareth Banks was at this very moment, just to make life a little easier for him.

PART IV
TROJAN FOOTBALL

CHAPTER 54

The mind of Gareth Banks had in part been successfully usurped by the placed instructions of William Chamberlain, but the psychotic and destructive madness that already lay there had also been stirred to focus on the *need* to kill, an urge Banks naturally displayed without any provocation. However, the intensity of William's manipulation and the suggestion of specific targets had served to confuse Banks, and in spite of William's intrusion of Banks' psyche, Banks had been able to decipher that he also had some time to kill, in addition to his potential victims. Time enough to pay a surprise visit to someone he knew very well.

"Gareth, my darling. It's so good to see you."

"Save it Mother. You didn't even let me know that you had moved."

"That's because I didn't know where you had gone, Gareth. You left London so swiftly. I had no idea where you were."

"Birmingham."

"Well, eventually I was able to work out that you were residing somewhere in the Midlands once you were arrested for the killing of those poor girls. I knew it couldn't have been you who had done those killing. Not my Gareth. You were always such a sweet and sensitive boy."

"Don't describe me like that; I don't want to be sweet and sensitive."

Gareth's venom and change in tone was lost on her. The terror he could project was yet to break through to a mother in denial.

"I tried to get in touch with you at the time, I wanted to show you my support but your lawyer told me that I wasn't welcome."

"I told him to tell you that. I didn't need you. I even changed my name to distance myself from you. I've never needed you, and it's a good thing I haven't, because you never really needed me did you, Mom?"

"That's not true, Gareth, I love you. It broke my heart when you took off without a word. Look, Son, let's not waste time squabbling. I'm glad that you have found me now."

"Yeah, and what a surprise to find you in St John's Wood. It's a bit different to the East End isn't it? What happened for you to end up here then? Have you started selling your body to millionaires now or something? Mind you, looking at the state of you, I wouldn't have thought that anyone is willing to pay even a fiver for your services these days."

"I'm no longer on the game Gareth, and that's my choice, it's not a circumstance of my appearance or age as you refer." She attempted to keep the mood light. "So what do you think of the apartment? I've done okay for myself in the end haven't I?"

Gareth didn't answer; he just stared coldly at his mother, enough to begin to scare her.

"Why have you come here today, Gareth? How were you able to find me?"

"I wanted to tell you about all the blood on your hands, Mother. You see in your wisdom, the life that you chose to give me turned me into a bit of a nutter some would say, and it's all your fault. Do you know what it was like knowing that your own mother was selling her body in order to feed her child? A child she didn't even want?"

"I'm sorry, Gareth. I did want you and I always tried to protect you when the clients came around. I've never been very clever upstairs, and as a kid I had even less guidance from my parents than I gave you, so I just kind of fell into prostitution. I simply had no other way of knowing how to survive and provide for you. I'd have done anything to feed and clothe my little boy."

"Shut up you old whore! Don't you realise that I would have rather we had lived on the streets than to have to hear you screwing those disgusting men through the thin walls of our shitty little flat"

"I'm sorry, Gareth."

"And you know what? I went to that shitty little flat today and you weren't there. I thought perhaps you were dead but I wanted to make sure before I started celebrating. I went into an internet café, searched for women named Penelope living in London and discovered that there were several women going by the name of Penelope Hibbett, but only one Penelope Zandretti. It seems we both changed our name from Hibbett.

"Not too common a name that one, Zandretti. That was his name wasn't it? That charlatan who you loved, the one who used to beat me senseless because every time he saw me it reminded him of the sin that he had committed. Father Marco Zandretti was his name. He was also my father. My father the dirty bastard. You couldn't marry him could you, that waste of a priest? But you still wanted to take his name. You make me sick.

"It wasn't too difficult for me to fill in the gaps to find you, Mom. I must admit though, I got a shock when I discovered that you were living in St John's Wood. You know I wouldn't have been able to find you if you had only taken the trouble to drop a letter to the website owners. They happily oblige in removing names and addresses from their website if people don't wish to be located."

"Why would I not want you to find me? I love you; you're my boy no matter what you think of me."

"Pretty soon you will wish that I hadn't found you, Mom."

"Gareth, please. You are beginning to scare me."

"Good."

"Look Gareth, have a cup of tea. I'll pop the kettle on. Sit down and let's catch up. What have you been up to?"

"Killing people."

"Don't joke like that, Gareth. It's not funny."

"Who's joking?"

Penny Zandretti felt her stomach roll over and a chill shivered up her spine.

"Gareth, did you kill those poor girls?"

"Yes."

It took all of Penny Zandretti's efforts not to get physically sick. "Oh my God, what have you done?" Her legs began to slightly give way at the knees in the realisation of her son's wickedness. "Gareth, I think you should leave."

"Oh, suddenly you are not so pleased to see me, Mom."

Penny was still winning her battle with the stirring of the contents of her stomach, but she was not as successful in suppressing her tears and she began to cry. "Why did you do it, Gareth? Why did you kill those poor innocent girls? They were prostitutes weren't they? Like me? Is that why you killed them, to punish me?"

"Partly, yes. Like I said, Mother, you have blood on your hands."

Penny surprised herself as she began to get angry. "I have never, ever told you that it is okay to kill people."

"I have to kill. I am the chosen one. And at the moment I've never been more focussed on killing with such amazing clarity. It is like I am being guided by another force, and I believe that it is God who is directing me."

"Gareth, you're not well. You need help."

"There is nothing wrong with me you ignorant woman. I'm simply doing God's work. He is known as God Almighty you see, because he is *the* almighty one, and there have been many imposters to that fact. Certain individuals use his name in vain, quite literally with their actions. That's why I had to kill the cult leader, he was just another imposter. And I will kill again; and this time I have a very significant target in mind."

"Who, Gareth, who?"

"The Pope."

"The Pope? Oh, Gareth, you'll never get away with it. They'll kill *you* if you try to kill the Pope."

"I am protected by God."

"If anyone is protected by God it is more likely to be the Pope than you."

"You still don't understand, Mother. God will not protect him because he too is an imposter. An imposter, who is the head of a religion simply because of a closed voting system of an old-boys network, based on man-made rules and perceived advantages for those who are allowed to vote. An imposter who is the head of a religion who allowed a priest to break the commitment of celibacy and father a child. A child who they also failed to protect as that priest was allowed to beat him. And that beaten child was me. It is simply a farce and I want my revenge."

"So this is what this is all about. Your father?"

"Yes, my father the Father." Gareth cackled at his own word play.

"Whatever you believe Gareth, you must stop killing people. Killing would never be God's way."

"You are wrong. God has called upon me. When I receive his instruction to stop killing then I shall, but right now I have a clear message to kill, and I have to kill imposters to God and next in line is the Pope."

"And you view the fact that your father was a priest to be a sign that the Pope must be your next target? Because as head of that religion he is accountable for you being born from an act of sin conducted between Marco and I, and the physical abuse that subsequently happened to you at the hands of your father?."

"Yes, it all makes sense."

"So you want to kill the Pope because he stands for the Catholic Church and your dad was a priest? A priest who is not meant to father a child in the laws of the Catholic Church?"

"I think that you are finally keeping up, Mother. I can't kill the actual priest who was my dad can I? He is already dead. Therefore the Pope has become my target?"

"Gareth, are you seeing the Pope as a living symbol of your dead father?

"Yes, of course."

"Would it make a difference if I told you that the priest wasn't your father?"

"What do you mean? You are lying just to stop me going after the Pope."

"I am not lying, Gareth. I am not going to lie to you anymore, look what it has turned you into. You are correct; I feel that I have got blood on my hands, so if the truth will stop you killing I will tell you the truth. Please believe me Gareth, what I told you originally about your father, I genuinely thought it was for the best. Now I have to live with the fact that you have killed innocent people because of what you have been led to believe all your life and I will always feel responsible. It is time for you to know who your father really is."

Gareth became confused. "You had better not be shitting me, Mom."

"I am going to tell you the truth, so help me God."

When Penny had woken up that morning she had naturally not prepared herself to break such overwhelming news to her son. She briefly composed herself as much as was possible before launching into her explanation. "Your father was not the priest Marco Zandretti, though I always wished that he had been. I loved that man and he would have been good for us. I know he would. He always told me that he would leave the church and we could be a proper family. I truly thought it would happen one day so I allowed you to think that he was your dad, Gareth. I also allowed Marco to believe that he was your father. I needed him more than the church did. We needed him.

"Your real dad was no good; he never wanted to know you, Gareth. He knew he was your father, I told him, but he didn't want you and he didn't want me, not like that anyway. It took me a long time to finally realise. I tried to make sure that he would do the right thing by you, that he would be a part of your life and support you financially; God knows he was in a position to help with money, but he never showed an interest in you and he could become very aggressive towards me.

"I did receive money from him, but only via our, erm, arrangement. But he never wanted to be your father. That was consistently clear. He had a family of his own you see and he persuaded me to agree that we wouldn't jeopardise their feelings or his career. He could be very manipulative. I also believed that there was no need to cause any hurt towards his wife and family. None of it was their fault after all. And scandal was big in those days."

"Yet you would have allowed a priest's career to be rocked by a scandal? So come on, who was my dad then? Why was his career so damn precious?"

"You have to remember I loved Marco and he loved me. Your real dad and I were never really in love. That made things different."

"That bastard hit me, yet you loved him."

"He would have stopped that once we had become a proper family. He used to tell me how he regretted hitting you; he just had difficulty dealing with his frustration and the complex situation. He loved you and he wanted to make it up to you. He wanted to be with us, Gareth."

"You stupid, delusional woman. If he hadn't died of a heart attack you would still be waiting for him now you desperate old goat."

"That's not true, but what is true for certain is that he loved you more than your real father ever did. And if you think Marco treated you badly, your real dad was far more capable of violence, believe me; I have the scars to prove it. He had a very nasty temper."

"So who is my real father?"

Penny looked down at the floor; it was clearly still difficult for her to find the correct words to release the secret she had held for all these years.

"Come on, who was this violent and selfish individual who is meant to be my dad?"

"Your father was a footballer, Gareth. I am sure that you will recognise his name and it may be difficult for you to take in at first. He goes by the name of Marlon Howell."

Gareth could hardly believe what he was hearing. So much so he let out a brief fit of laughter. "You are telling me that my dad is the England manager? You must think I'm really gullible, Mom."

The deadly serious look on his mother's face wasn't lost on Gareth. "What I tell you is true, Gareth. I wanted Marco to provide for us. He wanted me, he wanted us, and I loved him more than I ever loved Marlon but it wasn't to be. My arrangement with Marlon gradually faded away, and in the end I was glad of it. In the meantime I waited many years for Marco to leave the church and be with us, but he died before he fulfilled his promise to me.

"Perhaps you are right, Gareth. Perhaps I was a fool to believe that he would have left the church, but I know for certain that we were in love?

"Once Marco had died and I realised that him being your intended father figure was no longer a possibility, I approached Marlon again to see if he wanted to be your dad. I felt that you needed a dad to be around; I just wish it could have been Marco. Anyway, I showed Marlon a photo of you in your school uniform, one of those photos where they bring a photographer into school. The one I showed him has always been one of my favourites of you, you looked such a handsome boy but he hardly responded, and then do you know what he done? He went and watched you play football on the school football field from afar. He came back to me and said that the way you played football meant that you could not be any son of his. I hated him so much when he said that to me. At that time I hadn't 'entertained' him as a client for many years, but even though we were no longer acquainted and the hatred for him built up inside me, I didn't have the courage to do anything about it. Until now that is. Once he became the England manager I thought, you know what, enough is enough.

"It was time for him to begin to make amends. Why should I still be on the game in my fifties, while he Lords it up becoming the England manager, living a life of Riley compared to mine? I told him I was going to go to the press and shatter his little world. I told him as his kids are a lot older now they would cope with the news about their precious dad and his wife had a right to know what sort of a low-life she had been married to all these years. But he knew that it could certainly compromise the public perception of him and jeopardise his new found International management career.

"He wasn't best pleased and he showed me how his temper hadn't mellowed over the years, but instead of beating me senseless he found another way to silence me. He paid me off and bought me this flat. That's how I came to live in St John's Wood.

"He never had the courage to be a father to you, Gareth, and yet there he is being the manager of the England football team, the so called people's choice. I was going to go to the press and tell them about all those years he didn't provide for you and how he turned his back on his son.

"So nowadays I live well, Gareth and I am no longer on the game. I don't have to any more as Marlon Howell has paid me so much money I never have to work again."

"You should have received his money when I was growing up, he should have provided for me then, but you waited until now to get his money."

"I'm sorry. But you are here now; I can give you money Gareth, if that's what you want? You walked out of my life on the day of your 18th birthday, Gareth, it broke my heart. I know I failed you as a mother but I always loved you."

"You failed me alright, and so did my dad."

"Like you Gareth, your dad went to the Midlands; it was ironic how you were destined to follow each other. He moved to the Midlands to get away from me and you unconsciously moved to the Midlands after him."

"And that's why I got involved in football hooliganism. I was guided by God. The world laughed at me so I had to leave them with a permanent marking. I gave them a permanent smile as they liked to laugh so much."

"Gareth, what are you talking about?"

Gareth simply looked through his mother as if she wasn't there.

"Listen now you are here, son I have money. I have your father's money and a lot of it. He didn't provide for you all your life but now he can. What he has paid me I can share with you. There is no need to kill anymore. You don't need to kill the Pope. Religion has nothing to do with your real father. And if you need revenge on your real father I have done it in abundance for you. We're rich, Gareth. For the first time in our lives we're rich."

Confused, Banks took a moment to gather his thoughts and to digest what his mother had told him. No matter what she said he still felt an overwhelming necessity to kill. God had not asked him to relent. "You know, Mom, I joined up with a bunch of football hooligans in

Birmingham and they used to tell me that football was like a religion. Now it makes sense. I need to kill my father and that is what this has all been about. It was just more symbolic that's all. Football is an integral part of English life; football is an imposter to religion itself. Kids are more interested in a game than they are of the teachings of God. I now know what I need to do. Football has become the religion in England; England has forgotten its Christian values. And who is head of that religion, the religion of English football? My father that's who. The England manager. The England manager must die and at the same time my dad must die."

"No, Gareth, no you're wrong. That's not why I told you about, Marlon. I told you to stop the killing, not for you to go out and kill.

"And look, with all this money I can pay for some real help for you, Gareth, so that you never do anything like you did to those poor girls again. I don't think that you are well; Gareth, but now we can fix that. Let me help you. If you don't like St John's Wood we can move abroad, you can get away from your life in England and start a new life. "What do you say, son?"

Gareth Banks simply smiled as he pulled a knife from his inside pocket and drove into his own mother's stomach.

"All that Judd can do now is wait at St Pancras Station until the crazy lunatic shows up."

"I guess so, Sab. So near yet so far, hey? I just hope that Banks has no other avenues of mischief planned in the meantime. I wanted him to kill those two cult leaders and no more," said William as Sab handed him a cup of tea. William's grip failed and the hot liquid spilled across the desk.

"Sorry, William. I forgot that you don't grip so well these days."

"Please, allow me to help," offered Crystal. Crystal

pulled a packet of clean tissues from her handbag and mopped away frantically at the spilt tea, not making much headway. William brought his hand to Crystal's to stop her. "Thanks, but you'd best leave it, Crystal. Sab can go back to the kitchen and fetch a cloth that's a little more robust."

As Sab left her seat to search for a cloth, she noticed Crystal stop in her tracks and she grabbed William's hand tighter.

"Can you feel that?" Crystal asked William.

"Yes," answered William looking genuinely astonished. "It feels as if I have an electric current running straight through me."

"And can you see what I can see. In your mind's eye?"

"A man with a knife. A man pushing a knife into a woman."

"I can feel the same maternal connection that I often feel when receiving a message from the spirit world. The woman must be his mother."

"And the psycho is Gareth Banks. I can see him clear as day."

"What is happening?" enquired an unnerved Sabita Mistry.

"We have a psychic connection," explained Crystal. "The intensity of the situation, coupled with the mutual concentration that William and I have been applying on the same cause, has enabled us to generate a psychic reading when we joined hands."

"So both your energies are providing twice as much psychic activity in a single focus."

"That's about it," said Crystal.

Sab sat down and frantically typed away at the computer. Moments later she spoke. "There are a few Penelope Hibbetts in London, strangely none in the east of London, though. Hibbett was Banks' mom's name wasn't it, and she lived in the East End?"

"She's moved," offered William. "I have always kept

some form of intelligence ongoing where Banks is concerned, ever since we were acquainted with the scumbag. Banks' movements haven't always been easy to map, but I had PC Brownlow discreetly keep tabs on any developments or changes that ever came to light and he reliably informed me that Banks' mother had changed her name by deed poll to Penelope Zandretti; the priest whom she claimed to be Banks' dad was called Father Marco Zandretti. Get on the phone to Judd and tell him to get his arse over to St John's Wood. You'll find the exact address in Banks' file. Hopefully we have seen a vision of the future and not of the past."

Judd had taken some convincing to leave St Pancras Station, but he succumbed to his Detective Sergeant's pleas, and when he reached the property in St John's Wood, thankfully not the London home of Sir Paul McCartney only a few streets away, he didn't have to force entry as the door had been left ajar. He entered the property to find a woman slumped on the floor in a small pool of blood, clutching her stomach. Her eyes were closed and Judd thought that she was most likely dead.

Judd rushed over to the injured woman and cradled her head in his arms. "Ms Zandretti. Ms Zandretti, can you hear me?"

Penny Zandretti slowly opened her eyes, which offered a little sparkle in spite of the circumstances, and by looking into them, Judd could recognise the good nature nestled within. In that second he was sure that whatever had possessed Gareth Banks to do the things that he had done, it was not due to a genetic inheritance from his maternal parentage.

"Ms Zandretti, my name is Judd Stone. I know that your son Gareth has done this to you and I need to find him to prevent him from hurting anyone else."

"Please don't hurt him, Mr. Stone. He is a good boy."

Judd felt that it wasn't the time or place to correct Penny on her delusions about her monstrous son. "I do need to find him, Penny. Did he tell you he was going to Rome by any chance?"

"Yes."

"This may sound absurd but I think he is going to attempt to kill the Pope."

"It's not absurd, he was going to. But not anymore."

"Sorry?"

"He was going to kill the Pope. That was before he found out who his father was." Penny Zandretti winced in pain as she spoke.

"Let me call you an ambulance, Ms Zandretti. I think you need taking care of."

"I think you are too late to save me, Mr. Stone. I'm dying, I know I am."

"No, Ms Zandretti, let me call for an ambulance. There is still time."

"No, I don't think there is. You seem a nice boy; did you make your mother proud of you?"

"Yes, I think so. Eventually."

"What was her name?"

"Evelyn."

"Pretty name. A mother is always proud of her son, Judd."

"And a son is always proud of his mom."

"I wish I could believe that of Gareth, but I'm afraid he hates me." Penny writhed a little. "Oh, the pain in my stomach."

"Please let me get you an ambulance."

"Do you know my son, Judd?"

"Yes, you could say that."

"Did he ever talk about me?"

"Yes, often. He really loved you. He always spoke well of you whenever I met him."

"That's nice. Do you like football, Judd?"

"Err, yes."

"How would you feel if your dad was the England manager?"

"If it was the current England manager I wouldn't be too pleased. I know Marlon Howell from a long time ago and he is not the man people think he is."

"I couldn't agree more. I have told Gareth that Marlon is his father."

"I though Gareth's father was a priest?"

"That was a lie that I lived for too long. Until today that is. I have now told Gareth the truth. He isn't going to kill the Pope, Judd. Gareth is going to kill Marlon Howell. Please stop him; I don't want him to kill his own father as well as everything else, even if his father deserves it."

"Ms Zandretti. I think you are hallucinating. You are telling me that Gareth's father is the England manager?"

"I am, and it's true. Now please grant a dying mother one last request and stop my son from killing anybody else. Even if it is Marlon Howell."

"I promise."

Penny Zandretti found one last ounce of strength to stroke the cheek of Judd, wiping a smear of her blood across his bristled skin. "You're a good boy. You're mother would be proud of you."

The lifeless woman flopped into Judd's arms and he placed her on the floor, closed her eyes and covered her body with a nearby blanket applying all the dignity that he could in the circumstances.

Judd softly stroked her hair, placing it behind her ear before speaking to her. "Sleep well, Ms Zandretti. I promise to stop Gareth from killing anyone else so that you can rest in peace." Judd then stood up and walked away from the flat.

Gareth Banks walked up Wembley Way in his semi-robotic state with a clear focus on killing the England manager, Marlon Howell.

Incredibly he had hardly noticed the magnificent arch that covered Wembley Stadium. The arch now served as the defining image of Wembley since the removal of the twin towers and usually became everybody's focal point until inside the sports ground.

Inconspicuously a figure emerged from the shadows of the stalls and vans that were selling scarves, badges, match day programmes and burgers, and walked against the flow of human traffic in order to reach Banks.

In spite of his focussed determination to locate Howell, once in clear view of Banks he recognised the figure to be DI Lionel Scarrow of B.A.D Police, the sly man whom he had met with before.

Scarrow's wide mouth entered conversation first.

"I have a gun in my pocket pointing straight at you, Banks. Don't draw any attention to us and walk to the side of Wembley Way; we need to have a little chat."

Although in a much immersed state of his quest, Banks still sensed the logic to comply with Scarrow's request in order to avoid getting shot. Once in relative safety from the streams of football fans making their way to England's finest football stadium, the two individuals had the freedom to speak.

"What's this about, Scarrow? Why are you pointing a gun at me?"

"It's payback time. I'm taking you in. You are no good to me anymore; you just keep messing things up so you are worth more to me behind bars now. I'll be a hero if I take you in, and you my friend will rot in jail like your sorry and warped arse deserves."

"Messing things up?"

"Yes, you're useless. You failed to put an end to Chamberlain even though he was a sitting duck. I advised you how to find Haddock's daughter to have some fun with and instead you chose to use her in your little game with Stone. That little game could have backfired and how do I know that you wouldn't have implicated me to try and save yourself?

"Can you imagine how I felt when I saw that bastard Chamberlain enter the police station today? I thought the next time I saw him he would be in a coffin, opening a way for me to become DCI. That jerk Stone would have no chance of getting DCI, then imagine the real fun I could have with Stone if I was working above him in the hierarchy.

"But instead, you have chosen to let Chamberlain live and for some reason you've killed some random cult leader before driving a knife into your own mother you mixed-up freak. What's wrong with you?

"Chamberlain and Mistry are keeping things close to their chest up at B.A.D HQ, but I made sure that I heard enough to join the dots so I caught a train down to London to find you and steal the glory. I haven't quite worked out yet why you are at this football match but I don't really care. I've checked CCTV across London and tracked your movements, I have crooked friends all over this city you see, even in Scotland Yard for instance, so finding you has been quite easy and now the prize will be all mine.

"I've put my career on the line for you Banks, including lying in court to get you acquitted of killing those girls, and you can't even repay me by killing Chamberlain. You're becoming a liability; you are killing the wrong people."

"I'm killing the right people. William Chamberlain was not an imposter."

"What the hell are you talking about, you loony? You are one fucked up fruitcake, Banks. Turn around while I cuff you. I've made the arrest of the century so they may make me DCI after all even while Chamberlain lives."

"I won't let you cuff me. I need to kill."

"Who do you need to kill?"

"My father."

"Your father, is he at the match or something?"

"Yes, you could say that. I must kill him."

"You are killing no one else that you are not supposed to. Wait, this is great. As I have also seemingly foiled an attempt to kill your father, I can add that to my list of achievements in connection with arresting you. Now turn around or I swear I'll put a bullet in your crazy skull."

Suddenly the situation became disturbed as a loud Birmingham accent could be heard shouting across the crowd. It seemed that Scarrow hadn't quite achieved the amount of seclusion that he had hoped for in order to make his arrest. As he turned to look behind him, he saw a gang of men running towards him and Banks. Scarrow could see that they had their eyes firmly fixed on Banks and they had an intent in their eyes which signalled they meant to do him some real harm.

The guy leading the gang looked a real nasty piece of work, and the man positioned just behind him wouldn't have looked out of place in a bare-knuckled boxing contest.

The two evil slime balls were about to become acquainted with Eddie Goode, Hank Roderick and several other football hooligans.

"Banks," shouted Goode. "Start saying you're prayers, you are about to get the kicking of your life."

Scarrow pulled the gun from his pocket and pointed it at the football hooligans succeeding in stopping them in their tracks.

"What the fuck are you doing?" enquired Goode.

"You are not touching him. I don't quite know what your issue is with this man but he is wanted for murder so I am arresting him. Now back off."

"Are you a copper?"

"Yes, I am a detective inspector."

"Are you a friend of Judd's?"

"I am certainly no friend of Stone's." scoffed Scarrow. "How do you know him? Has he arrested you yobs at some point?"

"Never you mind how we know him, but you need to understand that Judd is a friend of ours and he asked me to specifically look out for Banks, and now I've found him I need to let him know," said Eddie.

"You have found no-one. And Stone is here, in London? I should have guessed. Now listen to me you big oaf I am arresting Banks and Stone isn't. That tosser is not having any of the glory, now you and your Neanderthal cronies had better turn around and walk away so that I can carry out my duty. I won't think twice about putting a bullet in your thick skulls."

"So, let me get this straight. You are going to take Banks in and not allow my friend Stone to reap the glory."

"Correct."

"Well that may be a little tricky as your detainee has just ran out of sight while you have been busy speaking a load of shit our way." Scarrow turned around and saw that it was true, Banks had got away. The turning of his head was enough time to allow Eddie to kick the gun from Scarrow's hand with Hank following up to retrieve it. Hank placed the gun in his pocket before landing the first punch on Scarrow's oversized, ugly and by now terrified face. Eddie took a turn before the gang of hooligans each reined punches and kicks into the helpless body and face of Lionel Scarrow.

It took no time at all to place Lionel Scarrow into a state of unconsciousness.

CHAPTER 55

The last thing that Judd Stone believed he would be able to do this evening was attend the International football match at Wembley Stadium. In light of the appointment of Marlon Howell as England manager, the fixture had been somewhat hastily arranged to allow Howell a chance to work with the players prior to the squad taking part in the remaining world cup qualifiers. Many followers of football often view a 'friendly' fixture as being a waste of time, but as this game was to be played against the auld enemy, Scotland, both sets of players would take the game seriously and it would be played out with a definite competitive edge.

Judd fondly remembered the home international tournaments as a young boy where each of the home nations played one another in an annual contest. He, like many other football fans, had always considered it a shame that the tournament had been withdrawn.

Judd had been surrounded by the atmosphere and pockets of supporters all day, but he had tried hard not to let the environment distract him from hunting down serial killer Gareth Banks. But now, as fate would have it, it had become necessary to attend the football match in order to try and catch the hunted.

Judd had been fortunate enough to purchase his ticket from a tout outside the ground. In normal circumstances, Judd wouldn't entertain purchasing a ticket from such an individual, but being so close to kick-off, Judd was grateful that a tout had been available.

Sab had confirmed to Judd that Banks had not purchased a match ticket via his credit card, leaving Judd with the assumption that he too must have purchased a ticket from a tout in order to gain access to Wembley with the intent of reaching Marlon Howell. This presented the very real difficulty of not knowing where Banks was hiding amongst the thousands of supporters.

Judd wanted to try and enjoy the game, but he realised that he needed to spend the majority of his time keeping a close eye on Marlon Howell to see at what point Banks would make his move. There was a part of him that willed Banks to achieve his aim of killing the newly-appointed England manager, because of what he had done to Bonnie Glass all those years ago, and it seemed he hadn't been an altogether pleasant character towards Penny Zandretti either. But Judd had promised Penny that he would prevent Banks from killing again, and besides, he realised that by catching Banks in the act he could become a national hero as well as hopefully being reinstated on the police force, his reputation once again intact.

Incredibly, the tout had a ticket positioned just five rows behind the England bench area, costing Judd almost twice the price that it had originally been sold for, but the location was a necessity for Judd to be able to see when Banks would approach Howell.

And for Judd to watch the football as well of course.

Judd knew that Eddie Goode and his cronies were also keeping a look out for Banks on Judd's behalf. Judd hoped that if they managed to get to Banks first, the serial killer would be left in a fit enough state for Judd to be able to arrest him, even though Banks deserved the kicking of his life, which Eddie Goode would be only too willing to oblige considering what Banks had done to Cassie, Olive and Kez. He wasn't sure where Eddie, Hank and the others would be sitting in the stadium, but he was grateful for the additional eyes, as before him were thousands upon thousands of bodies. Spotting Banks wasn't going to be easy.

Lionel Scarrow was in an unfamiliar place when he finally gained consciousness. His head throbbed from the almighty beating that he had taken, and as he attempted to move he realised it wasn't such a good idea as pain rushed through his body like an electric current.

His blurred sight however, did begin to clear as he lay there, and the kind face of an oriental woman came into focus.

"Hello, Detective Inspector Scarrow. We found your police badge in your pocket. My name is Dr Chow. It is perhaps a silly question but how are you feeling?"

"Like I've spent some time spinning around in a cement mixer before being thrown from a great height."

"It may not feel like it at the moment, but you have been very lucky. You were found unconscious not far away from Wembley Stadium, but fortunately I do not expect you to have any permanent damage from whatever beating you encountered. You'll be sore and in pain for a few days yet I'm afraid, and I would prefer to keep you in hospital overnight just for observational purposes. I'm sorry but this means that you are going to miss the football match."

"Football match? Oh yeah, I can live with that. What about my attackers?"

"They got clean away I'm afraid, and so far no-one has come forward to offer a witness's account. I suspect that your London counterparts will want to speak with you about the attack, but all in good time, your recovery is my primary concern. But when you do speak with them perhaps you can give them a description of your attackers?"

Lionel Scarrow wasn't entirely sure if that would be a good idea.

The two teams were led onto the pitch by their respective managers, with Marlon Howell receiving a colossal reception from the English supporters. Amongst the many faces and noise from the crowd, Judd realised that somehow he had to seek out Gareth Banks, knowing the psychopath could choose any given moment to strike, and now was as good a moment as any to gain maximum impact.

The teams lined up side by side in anticipation of the respective national anthems being played, and as the crowd focussed on this spectacle, Judd instead searched the sea of faces, some painted with the St George Cross, but he had not yet located a rogue, pistol-wielding hand in the crowd or any imminent intruder taking to the pitch.

As the opening bars of "Flower of Scotland" sang out, Judd's concentration was broken as he felt a hefty hand grab his shoulder. He turned around half-expecting Gareth Banks to be behind him, but instead it was the smiling, rugged features of Eddie Goode, with Hank Roderick sitting alongside him.

"Eddie, Hank!"

"Well of all the seats in Wembley Stadium look where we all end up sitting. "

"Have you seen him at all? Banks?"

"We have, and we would have got him too if it hadn't been for that stupid copper."

"Copper?"

"Some skinny, ugly looking prat, with a head so big that it looked as if his neck could collapse at any given moment with the responsibility of holding it aloft. He said that he knew you but didn't consider himself to be a friend of yours, so that seemed as good a reason as any to give him a good kicking for his insolence."

"Scarrow. How did he get involved in all this?"

"The cheeky bastard pulled a gun on us too, but we wrestled it off him and Hank has it in his safe keeping."

Hank pulled the gun from his pocket and showed it to Judd.

"Fucking hell Hank, don't flash that thing around in here. It's good to see that Wembley's 'stop and search' security measures are up to scratch. Listen, good work Hank, you did well but can you give the gun to me please?" Judd swiftly took the gun from Hank before he could provide an answer and placed it in his inside pocket. Judd realised that it may become handy later, and he wasn't altogether sure if it was wise for someone like Hank Roderick to have a firearm in his possession.

"I put it down my bollocks; they never touch you there when they search you."

"And who can blame them? Seriously though, nicely done, Hank."

"Okay ladies," interjected Eddie. "It's time to watch the match. It's about to kick-off."

Judd watched Marlon Howell walk towards the England bench to take his seat for the first time as England manager. It had been many years since Judd had encountered the displeasure of seeing him in the flesh again. All the feelings of hatred that he had for the man rose to the surface in an instant, and Judd considered pulling Scarrow's gun from his pocket and shooting the England manager himself. Instead, he managed to resist.

Judd scanned the immediate vicinity through the sea of red and white scarves, replica football tops and St George flags, but still he couldn't spot Gareth Banks.

Half time came and went without incident. Not from Gareth Banks or the England team. The score was 0-0 at half time. Judd had tried to enjoy the first-half as much as he could but he inevitably found his eyes searching the crowd for Gareth Banks, before always finishing his scanning activity by resting them on Marlon Howell to confirm that he hadn't suffered any injury.

Judd settled back into his seat for the second-half of the match after taking a leak and spending time with Eddie and Hank to sneak a quick pint of lager. It had been a long and intense day and Judd badly needed a drink.

There had still been no sign of Gareth Banks. Of course it had occurred to Judd that Banks could easily be nestled somewhere within the Scottish supporters, but it was unlikely as that would have made it more difficult for him to reach Howell.

As the teams entered the pitch for the second-half, Judd was pleased, in a bittersweet kind of way, to see Marlon Howell eventually trail behind them to return to his seat. Banks, it seemed, had not made a move during the half-time break to get to the England manager via the dressing room.

Finally, the match finished with no score, hardly a rip-roaring result for the 'people's choice' of England manager. With all due respect to Scotland, many would consider the result a poor one from England's point of view, who would have been expected to beat the Scottish who are ranked considerably below them in the world football rankings, and especially with the game being played at Wembley.

Marlon Howell's next test as England manager would quickly follow. He would need to try and offer an explanation via several awkward questions and interviews by the sports press, as to the reasons for the failure of not securing a victory.

And in truth, Scotland had deserved to win the match.

The Scottish fans were more than pleased with the result. Okay they hadn't won either, but gaining a draw at Wembley, the home of English football, would be considered a match well played. To celebrate, many of the Scottish fans managed to enter the pitch, running across the grass with a fairly even spread of yellow flags with a red dragon, and blue flags with a white cross on them. Many had the St Andrews flag painted on their face as well.

"Come on Hank, we're not standing for this," said Eddie, and pretty soon Eddie, Hank and scores of other England supporters were also on the pitch taking exception to the Scottish 'invasion' of their hallowed Wembley turf.

Fortunately these days, the police and associated security strategies that are in place to deal with football hooliganism are highly sophisticated. Mounted police and Wembley Stadium stewards soon had the matter in hand, but not before Eddie and Hank had cracked a couple of Scottish heads before avoiding arrest.

It was clear that the appetite for football hooliganism wasn't as wide spread across the thousands of supporters as yesteryear, and most simply left the stadium in a peaceful manner.

The pitch invasion had presented an opening for Judd to enter the field. Not to partake in any football violence, but to be able to get closer to Marlon Howell incase Gareth Banks made an appearance. Curiously it never happened.

Why had Banks not made an attempt to get to Howell at the football match? Had he viewed it too risky a proposition with so many people around? Had he planned to do it at the end of the game, but then the pitch invasion had spoiled his plans?

Whatever the reason, it seemed that Marlon Howell had managed to live another day.

CHAPTER 56

Marlon Howell had refused to speak to the press following the uninspiring goalless draw with Scotland. The consequence was a gathering of media personnel pitched outside his Berkshire home, each one of them determined to get a response from the England manager about his first game in charge.

After many hours of waiting they finally got their reward. The electronic gates to Howell's mansion opened, allowing the England manager to manoeuvre his Jaguar car out of his driveway. The frenzied crowd of media prevented Howell from driving any further as they surrounded his vehicle, and as tempting as it was, he resisted accelerating any harder as he would have surely ploughed into a good number of the journalists and photographers.

Baying for his blood, or at least a reaction to fill the pages of their newspapers, the mob swamped his car and Howell wound down his window to reveal a small gap of only about an inch in an attempt to diffuse their appetite. "Ok, ok, this will be my one and only statement regarding yesterday's match so I suggest that you all listen carefully. It wasn't a great performance but I fully understand where we went wrong on the pitch and I will endeavour to put those things right going forward. Both the players and I are 100% committed to English football and I can assure you that we will comfortably qualify for the World Cup Finals that are to be held in Brazil. I give full credit to the Scottish team for how well they played and being able to frustrate us yesterday, but I am not unduly concerned with the capability of the England Football team. Thank you that is all I have to say on the matter."

More questions were being fired at Marlon Howell as he managed to accelerate slightly and begin to pull away from the crowd, only to be halted by a car driving straight towards him.

"What the…"

The Ford Focus connected with the bonnet of Howell's Jaguar, which enraged him so much that he forgot about the swarming media and got out of his car to confront the driver.

"What the hell do you think you are doing?" screamed Howell as he approached the other car, but the driver didn't even bother to answer, instead he calmly got out of his car and pulled a shiny blade from inside his jacket.

"Keep the camera rolling, Reggie," said one savvy TV journalist, as other journalists simply gasped, shocked at what was unfolding before their eyes. It had become clear that the crashing of the cars had not been an accident and the young man walked steadily towards the now petrified England manager.

Howell thought about retreating to his car but realised that he would be unable to drive away as the Focus was preventing a means of escape. The angle of his own garden wall in proximity to both his Jaguar and the crowd of journalists would have required significant manoeuvring in order to find an alternative route, which would have ate into time he realised he didn't have.

The young man lunged at Howell who instinctively raised his arm to block the attack, preventing any fatal blows but still causing a nasty wound across his forearm.

"Why are you doing this?" spluttered Howell. "Who are you?"

The assailant didn't answer and Howell noticed the vacancy in his eyes. Instead, he took a second attempt to place the knife firmly into Howell. Fearing for his life, Howell realised that his only hope of survival was to fight back and he threw a punch towards his attacker. The movement of the punch was enough for the knife to glance the side of Howell's upper arm preventing a fatal blow for the second time, and not wishing to take a chance for a third time, Howell managed to follow up his punch with a kick to the attacker's hand that sent the knife spinning into the air, then a punch to the stomach as the attacker's natural instinct was to focus his eyes on the mid-air journey of the knife. This resulted in the attacker dropping to the floor. Howell saw his chance to finish off his attacker, but as he approached the man on the floor he was stopped in his tracks when the attacker pulled another weapon from his jacket. This time it was a gun and it was pointing straight at Howell.

The attacker now spoke for the first time as he cocked the barrel. "Back off."

Howell thought it best to comply and this allowed the attacker to get to his feet.

All of a sudden an individual broke through the crowd of astonished onlookers and retrieved the spilled knife from the floor.

Gareth Banks now pointed his gun towards Judd Stone, but Stone was clever. He grabbed hold of Marlon Howell and held the knife to the England manager's throat.

By this time the incident had become a live TV spectacle across both the conventional news and sports news networks, as it seemed that not only one, but now two people were making an attempt to take Marlon Howell's life. Okay so the England versus Scotland result hadn't been great but could it really provoke such a threat to the England manager?

"You want to kill this man don't you, Gareth?"

Banks simply nodded.

"He would be your latest victim, wouldn't he? With you being a serial killer and all, but Gareth, I know a bit about how serial killers operate and the primary reason that serial killers kill is for that supreme feeling of being in control. Well it's me who has that control now. It's me with a knife at his throat and it's me who is going to kill him, so what do you think about that?"

Both the TV audience and those present were gripped by the unbelievable incident that was unfolding. It was now seemingly becoming apparent that a serial killer wanted to kill the England manager as his next victim!

"You can't kill him, he is mine to kill. Mine."

"And why is that, Gareth? Why is he yours to kill? And what about Cassie Parker, Olive Jenas and Kez Raven? Were they yours to kill too?"

"They had to die. I had to do God's work and kill them all." The focus that William had applied to Banks' mind prevented him from being cautious in revealing information about his victims. To think that he had beaten the system throughout his court case, even toying and tormenting Judd beyond the unbelievable verdict, now his entire mind was focused on exercising his compulsion to being a killing machine and nothing else. Prostitutes needed to die and imposters to God needed to die. And that was that.

"Thank you Gareth, you have just told the world that you are 'The Crucifier'."

Gareth offered no emotion.

"And what is your motivation in wanting to kill Marlon Howell, Gareth? Is that carrying out God's work too?"

"He must be punished."

Judd continued to bring about Banks' confession in front of the TV cameras, whilst teasing out his rationale for killing. "So you are acting as God's vigilante then, Gareth? You kill prostitutes for somehow not following God's guidance? So why would you want to kill Howell then? He is a lot of things but he isn't a prostitute. At least I don't think he is? You may not know this Gareth, but I know Marlon Howell very well indeed and I have good reason to slit his throat, more reason I am sure than you could ever have. And believe me; I would be slitting this scumbag's throat because of the unprecedented life of sinning that he has led, far worse than any prostitute could ever lead."

Howell flinched as he felt Judd's blade nick his skin. "Judd Stone, it's you isn't it?"

"You bet it is, Howell. Long time, no see. Now why do you think I have good reason to slit your throat then?"

"It was a long time ago, Judd."

"That's irrelevant and you know it." Judd put further pressure on the blade causing a trickle of blood to run down Howell's neck.

"I didn't mean to do it, I didn't mean to."

"You didn't mean to do what, Howell?" Once more Judd pressed the knife against Howell's throat. Judd was now getting dangerously close to taking the wound beyond a superficial injury and it took all his self-control not to avenge Bonnie Glass right there and then. "Perhaps if you choose to confess your sins Howell, neither I nor the psycho opposite us will feel the need to kill you."

Genuinely terrified for his life, with a knife at his throat and a gun at his chest, Howell felt desperately like he needed to comply in order to save himself.

"Confess Howell and I might think about letting you live…" then Judd dropped his voice to a whisper, "But you don't use her name, you're not fit to use her name. If you do I'll kill you anyway, so choose your words very carefully. I'm only going to give you one chance to get this right."

"I raped her."

"Louder you prick, so everyone can hear."

Once more Howell confessed. "I raped her. I raped her. I'm sorry, Judd. I shouldn't have done it."

The witnesses were once again astonished at yet another twist of events. Now Marlon Howell, who less than a few seconds before looked as though he was about to become the victim of a murder by either one of two individuals, was seemingly confessing to a rape that he had committed.

Things were going well for Judd Stone. Banks had publicly confessed to murdering Cassie, Olive and Kez, and now Howell was confessing to the rape of Bonnie. Judd loosened his grip ever so slightly.

The perpetually confused Banks naturally thought Howell was confessing about the rape of his mother. "You raped my mother on top of everything else?"

"Your mother?" enquired Marlon, now looking confused himself.

"Yes, my mother. Don't you even recognise me you piece of shit? Apparently you didn't want me as I wasn't the kind of son that you could be proud of. I was shit at football and I wasn't a chip off the old block, so you disowned me and wouldn't even see my mom right to be able to support us properly. You had all that fame and money. A nice house, a nice job and a nice family while my mom had shit because of you. She had to carry on selling her body just to put food in my mouth. But you, you bastard. You could have given us a comfortable life. So now Daddy dear, you're going to take a bullet."

"Penny, your Penny's boy?"

"And I'm also *your* fucking boy. I'm your son."

Judd intervened. "Remember I'm in control at the moment, Gareth. I could slit his throat before your bullet reached him. If you don't have the control then you have lost the battle."

"He's an imposter, I have to kill him. He is just like that cult leader, abusing his position in charge of a false religion. Marlon Howell is a symbol of heresy. He is the England manager which makes him the head of the religion of football. Football was founded in this country and now more people follow football than the ways of the church and it is wrong. The words of the Lord Jesus Christ are gospel not the words of the England manager. God wants me to kill him in order to make people realise that football is not to be followed. Football matches are played on the Sabbath day, a day that is meant to praise the Lord. The same masses who attend football matches should be swarming the churches on a Sunday, and when I kill Marlon Howell everyone will finally understand. God's word is the only word that has to be followed. Marlon Howell is a charlatan and an imposter and imposters must die."

"But it is I who has the control, Gareth. Can you shoot either me or Howell before I slit his throat? Can you chance it? Once the killing becomes mine your quest has failed, so perhaps I am God's vigilante and not you. Perhaps he has chosen me to kill Marlon Howell. After all would God really send you to kill your own father?"

It was plain to see that Judd was playing with Banks' head. The serial killer was becoming agitated and very animated. He was clearly confused as he tried to make sense of why Judd Stone had arrived taking the control away from him on his mission to kill his final victim, Marlon Howell.

Gareth shut his eyes tight and held his hands to his head, agonisingly searching his confused and invaded brain for some kind of logic. His gun inadvertently moved away from its target and it allowed just enough time for Judd to receive a bit of help. Blended in the crowd were Eddie Goode and Hank Roderick, and Banks' momentary break of concentration allowed the two capable gentlemen to take Banks by surprise and overpower the serial killer? They were easily able to wrestle the gun out of the hand of Gareth Banks.

Reluctantly, Judd removed the knife from Howell's throat. He could so easily have slit his scrawny neck for what he had done to Bonnie all those years ago, but Judd knew that the imminent scandal that the fallen idol was about to face would be a significantly humiliating punishment for him. Now that Howell had confessed to the whole world that he had raped someone, he would stand trial for the rape of Bonnie Glass, and Judd would do all he could to preserve Bonnie's anonymity. Not that it mattered too much now, pondered Judd. After all this time, and because of Howell clearly admitting to his vile actions, Bonnie's good name would never be brought into question.

Furthermore, it would now become common knowledge that he had fathered an illegitimate child to a prostitute, and that this child, his son, had become one of Britain's most notorious serial killers, which some psychologists would claim, was in part due to having an absent father. Marlon Howell would never be free from scandal and that seemed like an apt punishment in itself for a man with such an inflated ego. His football career, and most likely his marriage was over.

Judd man-handled Howell towards the Jaguar and hand-cuffed him to the steering wheel. Then he took out another set of cuffs and approached Gareth Banks who was being held in a headlock by Hank and barely able to breathe, whilst Eddie sat on his legs holding the gun out of harm's way. Judd thanked his two unlikely assistants and cuffed Banks' hands behind his back just as two police cars arrived with their sirens wailing, after all the whole episode had just been played out live on national television.

Two policemen got out of the first car and walked towards the scene.

"Hi Gents, my name is Detective Inspector Judd Stone of Birmingham and District CID. I'll be more than happy to follow you down to the station as I think I can claim the arrests of these two clowns belonging to me, although there is just a slight technicality that I need to address." Judd turned his attention to Gareth Banks. "This time you're going to go down for the killing of Cassie Parker, Olive Jenas and Kez Raven. You confessed on national television you muppet and I'm also going to make sure that you're going down for the murder of Eli Zane and the attempted murders of Jaden Rivers and Marlon Howell, but it's the justice for those three girls that really makes my heart sing, Banks."

Programmed to kill by William Chamberlain, Gareth Banks had willingly confessed to the killings of the three women as an expression of his very entity. Although William had programmed Banks to kill Eli Zane and Jaden Rivers (though that one had gone slightly pear-shaped) Banks had chosen not to hide his previous killings, just as other assassins and attempted assassins had strangely been willing to confess to their killings over the years, such was the extent of their brainwashing.

Such was the extent of their minds being controlled.

Gareth Banks had become William Chamberlain's patsy. In order to control Banks, William hadn't needed weeks of grooming, providing subliminal messages, programming, formal hypnosis or anything else contrived to control the mind of his subject. Instead he had simply used a natural ability to control minds born out of the deterioration of his Multiple Sclerosis which somehow heightened the sensitivity of his telekinesis.

Lee Harvey Oswald had always stated that he had been a patsy up until his death. A fall guy meant to take the rap for killing the president, but of course could protest no more once Jack Ruby's bullet silenced him.

To this day, Sirhan Sirhan the convicted killer of Robert Kennedy declares that he never remembered shooting the man. This fuels theories that Sirhan Sirhan operated under the influence of a hypnotic trigger. His lawyers continually maintain that Sirhan Sirhan was an involuntary participant in the assassination of RFK and claim that he was subjected to sophisticated hypno programming and memory implantation techniques which rendered him unable to consciously control his thoughts and actions at the time the killing took place. Had mind control techniques progressed to such an extent that they ensured that memory could play no part in an assassination, suggesting that the lessons had been learned from Oswald's very vocal protest?

Lawrence Teeter, attorney for convicted assassin Sirhan Sirhan, believed Sirhan was under the influence of hypnosis when he fired his weapon at Robert F. Kennedy in 1968. Teeter linked records of mind control techniques to his claims.

And although Mark David Chapman recalls shooting John Lennon he speaks of hearing a voice over and over telling him to "do it" – again fuelling theories that a hypnotic or subliminal order had been implanted in his mind.

Conveniently all three of these 'killers' can easily be passed off as 'lone nuts'.

Gareth Banks was indeed a lone nut, and although he had blood on his hands already, he had unsuspectingly become William Chamberlain's programmed assassin…and patsy.

CHAPTER 57

The caption that ran along the foot of the TV screen read *Breaking News* as the lipstick-painted mouth that belonged to the striking face of the newsreader elaborated on the story. Judd Stone watched with interest as he chewed on his heavily-buttered wholemeal toast.

Judd was getting ready for his first day back on the force following the double capture of serial killer Gareth Banks and rapist Marlon Howell. At least he assumed it was his first day back at the workplace. The phone call from DSI Ben Francis had seemed promising enough. The DSI had certainly requested Judd's presence today and his tone was one of calmness, but the more Judd had thought about things since their conversation, the more he had realised that he was actually none the wiser about his future. He was after all suspended and removed from any official duties at the time of his heroics.

However, Judd's immediate attention had been temporarily captured by the newsreader as she continued with the news story… "*Following the shock revelations and scandal surrounding Marlon Howell, the English national team are once again searching for a new manager after the disgraced Howell was sacked following only a single game in charge. It is rumoured that the likelihood will be the reinstatement of the previous England manager whom Howell replaced. A statement from the Football Association clearly signals how they have distanced themselves from Howell and they state that there should never be a role in football again for the self-confessed rapist. They go on to say that if they had had any inkling of Howell's past crimes he would never have been appointed England manager in the first place. It has also been reported today that many other women are now coming forward to state that they too had fell victim to being raped by Howell in the past, with the rapes taking place over a period of as many as thirty years.*

"In a related development it appears that Gareth Banks, who is rumoured to be the illegitimate son of Howell, will stand trial once again for the murders of Cassie Parker, Kerry Raven and Olive Jenas as fresh evidence comes to light linking him to the Midlands' murders, known as The Crucifier killings, not least because of Banks' own astonishing confession on live TV, admitting to being responsible for the murders at the same time as Howell confessed to his crimes of rape.

"The re-trial of Banks seems to vindicate the dogged policing of one Detective Inspector Judd Stone who was also seen during the live broadcast securing the dramatic arrests of both Banks and Howell with the assistance of two plain clothes policemen. It is some turn around for the Detective Inspector who is now being hailed a hero, as he was once left humiliated as part of the team from Birmingham and District CID whom had seemingly failed to track down the correct serial killer. Yet Stone seems to have possessed an incredible determination to ensure that Banks is brought to justice in spite of the previous ruling, and now at last the world recognises that his targeting of Banks as being the Crucifier had indeed been correct all along. In addition to the Crucifier killings, Banks will also stand trial for the murder of religious cult leader Eli Zane and attempted murders of Jaden Rivers and incredibly Banks' own mother Penelope Zandretti. We will keep you informed of developments in this intriguing case as and when they occur…"

Judd couldn't help but smile. Firstly he was pleased to learn that Penny Zandretti had survived Banks' attack. He had initially feared that there had been no chance of her making it. Secondly, it appeared that the media didn't quite have all their facts right. Referring to Eddie Goode and Hank Roderick as plain clothes coppers was an absolute gem of wrong information and this tickled Judd somewhat. And as Judd himself was suspended from the force at the time of the dramatic incident, technically he couldn't officially arrest the two criminals. Nevertheless, their capture was a crucial intervention by him and he hoped that Francis and Haddock would be willing to overlook any technicalities considering the undoubted achievements of his police work, albeit on an unofficial basis.

Equally, Judd realised that both Francis and Haddock could be calling him in to the station today for a strong dressing down on the foundation that he could have endangered both his own and other civilian life by pursuing a serial killer without authorisation or authorised back-up. But that was typical of Judd Stone's methods – deliver the right result whatever it took! He just hoped on this occasion, with the results being so substantial, that for once his superiors would be able to agree that the means justified the end.

The overwhelming support from both the public and the media surely couldn't do any harm either.

Judd swallowed his last bite of toast and reached for his coffee, before being interrupted by a knock at his door. Feeling slightly curious, Judd opened the door and was pleased, if a little surprised, to be greeted by William Chamberlain and Crystal Stance. William was sitting in a wheelchair with the immaculately turned out Crystal standing behind him.

"Hello Judd, I think it's only fair that we have a little chat," said his friend.

CHAPTER 58

Judd watched with astonishment as his TV remote-controlled handset levitated in mid air. William allowed it to rest on the sofa before performing his next trick, which was to turn the pages of Judd's match day magazine from last week's football match, using only the power of his mind.

"All those years that I've known you and you never told me."

"What could I say, Judd? I can perform telekinetic magic tricks, oh, and by the way, please don't send me to the nearest funny farm."

"I've believed you now haven't I? All you ever had to do was show me that you can do these things."

"The time never seemed right. I always feared that somehow it would compromise our friendship, you may see me as a bit weird and perhaps I'd somehow freak you out."

"William, nothing could ever compromise our friendship."

Crystal then entered the conversation. "I convinced William that the time was right to open up to you, he was a little nervous not knowing if you'd accept things. I told him that true friends can always be honest with one another. I hope that we can help you to understand these sorts of things a little better."

"You mean there's more, Crystal?"

"All the answers are out there, Judd; they just need to be found, but sometimes the world just isn't ready for them."

"And Crystal and I now feel that you are ready for some of the ones that we can answer, even if you don't yet have the questions."

Judd listened to every word. He sat transfixed with a strong feeling of surrealism, absorbing all the incredible information that his friend and Crystal were telling him. He discovered that somehow William had managed to develop his telekinesis in order to control minds, and William had used this skill to save his own life when Banks came to finish him off in hospital. Somehow, in parallel, he had been able to plant a seed into the mind of Banks and send him to the Adonijah Truthsters to avenge what Eli Zane and Jaden Rivers had done to Tilda. They also informed Judd how their psychic connection had enabled them to direct Judd to Banks' mother, when William's abilities connected with Crystal's psychic abilities.

"So on that day when I had a fight with those thugs at the shop, that kid didn't stab himself did he? It was you controlling the knife with your mind."

William simply nodded.

"Wow, and now you can really control minds as well as objects. William, don't you see what an asset you could be to the police force?"

"That's something else I wanted to speak to you about, Judd. I've negotiated with Ben Francis and we have agreed that I am to be medically retired."

"Are you nuts, William? We have just discovered that you can control minds and you want to quit the force?"

"Yes, I do. I need to face up to the fact that I am not a well man, Judd. My telekinetic powers are increasing but my physical capabilities are decreasing. And frankly this whole mind control thing scares me, Judd. I don't understand enough about it to put it to good use, besides, remember what I said about the world not being ready for answers? Well that includes Francis and Haddock. There is no way that I could run the risk of telling them all of this. Even if they believed me they could arrest me as being an associate to murder. It was me who had sent Banks onto his latest victims wasn't it? And if they didn't believe me they would probably try and have me sectioned.

"Ok, so it is suspected, and a number of cases even known, that certain superior authorities have used mind control tactics for personal gain, but do you really think our little constabulary in the West Midlands are ready for it? Besides, I don't want to be a part of any law enforcement culture that controls people's minds, when has history ever told us that it was done for a good thing? Think about the slaying of all those political figures, activists and rock stars. Their message has simply become stronger at the attempt to silence them. My controlling of Banks was different; a 'one-off' to avenge Tilda and to help bring justice for the three unfortunate ladies that Banks had killed."

"So you don't want a job grooming assassins then?" Joked Judd, attempting to bring normality to the situation.

"William doesn't need to go through the processes of brainwashing; he doesn't need to groom individuals with subliminal messages and months of tedious techniques. His increasing ability to control minds and interfere with matter is deriving from the physical demise caused by his MS, with my help and confidential studies at the institution we hope to fully understand why this is happening. And if we can understand what is happening to William, we may even be able to channel the effects to perhaps find a cure for MS one day. We are faced with a terrible and debilitating illness which shows no mercy or discrimination. Rich or poor, MS doesn't care, and recently even the offspring of rock stars are known to have been diagnosed with MS.

"At first I was simply interested in William's ability to control physical mass with his brain," said an enthused Crystal. "But to be able to control a mind in order for the brain's messages to send signals to MS affected limbs, or even another source of limb paralysis, would be an amazing breakthrough for sufferers. And if we can work out a way to reverse the process in William he could self-heal."

"You see, I would prefer to channel my abilities to do some good, Judd. In the main brainwashing isn't ethical, it is an extreme force of social influence to get people to do things they wouldn't normally do. It's mental rape and both you and I know that any form of rape has to be wrong.

"Who am I to play God? I prefer the notion that people choose their actions, and if they are bad actions we have coppers like you Judd to put things right. That's how society is meant to function. Banks was one example where I controlled a mind, and yes I avenged my sister, but I also now know how things can go horribly wrong. I'm not skilled enough to fully control a designated programme of events; it scares me that Banks could have killed his mom and Marlon Howell because of me."

"Banks was well capable of doing that without your help, William," said Judd.

"Maybe."

"Well, I don't believe that anything supernatural, if that's what we are talking about here, needs to influence people like Gareth Banks to commit atrocities, unless they are being ultimately controlled by demons or devils perhaps. I mean, I've heard of exorcisms being performed by catholic priests to rid an evil spirit from an individual who has become possessed, but people like Banks are just born bad. It's as simple as that."

"That's an interesting point of view, Judd," offered

Crystal. "Believe it or not supernatural entities have always been taken very seriously by the authorities. The Americans once exercised an operation to explore the world of black magic in an attempt to harness the forces of darkness in order to reach parts of the mind that are considered beyond reach. They went deep into demonology, and attempted to liaise with chief exorcists of the Catholic Church, but the church wouldn't play ball. Nevertheless, even by going solo the authorities claimed to uncover 400 covens with witches and warlocks in their midst."

"Wow, but what was the point?" asked Judd.

"They were interested in discovering a powerful magic that could destroy the enemy."

"That would be some weapon."

"Possibly the greatest weapon there could ever be?"

"Ok, that makes sense. Scary, but I get it."

"They took it seriously. Researching agents went to fairground fortune tellers and they had 3 full time astrologers on the payroll to try and predict the future. Remember they wanted to identify and harness the forces of darkness. Would you believe me if I told you that on record somewhere, it is believed that some of the things predicted included Nixon facing a political disaster in his second term of presidency, but more remarkably perhaps that skyjacking would increase? Now these predictions were made a while back in the twentieth century but could it be that the predictor's realisation of skyjacking surfaced in its most horrific form when 9/11 occurred?"

"Wow. It seems there is a whole universe out there of things we don't yet understand."

"That's right Judd, there is. But with Crystal by my side I am determined to understand and channel the gift that I have, if it is a gift, in order to make the world a better place. And if I'm going to do that then I have no time on my hands for police work and I need to be honest with myself, physically police work no longer suits me."

Judd found it difficult to disagree all of a sudden. "I'll miss you, buddy."

"We'll still see each other you daft pillock. I'm going to need a best man for one thing."

Judd smiled. "You sly old fox. You and Crystal are getting married?"

"He proposed to me this morning and I gladly accepted." Crystal threw out her left hand to reveal a glittering emerald and diamond encrusted engagement ring.

"Unfortunately I couldn't get down on one knee, but Crystal is a very understanding lady which is one of the reasons I proposed of course."

"I think I need to keep an eye on him with all these hidden powers that he has, so I thought it best to keep him close."

"Well congratulations, I'm made up for the both of you. Retirement and marriage. They are big life changes, William."

"But nothing makes more sense to me, Judd. So, will you be my best man then?"

"Are you sure that you don't want to ask Scarrow first?"

"Now, there could be some unfinished business with controlling minds."

Crystal gave William a playful slap. "You're retired remember, William."

"I know, I'm only joking. I wouldn't waste my energy on that little runt. So how about it, Judd?"

"You know I will, it'll be a pleasure." Judd kissed Crystal on the cheek and shook the hand of his best friend.

The happy couple noticed a slight change in expression in Judd's face. "What's wrong?" enquired William. "Are you okay with the wedding?"

"Of course, it's not that."

"Well what is it?"

Judd turned to Crystal with the look of a little boy lost.

"What is it, Judd?" she gently asked.

"Well, you know what you were saying about being a medium and all that? Do you think you could contact someone for me?"

"Your wife?" William had informed Crystal of what had happened to Frankie, and she had spotted the framed photos of their wedding day on Judd's sideboard.

"I can try, but I warn you Judd, those that have passed over don't always want to be contacted and there are no guarantees. Spirits usually contact me when they feel like it, without warning usually, but perhaps if you hand me something of her's to hold it can sometimes help."

Judd went to the drawer and pulled out a dog-eared leather key ring with a metal insignia of a kitten. It had a single key hanging from it.

"This was her key to the front door of the house where we once lived together. She was buried wearing her wedding ring, but this would have been in her jeans pocket or handbag on a regular basis."

Crystal smiled as she gently took the key ring from Judd and held it in the palms of her hands. Both Judd and William watched with anticipation as Crystal closed her eyes. "Frankie, I have Judd here with me and if at all possible he would like you to make contact, no matter how small, just to help put his mind at ease. He misses you dreadfully and he would just like to know that you are at peace. Can you come through to me, dear?"

With baited breath Judd waited through a few seconds of silence.

"Are you there Frankie, love?" continued Crystal. More seconds passed.

"I am getting a strong feeling of peace Judd, but not much else I'm afraid. I'm sorry; she doesn't seem to be able to speak to me at the moment."

Judd looked a little dejected. "Okay, thanks for trying anyway."

"I'm convinced she is at peace, Judd. Perhaps she'll

reach you some other way, there is always time."

"Okay. It's just that I really loved her, I just never said it enough when she was alive. So you and William make a point of telling each other every single day because you never know when something can come along and ruin the dream that you are living. Can you just tell her that I love her, Crystal?"

"Wait, hold on something is coming through." A huge smile came on Crystal's face, followed by the medium becoming noticeably unsteady, but she managed to remain erect. "My word, that was intense, but I'm afraid she has gone again."

"Did she say anything?"

"Well, yes, she did. You may know best what she meant though?"

"What was it?"

"She said 'Yeah, me too. Love, love me do'."

Judd smiled. "That's what I used to say when she told me she loved me. I'd just casually reply 'yeah, me too. Love, love me do.'"

"It seems that she is affectionately getting her own back for your previous casualness, Judd."

"Did she say anything else?"

"She did, but this bit I don't understand. She said, you only have two-thirds of the catch and beware because the enemy lies within."

PART V
MILK AND HONEY

CHAPTER 59

On the journey from Sutton Coldfield to Birmingham city centre, and then onwards to DSI Ben Francis's office, Judd Stone could think of nothing else other than the message conveyed by Crystal. "You only have two-thirds of the catch and beware because the enemy lies within." None of the victims of Howell, that were now coming forward in significant numbers, had stated that there had been another individual involved in his crimes, so did this cryptic message from beyond the grave suggest that Banks wasn't working alone – "you only have two-thirds of the catch?"

But surely it was all over now? Banks had confessed to the killings of Cassie, Olive and Kez. But due to the message received from Frankie, fresh doubt had entered Judd's mind.

And who was the enemy within? Surely not William, the close friend and mentor whom he could trust with his life? The same William who had orchestrated Banks' final killing spree which had helped Judd to become a hero?

And Crystal? Surely not. After all it was Crystal who had conveyed Frankie's ambiguous message so why would she bother?

Sab? Unlikely, that girl didn't have a bad bone in her body.

Or perhaps it could be Francis or Haddock? Judd's mind boggled.

The obvious choice was Lionel Scarrow, but what could that little runt possibly do to hurt him? Judd had always been successful at keeping that low-life in his place.

Judd wasn't sure if the part of the message about 'the enemy lying within' would ever become clear, but he now knew more than ever to watch his back in future.

Judd believed that Crystal's connection with Frankie had been genuine due to the paraphrasing of his usual response back to her when she used to tell him that she loved him – "yeah, me too. Love, love me do." That was funny, and he could even sense the typical display of good humour from his bubbly departed lover. Perhaps he should just be thankful for receiving that special moment, the remainder of the message could easily have been misinterpreted by Crystal and perhaps it was best not to dwell on it.

As Judd sat down in the presence of DSI Ben Francis he wondered what his fate in Birmingham and District CID was to become. Whilst suspended from duty without any authorisation he had pursued an armed and dangerous criminal. Regardless of the positive response by the media, and both the public and his peers hailing him a hero, these were the facts. He had captured two criminals without any powers of arrest! Judd began to sweat as Francis looked him in the eye.

"Do you know that William is to be medically retired, Judd?"

"Yes, he came to see me earlier today. He is also getting married," smiled Judd.

Francis's facial expression could not be read.

"He was a good copper, one of the best I have ever had the pleasure to serve with. It leaves a huge gap in the form of a reliable and productive Detective Chief

Inspector, and incidentally there have been rumblings that perhaps I should have another gapped post to fill, concerning your position as Detective Inspector, following the reckless pursuit of an armed criminal whilst you were suspended from active duty."

"Yes, sir, I understand. But in my defence may I suggest that the end justified the means?"

Francis did not immediately answer. "You know that I like to do things by the book don't you Stone, as does the Chief Constable?"

Judd dreaded what was coming next. Over thirty years he had served on the force, clearing the streets of Birmingham from gun crime, drug smugglers, rapists, murderers and more, but it now appeared that it was about to come to an end. Is this what Frankie had been referring to, the 'enemy within' meant he was going to be fired?

"Yes, sir. I recognise that you like to do things by the book."

Francis stared hard at the man before him. "However, the way that you use your initiative, Stone cannot be matched by anyone else on this force. Your sense of go-getting and commitment to the cause is just what I need to achieve the unachievable and get the results that so often seem beyond us. However, when performing your duties in future I would prefer you to only bend the rules and boundaries a little and not to crash straight through them."

"You mean you are reinstating me to the force?" smiled Judd.

"What I mean Stone, is that I am offering you the vacant post of Detective Chief Inspector,"

"Wow, I don't know what to say. Thank you. But what about, Scarrow? I thought he'd be in the frame before me?"

"Not a chance. Most of the rumblings about making an example of you came from him. Frankly, I'm tired of his vendetta against you and I have no place for disharmony on my team. I need officers that display loyalty for one another and pull in the same direction. I look at you Judd, and I see someone who would go as far as to take a bullet for one of his fellow officers if need be, then I look at Scarrow and I can see that he wouldn't even urinate on one of his colleagues if they were on fire. I get that now; I just wish it hadn't taken me so long to realise just what a weasel he is.

"Banks has been convicted, which clearly shows that you and William were correct about him all along, and credit to you in particular Judd, for never accepting how things had initially turned out. And as I recall at Banks' original trial, Scarrow made a considerable effort to prevent his prosecution, even taking the stand against you. It didn't sit comfortably with me then and it certainly doesn't sit comfortably with me now. We now know for sure it was Banks, and I cannot allow Scarrow's actions to go unpunished. He influenced a perfectly sound intent to achieve justice and therefore Lionel Scarrow has permanently been relieved of his duties. There is no place for a man like that on my team or on any other police force in this country."

"Wow." This single word was all that the shell-shocked Judd Stone could muster as he attempted to take in the information conveyed by DSI Ben Francis.

"Now then Stone, are you going to accept the position of Detective Chief Inspector or do you need time to think about it, which is perfectly acceptable of course? I just need to smooth over the small misunderstanding regarding you and the Chief Constable's daughter, but even Haddock has recognised the good work you have done in catching a serial killer, albeit a little unconventionally.

"We are all content in senior management that those three unfortunate girls can finally rest in peace now that their killer is to be safely locked behind bars for the rest of his miserable life. There is no chance of him escaping his fate now that we have his confession articulated on live TV. And it's all thanks to you Judd; you finally brought this maniac to justice and for that alone you deserve promotion to Detective Chief Inspector."

"I don't need to think about it sir, I'd be glad to accept your kind offer to become Detective Chief Inspector. With the added responsibility I will try even harder at keeping the streets of Birmingham free of crime."

"That's what I'd hoped you'd say. Welcome back, Detective Chief Inspector Stone."

CHAPTER 60

New Year's Day 2013

Jaden Rivers woke groggily to the familiar surroundings of the metal-framed bed, low-budget furniture and dim artificial light. Since his arrival at the nursing home, directly following a lengthy stay in hospital following the attempt on his life, sleeping was pretty much all Jaden had to do, and the plethora of medication which he received contributed heavily to his feeling of fatigue. In-between sleeps; Jaden would read the pages of his Bible, typically interpreting the messages within the text to suit his own philosophy. Occasionally he would enter into television viewing. Jaden had reluctantly allowed himself to watch a limited amount of television. Under Eli's regime, television had been largely outlawed due to its "negative and improper influence" on society, and the television set had been known amongst the Adonijah Truthsters as the 'Devil's Box'.

Jaden had been told that he would never walk again. His faith remained strong; however there were things that puzzled him. For instance, how could God have allowed Eli to be taken from the Adonijah Truthsters? Their leader was gone and with him it seemed the direction and purpose of their cause.

Eli Zane was meant to have led the chosen few into shelter at the coming of Armageddon; yet the end of the world had clearly not occurred in 2012 as Eli had taught them. Was this because God had chosen to delay Armageddon due to the death of Eli? Wouldn't it have been simpler for God to have spared Eli's life, or had the Devil's influence triumphed at that fateful moment when the killer entered their Severn Valley home? It was all very difficult for Jaden to fathom. If Eli was such a great leader, which Jaden still believed he had been, why instead was it he, Jaden Rivers, that been saved? Jaden had been content to respond to Eli's requests, even recognised doing so as his duty in the quest for salvation, but he had no desire to become a leader himself.

And was the paralysis of his legs a punishment from God for something he had yet to understand?

And why had the Adonijah Truthsters not taken him in and nursed him at their house in the Severn Valley? Why instead had they chosen to place him in a nursing home and turn their back on him?

Under Eli's influence, The Adonijah Truthsters had believed that 2012 would be the end of the world for everyone except them, and it would be Eli Zane who would lead them from Armageddon.

Eli had informed them meticulously that in 1967 Israel occupied the city of Jerusalem through the 6 days war for the first time in 2000 years, therefore this was without doubt the fulfillment of the prophecy that said "Jerusalem will be taken down by the gentiles until the time of the gentiles be fulfilled." A Biblical generation is said to be of 40 years, therefore this belief would determine that the 1967 generation would be the ones to experience the second coming and would firmly look at the calendar as being 2012 for that second coming to arrive.

But with Eli gone and with Jaden resting in his bed on

the first day of the year 2013, all that the big man with the deep voice had taught his followers had now been brought into question.

Fortunately the risk of Zane's death being translated into making him a martyr hadn't seemed to materialise, and now that the year 2012 had passed without incident could the Adonijah Truthsters, and every other 2012 fuelled doomsday cult for that matter, ever be a unified entity again?

Jaden was confused.

Jaden was unsure if he had woken naturally or by the noises associated with the care nurse who was preparing his medication. The nurse was positioned with her back to Jaden, which was enough to determine that he didn't immediately recognise her, but he thought no more of it as she was wearing the standard aqua-coloured uniform that all the care nurses wore at the nursing home.

"Judging by the smell it seems we have parsnips on the menu today, nurse."

The nurse didn't answer; she just continued to prepare Jaden's medication.

When she did turn around, Jaden was a little baffled to discover that the nurse was wearing dark sunglasses.

"Hello, you must be a new addition to the nursing home?"

The nurse simply nodded as she approached the bed.

"My name is Jaden."

"Yes, I know who you are."

At last the creature speaks. The voice was familiar but Jaden couldn't quite place it.

The nurse placed Jaden's medication into his mouth and handed him a glass of water. He swallowed his painkillers with a large gulp of the water.

"Have you added something to the water, it tastes different?"

"We are trying out some new herbal remedies to complement the traditional medication. Please do drink it all up, every last drop. It is so good for you."

"Okay," Jaden completely swallowed the drink. "Not the best tasting remedy I have to say. What was it?"

"It comes from a plant named Hemlock. Six to eight leaves with a bit of the root usually does the trick, but I used a total of twelve leaves just to make sure it worked well on you."

None the wiser Jaden simply smiled and thanked her.

"How was your New Year's Eve?" enquired the nurse.

Oh, she seems quite chatty after all, Jaden reflected. *Perhaps she was just nervous at first with this being her first day?*

"I decided against being wheeled down to the communal area, I didn't want to particularly join in with the celebrations of seeing in the New Year. I stayed in my room reading my Bible. How about you?"

"I decided to stay in as well. I was kindly asked to spend the evening with my brother and his fiancée but I wasn't really in the mood for socialising. I sat by myself and watched Jools Holland's Hootenanny show on the TV instead. Roland Gift brought in the New Year singing his song "Good Thing." I like that song, I like Roland Gift too. He reminds me a little of my husband in appearance and my husband was most definitely a good thing in my life."

"Was?"

"He died. We used to watch Jools Holland's Hootenanny show every New Year's Eve together without fail, and dance the New Year in from our living room in Liverpool. I raised a glass to him last night as the chimes rang to mark the move to 2013."

"I'm sorry to hear about your husband's passing. He will be in a good place now I'm sure of it. A *Good Thing* in a good place, what do you say?"

"I couldn't agree more."

"You know, your voice sounds very familiar to me."

The nurse simply smiled and slowly removed her sunglasses.

At once Jaden realised why he had recognised the voice. Although the face was a little older there was no mistake who was standing before him.

"Tilda Chamberlain."

"My name is Tilda Blake these days, Jaden. My husband was Luther Blake; he was murdered by those crazy twins who were part of your sadistic religious cult."

"I had nothing to do with them, Tilda."

"Really."

"What do you want, Tilda?"

"Revenge of course. I want revenge for my husband's murder. As those two monsters were killed in a car crash some justice has already been partly achieved, but I also hold you partly responsible for his death, Jaden. You were a part of that warped and destructive machinery that led to my husband's untimely death. I also want revenge for what *you* subjected me to when I was held captive in that terrible cult."

"It wasn't a cult, Tilda. We were a religious gathering."

"Don't make me laugh, Jaden. I'm actually a bit of an expert in such things these days, and believe me The Adonijah Truthsters *were* most definitely a cult. And I use the past tense because after what Gareth Banks subjected you all to that day marked the end of the Adonijah Truthsters. Your little cult has simply folded, Jaden. There is no Eli Zane to lead anyone away from Armageddon, which hasn't actually happened by the way, has it? And you Jaden are in no shape to take over the reins are you? Look at you. You're pathetic."

Jaden, clearly unnerved by Tilda's presence, scrambled for the assistance button which caused Tilda to laugh.

"I moved the device out of harm's way while you slept, Jaden. It was quite an ironic sight actually; you lay there almost like a little angel. I could so easily have stuck a knife straight through your wicked heart giving you a quick and easy death, but then that would have been too good for you."

"Tilda, I only ever tried to look after you. Ever since that day I met you in Birmingham with that Yazoo album under your arm, I knew that you needed looking after. We've always had a special connection, Tilda. You and I."

"I already had a family to look after me," spat Tilda. "Including a big brother who I will always have a stronger connection with than I could ever have with you. I despise you Jaden Rivers."

"What did I ever do to you that was so wrong, Tilda?"

"You robbed me of my innocence, Jaden."

"It was what Eli wanted."

"It was what you wanted too."

"It was God's way."

"How dare you. You insult everyone who believes in God. It has never been God's way to rape girls, and doing it in his name only makes it worse."

Jaden simply looked away.

"But now look at you, my how the tides have changed. You lie there completely helpless and at my entire mercy. You look so pathetic I could almost feel sorry for you, but no I could never do that."

"Please, Tilda. Please leave me alone."

Tilda stepped closer. "You know, after what you did to me, all the nights I have lain awake, tormented, reliving all the sordid, horrible things that you subjected me too, I could slice off your vile manhood and insert it where the sun doesn't shine. That would then begin to let you know how I felt when you raped me all those times."

"Please Tilda; I beg you to let me be."

After a short silence, Tilda gave a wry smile. "Okay."

Confused, Jaden spoke. "What? You are going to leave me alone."

"Yes, the damage is in motion now anyway. My work here is done."

"What do you mean?"

"You always thought the end of the world was nigh, well I'm not going to disappoint you Jaden, however, I'll keep on living while you have your own personal Armageddon. It's the end of the world for you, Jaden. Just you."

"Oh no, the drink?"

"You really are a complete fool, Jaden. Hemlock is poisonous, it is fatal in fact. The twelve leaves and plenty of roots that I used will soon see you off, but it will be a long and unpleasant death which is something that you deserve."

"You bitch," he shouted. Overcome with fear, Jaden tried to get up but simply fell to the side of his bed and hung there like a limp puppet. Tilda laughed as she ironically helped to reposition him.

Jaden desperately made a grab for Tilda's throat, but a simple slap to his face was enough for him to loosen his grip and she was once more at a safe distance.

She moved to the foot of his bed and produced a small, translucent plastic box that seemed to hold a small yellow creature.

Tilda pulled aside the bedclothes and Jaden was helpless to intervene. Then Tilda opened the box and allowed the creature to enter the opening of Jaden's pyjamas at his ankle. With no feeling in his legs, he was unable to feel the scorpion climb up his limb, but he was still very much aware of its presence as he watched the bulging shape move closer beneath the cotton material.

"You should be familiar with that little critter, Jaden. It is a Centruroides Exilicauda, more commonly known as the Bark Scorpion, which is I believe is quite widespread in the southern states of America. I decided how fitting it would be for one poisonous creature from that region to be reacquainted with another.

"It will only attack when it feels trapped so that will most likely be when it reaches your groin area. It will provide some swelling at the point of sting, and from what I recall, you could really do with some help in getting bigger in that area, Jaden."

All Jaden could offer was a fearful gulp as sweat formed on his brow.

"Oh, I almost forgot, you will also experience some severe pain, frothing at the mouth and convulsions. When your respiratory muscles finally give in as your heart and lungs become starved of oxygen, you won't be able to tell if that will have been caused by the scorpion sting or the hemlock. In truth, the scorpion sting may not kill you, but the hemlock definitely will. However, I'm sure that both of their toxic effects mixed together are going to hurt like hell.

"It was the hemlock that smelled of parsnips you fool, not the cooking from the kitchens. Did you know that they once used hemlock, or conium as it is sometimes known, to punish condemned prisoners in Ancient Greece? And did you know that one such prisoner was none other than Socrates who was given the poison for impiety. How ironic is that, Jaden? Your death will be derived from the very same poison, a most suitable end.

"You won't notice the creeping paralysis at first of course; as your legs are fucked anyway, but you will notice your arms lose their power, followed by your respiratory muscles collapsing. You will eventually be put out of your misery when your lungs and heart become starved of oxygen.

"Oh, and by the way, with the help of my brother, who just happens to be a Detective Chief Inspector, I have a stone cast alibi so I was never here. Enjoy the rest of your life, Jaden. What you have left of it that is."

Jaden went to shout something at Tilda as she walked away, but instead his scream indicated that the scorpion had made a telling connection.

As Tilda opened the door she turned to say one final thing with a strong element of certainty. "Oh, Jaden, just one more thing. Rot in hell."

CHAPTER 61

Sisters of Mercy Convent, Handsworth Wood, Birmingham

"The weather is fierce tonight, Sister Marie," said Sister Cecilia in her soft Kerry accent.

"It is so," answered Sister Marie, her accent belonging to the slightly more eastern counties of Ireland. "The Lord in his wisdom has allowed it to rain all day today and it's coming down at an almighty rate just now."

The two Irish nuns were devotees to the Catholic faith, and were therefore brought together by circumstance to exist in the convent; but fortunately they had easily become firm friends and enjoyed one another's company immensely.

Marie was the more playful of the two, always looking to inject her mischievous sense of humour into the sphere – at times to the annoyance of the more senior nuns of the convent. But regardless of her frivolity, her faith was strong and she had a genuine heart of gold beneath her habit, feeling a distinct sense of duty to help and support the community around her. For example, Sister Marie took it upon herself to visit and nurse the sick on a regular basis– ironically a lot more often than the nuns who chose to belittle her ever did.

Cecilia, though not quite as playful, was equally as selfless in channelling her faith to help others. They both realised that praying all the days God sent didn't necessarily make you the most perfect nun; it was actions that spoke louder than words in their minds.

"Nice drop of cocoa, Sister Cecilia."

"It'll be the organic milk that is improving the taste, Sister Marie. I signed us up for a delivery service from that farm that sits on the borders of Great Barr and Walsall."

"They have farms in Walsall? Well I never."

"So they do. A young lad came knocking on the door and I didn't have the heart to send him away without committing to a regular delivery. Poor lad, he got a right shock when I opened the door in me habit, he didn't know where to put himself. By the look on his face I don't think he had ever seen a real life nun before. So anyway there you have it, as well as a delivery of four pints of milk a day, I've also committed us to two dozen free range eggs every week; they may even improve Sister Bernadette's home baking."

"I've been praying for something to improve her Victoria Sponge," Sister Marie looked up to the ceiling. "Thank you Lord for answering my prayers."

The two nuns giggled like naughty school girls.

As if in answer to their joviality, a loud crash of thunder shook the convent and a flash of lightning lit up the room through the sash window.

Not long after a knock came at the door.

"Who could that be, are we expecting anyone?" asked Sister Cecilia.

"I don't believe so; it's close to eleven o'clock. It's very late for someone to be calling."

"What shall we do?"

"It may be someone in need; it is our duty to answer the door and to help them."

"It could also be some drunken lout on the way back

from the pub…or worse."

The door knocked again, only this time louder and with more purpose.

"I'll go," offered Sister Marie, though clearly a little concerned due to the late hour.

"We'll both go."

The two nuns placed down their hot mugs of cocoa and apprehensively walked to the door. They had reached just short of half-way down the hallway when the door knocked for a third time.

"They're persistent whoever they are," said Sister Marie.

Sister Cecilia reached the door first and slowly turned the key. A flash of lightning lit up the frosted window of the door to reveal an eerie shadow of branches from the trees at the front of the house and the brief glimpse of a silhouette of a figure standing outside. The momentary glance gave away no clues to who the person could be.

Sister Cecilia finally opened the door. Standing before the two nuns was a bedraggled looking woman, her age possibly being somewhere between the ages of the two nuns. The woman had obviously fell victim to the weather, her hair was wet through and lank. She wore a vacant expression on her face as she raised her head to look at the two nuns.

"Hello child, can we help you?" spoke Sister Marie standing a little way behind her friend. She called most people child even when they clearly weren't one.

"I hope so. Have I reached the Sisters of Mercy?"

"Yes, my dear, that's us."

"Good, I need to speak with you."

"Of course my dear, but first please step in out of the awful weather. You look soaked through, so you do."

The mysterious visitor climbed the two steps into the convent and Sister Cecilia closed the door behind her. The visitor was so wet from rain that she dripped onto the tiled floor from every item of clothing.

"I notice you have a suitcase," spoke Sister Cecilia.

"Yes, I was hoping to stay."

"Do you not have a home, child?" enquired Sister Marie.

"Or any family, perhaps?"

"I thought I had a family once, but perhaps not in the sense that you mean. I do have a home but I can't live there anymore, the memories are too painful and it is a reminder of things that I don't care to remember. That's why I'm here. I need retribution and forgiveness. I need cleansing but I also have this overwhelming urge to belong to something worthwhile."

"Forgiveness from what?" enquired Sister Cecilia.

"I've seen…and I'm ashamed to say…I've done bad things."

"Such as?" pressed Sister Cecilia.

The visitor hung her head and gave out a sob.

"That can wait," interjected Sister Marie. "Sister Cecilia and I have just been enjoying a mug of cocoa, by the look of your wet clothes I'd say you could do with a hot drink as well. We have a small choice of spare rooms where you can stay for tonight at least; we are not in the habit of turning our flock away at times of need. We can figure out what's best for you in the morning after a good night's sleep."

"That sounds wonderful, but I already know what I want to do and what I want to be. I've had a calling you see. I want; no I need to become a nun, just like you."

"My, it seems we will be having a long chat, but all in good time. You go on up to the room; the second room on the left once you reach the top of the stairs is the nicest. Change into some dry clothes, there are plenty in the wardrobe should you need them, but I expect you have your own in the suitcase, and we'll put on another saucepan of milk for your cocoa. Sister Cecilia and I will be waiting for you in the kitchen just through there."

"Thank you, you are very kind."

"Do I detect a slight American accent?" enquired Sister Cecilia.

"Yeah, that obvious huh?"

"We don't have many Americans around here, that's all. But you are more than welcome."

"What's your name, child?" enquired Sister Marie.

"My name is Rowena. Rowena Baxter."

CHAPTER 62

Eddie Goode and Hank Roderick entered The Seraph Public House keen to quench their thirst following the balti curries they had both enjoyed not twenty minutes earlier in Birmingham's renowned Balti Triangle.

"It's killing me this is, Eddie."

"Yeah, ear infections can be painful."

"Not the ear infection mate, the lack of alcohol I can consume. The Doc warned me that the anti-biotics would make me sick if I were to have a skinful."

"Never mind mate, it was good to enjoy the taste of a decent balti while I was in a fit state for once. Usually it's beer first and the curry after, it made a refreshing change to do it this way round. I reckon we are getting quite civilised in our old age, Hank. We'll just have a couple and then call it a night, what do you say?"

"Yeah, a couple shouldn't hurt me. I'll get them in." Hank was quickly served by 'greasy' Gordan, his swiftness in service typically not matched by his natural charm.

"Cheers, bud," said Eddie, clanking his bottle against his friend's, before turning to face the wider view of the pub as he swigged his lager.

"Well I'll be a monkey's uncle! Hey, don't look straight

away, Hank, but we have a new face in the pub this evening and I'm sure that it is a face that seems familiar. Positioned at about Two O'clock sitting on his own, wearing a tweed jacket."

Hank turned around discreetly and spotted who Eddie had described. "Hey, isn't that the bent copper who we beat the shit out of at Wembley, the one who made life difficult for Judd?"

"Yeah, that's the ugly bastard alright. Lionel Scarrow, I'd recognise that weird-looking mug anywhere, he looks like he wears his face inside out." Eddie turned back to face the bar and signalled for Gordan to come to him. Leaning into the bar, Eddie whispered to the greasy-haired skinny barman. "Gordan, how long has that ugly-looking pillock been here? The stranger."

Gordan took a glance over at Scarrow. The Seraph pub wasn't usually frequented by strangers so it was easy to know who Eddie was referring to. "Let's think, about a couple of hours now, I'd say. He muttered something about needing to drown his sorrows. I didn't pay much attention, but he has been putting his hand in his pocket often enough which suits me."

Eddie straightened his posture and addressed his friend. "Hank, finish that beer pronto then meet me around the front in about 5 minutes. Leave the engine running; I think we can assist Mr. Scarrow in making this a night to remember. He is obviously craving for some excitement in his life. Gordan, give me a pint of what the twat's drinking."

Both men responded positively to their respective requests. Eddie walked over to the round oak table where Scarrow was sitting; realising there was a spare stool positioned next to the lowlife.

"Mind if I join you?"

"Be my guest." Eddie was pleased to discover that Scarrow hadn't recognised him from their previous encounter at Wembley. Eddie had chosen to grow a short beard recently and this assisted with the timely disguise, not that Scarrow had been allowed much time to decipher who his attackers had been on the day of his beating.

"I noticed that you are on the cider. I've bought you another one."

"Thanks."

"Are you here by yourself?"

Scarrow managed a wry smile. "Yeah, no-one would ever want to drink with me."

"I'm happy to drink with you."

"Is this a gay bar or something?"

Eddie laughed. "Don't worry, this isn't a gay bar. I'm just being friendly that's all, that's the sort of pub this is. The kind of pub that welcomes a new face. You looked like you needed company and I just happen to be out on my own too, that's all."

"It doesn't matter if this is a gay bar. I often go to the places around Hurst Street anyway; I'm just not that familiar with this pub. It's something else that people who know me, correction who think they know me, don't realise. That I'm gay, or at least I think I am, I'm not really sure."

"Are you in denial?"

"Maybe. I never have much luck with any gender if the truth be known, so I get my kicks in other ways."

"Yeah, I know what you mean," said Eddie. "There is much more to life than all that messy relationship stuff. The name's Eddie, by the way. Pleased to meet you."

Lionel Scarrow hesitated briefly before shaking the hand that was offered to him. Scarrow was feeling cautious, but the alcohol had helped erase the full extent of any distrust that he may ordinarily have displayed. Plus he was on such a downer it was difficult to neglect such a friendly approach.

"I'm Lionel."

"So what brings you to this part of town, Lionel?"

"I just fancied a change of scene, fancied somewhere

new to drown my sorrows."

"Why do you need to drown your sorrows?"

"You wouldn't want to know my troubles. I wouldn't want to burden you."

"Try me. I'm a good listener and you know what they say about a trouble shared being a trouble halved and all that. Anyway, I could do with the company myself; I'm on a bit of a downer as well you see, so let's get drunk together. We can help each other I reckon."

"Why not? You tell me your troubles first then."

"Well, I got into a bit of trouble at the football match, got into a scrap, you see. I reckon I may even get a prison sentence. It was self-defence I swear, but this copper caught me in the act and just wouldn't listen to my side of things. Even if I get off with a fine I will still have a criminal record and that means I'll lose my job."

"Welcome to my world, I lost my job and I was a copper."

"You're a copper? Well, if you were mixing with the likes of the bastard who stitched me up you are better off out of it mate."

"I dunno. I did love my job. Anyway, I can't say I ever operated fully within the law myself. It does sounds like you have got caught up with a bit of a jobsworth there though, Eddie."

"Too right. He's been harassing me and all sorts. I'm scared to answer the phone sometimes. The thing is he's a national hero, he has just exposed the England football manager for rape crimes and captured a serial killer to boot, so if I tried to complain who would listen? He is the blue-eyed boy of the police so I'm done for. Hey, you must know him, as you were a copper like? His name is Stone, Judd Stone."

Scarrow's body language changed for the first time. It was clear that Eddie had now gained his full attention. "Judd Stone! I know him alright. Eddie, it seems we both have something in common in that particular enemy. Judd

Stone totally wrecked my career. That's why I'm sitting here alone, with no job and my professional reputation in tatters. Judd Stone has ruined my life, while he gets a flaming promotion. He is the blue-eyed boy, just like you say."

"He did that to you? What a bastard that man is. If only there was some way to get even with him."

"Well, the thing is Eddie, for all the glory that son-of-a-bitch is swimming in now, I know that he still hurts inside." Lionel thumped his own stomach to emphasise his point.

"How do you mean?"

"A few years ago, Stone harassed another guy similar to the way it sounds like he is bothering you. He earned some brownie points with the force putting the villain away, his name was Delroy Whitton. So as you can imagine, when Whitton was released from prison he was gunning for Stone, but if he went directly for Stone I knew that there was a risk that the demented animal would beat the crap out of Whitton anyway. I managed to convince Whitton that there was more than one way to skin a cat and if he really wanted to hurt Stone properly, he didn't even need to lay a single hand on the bastard."

"Go on."

"For all his toughness, Stone had a weakness. He loved his wife. Frankie. To make Stone really suffer it was logical to hurt his wife. Whitton was so easy to wind up and manipulate, he was like an excited tiger when I left him that day and indeed, after I told him where Stone lived he went over and hurt Stone's wife. He hurt her real bad, he killed her Eddie." Scarrow began to grin; he too was getting excited as he blurted out the story. "Whitton killed Frankie and Stone has suffered ever since. Thanks to me that bastard can never be happy again, no matter how successful his career becomes, because he can never have his precious Frankie with him by his side."

It took a single punch for Eddie Goode to knock

Lionel Scarrow unconscious.

CHAPTER 63

When Lionel Scarrow awoke he was strapped to his own dining chair in his own flat.

And he wasn't alone.

Judd Stone had his face held just centimetres away from Scarrow's, uncomfortably invading the low-life's personal space. Judd was indifferent to just how unattractive Scarrow's face appeared at such close range, and Scarrow's appearance wasn't helped by the inclusion of a slight swelling on his already disproportioned chin.

From such a close angle, Judd's distorted face became the first thing that Scarrow saw upon awakening, and the unexpected sight caused the unpleasant character to have quite a shock. Once the moment of immediate menace had registered with Scarrow, Judd decided to move away for his own benefit, certainly not for Scarrow's.

"Hello Lionel, a little surprised to see me?"

"Stone. How did you get in?"

"Quite simple really, your key was in your pocket." Lionel looked beyond Judd for the first time and noticed two figures standing against the rear wall of the room.

Scarrow spoke to one of them. "You were in the pub. You told me you hated Stone, and that he harassed you."

"Oh, of course Lionel, you have already met Eddie haven't you? He told me about your little tete a tete in The Seraph and he has filled me in on all the details of your story."

Scarrow felt his stomach churn. He knew that he had drunk a lot of cider which could have easily clouded his judgment, but had he really told that stranger something that would compromise himself? For instance, had he shed any light on the time when he had informed the convicted criminal, Delroy Whitton, of Frankie Stone's whereabouts and encouraged him to kill her in order to torment Judd? Considering that he was now imprisoned in his own chair, Scarrow figured, yes, he really had been that stupid.

"Actually, you have met Eddie on a couple of occasions Lionel, and his friend Hank too."

Even more doomed clarity dawned on Scarrow. "Outside Wembley Stadium, they were part of the crowd that knocked me senseless."

"That's right; blimey you could make a detective yet, Scarrow. Oh, no I forgot. You have already played at being a detective and now you can't play anymore."

"Yes, that's right, Judd. I've lost my job so I'm already at my lowest point possible. You've had your fun, let me go and we'll say no more about it."

Judd shook his head and managed a very short laugh. "Sorry, Lionel, no can do. You see, I know the part that you played in getting Frankie killed. You told that piece of scum, Whitton, where he could find my wife and you arranged for him to kill her. You had her killed just to hurt me. You're really a piece of work Scarrow; you were able treat her life as something so insignificant, and you decided to use her just like a chess piece in your sick little game."

"No, it's not true."

"Are you calling me a liar," snarled Eddie stepping forward.

"Easy, Eddie," said Judd holding up a hand.

"No, Eddie. I'm not saying that you're a liar. I just said

what I said to you in the pub to make myself feel better, to make myself look big to you. Pathetic really I know, I never told Whitton anything, I simply made it up," snivelled Lionel.

"Sorry, Lionel, I can't tell when you are telling me the truth or not," said Judd. "You are a bit like that little boy who cried wolf in the storybook, and now you look just like a sad little boy as you sit there snivelling, with snot running down your big ugly face.

"You see, when I brought Whitton to justice he tried to say something to me not long before he was put out of his misery, but he wasn't really in great shape for his words to be in any way audible. But you know what, Lionel? I'm now sure Whitton was trying to grass you up with his dying breaths. The pathetic runt probably thought it would save his life but I had already worked him over far too well that he was never going to survive, and as if I was ever going to let him live after what he had done.

"The thing is I have always suspected that you had fed Whitton a story but I could never prove it. And now, if you are seriously asking me to not to believe the word of someone who has turned out to be an unlikely, yet very loyal friend to me, against someone who has spent his whole damn police career trying to upstage me and cause me nothing but trouble, who do you think I am going to believe?"

Scarrow squeezed his eyes shut and dropped his big head. "I'm sorry Judd, I was wrong. I can see that now. I was jealous of you, I looked up to you, and I just wanted to be like you."

"Fuck me you are desperate. Just save it Scarrow, you weasel. Now tell me, do you recognise this?"

"It…it's my gun."

"Yes that's correct, a very good observation considering what a shit copper you are. And now I have to express my disappointment in you, Scarrow. You see, I've worked hard to rid the streets of Birmingham from gun crime and then I discover that someone within the force, one of my own so to speak, actually owns a piece...tut….tut….tut. You see, Hank here got it from you the day he contributed to beating the shit out of you outside Wembley Stadium, the attack happening not long after it seems when you had met with Gareth Banks. Now, I ask myself this. What on Earth were you doing with Banks? And if you could have liaisons with the likes of Banks, then you could certainly have liaisons with scum like Whitton."

"I was arresting Banks, for the murder of that cult leader Eli Zane."

"Oh, really. Well I had arrested Banks a long time before that for the murder of three unfortunate girls, if he had gone down then as he should have done, then Eli Zane would still be alive wouldn't he? Not that he was necessarily a guy who deserved a long and fulfilling life. And as I recall you did everything in your power to discredit that prosecution of The Crucifier and make me look like a proper dickhead."

"No, you have it all wrong, Judd."

"Now come on Lionel, you know me better than that. You know, that I know, that you hate my guts."

"We could start again, Judd. I'm sorry, really I am."

"Well, what you may not know about me Lionel is that I am a big Spaghetti Western fan. I also like Quentin Tarantino movies. You see, I love the concept of revenge, it is always such a fitting reason to kill somebody, and as I have your gun in my possession have a guess what I could do?"

"I don't know."

"Well fucking try," shouted Judd, the sudden venom in his voice causing Scarrow to jump. "Don't tell me that you haven't learnt anything from being a detective inspector for all those years. Now try again. I have your gun and you are tied up, so what do you think I could quite easily do?"

"No, Judd. Please. I don't want to say."

"Stop your fucking snivelling and say it."

"You could kill me and make it look like suicide."

"Correct. I could shoot you with your own gun, from close range of course as forensics could work out if I fired it from way over here, and contrary to what you may think of me Scarrow, I am not that stupid to do that. So yes, I could kill you and make it look like suicide. I would make sure that I get the angle of bullet entry just right"

"Please, Judd. Please. I'll do anything."

"Okay, Lionel calm down. As I've already stated, I have worked damn hard to clear the Birmingham streets of gun crime and I do not like guns one bit, however I may just make an exception for you. What's that famous saying, 'If you live by the sword, you die by the sword', well how's about a slight re-work, 'If you live by the gun you die by the gun?'

"Now listen to me you piece of filth, and listen good. You have one chance and one chance only to walk out of here alive, and that is to start telling me the fucking truth. I will know instantly if you are shitting me Scarrow, and if I get one inkling of you telling me the tiniest, littlest fib I'm going to unload this little beauty right into your big fucking ugly face. You sung like a canary to Eddie, now it's time to sing like a fucking opera-singing eagle to me."

Lionel felt sick.

"Now, tell me about your liaisons with Banks. You knew that he was killing those girls didn't you?"

"No, I swear Judd; I swear I didn't know Banks until you were on to him after his three killings."

Judd cocked the trigger of the gun and pointed it at Scarrow. "You fucking liar, I'm going to blow your fucking brains out."

"I'm not lying, Judd. I swear."

Judd smiled which unnerved Scarrow even more. "Okay I believe you, but you had a part to play in the little game he played with Haddock's daughter, right?"

"Yes, Judd. It got out of hand, I'm sorry. Yes, I was

involved in setting Banks up with Haddock's daughter, but getting you involved was his idea, I swear."

"So let me get this clear, you would have gladly fed Chief Constable Agatha Haddock's daughter to Gareth Banks. You complete bastard, he could have killed her and you knew that."

"I'm sorry."

"You know what? I may just get Haddock over here as well; perhaps she would like the pleasure of pulling this trigger and blowing your brains out. It was her daughter you idiot."

"I'm sorry, I'm really sorry."

"Stop blubbering. You also sent Banks to kill William Chamberlain didn't you? You sent that psycho to kill another policeman while he was ill in a hospital bed."

"Yes Judd, I'm so ashamed. Honestly I am."

Judd uncocked the barrel and lowered the gun. "Okay, so I know where we are with you and Banks now. It is enough to shoot you dead right now but you've told me the truth so I will let you live. One thing that I am is a man of my word."

"Thank you, Judd."

"Now, that brings me to the little story that you fed Eddie in the pub. As you have already heard it Eddie, I wouldn't want you to have to sit through it again. Please wait outside for me; I'll be with you shortly."

"Okay Judd, if you want us we won't be far away."

"Thanks guys, but I'm firmly in control here." Eddie and Hank walked out of the room, closing the door behind them.

"So, I want to hear every last detail about how you arranged for Delroy Whitton to go over to my house and kill my wife. If you skip on the slightest detail I swear I will kill you, and remember I'm a man of my word. Now go."

Judd looked Lionel in the eye as the petrified low-life told the story of how he met up with Delroy Whitton and informed him of Judd's address, but then convinced him that a shrewder move would be to kill his wife and not Judd, as that would hurt Judd more.

Judd took a moment to compose himself after finally hearing Scarrow's confession of the awful truth.

"Thank you for sharing that with me Lionel, I know it couldn't have been easy for you. Now I could have my revenge I guess by taking a leaf out of your book and hurting someone who is close to you, you know an eye for an eye and all that. The problem is you are a fucking loser, with no friends or close family. You have nobody who gives a shit about you in the whole wide world so what am I to do?"

"I did what you asked Judd, I told you the truth. Please, you said you'd let me go."

"I said I'd let you go if you told me the truth."

"But I did Judd, I did."

"You see I don't think that you did tell me the truth, the whole truth and nothing but the truth."

"I did, I did, I told you everything. For fuck's sake, Judd." Scarrow's escalating desperation could clearly be heard in his voice.

Judd shook his head. "No mate, you told me that you were sorry. Now I think you said that just to make me feel a little better, to try and save your sad and pathetic life. But you see I don't believe that you are sorry, you enjoyed watching me suffer when I lost my Frankie. That was the whole damn point you sick fuck. I think you lied when you said 'sorry' so for that reason I have to kill you, because you didn't tell me the truth."

Judd walked over to Lionel Scarrow and placed the gun at his head, cocking the trigger ready for its imminent activity.

"You won't get away with this, Stone."

"Oh, but I already have. And this is for Frankie." And with those words Judd pulled the trigger, ending the miserable life of Lionel Scarrow.

CHAPTER 64

Judd had recorded the whole thing and burnt an edited version to CD. He played it to Chief Constable Agatha Haddock.

"So let me get this clear, you would have gladly fed Chief Constable Agatha Haddock's daughter to Gareth Banks. You complete bastard, he could have killed her and you knew that.

"You know what? I may just get Haddock over here as well; perhaps she would like the pleasure of pulling this trigger and blowing your brains out. It was her daughter you idiot."

"I'm sorry, I'm really sorry."

"Stop blubbering. You also sent Banks to kill William Chamberlain didn't you? You sent that psycho to kill another policeman while he was ill in a hospital bed."

"Yes Judd, I'm so ashamed. Honestly I am."

"Okay, so I know where we are with you and Banks now. It is enough to shoot you dead right now but you've told me the truth so I will let you live. One thing I am is a man of my word."

"Thank you, Judd."

An open-jawed Agatha Haddock looked at Judd. "My God, I never knew Scarrow could be capable of this. He could have got my daughter killed."

"He used her as bait, ma'am, to frame me and to fuel

his warped mind with the game he had going on with Banks. My only intent regarding your daughter was to save her life."

"Where is he? I'll kill him."

"Well after he had confessed I left him alone, I wanted to give him the chance to do something decent for once and hand himself in. But it seems that the guilt was too much. He was found by a neighbour with a gunshot wound to the head."

"Are you sure that you didn't kill him, Stone? You clearly had a gun pointing at him to generate his confession, but you said on the recording that you were not going to kill him."

"And I didn't, ma'am. I wanted to bring him to justice in the correct way, just like I have done with Gareth Banks. And when I stopped recording Scarrow, the extent of his despicable actions finally seemed to hit home. He went ahead and told me that he wanted to face you and tell you everything himself. He said he now knew that he had been a disgrace to the force and he wanted to do the decent thing and offer you an apology. I figured who was I to deny him that final chance of absolution? But it seems that after I left he must have mulled things over and decided to take his own life. I should have brought him in and perhaps he could have received some help, he was obviously a sick individual."

"One thing I've learned in all my years in the police force, Stone, is that there are mad people and there are bad people. I think Scarrow belonged to the latter so don't beat yourself up if he chose to take an easy way out, you weren't too know. Another thing I have learned over the years is when people are bullshitting me. It does strike me as curious that you didn't arrest him and bring him in to the station there and then. He could have absconded instead of taking his own life."

"Yes ma'am. My mistake."

"So anyway, is that the official verdict, suicide?"

"I believe so, ma'am."

"Which has prevented a long and unpleasant trial with the potential to drag this police force through months of unfavourable press, just when the media are being so positive about your achievements, Stone? So suicide it is then. It seems to me that we shouldn't have to waste police resource on investigating such a clear cut case, I'll personally see to it that this case is finalised and put to bed as quickly as possible. Thank you, Judd."

"No, ma'am. Thank you."

"And how is William? The recording states that Scarrow had sent Banks to kill him in hospital."

"William tells me he never met Banks that day. The hospital CCTV shows Banks entering the hospital but it seems he must have got spooked and luckily for William he decided against following through on Scarrow's instructions. The CCTV also shows Banks leaving the hospital again minutes later with no incident in-between. And William's doing well, ma'am. Thanks for asking."

"I'm glad to hear it. You take care, Stone."

As Judd went to leave, placing his hand on the door handle, the Chief Constable spoke again. "And Stone, I never really faced up to the erm, career choice that Tabitha had chosen, it was certainly not what my husband and I had intended for her after years of private schooling."

"No, ma'am."

"Yet even as I deflected my anger on you, you still protected her name as well as protecting her life that night Banks was with her."

"I was just doing my duty, ma'am."

"You are far too modest. And were you simply doing your duty pursuing a crazed serial killer while you were suspended from the force?"

"In my mind, ma'am, yes I was. I found it difficult to stop being a detective, and although sometimes I guess I go about doing things a little differently to others, I always try to end up doing the right thing."

"You were very brave to do what you did with no real back-up, a little foolish perhaps, but brave nonetheless, especially under the circumstances. And I understand why you did it, you went with your instincts rather than waste time trying to convince your colleagues that Banks was our man. It seems it was our failing not to make you Detective Chief Inspector sooner. Anyway that'll be all for now, Stone."

"Thank you, ma'am."

CHAPTER 65

Marlon Howell placed his face in the soapy water and for a few seconds he contemplated keeping it there allowing his life to slip away from him.

For what life did he have now?

His predecessor as England manager had been reinstated to the position with a public apology by the FA, and he had improved the team way beyond Howell's capability.

His wife had publicly disowned him, and with the help of a clever divorce lawyer had wrestled the luxurious house they once shared from his ownership, along with most of his finances.

His reputation was in tatters and even if he did eventually get out of this stinking prison, which was many years away from now running the very real risk that he could actually die behind bars, he would probably be too old to work in football again.

Who would want to employ a convicted rapist anyway?

As news broke that he was standing trial for the rape of Bonnie Glass, whose name was kept anonymous for the most part, a number of women had gained the courage to come forward and claim that Marlon Howell had raped them also. He was eventually convicted of raping nine different women, including Bonnie. The shame falling squarely on his shoulders and on none of his victims.

Still, even now Marlon Howell loved himself far more than he could ever love anyone else, and taking his own life was something he quickly decided against doing.

As he pulled his head from the water, his eyes caught the glimpse of a blurry figure standing behind him in the mirror. He was soon shocked to his senses when he felt the cold touch of a metal blade against his throat.

"Hello, Daddy."

As the water cleared from his eyes, it became clear to Howell that the figure standing behind him holding a knife to his throat was Gareth Banks, his son.

"Have you noticed the improvement in the food here lately, Dad?"

Howell frowned, unable to provide an adequate answer.

"Well, due to my good behaviour in here and my experience of culinary skills they gave me a job working in the kitchen as a chef, can you believe it? The bloody fools didn't consider how ridiculous it would be, to place me of all people amongst a few sets of knives. It's like employing Dracula in a blood bank, or perhaps even putting you dear Daddy, in charge of an all girl's school, the temptation simply becomes too much."

"What are you going to do to me?"

"That will become clear in the next few minutes but for now you're going to listen. You see, it all seems so clear to me now Dad, why I am the way I am? I know my gene pool is messed up, it has to be doesn't it to do the things that I've done. I mean, having two parents, I naturally have a fifty-fifty chance of inheriting the genes of either my mother or my father, I guess. The old lady was a bit misguided, a bit desperate going on the game and all, but was she evil? No way, my mom hasn't got a bad bone in her body. And do you know what I done? I stabbed her for fuck's sake. Left her for dead, yet she still visits me in this stinking place. She still sends me letters of warmth and hope and she still forgives me after all I've done. But you? A dirty rapist who wouldn't give his son or the mother of his child the time of day, well it doesn't take Einstein to work out why I'm so messed up does it, Dad?" Banks increased the pressure on the knife, causing it to draw blood on Howell's terrified neck, as Banks became increasingly more agitated at his own words.

"I'm sorry, Son."

"Don't you dare call me that. You have no right. You're only sorry because I have a knife at your throat."

"I'm a rapist Gareth, but I'm not a killer. You can't blame me for all the killing that you have done."

"I inherited my messed up genes from you so take some responsibility for once in your life. I admit I had my own agenda to carry out God's work and that duty hasn't left me in spite of the hours I have talking with the prison shrink. But I believe that it is your genes that allow me to have the inclination to kill. You rape, I kill, and both are aggressive acts of an unnatural nature, although even now we both feel totally justified in the acts that we have done."

Gareth's words rang true with his father. He didn't regret raping those women, they deserved it, they needed to be taught a lesson the dirty teases. He only regretted being caught and ending up behind bars.

"You know, the shrink struggles to understand why I killed those people. I killed those three girls, I remember their killings so vividly, but apparently I also killed a religious cult leader called Eli Zane. I understand my motive, he was an imposter to the teachings of God, but I don't remember a thing about killing him, not one single thing. I have a slight hazy memory of driving my knife into Mom, and a slightly better recollection of turning up to kill you, but why are my slayings of those three girls as clear as day, yet my killing of the cult freak non-existent? It doesn't make sense. Tell me Daddy, have you ever heard of a man named, Sirhan Sirhan?"

"Yes, he's the guy who shot Robert Kennedy."

"So the story goes. Well to this day Sirhan Sirhan claims that he never remembers killing one of those unfortunate Kennedy brothers. Just like I don't remember killing Eli Zane. I think my shrink is a bit of a conspiracy theorist. At first he suggested I had been programmed to assassinate both Zane and you, but I keep throwing back at him what possible gain does anyone have to take the pair of you off this planet?

"He has suggested that Eli Zane was assassinated simply because he pissed off the US authorities and continued to promote a dangerous take on religion outside of the accepted organised religious movements, hence he was still around to corrupt young minds. I've had time to do a lot of reading in prison, and one thing my shrink has done for me is to get me interested in famous murders from history. I pointed out to him that I have never been to the USA, or ever owned a copy of *The Catcher in the Rye*, which both Mark David Chapman, John Lennon's killer, and John Hinkley, Ronald Reagan's would be killer, both had as a suggested trigger planted in their brains. The book allegedly gave the signal to go after these famous people.

"So I simply can't see how I've been programmed under any mind control programme because there simply hasn't been the window of opportunity. So now my shrink wonders if British intelligence have adopted such methods of using lone nuts to brainwash and use as patsies to carry out assassinations, but the only people I've ever been close enough to that bears any kind of resemblance to British Intelligence is Judd Stone, whom I admit I underestimated somewhat, but to describe him as British Intelligence is completely unintelligent in itself. Similarly, his boss, William Chamberlain is not cut from that cloth either. Now I do admit that after paying Chamberlain a visit in hospital I seemed to go off on a killing spree, but this man is not in a good state of health and hardly carries the rank in his force to run Mind Control programmes in Great Britain. He is just a Brummie plod for fuck's sake. So weighing everything up, my shrink now believes that I probably just hit some type of temporary insanity where I didn't know what I was doing, you know like some sort of diminished responsibility.

"But then I got thinking. If I was meant to assassinate you, I failed didn't I? Just like John Hinkley failed to kill Reagan and Ali what's-his-name failed to kill the Pope. But now I have a chance again to finish what I started."

"No please Son, don't kill me."

"Don't worry Dad; I'm not going to kill you. You see, I don't think I was programmed to kill you because you are simply not important enough. How on Earth could any government or movement benefit from killing the England football manager?

"Now I realise that John Lennon was a celebrity too, but come on Dad, you are not in his league, no pun intended. Lennon was world famous, and had a voice that was listened to. He was listened to about peace and political viewpoints. He was a musician whom a lot of people worldwide could be influenced by, but you? All anyone has ever been bothered about listening to you about is football, not something that springs to mind for the deployment of a programmed assassin to be involved in is it? I realise that now.

"And like I said Dad, I'm not going to kill you. You see all these victims of assassination become even more famous in death, so assassination doesn't actually work. John Lennon's message took on a new life after his death, his message never went away and neither did JFK's or Martin Luther King's. These people were special in life but in death their message magnified thousand fold. It's ironic don't you think considering that they were meant to be silenced.

"Now I'm not sure what message yours could be, but I

am not going to kill you. I hate to admit that you were a celebrity and a household name, and I don't want to risk the tiny chance of you being turned into a martyr. I mean you would be the first England football manager ever to be assassinated wouldn't you? And I don't want to run the risk of that. I can't have you coming up smelling of roses, what if people began to forget that you had raped nine innocent women?

"Now when I found out from Mom that you were my dad I came to kill you. Fate has it that that hasn't happened. But you spent your whole life laughing at me and my mom. You laughed at me playing football, you laughed that I could be your son and you laughed at my mom as she struggled to make ends meet on the game, while you simply took what you wanted from her as you gloated in your privileged position. So as you like laughing so much I'm going to make sure that you permanently have a grin on your face, and every time you look in the mirror you will be reminded of how you laughed at me and my mom. But ultimately Dad, it is us, Mom and me who have had the last laugh."

And with those words Gareth Banks sliced the blade across Marlon Howell's mouth and face giving him the lasting impression of a *Chelsea Smile*.

As Howell writhed on the floor, screaming and clutching his face with blood seeping through his fingers, an unremorseful Banks casually glanced back at his victim.

"You had better hope that I never do discover that you have a message for the world that has to be silenced, or that my mind becomes not my own again, because next time you won't be so lucky. Keep smiling, Dad."

CHAPTER 66

After Judd had secured the capture of both Gareth Banks and Marlon Howell during the incredible incident that had unfolded before the nation on live TV, he went on to do one final thing before he left London. Judd had visited the grave of Bonnie Glass, and whilst laying down a bunch of fresh flowers, updated her on the success of finally being able to nail Howell. As he left the grave, Judd finally felt an element of satisfaction and for the first time felt that Bonnie could finally rest in peace now that justice had prevailed.

Today, Judd was back in Birmingham to visit the grave of his deceased wife.

"I'll wait here," said Brooke. "I'll give you some time alone."

"Thanks," smiled Judd.

Minutes earlier, Brooke had already accompanied Judd to the grave of Evelyn Craig, and the short walk through Witton cemetery had brought them to the oak tree that always served as a useful marker for Frankie's grave, though Judd would probably be able to locate it blindfolded.

Frankie's resting place wasn't too far from the path and

Judd left Brooke by the tree as he trod onto the grassed area, pleased to find that the earth wasn't as sodden as usual and his shoes didn't surrender to any emerging patches of wetness. Not that walking to Frankie's grave could ever be considered to be a burden to Judd. He had visited her grave in rain, sleet and snow many times before now.

Judd had agonised over choosing Frankie's head stone, wanting to mark her resting place as perfectly as he could. He needn't have worried, he had got it right.

Not long after stepping away from Brooke, Judd reached the black heart-shaped marble that bore his wife's name: *Francesca "Frankie" Stone, beloved wife of Judd*. Judd, not a natural with words unlike his idol John Lennon, had still managed to come up with the simple yet poignant tribute of *"Heaven has gained an angel as special as can be, each painful day without you is one closer until you're back with me"*.

"Good morning, Frankie. It's a bit early in the day for a drink but it's never stopped us before has it, girl?" Judd pulled two wine glasses and a bottle of Merlot from a plastic bag; he placed the glasses on the lawn and screwed the top off the bottle. "They're a lot easier to open these days Frankie, remember all that messing around with a cork?" Judd proceeded to pour two glasses of the wine and then promptly poured one glass onto his wife's grave.

"There you go girl, you enjoy that." Judd then took a sip of his own glass. "Mmmm, not bad. It reminds me of all those nights we used to drink Merlot whilst watching some sad chick-flick that you insisted I watched with you. I used to enjoy the wine but never the film. Still, I'd swap anything to be able to watch one more chick-flick with you again.

"I've had a very eventful year or so, Frankie, but it's all worked out okay in the end. And thanks for that message about only having two-thirds of the catch and the enemy lying within. You must have been so tormented knowing that Scarrow had stitched us up with Whitton, and then

Banks too. It took some figuring out but justice has been done in the end I guess. In fact, I find myself in a bit of a strange position, Frankie. It's a bit scary in a way, but I don't seem to have anything to concern myself with these days. I'm not sure that I can ever get used to peace and tranquility.

"I still miss you though, Frankie, but William and Sab tell me that you would want me to be happy and the time is now right for me to try and move on a bit. And knowing you, the way I knew you, I know they're right. You would want me to be happy. Being happy since you went has never been easy, but I've started seeing someone now you see, Frankie. She can never replace you of course and I don't think she wants too. She seems a good sort, Frankie. She's very caring; in fact she's even been looking after William the old fart. That's how I met her, she's a nurse.

"And guess what. The old git's also got himself a bird these days. Some posh bit called Crystal; she seems good for him though. Oh, I forgot, you've already met her, haven't you? Sort of anyway."

"I hope you don't mind that I have met someone, Frankie. There is not a day goes by when I don't think of you but I get lonely sometimes, and don't you go telling that to William and Sab. I have my reputation to think of. So anyway, what do you think of the Merlot? And what do you think of me seeing someone? Are you cool with it?"

Judd took another sip of his wine and looked down at the lush grass beneath his feet. From nowhere a single white feather of significant proportion drifted down to complement the colour scheme before him. He looked up to the blue suburban sky and was slightly puzzled to discover that there was no bird or creature of any description circling above him to suggest that the feather had derived from any tangible source. The entry of the white feather seemed a complete mystery.

Judd used his free hand to collect the white feather; he examined it and felt its soft texture. Judd couldn't begin to guess which type of bird it could have belonged to. He looked around again to see if a bird was perched on one of the larger and older gothic gravestones of Witton cemetery. All he could spot was the odd black raven or crow in the distance, but definitely not a single creature that could host a white feather of such a considerable size.

"That's strange, Frankie. Where has this come from? It's a beautiful feather though, I may just keep it for a while – place it in a vase or something. It seems too lovely to simply discard."

Judd finished off his glass of wine. "Well here's until the next time, Frankie. I'll be back to see you soon and share another bottle of Merlot with you. Sleep tight my darling."

Judd collected the wine glasses and slightly depleted bottle of wine and placed them back into his plastic bag. For some reason he felt the feather was too special to place into a crumpled plastic bag, so he simply left that resting in his free hand. Judd moved away from his departed wife's grave and was greeted by Brooke's large dark-brown eyes and beautiful smile. Brooke's perfect teeth were almost as white as the mysterious feather. She was also just as beautiful.

"Are you okay, Judd?"

"Yes thanks, we had one of our little chats."

"Good, that's nice. What do you have there?"

"It's a white feather. It's quite significant in size and really quite beautiful. You didn't see a bird with white feathers flying around the place did you?"

"Not so I noticed."

"It seemed to appear from out of nowhere! One minute I was speaking to Frankie, about you as it happens, and the next thing this beautiful white feather floated down."

"It's a sign."

"A sign?"

"Yeah, for sure. The mysterious appearance of a white

feather often means it's a sign from a departed one. It's a way of communicating with their loved ones to show that that they are at peace and all is okay. You see, when we die the energy doesn't die only our physical state. The shell of our body that happened to house our spirit for however many years it walked the Earth dies, but the spirit itself lives on, that can never die. There are other ways in how the spirit world connects with us too; the spirit can visit us in the form of a bird, a butterfly or another creature. Pennies scattered from nowhere can also be a sign, in particular on a path that the departed one used a lot when their physical form was alive. What exactly were you saying to Frankie at the time the feather appeared?"

"Well, I was telling her that William had met Crystal and I told her that I had met you. I explained that although I still miss her perhaps it was time that I allowed myself a little happiness while I'm still on this planet. I told her that you were a nurse and was a very caring person."

"Well the white feather is clearly a sign from Frankie to tell you that she approves of you seeking some happiness and therefore it seems she approves of us."

"You reckon?"

"What other explanation is there? Trust me I know about these things. Crystal Stance is not the only spiritual one around here you know."

"Wow, that's incredible, it makes sense I guess. It would be nice to know that Frankie is sending me a sign."

"I thought you were a Beatles fan, Judd?"

Judd frowned. "I am?"

"Well, have you never heard of the White Feather Foundation?"

"I've heard of the White album, a unique collection of diverse music by the best group ever, but the album was actually called *The Beatles*, you know."

"I didn't know, but let me tell you something. Julian Lennon had been told by his father, that should he ever pass away he would let him know that he was okay through the form of a white feather. Some years later whilst Julian was in Australia, he was presented with a white feather by an aboriginal tribal elder. Julian obviously recognised this as his father contacting him; and it eventually inspired Julian to create the White Feather Foundation. The White Feather Foundation is a gateway to many charities that support the well being of the planet and its people."

"Well I never. I thought I knew all there is to know about the Beatles, but it just goes to show that I don't. So even after his death, John Lennon has been able to contact his son, through a white feather, and sustained his desire to have Peace on Earth." Judd looked around the sky, which was unusually blue for a typical day in Birmingham, and he felt a definite connection with Frankie somehow. "She's all around us Brooke, she's still with me."

"She will always be with you, Judd."

Judd looked into the beautiful eyes of his new girlfriend. It had been so long since he had dared to allow anyone into his life he felt a little scared. Scared mainly that his emotions would inadvertently cause him to be harsh and unloving towards Brooke who clearly didn't deserve such a relationship, but he was also scared to allow himself to release love again, because the people he loved usually ended up being taken away from him.

The pain he had felt when Frankie died had been unbearable, and had shaped Judd's persona from that day forward. But this white feather surely proved that all was okay. Even if he were to lose his love on Earth, they could still be okay somewhere else, and he would know this through the connection of a white feather. There was a time that he would have dismissed such things as being mumbo-jumbo, but he now knew that there were things that could happen that he could never fully understand, but his mind had been opened to accept that unexplained things can happen.

His best friend William had a debilitating illness in

Multiple Sclerosis, but somehow his physical state did not prevent him from controlling things with his mind. William could clearly perform acts of telekinesis. Crystal Stance it appeared had the gift to speak to those that had passed over, and even Judd, a macho and uncompromising individual could even be reached from a departed loved one via the mysterious appearance of a white feather.

"I like you, Brooke. I like you a lot but I have baggage."

"Well it's a good job I have strong arms then isn't it? Besides, we all have baggage."

"Look what happens to women I care for. They end up dead."

"That doesn't mean it will happen to me does it? You are not cursed, Judd."

"I sometimes wonder."

"Believe me, I don't plan going anywhere just at the moment, except back to your flat to finish off that bottle of Merlot."

"Well it would be a shame to waste it."

"And it would be a shame to waste anymore of your life, the life which is in its current physical form of Judd Stone. It is time to enjoy this life again Judd, and I'm here to enjoy it with you, for as long as you want me to."

"You may not find me much fun too often. I leave toothpaste in the sink, I'm used to leaving the toilet seat up, I fart and swear at will and I can wake up in the morning like a man far grumpier than my years would suggest."

"Well you certainly sound a catch don't you? I also know that underneath that grizzly bear exterior of yours is a guy with a genuine willingness to make this world a better place, and I have seen that you have even tried to make that happen which is an extremely admirable quality. Anyway, I'll have some help to keep you in check won't I, Detective Chief Inspector Stone? You just keep looking out for those white feathers."

And as Judd slowly began his journey to allow a little sunlight into his heart, he knew that there would undoubtedly be challenges along the way, but after everything that he had gone through and witnessed, not least in recent times, one thing Judd Stone now knew for sure. Nothing, absolutely nothing was impossible.

CHAPTER 67

Cannon Hill Park was a fitting location to construct a Garden of Remembrance for Cassie Parker, Olive Jenas and Kez Raven. Situated less than 2 miles from Birmingham's city centre, it is widely regarded as the park closest to the heart of Birmingham. It was therefore especially appropriate that the three girls who had touched the hearts of the people of the West Midlands should be remembered in the heart of the city where they lived.

The Remembrance Garden would complement the already wonderful attributes of the park including lakes, pools, lush green lawns and a diverse collection of trees. Made up of 80 acres of formal parkland and 120 acres of conservation and woodland plantation, Cannon Hill Park has successfully achieved Green Flag status, an award scheme which recognises and rewards the most excellent green spaces in the UK. This is an amazing achievement for a location that sits in the heart of industrial Birmingham.

Looking around at the park these days it is difficult to envisage its rich industrial history. In the 16th Century it was a site dedicated to the manufacturing properties of forges and mills, with related noises and smells filling the air. By stark contrast in the days, months and years to come, the Garden of Remembrance would be visited by the people of Birmingham as a peaceful and beautiful place to sit and pay their respects to three of the city's daughters.

The park runs along the River Rea and also incorporates Birmingham's Nature Centre and Midlands Arts Centre, more commonly known as simply the MAC, so it is likely that the Garden of Remembrance will now also fall into the schedule of those visiting these establishments too.

The Lord Mayor of Birmingham had opened proceedings at the event, thanking those in the crowd for attending. Some had been cordially invited to occupy the front section of temporary seating, but there had been no restriction placed on the amount of people who wished to attend, with large screens being placed around the park to broadcast live proceedings to those who couldn't quite squeeze into the garden itself. A fitting crowd had indeed gathered to pay their respects to the three girls who had tragically being taken away from Birmingham.

The Lord Mayor had spoken warmly about the three girls, giving an insight far beyond their career choice that had helped orchestrate their downfall, and the crowd learnt how Olive had been a keen ballet dancer in her youth, whilst Kez had ironically been a bit of a tomboy, having a love of football and cars, whilst Cassie had enjoyed years of horse riding. Although the Lord Mayor had been content to open proceedings, he insisted that Judd should have the honour of cutting the ribbon to officially declare the Garden of Remembrance open.

The Lord Mayor introduced Judd, describing him nothing short of a hero. A police detective with a dogged determination to ensure that justice was achieved for Cassie, Olive and Kez, and he achieved this justice against all the odds and in the face of many doubters. As he made his way to the temporary podium, Judd felt a little embarrassed by the Lord Mayor's kind words and the level of lengthy applause generated from the crowd. Once standing on the podium, Judd had to wait to speak as the applause continued. He was overwhelmed at the adoration being directed at him and a lump began to form in his throat. He looked out at the crowd and he could see people that he recognised and people that he didn't, but he felt genuine emotion that such a unification of people had gathered in honour of the three girls.

Judd spotted Brooke in the crowd, sweet selfless Brooke, someone who at last could provide a sense of purpose in his personal life. Since Frankie's death he had only been able to recognise a reason for living through his work.

Then Judd noticed William and Crystal with Agatha Haddock, Ben Francis and Sabita Mistry sitting close by.

He spotted senior representatives from all the many faiths that existed in this great city of diversity and inclusion, and although not a religious man himself, Judd felt proud that his city could achieve such unity.

Then he spotted the most important guests of all, the families and friends of Cassie, Olive and Kez, many quietly crying into tissues even after all this time, but Judd knew only too well that losing someone in such violent and untimely circumstances never really heals, instead you simply nurse an open wound the best way you can. Judd was humbled as he stood before them, and he could recognise a genuine gratitude in the eyes of the parents of the three victims. It was he that had been able to bring justice for their little girls and a sense of closure.

Today's sentiment reminded Judd a little of the Strawberry Fields garden in New York's Central Park created in remembrance of John Lennon, which hosted a flower from every country in the world. Looking out from Strawberry Fields, one can see the Dakota building where Lennon lived, and died, as well as other typical NYC buildings. Looking beyond Cannon Hill Park, Judd could see elements of Birmingham's skyline, including blocks of council flats and student accommodation – a long way removed from the luxurious Dakota residence, but nevertheless necessary dwellings for some of the people of Birmingham. As Judd looked beyond the crowd he could also see the Edgbaston cricket ground where Warwickshire and England play the sport.

Judd looked a little closer at the garden before him. It was beautiful and had been expertly created with a great deal of thought and pride. Much of the blooming foliage had been developed at the nearby Botanical gardens. The section with lilac and lavender blooms took Judd back to the colour scheme in Cassie's waterside apartment where he had experienced the sight of Gareth Banks' horrific handy work for the first time. Nevertheless, Judd found it fitting that such colours should be included in her honour. The families of the dead girls had been consulted about what type of flowers and plants should be included. There was a sea of roses of varied shades, cultivated in nearby Albrighton, placed around the borders of the garden. At times the Birmingham climate could be harsh, yet palm trees had been included, a request by Kez's family as she had always loved holidays in the sun. The garden represented quintessential England as well as hosting a range of exotic plants, something Judd saw fitting to once again represent and celebrate the diversity of this great city.

The applause eventually died down and Judd began to say a few words. "It is with deep regret that I never had the opportunity to meet Cassie, Olive and Kez, in life, but my investigations into the abysmal crimes committed against them, and the hours I willingly spent speaking with their families and friends enabled me to at least get to learn a bit about them. It is clear to me that all three girls were warm and bright individuals, that they were very much loved and now sadly missed. It also remains clear that this world benefitted from having them with us for the short time that they were able to be here. I am not exactly sure what awaits us beyond this life but my mind is being opened all the time to learn that there is definitely something and for people like Cassie, Olive and Kez it can only be a good thing otherwise nothing makes sense. This Garden of Remembrance is also a good thing to recognise their influence on us all, and to celebrate with genuine fondness the short lives they lived. It is a fitting and beautiful place for us to come and reflect, and for many of you to remember the good times that you had the opportunity and honour to share with Cassie, Olive and Kez. I only wish that I too had had the opportunity and pleasure to share a moment or two with these three special daughters of our city, but through the beautiful foliage and flowers in this garden, those like me who didn't have the pleasure first hand can now experience a flavour of what these three wonderful girls were all about. So with no further ado I shall ask Mrs. Parker, Mrs. Jenas and Mrs. Raven to step forward and unveil the memorial."

The three women stepped forward with a definite air of togetherness, brought together in a unified and distinct grief which only they could understand. Holding hands as they walked forward, they would be forever connected by the cruel act of a unique kind of murder.

The cover was lifted and Judd cut the ribbon, but not before each one of the mothers had kissed him on the cheek.

"It is my great pleasure to declare this Garden of Remembrance for Cassie, Olive and, Kez open."

Situated on the western boundary of Cannon Hill Park, a granite and bronze memorial to the dead of the Second Boer War was erected in 1906. Now more than a century later a new memorial had been erected in honour of three daughters of Birmingham who had also lost their life at an untimely intervention. The three grieving mothers wept emotionally as the memorial was now officially revealed with the inscription of their daughter's names and an accompanying simple message – *In loving memory of Cassie Parker, Olive Jenas and Kerry "Kez" Raven. Forever in our hearts.*

Birmingham will never forget you.

The memorial was a bronze sculpture of three sunflowers reaching up to the heavens, each sunflower representing one of the girls. Nestled amongst the bronze stems that rooted from a single point was a dove made from white marble. It was a truly exceptional structure and one that served as a very fitting memorial.

As Judd looked closer he noticed three small white feathers resting beneath the dove's breast. He looked closer still and he could tell that these were real feathers and in no way could be interpreted as an extension of the sculpture. With the memorial being previously shrouded until now there was no explanation to how the three white feathers had come to rest there.

Judd smiled to himself as he realised their significance and understood just how and why they had appeared. Quietly he spoke under his breath as he looked up to the blue suburban sky. "Hello, girls. I take it that you approve."

ABOUT THE AUTHOR

Martin Tracey is an author who likes to push the boundaries of reality. He lives in Birmingham and is married with two daughters.

Printed in Great Britain
by Amazon